Reconstructing Amelia

Reconstructing
Amelia

a novel

KIMBERLY McCREIGHT

HARPER  PERENNIAL

NEW YORK • LONDON • TORONTO • SYDNEY • NEW DELHI • AUCKLAND

HARPER ● PERENNIAL

A hardcover edition of this book was published in 2013 by HarperCollins Publishers.

FIRST HARPER PERENNIAL EDITION PUBLISHED 2013.

Designed by Fritz Metsch

Library of Congress Cataloging-in-Publication Data has been applied for.

ISBN 978-0-06-222544-3 (pbk.)

13 14 15 16 17   OV/RRD   10 9 8 7 6 5 4 3 2 1

For Tony,
my light home

Let us again pretend that life is a solid substance, shaped like a globe, which we turn about in our fingers. Let us pretend that we can make out a plain and logical story . . . Virginia Woolf, *The Waves*

Reconstructing Amelia

gRaCeFULLY

Because there are 176 definitions for the word *loser* on urbandictionary.com. Don't Be a Statistic

Hey bitches!

Ah, the beginning of another school year. And I'm back with all the shit that's not fit to print . . .

So while you've all been whiling away the summer in Southampton, or on Nantucket or in the South of France, perfecting your tennis game or your pas de deux, or training for your first marathon, or basking in your latest chess championship, I've spent the summer keeping track of the back and forth of our dear faculty members. Mr. Zaritski went out to UC Berkeley to teach at a science camp for crazy-smart kids. Word has it the parents had him fired week two because he SMELLED. Mrs. Pearl took a Latin lover and learned to pole dance in Miami. Kidding. She didn't actually have a lover, of course. Who would ever want to sleep with her?

Ah, and sweet delicious Mr. Woodhouse. Who wouldn't have wanted to see him in a Speedo somewhere? Alas, his whereabouts lo these sultry months is unknown, though I have it on good authority that he spent at least one long weekend snuggled up with our beloved English prof Liv. To which I say, bravo.

As for all of you, I'll be covering a summer wrap-up as the updates flow in over the next few days—and do send them along to gracefullyblog@ gmail.com. Because here we are, another year where every loser has the chance to finally be cool and the fat kids might turn up skinny.

And the same old questions: Will lovely little Dylan ever come clean about who she's screwing? Will Heather and Rachel ever admit they're screwing each other? Will Zadie stay out of jail long enough to graduate? Which senior girl will our resident sophomore hottie Carter sleep with first? And who is this Ian Greene and is he as sizzlin' as his meet book pictures suggest? Outlook doubtful says my own personal eight ball. But y'all will be the first to know.

In the meantime, keep those new shoes shiny and those smiles bright. And buckle up. Because it's going to be one hell of a ride . . .

Amelia

AMELIA

when did u know?

BEN

know what?

AMELIA

that you liked boys?

BEN

idk, always I guess

AMELIA

no way

BEN

it's true, seriously

AMELIA

and you just told everybody

BEN

pretty much; who cares what people think

AMELIA

I can't imagine being that sure about anything. or that brave.

BEN

u might surprise yourself

AMELIA

nah

BEN

u r stronger than you think

AMELIA

thx. what wld I do w/o u to pump me up?

BEN

die? I like to think lives depend on me

AMELIA

ha ha. when are we going to hang out 4 real?

BEN

this isn't real?

AMELIA

u know what I mean

BEN

I might come to NYC in a few weeks; my dad's going on a business trip

AMELIA

and I'd get to see you?

BEN

totally

AMELIA

OMG! Seriously? I can't wait!!!

Kate

Kate knew Victor wasn't happy, even before she looked up from her notes to see the anger settling over his face in a heavy cloud. The room was silent, everyone—five lawyers from Slone, Thayer; ten from Associated Mutual Bank—waiting for him to say something. Instead, Victor leaned back in his conference room chair, hands folded neatly in his lap. With his salt-and-pepper hair and perfectly tailored suit, he looked handsome and dignified, despite his obvious annoyance.

Amid the uncomfortable quiet, Kate's stomach growled. She cleared her throat and shifted in her chair, hoping no one had heard. She'd been too nervous this morning to eat. There'd been the meeting, but there'd also been the argument she'd been bracing to have with Amelia. The argument had never materialized. Instead, Amelia had left for school with a smile and a cheerful wave, leaving Kate late for work and with an excess of unused adrenaline.

Kate glanced longingly at the endless array of bagels and fruit and sweets laid out on the conference room sideboard. But when you were running a client meeting in the place of Jeremy Firth, the beloved head of litigation at Slone, Thayer, you didn't get up to grab a snack in the middle of it.

"You do realize," Victor said, pointing at Kate, "that complying with this subpoena will nullify any later objections."

"I understand your frustration, Victor," Kate said calmly. "But the SEC is within its rights to—"

"Within its rights?" Victor snapped. "Overcompensating is more like it."

Kate held Victor's stare, which had morphed into something more of a glare. Vacillating now, even in the slightest, would be fatal. Victor would surely demand to see Jeremy, and while Kate might be a partner, she was still a junior one. She needed to be able to handle this on her own.

"And what about merit? Doesn't that—" Before Victor could finish his thought, the phone in the conference room rang, startling everyone. Rebecca, the junior associate, dutifully hustled to answer it as Victor turned back to Kate. "I want our objections made part of the official record, and I want a budget for this whole mess before anyone opens a single box of documents. Do that and you've got your document collection, agreed?"

As though Kate would be pocketing the extra firm earnings herself. In fact, she wouldn't benefit at all, beyond Jeremy's appreciation. That wasn't inconsequential, of course. Remaining one of Jeremy's favored disciples mattered, a lot.

"Absolutely, Victor," Kate said. "We'll certainly do our best to—"

"Excuse me, Kate," said a voice in her ear. When Kate glanced up, Rebecca looked petrified to be interrupting. "Sorry, but your secretary's on the phone. She says there's a call you need to take."

Kate felt her face flush. Taking a call in the middle of a meeting with Victor Starke was even worse than grabbing a bagel. Kate's secretary, Beatrice, would never have interrupted that kind of meeting, but she was out sick. Kate had told her replacement not to disturb her unless it was an absolute emergency, but the girl had had such a blank look on her face that Kate was convinced she was high. Unfortunately, refusing the call wasn't an option either. Kate was waiting to hear back from a judge's clerk about her application for a temporary restraining order for another client.

"Excuse me, for one moment, please," Kate said, trying to make it seem as though the interruption was all very expected. "I'll just be a second."

The room was quiet as she made her way over to pick up the receiver. She could feel everyone staring at her. Luckily, as she pressed down on the flashing Hold button, the conversation behind her finally picked back up. Victor's associates laughed obediently, probably at one of his jokes.

"This is Kate Baron."

"Yes, Ms. Baron," said the woman on the other end. "This is Mrs. Pearl, the dean of students at Grace Hall."

A call she needed to take. How could her daughter not have even crossed her mind?

"Is Amelia okay?" Kate's heart had picked up speed.

"Yes, yes, she's fine," Mrs. Pearl said, with a hint of annoyance. "But there has been an incident. Amelia's been suspended for three days, effective immediately. You'll need to come down and sign an acknowledgment form and take her home."

"Suspended? What do you mean?"

Amelia had never been in trouble in her entire life. Her teachers called her a delight—bright, creative, thoughtful, focused. She excelled in athletics and was involved in every extracurricular activity under the sun. She volunteered once a month at CHIPS, a local soup kitchen, and regularly helped out at school events. Suspended from school? No, not Amelia. Despite Kate's crushing work hours, she knew her daughter. *Really* knew her. There had been a mistake.

"Yes, Amelia has been suspended for three days," Mrs. Pearl repeated, as though that answered the question of why. "For obvious reasons, we can only release her to a parent or guardian. Is that going to be a problem, Ms. Baron, for you to come and pick her up? We are aware that you work in Manhattan and that Amelia's father is unavailable. But unfortunately, school policy is school policy."

Kate tried not to feel defensive. She wasn't even sure that it was judgment she was hearing in Mrs. Pearl's voice. But Kate had suffered her share of uncomfortable questions, quizzical looks, and thinly

veiled disapproval over the years. Her own parents still seemed to re-
gard her decision to carry her unplanned pregnancy to term while still
in law school as an especially depraved form of criminal insanity. The
decision had certainly been out of character. Her whole life, Kate had
always done the right thing at the right time, at least in all respects
other than with men. The truth was, with men, Kate's judgment had
always been somewhat flawed. Keeping her baby had not been a decision Kate had made lightly, though, nor was it one she regretted.

"I'll come right now, immediately. But can you at least tell me what
she—" Kate paused, the lawyer in her suddenly aware that she should
choose her words carefully. She wasn't about to admit her daughter's
guilt. "What is Amelia accused of doing exactly?"

"I'm afraid disciplinary issues can't be discussed by telephone," Mrs.
Pearl said. "There are confidentiality rules, procedures set in place. I'm
sure you understand. Mr. Woodhouse, the headmaster, can provide
you with details when you arrive. Which will be when exactly?"

Kate looked down at her watch. "I'll be there in twenty minutes."

"If twenty minutes is the best you can do," Mrs. Pearl said, sounding as if she really wanted to say something far less accommodating. "I
suppose that will be fine."

Twenty minutes had been a vast overstatement. Victor had balked,
loudly, when Kate tried to end the meeting early. In the end, she'd had
no choice but to call Jeremy.

"I hate to do this," she said to him in the hallway outside the conference room. And she did hate leaving. It was something that childless
and long-divorced Daniel—her ultracompetitive former law school
classmate, now fellow junior partner—would never have done, even if
he'd been hemorrhaging internally. "But Amelia's school called. I have
to go pick her up."

"Not a problem. In fact, you've just saved me from having to meet
with Vera and the contractors at the new apartment. I'd take a client
meeting with Attila the Hun over conversations about load-bearing
walls any day," Jeremy said, with one of his trademark smiles. He ran

a hand over his prematurely silver hair. He was tall and handsome and, as usual, looked elegant in his pink-striped shirt. "Is everything all right?"

"I don't know," Kate said. "Apparently Amelia's gotten into some kind of trouble, which doesn't make sense. She doesn't get into trouble."

"Amelia? I'm fresh off singing her praises in that recommendation for the summer program at Princeton, so I may be biased, but I certainly don't buy it." Jeremy put a sympathetic hand momentarily on Kate's shoulder and smiled again. "You know these private schools. They blame first, ask questions later. Whatever happened, I'm sure there's a reasonable explanation."

And just like that, Kate felt a little better. That was Jeremy, always with the perfect empathetic aside. It came across as genuine, too, even for Kate, who should have known better.

"Victor isn't happy," she said, gesturing toward the closed conference room door. "I feel like I'm throwing you to the wolves a bit."

"Don't worry." Jeremy waved a nonchalant hand. He could work until dawn, head into court with a losing case to confront an agitated adversary and a dissatisfied client all at once, and never lose his we're-all-friends-here air. "I can handle Victor Starke. You go take care of Amelia."

Kate opted for the subway to avoid Midtown traffic, but she was still forty-five minutes late when the number 2 train lurched to an unexplained halt just before Nevins Street. Fifty, fifty-five minutes late, that's what she'd end up being by the time she got to Grace Hall. *If* she was lucky. Surely the school would take it as a sign of her poor parenting. Mother late, derelict child. It was an exceedingly direct line.

And the more Kate thought about it, the more she was convinced that whatever Amelia was accused of doing must have been bad. Grace Hall prided itself on being liberal, open-minded, student-driven. Founded two hundred years earlier by a group of New York City intellectuals—playwrights, artists, and politicians—the school was revered for its excellent academics and unparalleled arts program. While it was often spoken about alongside the old vanguard of Manhattan private schools—Dalton, Collegiate, Trinity—Grace Hall was in Brooklyn, and so came with a more bohemian pedigree. As such, the school shunned textbooks and standardized tests alike, in favor of experiential learning. Given the school's dearth of formal rules, Kate could not imagine what a student would have to do to warrant suspension.

Suddenly, the train hissed and sputtered forward a few feet, before jerking again to a halt. Kate checked her watch. One hour and five minutes late, at least. Still four stops away. *Goddamnit.* She was always late, for everything. She stood up and went to hover near the subway door, doubt creeping up on her.

Recently, Amelia had seemed distracted, even a little moody. She was fifteen, and moods were a part of being a teenager, but it did seem like more than just that. There had been Amelia's questions about her dad, for instance. Apparently, Kate's stock explanation for why she didn't have a daddy—that, after a single brief encounter, he'd gone off to teach children in Ghana and had never returned—was no longer holding water. There'd also been Amelia asking to go on that absurd semester-abroad program just the morning before.

"Mom, can't you just stay and listen to me for *one* minute right now?"

Amelia had been leaning with her arms crossed against the kitchen counter in their narrow brownstone. With her long blond hair falling in waves over her shoulders and her miraculous eyes—one blue, one hazel—glinting in the warm morning light, Amelia had looked so much older, and taller, than she had only the day before. With Kate's high cheekbones and heart-shaped face, Amelia was a beautiful girl. Sexy now, too, in her low-rise jeans and fitted tank top. Thankfully, she was also still a bit of a tomboy.

"Yes, Amelia, I can listen, for a minute," Kate had said, trying not to lose her patience. From the sour look on her daughter's face, the Thanksgiving trip to Bermuda Kate'd just suggested had been akin to offering up a weekend of dental work. "I'm always here to listen."

"I want to spend next semester in Paris," Amelia said.

"Paris?" Kate jammed her laptop and a handful of files into her bag, then resumed her search for her phone, which she thought she'd left on the counter. Kate ran a hand over her hair as Amelia stared at her. It was still wet, and yet she could have sworn she'd dried it. "For a whole *semester*? And Paris is so far away."

Despite Kate's best intentions, she was getting aggravated. It was hard not to see it as intentional that Amelia was insisting on having this conversation when she knew Kate was already running late. Kate wondered sometimes if Amelia wasn't more strategic than she gave her credit for. She said yes to a lot of things—late nights out, sleepovers, parties—because Amelia asked when Kate was stressed or in a rush. But a semester in Europe was a different story. Kate wasn't going to cave to that simply because it would be easier. But it would have been. Much, much easier.

"What does it even matter?" Amelia made an annoyed, guttural noise. "You're never here anyway."

Kate's long work hours weren't something Amelia usually complained about. Kate had always assumed—*hoped* maybe was a better word—that it was because having a single mother with a demanding career was the only life her daughter had ever known. But Kate was always bracing herself to discover that her daughter still felt the holes, despite her frantic efforts to cram them full of love.

"Amelia, come on, that's not fair. And a semester abroad is for college, not high school."

"It'll be educational."

Kate looked over at her daughter, hoping she'd see some hint of humor around her eyes. There was none. She was completely serious.

"Amelia, I wish I could just blow off my meeting and stay to talk this out," Kate had said, and she'd meant it. "But I honestly can't. Can we please talk more about it tonight, when I get home?"

"Just say yes, Mom!" Amelia had yelled then, startling Kate. Her daughter wasn't a yeller, certainly not *at* Kate. "It's really easy, listen: yes. Just like that."

This is it, Kate had thought. *She's officially a teenager. It'll be her against me from now on, not us against the world.*

The worst part about their argument was that Kate had then ended up getting home the night before too late—late again, late always—to talk about the semester abroad. But she'd been ready when she'd gotten up the next morning—that morning. She'd even woken up early— despite the fact that the meeting with Victor was bound to be one of the most stressful of her career—so she'd have plenty of time to talk to Amelia about Paris. She'd planned to stay firm on her no, but had decided to offer up a trip there together at Christmas. Kate had planned to apologize for not being home more, too, especially lately. She'd still been managing to keep her and Amelia's Friday dinner dates and their Sunday movie nights. But their weekend adventures had been in much shorter supply.

Ever since Amelia was little, Kate had always tried to be sure they took at least one field trip together every weekend—a Broadway show, an exhibit at the Met, the cherry blossom festival at the Brooklyn Botanic Garden, or the Mermaid Parade in Coney Island. But it had been harder with the metastasizing Associated Mutual Bank case, not to mention Amelia's own commitments—field hockey and French club and volunteering and friends. These days, it seemed she was always headed off somewhere, too.

Kate was still standing up near the subway doors, studying her tired reflection in the long window, when the subway's automated conductor came over the PA system.

"We are being held momentarily because of train traffic ahead," the computerized voice said. "Please be patient."

In the end, Kate hadn't had any conversation with Amelia that morning about her job or Paris or anything else. After all that preparation and worry, Amelia had simply sauntered down the stairs all sunshine and light, saying she didn't want to go to Paris after all. Now, of course, that sudden change of heart seemed suspect. Kate still didn't believe that Amelia would have ever done something bad enough to warrant a suspension. But with the erratic way she'd been acting the past couple of days, maybe she could have done something a tiny bit bad.

Kate checked her watch again. One hour and ten minutes late. *Shit.* She was a terrible, terrible mother. It was too much, juggling her job and parenting by herself. She had no margin for error. There were other law jobs that would have allowed her more flexibility—less money, too, though she and Amelia could have made do with much less. Money wasn't the real reason Kate stayed at her job anyway. She liked her job, and she was good at it, and that made her feel capable and secure. Success—first academic, later professional—had always made her feel that way: safe. And that was no small matter given that there was no knight in shining armor on the horizon.

Not that Kate was in the market for a rescue. She wasn't in the market, period. She'd gone on a few dates over the years, mostly because she'd felt like she should. Friends had often insisted on setting her up, too. But Kate had never had good luck with relationships, not in high school, not in college, and not in law school. In fact, her healthiest relationship had been with Seth, whose biggest takeaway from Kate was that he was actually gay. Before Seth, Kate had had other boyfriends, usually the emotionally distant type. At least she was old enough now to recognize that her poor taste in partners had everything to do with her upbringing, though that did not mean it was something she could change.

These days, it was hard to say whether the men she went out with were wrong or if between Amelia and her job Kate couldn't make space for them. Regardless, nothing—no one—had ever stuck. And life had almost seemed easier that way. Except that now, at thirty-eight, Kate's accidental baby—her mother's charming term, one that she used glibly even when Amelia was old enough to understand—might be her only baby. The notion of Kate being the mother of an only child didn't exactly feel wrong, but it *was* recklessly economical.

By the time the train was finally pulling into Grand Army Plaza, Kate was one hour and fifteen minutes late. She sprang off when the train doors finally hissed open, her heart picking up speed as she jogged for the station steps.

Up on the sidewalk, she blinked back the brightness. Shielding her eyes with a hand, she walked briskly, turning onto Prospect Park West. The two-lane, one-way street was quiet at that hour, and Kate's very high client-meeting heels clicked loudly against the concrete. The park, with its brightly hued, late October maples, was across the street on her left. The leaves had begun to fall, gathering in a thick ridge along the wall lining the park, a park Kate hadn't been inside in years.

After fifteen years in Park Slope, Kate still felt more at home in her office than on her own Brooklyn block. She had wanted a cozy, neighborly, open-minded place to raise Amelia, and Park Slope was certainly all of those things. But the Food Coop walkers, the piles of recycled goods left out for the taking, and the tight cliques of shabby-chic families gathered on playgrounds adjacent to their multimillion-dollar brownstones still felt like charming details from someone else's life.

Up ahead, Kate watched two quintessential Park Slope moms, attractive and urban without being overtly hip, chatting as they came out of the park. Each pushed a sleek jogging stroller, a small child gripped in their one free hand, an eco-friendly water bottle in their cup holders. They were laughing as they walked on, unbothered by the little ones tugging at their hands. Watching them, Kate felt as if she'd never had a child of her own.

Kate had always planned on having a family. At least two children, maybe even three. She'd originally hoped to avoid having an only child, given her own less-than-happy solitary girlhood. She had come to realize, though, that having an "only" did not actually require that you treat them from birth like a mini adult. Kate had also assumed that— however many children she did one day have—they would come later. Much, much later. Kate was going to focus on her career first, make some headway, as her mother, Gretchen—professor emeritus of neurology at the University of Chicago School of Medicine—had drilled into her. Career first, kids only if there was time.

But her life had taken a different turn. And in the end, she hadn't wanted to take advantage of any of the "options" Gretchen had pressed on her to "handle" her "unfortunate situation." Because Kate may have admired her mother's professional success, but she had no wish to emulate her in any other way. Instead, Kate took her pregnancy as a sign, one that she would ignore at her peril. And also as a chance for something more.

Motherhood, of course, had been hard, especially single motherhood at the age of twenty-four while still attending law school. But she—they—had survived. Kate and Amelia's true salvation had been Leelah, the nanny who'd cared for Amelia for fifteen straight years. It was Leelah's warmth and compassion and excellent cooking that had truly kept their heads above water. It was with great regret that Kate had scaled back Leelah's hours to only cooking and cleaning while Amelia was at school. Amelia had been insisting since last fall that she was too old for a nanny, and Kate had finally lacked the fortitude to fight her anymore. They both missed Leelah, though: Amelia more than she would admit; Kate more than she could sometimes bear.

Kate paused as the two women with their strollers crossed the street in front of her, then followed them as they headed across Garfield. She watched their narrow hips in their yoga pants, their high, matching ponytails swishing right, then left.

"Look at all those fire trucks," gasped one of the women, stopping so abruptly on the opposite corner that Kate almost crashed into her perfectly sculpted rear end. "Are they at the school?"

"Oh God, I hope not," the other one said, pushing up onto her toes to get a better look. "They're not rushing anywhere at least. It must be a false alarm."

Kate looked toward the fire trucks blocking half of Garfield Street. They were parked in front of a side entrance to Grace Hall's Upper School, an ornate old mansion that looked like a grand public library. Several police cars were in front of the adjacent Grace Hall Lower School, two brownstones that had been overtaken long ago and refurbished in a similar style. The firemen were loitering around the sidewalk, chatting in groups, leaning against their trucks.

There was also an ambulance sitting there with its lights off, doors closed. If there had been an actual fire or some other emergency, it was over now. Or maybe it had been a false alarm.

Amelia couldn't have pulled the fire alarm, could she have? No, only juvenile delinquents did things like pull fire alarms. Whatever Amelia's mood lately, whatever that junior-year-abroad nonsense had been about and however deep her sudden existential crises about her absent dad, Amelia was not, and would never be, a juvenile delinquent.

Kate took a deep breath and exhaled loudly, which caused the taller mother standing in front of her to startle and spin around. She tugged her cherub-faced little girl in the puffy pink vest closer. Kate smiled awkwardly as she stepped around them. She tried to see past the ambulance. There, on the side, was a uniformed officer talking to an older, gray-haired woman in a long brown sweater. She was walking a tiny, shivering dog and was hugging herself, hard.

People weren't interviewed for fire alarms. Kate looked up at the classroom windows. And where were all the kids? The ones whose faces should have been pressed up against the glass, investigating the commotion? Kate found herself moving closer.

"So you heard the scream first?" the police officer asked the gray-haired woman. "Or the sound?"

Scream. Sound. Kate watched two police officers come out of the school's front door, head down the steps, then turn into the school's side yard. When she peered after them, she could finally see that that was where the real action was. At least a dozen police officers were gathered in a large pack. And still, there was no rushing. It no longer seemed like a good sign. In fact, it was beginning to seem like a terrible one.

"Ma'am," came a loud voice then, right in Kate's ear. "I'm going to need you to head back over to the other side of the street there. We need to keep this area clear."

There was a hand on her arm, too, hard and unfriendly. Kate turned to see a huge police officer towering over her. He had a doughy, boyish face.

"I'm sorry, ma'am," he said again, a tiny bit less forcefully. "But this side of the street is closed to pedestrians."

"But my daughter's inside the school." Kate turned back to look at

the building. A bomb threat, an anthrax scare, a school shooting—
where were all the children? Kate's heart was picking up speed. "I
need to get my daughter. I'm supposed to. They called me. I'm already late."

The officer squinted at her for a long time, as though he was willing her to disappear.

"Okay, I guess I can go check it out," he said finally, looking skeptical. "But you still got to go wait over there." He pointed to the other
side of Garfield. "What's your daughter's name?"

"Amelia. Amelia Baron. They called from the headmaster's office
to say she'd been suspended. They said I had to come get her." Immediately, Kate wished she'd left that part out. The officer might be less
inclined to help if he thought Amelia was a troublemaker. Maybe even
the troublemaker. "Wait, before you go," Kate called after him, "can
you at least tell me what happened?"

"We're still trying to figure that out." His voice drifted as he turned
to stare at the building for a minute. Then he turned back to Kate and
pointed again. "Now, go there. I'll be right back."

Kate didn't go where he'd pointed. Instead, she stood on her toes
to see if she could make out what was in the backyard. She could see
there were actually more than a dozen officers back there—some in
uniforms, some in dark suits—clustered up near the side of the building, their backs forming a curved wall. It was as if they were hiding
something. Something awful.

Someone had been hurt, or worse. Kate felt sure of it now. Had
there been a fight? A stray bullet? This was brownstone Brooklyn, but
it was still Brooklyn. Things happened.

As soon as the police officer who'd stopped Kate was through the
school's front doors, she darted up to the fence at the side yard. Officers
were shielding their eyes as they stared up the side of the building toward the roof. Kate stared up there, too. She could see nothing except
the immaculately maintained facade of the old stone building.

When she looked back down, the officers had shifted. And there,
in the center of their protective circle, was a boot. Black, flat-heeled,

rugged, it lay there on its side like a felled animal. But there was something else there, too, something much larger. Something covered with a sheet.

Kate's heart was pounding as she wrapped her fingers around the bars of the wrought iron fence and squeezed. She looked at the boot again. It was the kind that lots of girls wore with skinny jeans or leggings. But Amelia's were brown, weren't they? Kate should know. She should know the color of her own daughter's shoes.

"Mrs. Baron?" came a man's voice then.

Kate whipped around, bracing to be told by the same baby-faced policeman that she wasn't where he'd told her to be. Instead, behind her was an attractive but tough-looking guy in jeans and a hooded sweatshirt. He was about Kate's age, with a strong, square face, a tightly shaved head, and the bound-up energy of a boxer, or maybe a criminal about to make a break for it. There was a badge hanging from a cord around his neck.

"You're Kate Baron?" he asked, taking a step closer.

He had a tough Brooklyn twang that went with the rest of him. But he was trying to seem soft. Kate didn't like his trying to be gentle with her. It made her nervous. Behind him, Kate could see the uniformed officer she'd talked to before, standing on the steps with a gray-haired woman in red reading glasses. They were staring at her.

"Where is Amelia?" Kate heard herself shout. Or had it been someone else? It sounded like her voice, but she hadn't felt the words coming out of her mouth. "What's happened?"

"I'm Detective Molina." He reached out a hand but stopped short of actually putting it on Kate's arm. A tattoo on his forearm—a cross—peeked out from under the sleeve of his sweatshirt. "Could you please come with me, ma'am?"

This wasn't right. She didn't want to go somewhere with this detective. She wanted to be sent somewhere out of the way. Where all the other irrelevant spectators were sent.

"No." Kate jerked away. Her heart was racing. "Why?"

"It's okay, ma'am," he said, putting a strong hand on her elbow and tugging her toward him. Now his voice was lower, more careful, as if Kate had a horrific head wound she was unaware of. "Why don't you just come over here with me and have a seat."

Kate closed her eyes and tried to picture Amelia's feet that morning when she'd happily bounded out the door. Mothers were supposed to know what kind of shoes their children were wearing. They were supposed to check. Kate felt light-headed.

"I don't want to have a seat," she said, her panic rising, "Just tell me what's wrong. Tell me now!"

"Okay, Mrs. Baron, okay," Detective Molina said quietly. "There's been an accident."

"But Amelia's okay, right?" Kate demanded, leaning back against the fence. Why weren't they rushing? Why was the ambulance just sitting there? Where were all the flashing lights? "She has to be okay. I need to see her. I need her. Where is she?"

Kate should run. She felt sure of it. She needed to go somewhere far away where no one could tell her anything. But instead, she was sinking, sliding down to the cold, hard sidewalk. There she sat, balled up against her knees, mouth pressed hard against them as if she were bracing herself for a crash landing.

Run, she told herself, *run*. But it was too late.

And for one long, last moment, there was only the sound of her heart beating. The pressure of her tight, shallow pants.

"Your daughter, Amelia"—the detective was crouched next to her now—"she fell from the roof, Mrs. Baron. She was . . . she unfortunately didn't survive the fall. I'm sorry, Mrs. Baron. But your daughter, Amelia, is dead."

gRaCeFULLY

Because there are 176 definitions for the word *loser* on urbandictionary.com. Don't Be a Statistic

---

Hey bitches,
Here with the shit that's not fit to print . . .

Ah, the clubs. The place where all you desperate social climbers might finally get your slippery hands on that higher rung. Just remember that there isn't actually any honor in your boobs or your wee-wee getting sized up against the pledge next to you, no matter how many hundreds of years they've being doing it.

Then again, could be I just think that because I'm still waiting to get tapped.

Word on the street is that the Tudors and Devonkill are trying to lift their street cred by going hard core with hazing, the Magpies are thinking outside the box—ha-ha—on invites this year, and Wolf's Gate is staking out a great British invasion.

Speaking of great British invasions, how many people is Ian Greene going to bed down? It's only the second week of school, and from what I hear he's approaching double digits with lots more fair ladies lining up to be laid—our resident harlots Sylvia Golde, Susan Dolan, and Kendall Valen just to name three.

And Dylan Crosby? Dear, beautiful, mysterious Dylan? No, she's not one of them. Not sure who she's getting with, but she's not the kind to queue up for anything.

Word is George McDonnell and Hannah Albert finally consummated their decade-long obsession with each other. And Carter Rose has his eye on one tight-legged sophomore. Oh poor Carter, don't bother. That chastity belt snaps open for no man.

And stayed tuned, everyone. I've got mad scoop on the academic probation roll . . . I'm thinking I'll just put it up in its entirety in the next issue. I mean—imho—if you can't keep your head above water in a cush school like this, you deserve to get made a fool out of.

facebook

Amelia Baron

Can't believe she let her best friend talk her into wearing skinny jeans during a heat wave

George McDonnell and **2 others** like this

Sylvia Golde can't believe her best friend is such an epic fashion failure; u should be thanking me you know . . .

Amelia

Halfway down our front steps, I could already see Sylvia waiting up in the usual spot—Garfield and Eighth Avenue, the near corner. Sylvia lived on Berkeley between Seventh and Eighth, around the corner from Mr. Wonton and one block over from Ozzie's, the coffee place where they would sometimes give you free refills on hot chocolate and had huge samples of cookies practically every day. For four years, Sylvia and I had been meeting on the same corner every day to walk the last couple of blocks to school together. Four years ago—when we were eleven—was the first year that Sylvia's mom would let her walk to school on her own. And she had all sorts of tests Sylvia had to pass first, about what to do in an emergency, who to go to for help, what to do if someone tried to grab her.

My mom finally said I could walk to school alone when I was eleven, too. She had her own tests. But I think she got them from Sylvia's mom. I love my mom, but she gets most of her ideas about how to be a mom from other moms. Pretty much whatever Sylvia was allowed to do, I was allowed to do, too.

But Sylvia had never had a nanny, so getting rid of Leelah was on me. I liked Leelah and all, but what sophomore in high school had a nanny? That was pretty much my argument. And I was psyched when my mom finally said okay. Now that school had started, I did kind of miss Leelah. I never would have told my mom—I didn't want her to feel bad or whatever—but it was weird being alone, like, all the time.

I waved at Sylvia, and she held up a hand in one of her two-finger, too-cool-for-school salutes. It was the second week of September, but it was still that disgusting, soupy New York City hot where you feel like you're walking through mesh and everywhere smells like garbage, or pee. Of course, Sylvia wasn't about to let a little heat keep her from busting out her new fall styles. Clothes were to Sylvia what books were to me: the only thing that really mattered. So there was Sylvia, up at the corner in skinny jeans, platform sandals, and a long, sleeveless sweater. Sleeveless yes, but it was still a sweater. She'd showed it to me the afternoon before—it was a cool purplish-eggplant color with a big loose collar. Funky and almost a little weird, the kind of thing I would have looked stupid in. But it totally worked on Sylvia.

I waved back to her as I stuffed *The Handmaid's Tale* into my bag to finish reading at lunch. For the first time ever, Sylvia and I weren't in the same lunch period except on Fridays. I could always sit with Chloe or Ainsley or someone from the field hockey team. Sylvia and I weren't each other's only friends, but we didn't have a posse like a lot of other kids. We'd never be asked to join one of those clubs either. Not that we wanted to. The clubs were a stupid idea, with all their dumb secrets and hazing crap. They'd been around at Grace Hall from like the 1920s up through the 1980s, when some freshman kid pledging the all-boys club tried to go train surfing drunk and got his head cut off. After that the school banned the clubs.

Then a couple of years ago someone started bringing the clubs back. Woodhouse, the new headmaster, went all schizoid at first, saying he was going to expel people and whatnot. Then it was, like, radio silence. Rumor was that some of the parents of kids in the clubs had paid him to butt out because they were worried about their kids' college apps.

But Sylvia and I had made a pact that we'd never join a club anyway, at least not unless we were both invited and even then probably not. We had other things. Sylvia had her boyfriends, and I had my books and my new friend Ben. But mostly we'd had each other. It had always been that way. We might have seemed like oddball friends to some people—me the virginy, brainy jock and Sylvia the slutty fashion queen—but we were alike in ways that mattered, especially when you were like five, which was when we started out being BFFs. We became friends in kindergarten, mostly because we'd both hated playing dress up. I'd thought that kind of girly thing was dumb in general. Sylvia had hated dress up because the clothes on offer were always shitty. That was us. We always ended up in the same place, just for different reasons. Plus, we had history. A lot of it.

Up on the corner, Sylvia tugged at the neck of her sweater, pretended to look at the watch she wasn't wearing, and waved for me to hurry. She was probably sweating to death in that stupid sweater. But Sylvia would have gotten totally hurt if I'd pointed out that she looked kind of silly wearing it in that heat. Then she'd say something mean. Sylvia was like a crab that way: if you poked her wrong, she'd snap your finger right off.

Besides, Sylvia did look good. She might not have been so practical, but she was always stylish. Sylvia read British *Vogue* and fashion blogs like *Style Rookie* and dreamed of turning into the next fifteen-year-old fashion phenom. Ick—that was what I thought, in general, about the whole stupid fashion thing. But Sylvia thought the books I read for fun were pretentious, and she wasn't totally wrong. All in all, it was safer to keep my mouth shut in my own glass house.

I tried to pick up the pace before Sylvia had an aneurysm, but between my field hockey bag and my backpack and the fact that my legs were starting to sweat under my own skinny jeans, it was hard to move very fast.

"Jesus, you're slow," Sylvia said when I finally made it to her.

"It's these jeans," I said, pinching at the sticky fabric. "Which—do I have to remind you—were your idea."

Sylvia smiled. "They make you slow as all get out, but they do look good." Then she frowned, pointing at my T-shirt. "But what's up with that gross top? That's not what I said to wear with them."

"The shirt didn't fit right." That was a lie. I hadn't even tried it on. When Sylvia had left it for me, I'd known there was no way I'd be caught dead in it. "It had these, like, puffy shoulders that made me look, I don't know, like—"

"Like a girl?" Sylvia crossed her arms.

"I was going to say like a doily."

"Your problem is you confuse feminist with frumpy. Have you ever seen pictures of Betty Friedan? She was actually kind of fabulous."

"How do you even know who Betty Friedan is?"

"I'm not an idiot." Sylvia rolled her eyes as she started toward school. "I just like my social activism with a little style."

Sylvia readjusted her books on her narrow hip. They were tied together with their usual satiny brown ribbon. On style principles, Sylvia refused to carry any kind of book bag. Secretly, I think she'd been hoping to start a trend. She'd tried to launch a bunch of different ones. So far, none had taken off. But nobody at Grace Hall made fun of any of Sylvia's weirdo fashion statements either—not her crazy hats or huge sunglasses or purses covered in Skittles—which was like a victory, you know, full stop. I might have been a better student, and a better athlete. But Sylvia had always been way better at being herself.

When we turned onto Prospect Park West, the sidewalk was jammed. It was like that every morning on the way to school. And every morning beating your way through it totally sucked ass. There were stressed-out, lower-school parents ramming their strollers into your ankles or huffing in your ears as they dragged their little kids to school. There were middle-school kids on scooters crashing into you, and all of the high-school cliques screaming at one another up and down the block, most of it swears. As if that could turn them from rich prep-school kids into the Brooklyn thugs they wanted to be.

That stretch of Prospect Park West leading up to the school's main doors was where a lot of the real Upper School drama played out.

People broke up with each other, got into fights, made plans to hook up. And whenever something real bad happened—like when George Mc-Donnell gave some first-grade girl a bloody nose when he accidentally clocked her with his backpack while chasing some other idiot down the sidewalk—Mrs. Pearl would jump on the PA system first thing, sounding like she'd been dying for an excuse to ream everybody out.

"Misbehavior en route to school is equivalent to misbehavior *on school grounds*," she'd screech, like that was going to make us all listen more. "Once you leave your parents' guardianship you are deemed under the supervision of Grace Hall. Fighting will not be tolerated, nor will horseplay involving rough bodily contact. Punishments will be imposed for such conduct in accordance with the Grace Hall Student Code of Conduct."

I wasn't any expert, but that didn't even sound constitutional. The first time I heard Mrs. Pearl say it, I'd tried to stay awake late enough to ask my mom her professional opinion, but I'd fallen asleep waiting for her to get home.

"Ouch," I yelped when we were still a block away from school. I grabbed the back of my head where something had whacked into me.

When I looked up, Carter Rose was smiling back at me. He pointed a finger in my direction, then darted off toward the school. This was how the sophomore boys flirted: by hitting you on the head.

"Did Carter seriously just smack me on the back of the head?" I asked, my ears still ringing.

"He likes you." Sylvia grinned, as we watched him dive into the mess of people slowing down in front of us. "You should give him a chance. He's supercute *and* he's a lacrosse player. You guys have so much in common."

"I play field hockey. They are two totally different sports. You know that, right?" I asked, kind of annoyed. Sylvia was always pushing me toward guys, any guy. "Besides, Carter's like a big hyper dog. No thanks."

"Yes, but he is a *cute* hyper dog."

With his lanky body, shaggy blond hair, and high cheekbones, Carter was widely crushed upon. But not by me. I wasn't sure yet what my type was, but it wasn't him.

"Yeah, no thanks," I muttered. "When I need a matchmaker, I'll let you know."

"Suit yourself." Sylvia shrugged as the school's front steps came into view, the crowd clogged up into a big pile around them.

The security guard, Will, was standing at the top, waving everyone inside with his big puffy hands. As we slowed to a stop on the edge of the pack, Sylvia grabbed my arm hard, jerking me toward the bushes.

"Ouch, Sylvia. What are you doing?"

"Sorry," she said. Her voice was wired all of a sudden, and her eyes were jumping around like she wanted to be sure no one was listening. "I was going to keep this a secret so I didn't jinx it, but I can't stand it anymore. I *have* to tell you."

"Tell me what?" I had to give Sylvia credit, it was a good opening. Then again, I knew not to get my hopes up. Sylvia could find crazy high drama in the way somebody stopped to tie his shoes.

"I said hi to him yesterday"—she leaned in even closer—"and you are *not* going to believe what happened!"

"Him who?" I asked. I could tell I was supposed to know. But then I got suspicious. Sylvia was acting like such a whack job all of a sudden. The last time she'd been that way it had been for a bad reason. "You didn't take one of your mom's Ativans again, did you, Sylvia? You shouldn't go into school if—"

"I didn't take anything!" Sylvia yelled so loud a bunch of people, mostly moms, turned to look at us.

"Whatever—sorry," I mumbled. I folded my arms out of reach so she couldn't manhandle me again. "I was just trying to help."

"I don't need your help, okay?" she said. "*I* have a mom, remember?"

"Okay, ouch."

That was Sylvia. She had no filter. She said really mean stuff: about my MIA dad, my mom not being home. *Little Orphan Amelia*, she'd even called me once. She did it when she felt like you'd hurt her feelings first. It wasn't the best part of her. And sometimes I yelled at her about it. But I tried to overlook the stuff she said about my mom because I actually think she was jealous. My mom was all I had, and she wasn't home a lot, but the time we had together was awesome, and when my mom wasn't there, I knew she wished she was. We fought sometimes about stupid stuff, but I always knew she loved me. *Really* knew it. Sylvia's mom, Julia, seemed great to me, but Sylvia kind of hated her. I never really understood why.

"I was just trying to tell you something that happened." Sylvia was all sour now. "It was important to me, but if you don't care—"

"I care," I said, swallowing the dig about my mom. Because Sylvia couldn't help being Sylvia. "Come on, tell me. I'm totally listening now."

Sylvia looked around with a crunched-up face for a minute more, as if there was any chance she wouldn't tell me her secret. Who else was she going to tell?

"Okay, fine," Sylvia said finally, her face bouncing back to a mischievous grin. "Ian Greene," she breathed. "I finally said hi to him yesterday, and guess what happened?"

Sylvia was more obsessed with Ian Greene than she had ever been with any guy, ever. And that was saying *a lot*.

The first time we'd both seen him was the week before school started. We'd been lying side by side on my bed, my laptop resting on our knees as we went through the new Grace Hall "meet book," which had just been posted online. Ian Greene was new. And with his perfectly imperfect hair and dark, moody eyes, he was hot, no question. Even I could see that. Plus, it said HAMPSTEAD HEATH, UK, under his name, which meant he was also going to have an accent. Hampstead Heath sounded fancy, too. Noble even. For all we knew, Ian Greene might be royalty.

"Don't be stupid," Sylvia had said when I'd suggested as much. She'd been to England several times. "Hampstead Heath is like the Brooklyn of London, except there they all live in these gazillion-dollar minimansions." Then she'd turned to me and smiled. "But you never know, he could be, like, a count or something."

Not surprisingly, Sylvia wasn't the only person jacked up about Ian Greene's arrival. Half the girls in the Grace Hall Upper School had their sights set on him before the first day of classes. And in person, even I had to admit he was a lot of a lot. He had a natural, bad-boy charisma and a quick, lopsided grin that made him hard to look away from. He played acoustic guitar and wrote music, too, but his real talent lay in photography, as did his father's, whose photographs were supposedly hanging in MoMA. The Greene family had moved to Brooklyn so that Ian's mother could take over as chief curator of the Brooklyn Museum.

Ian hadn't wasted any time taking advantage of all the female attention either. But somehow, the very unassuming way he'd gone about sleeping with every girl who came his way made the whole thing seem sort of civilized.

"Aren't you even going to ask me?" Sylvia demanded, glancing in the direction of the Grace Hall steps.

"Ask you what?" I'd completely lost track of what we'd been talking about.

"What happened when I said hi to Ian," Sylvia snorted, stamping her foot.

"Oh yeah, totally. What happened?"

She squinted at me for a second. "He came over *to my house*." She gushed finally. "And . . ." Sylvia looked around again, but the crowd on the sidewalk was thinning as most kids—the nonlate ones—had streamed inside. Her eyes got wide as she put a hand to her lips. "And we *totally* kissed."

"Really?" I asked, trying to sound excited. But really I was kind of aggravated. I didn't even know why. "That's amazing!"

Because I had to give it to Sylvia. A lot of times she exaggerated, but this was big. Ian Greene had his choice of girls, but he'd picked Sylvia, at least for one afternoon and one kiss. It wasn't actually that much of a surprise that she'd snagged his attention. Boys had always loved Sylvia. She was pretty and curvy in just the right way, but lots of girls at Grace Hall were. Sylvia had something more than that. She had a wildness tucked inside her that made her seem fun and unpredictable and just a little tiny bit dangerous. Of course, it was also the exact same thing that eventually ended up driving the boys away. After all, there's a fine line between wild and full-on whack job.

So if getting with Ian was serious news, why was I so annoyed? Oh my God, was I jealous? Not jealous that Sylvia had kissed Ian Greene, though. It was more like I was jealous that she had wanted to kiss him and she had. I couldn't imagine feeling that way about someone, much less acting normal enough to pull it off.

"I know—it's crazy, isn't it?" Sylvia nodded quickly, biting on her lip. She looked nervous now. "Except I don't know what to do when I see him now. Do I just act like nothing happened? If I'm too nice, he'll think I'm a loser. But I don't want him to think I'm a bitch either." She looked like she was in pain. "I know you're basically totally clueless about this stuff, but do you think I should go up to him?"

"Um, I don't think you should, like, chase him down," I said, trying to sound sure. "But don't ignore him either. Ian's the kind of guy who would think that was stupid, too."

"That's totally *not* helpful *at all*, Amelia. I need specifics." As she moved closer, I stepped back. I was worried she was going to yank one of my arms again. "You have to tell me *exactly* what to do."

"First of all, breathe," I said. Whatever weird jealousy thing had popped up in me was gone just as fast as it had come. I was there to help Sylvia 100 percent now. I put my hands on her shoulders, holding them until she took one deep breath and then another. "This is good, remember? Ian wouldn't have kissed you if he didn't like you."

Sylvia looked down, shuffling her feet back and forth. It was getting late. There were only a few people left out on the sidewalk. Will was still standing next to the open front door, but he was going to let it drop shut any second. When he did, we'd officially be late. I could probably be late for six weeks straight before the school would even think about doing anything about it. So I tried not to care. But I totally did anyway. Especially because I wasn't even *actually* late.

"But what if *I* kissed *him*?" she asked. "I mean, he walked me home and we were talking about photography and then we sat down on my stoop and we were talking about music and fashion, of course, and then . . . I just—" She put a hand over her mouth again and turned to look at me with these crazy, bugged-out eyes. "Oh my God. I think I did. *I* kissed him."

"He kissed you back, right?"

"What if he didn't?" Sylvia's voice was high and screechy.

"Come on, you would have noticed if he wasn't kissing you back."

"How would *you* know?" she snapped, then looked down. "Sorry, but it's true. Anyway, even if he did kiss me back, maybe he was just being polite."

This was starting to get seriously painful. I knew the only surefire way out was to give Sylvia what she really wanted—to have her ego pumped up. It was pretty much what she always wanted in life, just in general.

"Ian Greene seems pretty smart to me. I'm sure he sees how great you are. Now, all you have to do is *not* act like a freak around him."

I linked my arm through Sylvia's, tugging her toward school. Will squinted in our direction. I waved, hoping he'd wait. He leaned forward and shielded his eyes with a hand. Then he shook his head and started talking to himself. I tugged Sylvia a little harder.

"Sorry! We're coming!" I called out, then snaked around to glare at Sylvia. "Come on, being late isn't going to help anything."

"It'll take a lot more than being tardy once to keep you out of Harvard." Sylvia rolled her eyes. "Besides, weren't you *face painting* kids or some shit at the Harvest Fest last weekend? I feel like that has got to earn you, like, a free pass for at least a week."

"I helped set up, that's all," I said, though I had painted one kid's face. Turned out it was less fun than it looked. "And anyway, Harvard? Ick, who said anything about—"

My phone pinged with a text message then. I tried to keep walking as I dug it out of my bag. It was from Ben.

Forgot to tell you. I think u r awesome. Exactly the way you are.

"Oh gross," Sylvia said over my shoulder. She was looking down at my phone. "Are you seriously *still* talking to that freak?"

I never should have told Sylvia about Ben in the first place. Actually, I hadn't told her. Two weeks earlier, she'd picked up my phone—totally without asking me—and read a text I'd gotten from him while I was in the bathroom.

"Oooh, keeping secrets, huh?" she'd asked, rolling onto my bed with my phone up above her head. " 'I feel like no one understands me the way you do?' I have to say, I'm kind of personally insulted by that one, Amelia. Unless, of course, you're getting laid by this Ben character, in which case kudos to you. But then, I'm offended you didn't tell me." I'd stood in the doorway with my arms crossed, squeezing my teeth together so hard it felt like they might crack. I hadn't wanted to explain Ben to Sylvia. I knew she'd make me feel stupid. She bolted upright in my bed. "OMG! You did! You had sex with this guy!"

"No, I didn't, Sylvia. Stop it, seriously."

"OMG, you totally did. Who is he? What does he look like? I can't believe this: my little girl, all grown up, and you left me out of the *entire thing*." But really she'd sounded mostly psyched for me. "Okay, I'll be willing to forgive you for not telling me before, *if* you tell me everything, right now. Starting with a picture of this Ben person. You do have a picture of the boy who deflowered you, don't you? It's that kid from Packard you met at that field hockey game, isn't it?"

I marched over and snatched my phone out of her hand. "No, he isn't that kid from Packard," I said, stuffing the phone in my back pocket. "And he didn't deflower me, which is, by the way, like, the grossest thing you've ever said."

"Gross?" Sylvia asked, putting her clasped hands to her chest and batting her eyes. "Losing your virginity is a beautiful thing. Oh, my little girl."

"Sylvia, stop it!" I yelled. "Just because you're a slut doesn't mean everybody else has to be."

I'd heard myself say it, but I kind of couldn't believe I had.

"A slut?" Sylvia looked like I'd slapped her. "Nice. Thanks, friend."

The worst part was that it was true—Sylvia had slept with nine guys since she'd lost her virginity in the seventh grade. Most of the time she acted like she didn't care. But I knew better. I was her best friend. And Sylvia might have said mean things to me all the time, but that didn't mean she could take what she dished out.

"You know I didn't mean that," I said. "I just . . . I really don't want you to make fun of me about this."

"I wasn't making fun of you," Sylvia said, crossing her arms in a huff. "But I can't believe you have some whole thing going on with a guy and you didn't even tell me. I tell you *everything*."

"He's just a friend," I said, and Sylvia rolled her eyes. "Seriously. I've never even met him in real life."

"What do you mean?"

"He applied to that Princeton summer program, too." I said, already bracing myself for how Sylvia was going to respond. "We e-mail and text and whatever. That's all."

"That's *all*?" Sylvia's mouth was open. "Are you e-mailing *other* kids who applied to that geekfest?"

"No." I rolled my eyes. "Ben's the only one who contacted me. I think he asked the program for the names of the other people who applied from New York."

"Uh-huh," Sylvia said with a smirk. "And what do you want to bet he's not e-mailing any of the boys on that list?"

The worst part was that, at the beginning, I had actually kind of been hoping that Ben and I could maybe turn into a girlfriend-boyfriend thing. I'd never been able to talk to a boy the way I could talk to Ben, and I'd started thinking: Wow, this is finally it. I'm not a freak, after all. I just needed to meet the *right* guy. But it was almost like Ben knew exactly what I'd been thinking, because the very next day he told me he was gay.

"Sylvia, stop it." I was starting to get kind of mad. She could never leave anything alone. "Seriously."

I could have told Sylvia the part about Ben being gay, right then. It probably would have ended the whole conversation. But I kind of liked her thinking there was stuff about me she didn't know.

"Uh-huh. And where does this Ben person go to school?"

She sounded like she *might* consider Ben being okay friend material for me, provided he met certain criteria. Like going to an acceptable school. To Sylvia, Packer, Trinity, and St. Anne's got a thumbs-up. But everybody at Collegiate and Dalton were assholes— meaning that Sylvia had slept with more than one boy from those schools and had been blown off by them.

"He goes to public school, in Albany."

"He lives in *Albany*?" Sylvia had said, like it was herpes. "You *are* joking? That basically doesn't even count as New York. I can't believe you're going to have, like, a long-distance love affair with some dork from *Albany*."

"For the last time, Sylvia, we're just friends!" I'd shouted. "Why can't I just be friends with somebody and have that be that? Maybe I don't even want a boyfriend."

It wasn't until the words had come out of my mouth that I'd realized how very true they were.

As of two weeks later, I still did not want a boyfriend. And there was nothing wrong with a fifteen-year-old girl not wanting a boyfriend. Like Ben had said, there was nothing wrong with *me*. Sylvia being boy crazy didn't change that. *She* had the problem. Not me.

"Ben is my *friend*, Sylvia, for the three hundredth time," I said as I paused at the base of Grace Hall's steps to write back to him. "And like I've also told you three hundred times, he's *gay*, remember?"

Because by then, I had told her. She'd been driving me too crazy about the whole thing not to.

"I'm gonna shut this door in thirty seconds!" Will yelled then.

But I could be late, Sylvia was right. And if I didn't answer Ben now, I wouldn't be able to all day. As I typed, Sylvia snorted, then started up the school steps. She was jealous. And kind of for good reason. It wasn't that I liked Ben *better* than her—Sylvia would always be my best friend—but sometimes he was a lot easier to be friends with.

"*Him* you'll be late for, huh? And you think *I* put boys ahead of you." Sylvia shook her head as she marched on. "Catch you later, I guess. Maybe then you'll have more time for me and my boring Ian drama. And BTW, there's no way that Ben kid is gay. I don't care if he sends you a picture of him doing it with a dude."

Sylvia slid inside just as Will dropped the door. I watched it click shut. There wasn't any rush now. I was already officially late, which was kind of liberating in a weird way.

Thx, I wrote back to Ben. Idk what I'd do w/o u.

I hit Send, then waited.

When my phone pinged again, I looked down to see what Ben had written back. But the text wasn't from him. It was from a blocked number.

Prospect Park Long Meadow, 3:00 p.m. Be there. But only birds of a feather can flock together—come solo, or don't come at all.

Kate

I took eight tests in all.

But the little plus sign in the window never changed. It didn't matter if I took them late at night. Or early in the morning. Or after three glasses of wine. Every single test was still positive.

Today, the on-campus doctor confirmed the pee tests with another pee test. Part of me—the ridiculous part that made all the choices that got me here—thought maybe number nine might do the trick. It didn't. Campus doctors referred me to an OB.

The OB confirmed "the pregnancy" with an ultrasound. They don't say "baby" when they think you might not want to be pregnant. Might decide not to stay that way.

I'm nine weeks, approximately. They can't say for sure, and neither can I.

Because it wasn't just one mistake, one time. It was a summer of bad decisions, brought on by a lifetime of too many of the right ones. Apparently, I know only one way to screw up: royally.

As a little girl, I practiced piano without being told and always did the extra credit. I was class valedictorian at my fancy Chicago prep school. I graduated with honors from Duke and went on to Columbia Law School. I'm an assistant editor of the Columbia Law Review *for Christ's sake.*

Of course, that's a résumé, not a person. A person is what's growing inside me. And that tiny, little germ of a he or a she won't care about any of that. They'll just want me to love them.

And how can I not, when that's the only thing I've ever really wanted, too? Of course, at twenty-four years old, love is the one thing I've never come close to succeeding at.

So maybe I can't promise to love this baby right. But I can promise to try.

Kate

It was only eight thirty a.m. when Kate stepped off the elevator on her office floor. Most of the lights were off, and it was utterly still. A single overhead light shone down on top of the empty receptionist's desk, casting an eerie spotlight on the huge vase of lilies sitting there. It was an awful joke, those flowers being the first thing Kate saw on her first day back at the office. Her mother, Gretchen—in her sole and largely token effort to be helpful—had selected lilies for Amelia's funeral. They were lovely and tasteful. And terrible.

Looking at them, that familiar burn flared up in the back of Kate's throat. The one that was always followed these days by a mad dash to the bathroom where Kate would spend the next ten minutes huddled over the toilet, vomiting, or, more often, dry heaving. The bouts of nausea could be triggered by almost anything, too—the sight of Amelia's favorite cereal in the grocery store, a catalogue for field hockey gear arriving in the mail, a teenage girl's boots. Avoiding food entirely was the only thing that seemed to help at all. In the month since Amelia had died, Kate had lost fourteen pounds. She'd taken to wearing baggy clothes to hide her skeletal frame.

"How do you manage to stay so trim, dear?" a sweet old lady had asked her the other day in Rite Aid.

Simple, Kate had wanted to say. *I'm already dead.*

Instead, she'd pressed her lips together so hard it had made her eyes water as she'd grabbed her prescriptions. The ones her therapist had assured her would help with the nausea and the insomnia. In reality, they'd done nothing except make her feel as if she were underwater. Kate kept taking them in the hope she might eventually drown.

Coming back to work had been a bad idea. At a minimum, Kate needed to get out of the vestibule and into her office. But she couldn't tear her eyes away from the flowers. Frozen there in the elevator bank, she was glad at least that she'd decided to come in early. That way, if she vomited on the floor, there would be time to clean it up. And perhaps she wouldn't actually have to see anyone. That had been her plan: to stay inside her office all day, comforted by the knowledge that there were people—living, breathing people—safely secured on the other side of her locked office door.

Certainly she could never have exchanged pleasantries with anyone. What would there be for them to say to her anyway? Sorry? Sorry your daughter is dead. Sorry your daughter jumped off the roof of her school when you were on your way to pick her up. Sorry you were late. Too bad you'll be reliving that failure for the rest of your miserable life.

As much as Kate didn't want to have small talk with anyone, surely people wanted to avoid her, too. No one wanted to talk to a mother whose only child had just killed herself. Kate could have spared everyone the discomfort by staying home for much longer.

"Take three months at least, then work a couple more from home," Jeremy had said at the funeral. His eyes had been damp and red-rimmed, and for the first time Kate had felt sure that all of his caring overtures over the years had not been an act. No one was that good an actor. His beautiful, teary-eyed wife, Vera, and his three tall sons, all staring at their shoes, had flanked him. The sight of them together like that—handsome, well matched, complete—had almost brought Kate to her knees. "You know how much everyone at the firm loves you, Kate. But we can hold down the fort without you for as long as we need to."

When Vera had stepped forward to hug her, Kate had clutched her back, burying her face into Vera's long, sweet-smelling hair. It had been too much, inappropriate even, given how little the two women actually knew each other. But there was so much life around Vera. Kate had been terrified of what would happen when she let go.

Staying home ended up being easier said than done. Kate had spent the first days after Amelia's death surrounded by her three closest friends from college. They'd swooped in and propped her upright, had seen to it that she ate and bathed and breathed. But they all had families of their own whom they'd had to return to shortly after the funeral. Even Seth—Kate's onetime law school boyfriend, now de facto best friend, who had been so sweet and wonderful—had eventually come round less and less. Kate had insisted. Their days of comfortably impossible, pseudomarital status had long since passed. Seth had a husband now, Thomas, and a daughter of his own who needed him.

Kate's mom and dad had been there, too. Strategically, they had arrived somewhat later, not until the eve of the funeral. Allowing, conveniently, for the messiest of Kate's grief to subside. Her parents had always disdained big displays of any kind of emotion—anger, despair, joy, love—from anyone. But especially their only child. Kate had learned early on the value of swallowing her feelings whole. With Amelia's death, though, her parents must have suspected that there would be no controlling anything this time, and they'd wisely waited a couple of days before arriving in Brooklyn. So they'd missed the part where Kate had scratched her arms until they bled and sobbed so hard that she had broken capillaries in her face. They had quickly departed, too, probably once it became apparent that Kate would not be pulling it together anytime soon.

After her parents had gone and her friends had all returned to their very full lives, Kate was alone. Again. As she always had been before Amelia.

For two weeks, she'd sat in her deathly quiet brownstone sheathed in her guilt and grief, feeling like her skin was being sloughed off in strips and discarded like sheets of cellophane. She'd stared at the ceiling and sobbed until her insides were a burned-out hull. She'd thought about how her life without Amelia would be nothing but an inexplicable void. Nothing but her. Alone. Forever.

Every night she actually managed to fall asleep, Kate would dream she was falling—from the roof of Grace Hall, her office window, the top of the stairs—jolting awake just before she smacked into pavement. And every morning when she awoke she'd be compelled to the top floor of her brownstone, where she'd open a window and lean out, hands pressed against the frame, staring down. Not that forcing herself to see what Amelia had in those last seconds of her life would ever be punishment enough. Nothing would ever be punishment enough.

Because it was Kate's fault, of course, that Amelia was dead. That she had *killed* herself. It was a mother's job to protect her child, even from herself. And Kate had failed, utterly and completely and awfully.

Kate thought often about killing herself, too. About how to do it— her many tranquilizers; where—in her bed; and when—immediately. Thinking she needed to pay for her catastrophic failings by living with her guilt was the only real reason she hadn't gone through with it. Kate went back to work when she could no longer bear sitting there, waiting to slowly decompose.

And so there Kate stood in one of the many reception areas of the illustrious Slone, Thayer—four weeks, two days, and sixteen hours since Amelia had leaped off the roof of Grace Hall—wondering how she could have ever cared what went on there. Because she didn't. Not anymore. Not in the least. She didn't care about anything.

An arriving elevator chimed behind Kate, and she lurched forward down the hallway toward her office before anyone could emerge from behind the doors. She picked up the pace around the corner as a light in an office down the hall went on. She should have known there would be someone already there, no matter how early she arrived. At a place like Slone, Thayer, there always was.

"Hey!" Someone shouted just as she was about to open her door. Kate startled and dropped her keys. Daniel Moore, of all people. Kate knew it was him without looking up. He was the last person she felt like seeing at that moment. Rushing over, he grabbed her keys from the floor before she could bend to pick them up. "I didn't mean to scare you. I was just . . . I'm surprised to see you. I thought you were going to work from home for a while."

He sounded disappointed, but he was trying to hide it. Kate wasn't surprised. For Daniel, one less junior partner was one less person to compete with. Not that their relationship was as simple as being fellow partners. Ever since the two had met their first week of Columbia Law School, they'd swung between distant respect, outright hostility, and something else—something substantially more humiliating—that Kate had worked hard for a long time to forget. Surprisingly, perhaps, she'd often succeeded. Right now, though, that ugly ancient history loomed over her.

"Being alone in my house day after day . . . I needed to go some-where," Kate said, meeting eyes with Daniel for the first time as he handed her keys back to her. He had on a tie, loosened at the neck, and a rumpled shirt. He was unshaven, and his eyes were bloodshot, as if he'd been up all night. But on Daniel, the effect was flattering. His perfectly shorn blond hair and meticulously preppy clothes had, for Kate, always been some of the least attractive things about him. But not *the* least. The least attractive thing about Daniel was his utter lack of compassion. "You look like you've been here all night."

Daniel looked down at his clothes and smiled sheepishly. "This As-sociated thing has kind of exploded."

His voice was trying to make that sound as if it was a bad thing, but the glint in his eye said differently. Kate's and Daniel's careers at Slone, Thayer had been in lockstep ever since they'd both joined the firm as summer associates. A decade and a half later, they were both well-respected litigation partners. But only Kate was one of Jeremy's disciples, an inequity that seemed to drive Daniel to quiet, but utter, distraction. Handling Associated in her absence had been a huge op-portunity for him.

Kate could tell that Daniel was desperate for her to inquire further

about Associated. But she didn't care if the big news was that the SEC
had come down and subjected Victor Starke to a cavity search. Jeremy
had gone to great lengths to assure her that she didn't have to worry
about Victor or Associated Mutual Bank while she was on leave, and
she hadn't. Now that she was back, she couldn't have forced herself to
care about it if she'd tried.

"Exploded." Kate heard herself say. It was more statement than
question. Still, she hated giving Daniel the satisfaction of even her perceived curiosity.

"Not in a bad way," Daniel said eagerly. "Turns out we got the subpoena quashed after all. SEC appealed, of course." He shrugged as if
it was all in a day's work. "Arguments are later today. I was up half the
night briefing Jeremy by phone. You know him, smart enough to pull
his all-nighter from home so he won't look like crap when he gets here.
Speaking of which, I should probably go shower. Jeremy said I could
argue part of the brief. Don't want to give him any reason to leave me
at the courthouse door."

"Right." Kate tried to smile but couldn't really. She wanted to get
away from Daniel, *now*. "Don't let me hold you up. I should probably
be getting inside anyway. I'm not exactly fit for public consumption."

"Okay," Daniel said, narrowing his eyes slightly, as if he was contemplating saying something more but then decided not to. "It's good
to see you, Kate. I'm glad you've made it back. We . . . the firm missed
you. Let me know if there's anything I can do."

Daniel was trying his best to be nice, Kate could see that. And he
meant well—or at least didn't mean terribly—even if there was nothing on earth he, of all people, could possibly do for her.

"I appreciate that, Daniel," she said. "Now you should go. Good
luck."

"Thanks," Daniel said, blowing some air out of his puffed-up
cheeks. "I think I might need it."

Kate closed her office door and leaned back against it for a minute
before pushing herself forward and dumping her things on her desk.

She made a point of not looking out her wide window at the jumbled cityscape below. Kate's office was on the twenty-eighth floor, near the corner, so that if she leaned into her window and looked down, she could see both Forty-third Street and Seventh Avenue. But looking down from that height, imagining—as she surely would—the sensation Amelia must have felt as she was falling, would only bring the nausea right back.

Her computer hadn't even fully started up when her office phone rang. UNIVERSITY OF CHICAGO, the caller ID read, followed by the main campus number. Theoretically, it could be either of her parents. With many years of illustrious work in their respective fields, Gretchen Deal and Robert Baron were both professors, her mother at the medical school and her father at the business school. But Robert—the more distant but comparatively warmer of the two—never called Kate. He'd e-mail occasionally, and they had nice talks when they saw each other once a year at Christmas, but for Robert the telephone was far too intimate and much too deliberate.

Kate stared at her phone, debating whether to let the call go to voice mail. But Gretchen was relentless. If she had something she wanted Kate to hear, she would hunt her daughter down and make her listen to every last keen, insightful word. Finally, Kate took a deep breath and picked up the phone.

"Kate Baron," she said quietly, pretending she didn't know who was on the other end, as if that could magically make it be someone different.

"You're there!" her mother called out cheerfully. "I was hoping you'd make it."

Gretchen had been the biggest advocate of Kate's returning to work as soon as possible. Immediately, preferably. Gretchen made clear this was only because she felt it was in Kate's best interest to get out of the house, to be distracted. But Kate knew her mother better than that. In reality, Gretchen was probably more worried about Kate's missing out on important advancement opportunities at work.

"Yes, here I am." Kate exhaled. "I made it."

"Really, I think that's for the best, Katherine," Gretchen said in her usual rapid-fire staccato, the one that always made Kate feel as if a timer was about to go off. "I'm sure they've missed having you there. Jeremy especially. He depends on you more than you think."

"He works with two dozen junior partners. He depends on all of us," Kate said flatly. She was annoyed that this was why her mother was calling her. And even more annoyed that she was annoyed. By now, Kate should have been used to her work being her mother's focus. Gretchen had called every couple of days since Amelia's death, and in each conversation she'd been far more concerned about the state of Kate's career than her grief. "I'm sure he survived just fine without me."

"I wouldn't be so sure," Gretchen said, her voice lifting into an I-told-you-so singsong. "In any case, I think it's good progress. Forward momentum. A look on the bright side."

Kate felt her stomach tighten. "Bright side?"

"Yes, Katherine, to this whole, terrible mess."

"Mess?" As though Amelia's memory were a thing that could be swept up and discarded into a trash can.

"You'll get angry at me for saying this, but someone needs to."

Gretchen could always render herself simultaneously the hero and martyr, even in situations that had nothing to do with her.

"Needs to say what?" Kate heard herself ask, even though she did not want to know.

"Amelia is gone, Katherine, and that is a horrific tragedy," Gretchen said briskly. "But it's also a fact of life. A life which, last I checked, you were still here living. Personally, I think it would be easier for you to move on if you took advantage of some of your newfound freedom."

"Freedom?" The word came out sounding gummy.

"Come now, dear, don't be deliberately obtuse," Gretchen said. "*I* was a working mother, too, remember? I know the stress of being forever torn between work and home. Freedom from that, that's what I mean. Who knows, maybe you'll even have time to meet someone now.

Stranger things have happened. You could start all over again. And Amelia would want that for you. She would want you to be happy."

Kate's heart was pounding in her ears. She could have imagined that in some small, dark corner of her mother's heart, she would see Amelia's death as a chance for Kate to get on the straight and narrow. But saying it out loud was monstrous, even for Gretchen. Kate was gripping the phone so hard she thought she might snap it in half.

"Mom?"

"Yes, dear?" Gretchen sounded so pleased with herself. Like having offered Kate this brutal insight had been a grand act of selfless charity. "Oh, wait, hold on." There were some voices in the background on Gretchen's end. "Lee just popped in. There's a *Times* reporter on the other line for me. Apparently, I agreed to do some interview. I don't even recall what this one's about." She laughed breezily. "In any case, what was it you were going to say?"

"Fuck you, Mom," Kate said calmly. "That's what I was going to say: fuck you."

Kate placed her phone gently down into its cradle and stared at it. She kept waiting for the receiver to explode. It didn't. Nothing happened. It was liberating, and oddly embarrassing, that it had taken her this long to stand up to Gretchen, to tell her mother how she really felt about anything. But she was done making people happy, behaving well, being polite. She was done being a good girl.

Kate exhaled in a long stream, her shoulders sagging forward. Her computer had finally started up, her e-mail in-box open in front of her. There were only a handful of new messages since she'd checked from home the evening before, far fewer than there would have been in the days before Amelia died. Now that Kate was back in the office, though, people would probably take that as an invitation to stop pulling punches. And a part of Kate was looking forward to getting swallowed by the grind of her job, even if it was a job that meant nothing to her anymore. Kate was still staring at her e-mail in-box when her cell phone alerted her that she had a text message.

"Here we go," she muttered as she dug around in her bag.

Gretchen was never just going to take being told to fuck off.

Finally, Kate laid her hands on her phone and pulled it from her bag. She looked down at the message on the screen.

Amelia didn't jump.

Kate snapped her eyes closed. No, that message hadn't said what she thought it had. It wasn't possible. Kate squeezed her eyes even tighter before finally opening them. But when she looked down at her phone again, the message was still there. Amelia didn't jump. She read it three times more, and yet the words remained the same. Kate's heart was pounding as she rested her phone gently on the center of her desk. Then she rolled her chair slowly away so that she could stare at the phone from a safe distance.

Please, was all she could think. *Please don't do this to me. Please don't torture me.*

Why would someone play such a sick joke? And *who*? Kate had been too startled even to check whom the message was from. She was leaning over her desk, peering at her phone for the sender, when her office door opened. Kate bolted upright.

"What in the world?" Kate's secretary, Beatrice, asked. She was staring at Kate as if she'd lost her mind. "I was about to call security when I saw your lights on. What are you doing here?"

"Beatrice, you scared me," Kate panted, a hand to her chest.

"I can see *that*." Beatrice looked Kate up and down with wide, disapproving eyes. Beatrice, a mother of six children, treated Kate and her other assigned lawyer as if they were her seventh and eighth. "I thought we'd agreed you'd take at least six more weeks working from home. Jeremy didn't pull some of his oh-please, you're-so-talented, you're-the-only-one garbage, did he? Because I swear, I'll—"

"Jeremy didn't call me back in." Kate shook her head. "I needed to get out of the house."

"So you came here?" Beatrice asked. "Back to *work*?"

"I didn't have anywhere else to go." Kate glanced over at her phone. She thought for a second she might tell Beatrice about the message, but it felt premature. She was still hoping she'd imagined it.

"You had best keep your door closed," Beatrice said. "Otherwise, these vultures will have your carcass picked clean by lunchtime."

Beatrice's face froze then, as though she wanted to stuff her inadvertent reference to death back into her mouth. Kate wanted to tell Beatrice not to worry, that it was okay. But all she could think about was that text.

Amelia didn't jump.

It was especially cruel, given how long it had taken for Kate to accept that Amelia *had* killed herself. The notion that Amelia had been caught cheating—on an English paper, no less—was especially absurd. Detective Molina informing Kate that all the preliminary physical evidence pointed to Amelia's having committed suicide hadn't really convinced her, at least at first.

Instead, Kate had wanted someone to blame, and the school had been her primary candidate—a faulty lock on the roof, inadequate supervision, an inherently dangerous condition. Kate had also considered the possibility that Amelia had been pushed, but not very seriously. Someone wanting to hurt Amelia was almost as unbelievable as her wanting to hurt herself.

And Detective Molina had done his investigating—he'd searched Amelia's room and talked to her teachers and friends; he'd checked her computer and her phone; he'd looked for signs of something that could have caused a fall, a dip in the roof surface, something that Amelia could have tripped on. He'd looked for evidence of a struggle, too. But there had been nothing, except the word *sorry* on the wall. A week later, Molina had called to inform Kate that the medical examiner had made the preliminary finding of suicide official. And that was that: Amelia had killed herself.

The whole thing had taken nine days. Nine days to be told that the daughter she had been best friends with, the daughter she had looked after and laughed with and loved, had been someone she hadn't really known. That she'd been someone filled with a sadness so great it had taken her last breath and yet Kate had somehow missed all the signs.

They'd had a handy explanation for that, too: impulsive suicide. It happened more than anyone knew, or so said Dr. Lipton, the school psychologist from Grace Hall. People apparently routinely decided to kill themselves and then went ahead and did it all within hours. No giving away prized possessions, no suicide note like in the after-school specials of Kate's youth. According to Dr. Lipton, Amelia's getting caught cheating could easily have been the trigger, especially if she'd already been feeling emotionally overwhelmed by problems with a friend, a breakup, trouble at home. Just the ordinary stress of being a teenager could have been enough to set the stage. And Kate's arguing otherwise only made her feel more responsible.

"You sure you should be here?" Beatrice asked. She sounded even more concerned now, probably because Kate had been sitting there, staring at the floor, for God knows how long. "You really don't look okay."

There was a knock on Kate's office door before Beatrice could press her for an answer. Standing there in the doorway behind Beatrice was Jeremy. He was wearing a sharp navy suit and striped tie that set off his blue eyes. Kate hadn't seen him since the funeral, but they'd talked a couple of times by phone, and Jeremy had sent several e-mails— brief, but flawlessly kind—checking in on her.

"Hi," he said quietly, staying near the door.

"Hi," Kate said, trying to pull herself together.

"You're back."

"I'm back."

As they stared at each other, Kate could feel Beatrice watching them, looking from Jeremy to Kate then back to Jeremy. Kate knew Beatrice's eyebrows were raised without even having to look at her. People talked about Jeremy and everything he did and everyone he did it with. They always had. Much was made of too many cases assigned here, too many dinners behind closed doors there. Some of it might have been true—parts definitely were—but most of it certainly wasn't.

Kate's phone vibrated again then, rattling loudly against her desk. A second message. Kate sucked in some air as she leaned tentatively to look at it.

Amelia didn't jump. You know it and I know it

Kate clamped a hand over her mouth and tried not to cry.

"Whoa, what's the matter?" Jeremy asked, stepping inside the office.

He headed straight for her desk and picked up the phone. His brow was wrinkled as he looked down at the message.

"Who sent this?"

Getting the messages was bad enough. But Jeremy standing there, looking at Kate as if she was some kind of maimed animal? It was entirely too much.

"I have no idea," Kate said, trying to swallow back her rising tears. "I got another one a couple of minutes ago. Someone trying to get their kicks, I guess."

"Kicks? That doesn't make any sense," Jeremy said skeptically. "You don't think there could be any truth to it, do you?"

"Truth? No, I don't think so. The police—" Kate shook her head. Despite her efforts, tears had made their way into her eyes. She looked down at her desk, hoping no one would notice. The worst part was that its being an actual, legitimate message hadn't even really occurred to her. Kate had assumed that it was just someone harassing her. "But I guess . . . I honestly don't know."

"Well, it's a blocked number," Jeremy said, looking back down at Kate's phone. "At a minimum, we should find out who sent it." He turned and held the phone out to Beatrice. "Would you mind taking Kate's phone to Duncan in IT? I'm sure he can help us get a number for the person who sent it."

"Good idea," Beatrice said, snatching the phone from Jeremy and striding out the door. "Blocked number, my ass."

Jeremy watched Beatrice leave, then looked down at the floor. Kate felt as if he was looking for a way to leave gracefully.

"Thanks for that. But I don't want to hold you up, dealing with this. I'm sure it's nothing, and anyway, aren't you going to be late for court?" she asked, trying to let him off the hook. "Daniel told me about the subpoena getting quashed. Victor must be happy."

"Victor, happy? I'm not sure I'd go that far," Jeremy said finally, looking up at Kate. The morning sun coming in the windows behind her had turned his eyes a sad, watery blue. "For the record, I agreed with you about the Motion to Quash being pointless. You were giving your client sound advice. I thought pursuing it might even open us up to sanctions. But Daniel—" Jeremy shook his head and clenched his jaw. "You know how he is, like some kind of little yapping dog. He wore me down. But I said he'd have to pay any sanctions out of his own pocket. Looking forward to that possibility might have been the real reason I gave the go-ahead. That and we moved into the new apartment that same week. Exhaustion had left me vulnerable."

Jeremy had never liked Daniel, starting back when he was a summer associate in the same class as Kate, buzzing around Jeremy like an insistent fly. Bald-faced ambition was not a quality Jeremy tolerated, probably because he was so very good at camouflaging his own. But his disdain of Daniel did seem to be about something more. What, Kate did not allow herself to contemplate too deeply. She could have been imagining it anyway. In any case, Daniel wasn't going anywhere anytime soon. Jeremy's personal opinions notwithstanding, Daniel was an exceptional lawyer, one of the best in the firm. And Jeremy liked winning more than he disliked Daniel.

"It seems to have turned out all right," Kate said.

"The fact that it turned out okay doesn't mean that challenging the subpoena was the prudent course. Good luck is not the same thing as wise counsel. And by the way, we're going to lose today on appeal, no question. Why do you think I have Daniel arguing the second half of the brief?" Jeremy smiled, looking very pleased with himself. Then his face changed, turned serious again. "Listen, it may not be my place here even to ask—actually, it definitely isn't. But with this message and everything, are you *sure* Amelia's death was a suicide? I know they talked about that 'note' she supposedly left on that wall near where she fell. But it was really just *one* word, wasn't it?"

"Yeah. 'sorry.' That was it. I kept telling the police that Amelia took writing and words so seriously. That if she'd left a suicide note, it would have been epic." Kate shrugged, then shook her head. "But maybe I'm just deluding myself. The police certainly thought I was."

"They confirmed that it's her handwriting?" Jeremy asked.

Kate blinked at him. Such a simple, simple question. Why hadn't she thought about getting the handwriting analyzed? She'd been so overwhelmed, upset, vulnerable. Alone. And Detective Molina had acted as if there was something wrong with her whenever she'd asked one too many questions. It was bad enough being the mother of a child who had killed herself. Being regarded as a mother in denial was just unbearable.

"God, I am so stupid," Kate breathed. "I never questioned it when they said it was Amelia's. You're right. I should have had it analyzed myself."

"Taking the police at their word is reasonable, not stupid," Jeremy said with his usual ease. "But now, with this text, maybe it's time to take a closer look . . . at everything."

"I think maybe I've been afraid this whole time to question too much. Maybe I'm afraid of what I might find. I don't know."

"Amelia was a good kid," Jeremy said. "And you were a good mother. Nothing you find is going to change that."

Kate smiled sadly, tears filling her eyes again. Jeremy always knew the perfect thing to say, to everyone, about everything. He couldn't help himself.

"Listen, I know the police commissioner. Well, 'know' might be a stretch, but we're both on the board of the Boys and Girls Club. Let me make a few calls, see if maybe we can get that handwriting analyzed. We'll start there and see where it leads."

Kate nodded. There was a part of her that was worried about letting Jeremy do this. Of letting him get too involved, especially when she so desperately wanted him to.

"That would be great, thank you," she said, feeling as if she was betraying someone. She wasn't sure whom. "It's . . . I've been . . . thank you."

Jeremy turned back at the door.

"Please." He smiled, but with a tinge of melancholy. "It's the least I can do."

Amelia

AMELIA

shld I go?

BEN

go where?

AMELIA

to the thing in the park; you know, birds of a feather flock together

BEN

Idk come alone? snds like a trap to me

AMELIA

but I'm curious

BEN

so was the cat

AMELIA

good point

BEN

your school is filled with crazies

AMELIA

u r freaking me out

BEN

good. Scared is safer.

AMELIA

   grt. Thx.

BEN

   have Sylvia go w/ u

AMELIA

   she wasn't invited

BEN

   oh my

AMELIA

   yup. oh my

BEN

   she will b mad

AMELIA

   yup

BEN

   yikes and b careful.

AMELIA

   I will . . . love u!

BEN

   luv u 2; text me aftr. byeee

facebook

Amelia Baron

is flirting with disaster

Carter Rose	that's hot
Sylvia Golde	flirting? Sorry, but I'm gonna have to call bullshit on that one
Carter Rose	you kiss your momma with that mouth
Sylvia Golde	f-off carter

Amelia

When I poked my head out from the little path that ended at the Picnic House in Prospect Park, I could see them in a big pack up by the edge of a clump of trees. At least I figured it was them, and I was actually kind of surprised they were there. I'd been pretty sure that I'd go to the trouble of lying to Sylvia about where I was going and haul my butt all the way to the park, only to find nobody anywhere. Like it would all be one big joke. But there they were, all girls, it looked like, hanging out under the old, crooked trees, waiting.

The Magpies. They had to be.

They'd brought four of the clubs back—the Maggies were all girls, Wolf's Gate was all boys, and Devonkill and the Tudors were coed. They were all crazy about keeping who was in them and what they did a big secret. But people talked in the hallways and on Facebook, and there was stuff about them on *gRaCeFULLY*, too. Word was that the Maggies had contests about who gave the most blow jobs, and that boys from Wolf's Gate had broken into the school and stolen iPads. But people were careful about what they said. Nobody wanted to get on the clubs' bad sides. There were rumors about what happened then, too.

Half of it was probably true. But half was plenty. Mostly, the clubs supposedly did pretty much what you'd expect—hung out, had parties and sex, and decided who could and who couldn't be in them. Actually, it seemed like they spent most of their time doing that. Wolf's Gate and the Maggies were Grace Hall's version of football players and cheerleaders—the coolest kids. Kids in Devonkill and the Tudors were more like second-tier cool.

It wasn't like I'd been looking for an invite into one of the clubs. The people in them were basically sheep, at least most of them, and Sylvia and I had our pact about not joining. Unless and until we changed our minds together, and then only if we were both invited. Because any club that didn't want the both of us wasn't a club either of us wanted to be part of. And my being curious and showing up didn't change that.

I never thought in a million years *I'd* get tapped anyway—if that was even what was going on. And definitely not by the Maggies. Which was another reason I didn't feel so bad about going to check out the whole thing. I was still pretty sure it was all some messed-up joke. But I had to know. It wasn't like I *cared* about being cool, but then again I'd never had the chance to be cool before. Also, it felt kind of good getting picked for something that wouldn't have anything to do with how smart I was or how fast I could run. If the Maggies wanted me, it would just be for me being me.

Besides, it wasn't like Sylvia brought me along every time she got a new boyfriend either, and I didn't blame her for that. But maybe I didn't have to sit around and do nothing all by myself until she got dumped this time. Because Sylvia *always* got dumped, eventually. And I was *always* there, picking up the pieces.

I squinted into the crazy-bright sun as I turned at the Picnic House, then pushed my hands deep into my pockets. They were shaking. I didn't know why. It wasn't like I was *that* nervous, or whatever.

When I was a little closer, I could finally make out what looked like twenty or so girls—only girls as I'd thought—leaning or squatting in the shadows under a clump of trees. They were still too far away for me to make out any of their faces, but I saw one point in my direction. A few others turned to look. Someone raised a hand. It wasn't so much a wave as, like, a signal.

They were definitely waiting for me. The Magpies: beautiful, vicious birds known for pecking people's eyes out.

I tried not to speed up. I didn't want to look like I was in any hurry to do what they wanted me to do. No, I was laid back and cool and not stressed about the whole thing. Because it was one thing to let the Maggies try to play me. It was another for me to run over there so they could do it.

When I was about halfway there, I saw two other girls coming from the opposite direction. It was a relief—and kind of a letdown—to see that the whole mess wasn't just for me. On the upside, if it was a joke, at least it wouldn't be only me that the Magpies were playing it on.

I was almost there, but the sun was still so bright that I couldn't make out much of who it was under the trees, except that there were five people standing. One of them I recognized from her huge head of long reddish curls. In a school full of blend-in people, it was wild, stand-out hair, and it belonged to Dylan Crosby—beautiful, popular, junior. Dylan was the kind of girl you'd expect to be a Magpie, except she was so ultracool that she was like above the cool kids. An actress who'd had the lead in almost every Grace Hall play I could remember, Dylan didn't seem to care what anyone thought, which, of course, made everyone want to be her best friend. It was exactly the way that Sylvia and I thought of ourselves. Except when we colored outside the lines, no one tried to follow.

Dylan had never had a boyfriend at Grace Hall. And a girl like her was too pretty not to. Half the school thought she was frigid; the other half figured she must have some secret boyfriend somewhere—someone older, maybe even married. Or famous. For a while there was even a piece on *gRaCeFULLY* called Dylanwatch—everyone holding her breath to see whom she'd finally decide to give the green light to. But the column fizzled when no dirt on Dylan ever got dug up. There were even some rumors for a while that Dylan was still a virgin—which I took as like a personal endorsement. But then people seemed to decide that that was too stupid even to joke about.

Finally, I hit some shade on the path, and I could make out the faces

of the four other girls who were standing: Zadie, Bethany, Rachel, and
Heather. Along with Dylan, the five of them looked like the ones who
were in charge. It made sense. They were the main crew of popular
senior girls, except for Dylan, who'd made the cut even though she was
a junior. That was probably because she was Zadie's best friend—a
match that was almost as weird as Sylvia and me. Those five girls were
the ones all the boys at Grace Hall wanted to sleep with and all the
girls wanted to be. They were always together, too, even if it didn't
seem like they necessarily liked one another very much.

I knew Rachel and Heather from the field hockey team. They were
cocaptains. Heather was an old-school, upper-crust preppy with May-
flower looks and Rockefeller money. She spent summers in Nantucket
and winter break at horse shows in West Palm Beach. The weirdest part
about her was that she lived in Brooklyn and not on the Upper East Side.
Rachel was from Paris and swore in French, which pretty much sealed
her coolness. They both had thick, straight blond hair—Heather's
chin length, Rachel's much longer—and could have passed for twins.
Heather and Rachel were both really bitchy to all the other players on
the field hockey team. So far, they'd mostly left me alone. It helped that,
even as a freshman, I'd been twice the player they would ever be.

I didn't know Bethany personally, but I knew she was the group's
comic relief. She made sure everyone at school knew that. Ballsy and
a little on the heavy side, she got suspended all the time for these big
school pranks. She had a vicious sense of humor, too. She made kids
cry all the time. That was probably part of how she got in with the
Magpies: they were too afraid to keep her out. Rumor was that she was
also willing to sleep with just about anyone, anywhere, too. In the Grace
Hall world of emaciated skeletons, that could have helped make up for
her extra poundage.

And everyone knew Zadie. Dylan's best friend and Grace Hall's
wildest child. Pale and wiry, Zadie had short, shaggy black hair that
covered her bright blue eyes, and a nose ring. She also had a big stripe
of white hair on one side of her head, almost like a skunk. I wasn't
the only person who wondered if she'd put it there on purpose. I also

wasn't the only person way too afraid to ask. Zadie was always dressed in skinny jeans and a rumpled army jacket that was more couture than standard issue. She even had a little tattoo, on her forearm: CAVEAT EMPTOR. Word was that Zadie's parents were totally lax—I mean, she was seventeen and had a tattoo—and that they even let her drink at home and went clubbing downtown with her sometimes. I was most surprised and most unpsyched to see Zadie there. I would have thought some dumb high-school club would have been way beneath her.

When I stopped walking, I could finally see the faces of the two girls coming up the opposite hill: Charlie Kugler and Tempest Bain. They were sophomores, too, and looked as nervous as I felt. Neither of them was exactly mainstream popular either. Tempest, a ballet dancer, was new to school. She was a tall reed of muscle, with purplish streaks in her jet-black hair. Charlie was a teeny girl with cute, droopy eyes, baggy clothes, and, rumor had it, a $50 million trust fund, which included an original Warhol hanging in her bedroom.

Charlie and Tempest and I looked at one another with the same confused, kind-of-spooked expression, shrugging as we met in front of the pack sunk in the trees. It seemed like the only thing the three of us could possibly have in common was that we'd all been curious enough—or dumb enough—to show up.

"*Finally*, for fuck's sake," Zadie said, clapping her hands together. She looked down at her big black watch. "You guys better not fucking be late again."

When I looked down at my own watch, it was 3:02, two minutes past our appointed meeting time.

"What is this anyway?" Tempest shot back, working her head like she couldn't have cared less who Zadie and her friends were, only that they were wasting her time. "Why don't you people start by telling me what the hell it is I'm supposedly late for."

Zadie fluttered her eyes shut, then took a deep satisfied breath like she was inhaling something delightful.

"See," she said, looking back over her shoulder at the other girls. "What did I tell you? A badass ballerina. How fucking great is that?"

"What are you talking about, badass baller—"

"Tsst." Zadie sliced an index finger in front of Tempest's nose. "Shut the fuck up. I like you, but not that much."

My heart was beating hard. I didn't belong there. I was not a badass anything. The whole thing was just . . . it wasn't me. I wanted to run and hide back in my safe little world with Sylvia. So what if lately it seemed like she treated me well only when a guy dumped her? That was okay. We'd been friends for a long time. She'd get back to being the friend she used to be, sooner or later. And I had Ben now. I didn't need anyone else.

But now I'd seen them. Seen the Magpies. They weren't just going to let me go. There'd be a price to pay. How high, I could only guess. But it wasn't one I wanted to pay, that I was sure of.

Dylan came forward then. "Why don't you guys come over, have a seat," she said. Her voice was nice and her smile friendly. "I know all the secrecy stuff is a little weird. But it ends up being part of the fun, I promise." She smiled wide and waved us forward. With her face lit in the sun, her eyes warm and twinkling, she was even prettier than I'd realized. When she smiled a second time, it was right at me. "Come on."

I felt myself moving before I'd fully decided to. I headed toward the tangle of low, heavy trees where the rest of the girls were propped against limbs, sitting on book bags, and sprawled out on blankets. I knew most of their names. I'd been going to Grace Hall with them for practically my whole life. Except for one or two surprises, they were exactly the girls I'd have expected to be in the Magpies—pretty, popular, well dressed, and well connected. They all made sense—even Tempest and Charlie, in their own, offbeat ways. Everybody except for me. But my not fitting in wasn't nearly as weird as how much I wanted to all of a sudden. *Really* wanted to. I knew I should leave. I was doing wrong by Sylvia still being there. I was doing wrong by myself. But I didn't want to go. I couldn't. Not yet.

Zadie and Dylan were still standing out in the sun, whispering to each other. Zadie looked pissed. Dylan looked a little spacey and kind of sad all of a sudden. People talked about the two of them, Dylan and Zadie, the way Zadie was always circling around Dylan like a bulldog. People thought it was creepy. And it was. It was weird.

"I'm serious," was the last thing Zadie said, pointing hard at Dylan. "Don't."

Dylan drifted away then, smiling and blinking fast as she took a seat under the trees on a low boulder. She was trying to look happy but didn't. Zadie stayed on the path in the sun for a minute longer, then crossed her arms and frowned. She looked right, then left down the long sidewalks that wove through the park, like maybe she was considering taking off down one of them. But instead, she finally stepped forward and took her rightful place at the front of the group under the trees. Heather, Rachel, and Bethany flanked her on either side.

When Zadie finally turned to look at the three of us, it was in a not-so-nice way. Actually, she seemed kind of disgusted. All I could think about was the story I'd once heard about her making a girl at some party swallow a bottle cap. Which made me wonder what exactly they were doing to keep everybody in the club so quiet. Because with that many girls you'd have thought that somebody would have talked. Unless they had a *really* good reason to keep their mouths shut.

"So we're the Magpies, the oldest and most fucking cool club at this lame-ass school," Zadie began, sounding kind of annoyed. "Founded way the fuck back in nineteen-twenty-something, the motto was '*support, sisterhood, spirit.*' Now that we've brought it back from the dead, I've added, '*or suck it.*' You've heard of the club, right?"

She glared at us. One of the three of us started nodding—I don't know who—then we all joined in.

"Good," Zadie said. "Because otherwise, I'd have to kick your asses to the fucking curb straight out of the box."

I saw Tempest's body coil up like she was going to tell Zadie to go to hell, but she stayed quiet, even shrinking up some when Zadie's eyes flashed in her direction.

"But why us?" Charlie asked quietly. "I mean, the three of us are totally different."

And if they were assigning categories, I was definitely the nerd of the group.

"Come on, Charlie, you know this is just some kind of fucked-up joke," Tempest said, finding her backbone again. She pushed herself off the tree she'd been leaning against. "They get us to say we want to join and then they make us eat, like, ten gallons of vodka and Jell-O and take pictures of us throwing up or something. And then we get to be *in* the club and they get to keep on doing even more messed-up stuff to us."

Zadie smiled viciously. "Basically."

Dylan moved forward, putting a hand on Zadie's shoulder.

"No," Dylan said, "that's not what we're doing. I promise. This club is supposed to be fun. It is fun."

"Hold up. I don't know why you're kissing their asses. It's not like they're even fucking *in* yet." Zadie glared at Dylan, then turned back to us. "You three have got shit ass-backwards too, if you think we're going to fucking sell you on joining. You don't want to be here, turn the fuck around and take off. We'll see you around."

She didn't make it sound like anything bad would happen if we left, which meant I should go, now. Take her up on her offer. I waited for my body to lurch for the sidewalk. But it didn't. Something in me still wasn't ready to go.

"Listen, I know this probably seems kind of weird," Dylan said, stepping in front of Zadie. "We know there are other sophomore girls who are, like, more popular or whatever. But we think all those girls are boring. We think *you* guys have, I don't know, personality. You're not trying too hard or pretending to be something you're not. You're not all obsessed with being cool, which is so *not* cool."

I felt the air get sucked out of me when Zadie suddenly swiveled her black-lined eyes in my direction.

"But I'll say it again. If you don't want to be here," she hissed in my direction, "leave right now. Get the fuck out. No hard feelings." Zadie walked closer to us, pulled out a cigarette, lit it, and inhaled heavily. She exhaled in a long steady stream, directly in our faces. "Because if you do stay *and* we decide to let you pledge in, there won't be any leaving after that. At least, not any *easy* way."

My heart was beating so fast I worried that Zadie would be able to see it. That she'd pounce if she did. I could leave right then. She'd said I could and it would be like nothing happened. Like I'd never betrayed Sylvia or let myself down. Leaving was what I should do. I knew it. No doubt about it. Except just thinking about taking off made me feel so let down.

So I stood there instead. I watched Dylan go back and sit on her low gray boulder. Relaxed, carefree, at ease, she stretched her legs out in front of her and crossed them at the ankles. Dylan looked up at me then like she'd heard me thinking about her. She smiled once, her cheeks lifting into warm red apples.

"It's okay," she mouthed. Then she smiled again, and nodded once. "Stay."

"So, what's it going to be, ladies?" Zadie asked, sticking her cigarette between her lips and clapping her hands together, hard. "Speak now, or forever hold your fucking peace."

Amelia

BEN

sounds all Skull & Bones

AMELIA

kind of, I guess; can't even use their names in texts; have to call them
Maggie #1 & #2, etc, kind of crazy

BEN

yeah, crazy. We have a computer club at my school

AMELIA

ha, ha

BEN

french club too. that's kind of cool right?

AMELIA

sort of, yeah

BEN

for albany

AMELIA

i guess

BEN

is there a secret handshake?

AMELIA

no

BEN

do you like wear masks and do weird creepy stuff

AMELIA

not yet

BEN

that was a joke; u r not laughing; tough crowd today . . .

AMELIA

u r making me feel even more stupid

BEN

sorry

AMELIA

no u r not

BEN

i am, seriously. it sounds cool. I'm just jealous.

AMELIA

cool?

BEN

come on, you know it is. u live in New York City. everything there is cool.

AMELIA

brooklyn

BEN

same difference to us up here in the sticks

SEPTEMBER 14, 7:41 PM

SYLVIA

hello??? where the hell were you after school?

AMELIA

sorry! Xtra field hockey practice

SYLVIA

Jesus will that woman ever chill out?

AMELIA

state is coming up

SYLVIA

state? U sound like such a jock; ew

AMELIA

yeah, that's me; see you tomorrow a.m. usual time?

SYLVIA

yeah; maybe THEN I can give you an Ian update, finally

SEPTEMBER 14, 8:03 PM

BLOCKED NUMBER

no underwear or bra tomorrow fledgling; we'll be checking. And wear a skirt. Meet same time, same place

SEPTEMBER 14, 8:07 PM

BLOCKED NUMBER

don't worry about Maggie #1; she's all bark and no bite. Xoxo Maggie #2

AMELIA

thx I needed that

BLOCKED NUMBER

anytime; and I went commando too. Key is a loooong skirt.

SEPTEMBER 14, 8:11 PM

BLOCKED NUMBER

who's your daddy?

facebook

Amelia Baron

is cautiously optimistic

Ainsley Brown and **4 others** like this

Kate

When Kate got home, she headed straight upstairs to Amelia's room. She was hoping that the rapid forward momentum might help her outsmart herself. She'd been unable to get herself to go inside Amelia's room since she'd died. Seth had picked out Amelia's clothes for the funeral. He'd even straightened up a little—threw out a half-eaten apple, collected the dirty clothes, and made the bed—so Kate wouldn't have to go in until she was ready. Since then, the door to her dead daughter's room had stayed closed. Kate wasn't any more ready to open it now. And so there she stood, hand on the doorknob, her stomach twisting into a knot.

All she'd been able to think about since getting the text that said Amelia hadn't jumped was how she should have been more involved in the investigation in the first place. How could she have trusted all of it to some detective who she suspected might care more about closing cases than finding out the truth? She should have looked through Amelia's things herself. She should have thought more about the right questions to ask and had the courage to ask them, no matter how much people had wanted her to be good and stay quiet. No matter how guilty she had felt. Instead, Kate had folded in on herself and around her grief, accepting an explanation for her daughter's death that she never fully believed. Because blocking it out had been easier than fighting. It had been the only possible way to survive.

But Kate could do this now. She was stronger than she'd been right after Amelia died. Not much, but a little. And she would need to be. Because as horrible as it had been trying to get herself to accept that Amelia had killed herself, Kate knew that there could be even worse things to come.

She took a deep breath and went to turn the knob. But before the door opened, the house phone rang. Kate exhaled in a relieved gasp, then looked around for the upstairs extension, which wasn't on its cradle. When the phone rang again, Kate realized the sound was coming from downstairs, where she must have left it. She raced down the steps, glad to be headed far away from her daughter's room. When she finally laid her hands on the phone in the kitchen, it took her a minute to believe that she was seeing NYPD on the caller ID. It had been so long since anyone had called her. And on that day, of all days? It couldn't be a coincidence. Maybe the police had gotten some kind of message, too.

"Hello?"

"Ms. Baron? Detective Molina here."

"Hi, yeah, it's me, Kate." She was already bracing herself. As much as she was hoping Molina was calling with news about Amelia, she was afraid of what that news might be. "Is there . . . do you have some . . . How are you?"

"Been better, to be honest," he said. "At the moment, I'm wondering why, out of nowhere, I'm hearing complaints about my work on your daughter's case. If you had concerns, you've got my number."

Jeremy had already called the police commissioner? Kate didn't know why she was surprised. Jeremy didn't generally make empty promises. Still, she hadn't expected anything to come of it, certainly not within hours.

"Oh, um, sorry," Kate said. "I think that was my boss. He was trying to be helpful."

"Helpful to who?" Molina muttered, as if he was talking half to Kate, half to himself. "What would have been worth your doing was asking me a question that I could have just answered. Because, not for nothing, this wasn't exactly how I wanted to get on the commissioner's radar."

Molina was worried about his career prospects? This conversation was bringing back everything Kate hadn't liked about him. The aggressive way that Molina had hammered Kate with questions in those early days. Like gunfire. So that Kate had ended up constantly on the defensive, focused less on the answers she'd wanted and more on ducking for cover. Kate had waited and waited for Molina's bad-boy harshness to break open and reveal a heart of gold. It never had.

"I'm sorry that you've been *inconvenienced*." Kate hadn't realized the depth of her anger until she heard it in her own voice. "But I got a message today saying my daughter didn't jump. As you can imagine, it raises questions that I'd frankly like answers to. Now."

"Oh yeah?" Molina asked. "A message from who?"

"I don't know. It was an anonymous text."

Duncan had returned Kate's phone to her, able to tell her only that the message had been sent using a telephone company website, making it effectively untraceable.

"Ah, anonymous, huh?" His sarcasm was palpable.

"Yeah, anonymous. That doesn't mean it's not true," Kate said, wishing she sounded more firm and less defensive. But she wasn't going to let herself get bullied by Molina. Not this time. "I want the text looked into. And I want someone to do a handwriting analysis on the *one* word that was written on that wall. I assume you have a photograph? Because that wasn't any suicide note, and Amelia didn't write it. I've known that from the start. She didn't kill herself either. I've known that all along, too."

Kate didn't realize how true that was, until now. Amelia hadn't killed herself. Amelia hadn't jumped. There was no question about it anymore.

"So I take it, then, that it doesn't matter to you anymore that the ME's official findings were to the contrary?" Molina asked.

"I *knew* my daughter. I *know* she didn't kill herself," Kate said, struggling to keep her voice steady, but the floodgates were open now, and all the doubt she'd kept so tightly bottled up was rushing out. "I'm going to find out who or what did kill her, Detective. You can help me, or you can get out of the way. But I promise you that I am not going to stay quiet because you want me to. Not anymore."

"That so?" Molina sounded as if he was smiling. "Then why don't you—"

Kate hung up, then threw the phone down too hard onto the long farmhouse table. It shot across the top and crashed onto the floor, where she heard it crack into pieces.

"Shit," Kate said, welling up as she dropped herself down hard onto one of benches that ran the length of the table. She buried her face in her hands. "Goddamnit."

What was she doing? Her new no-more-Mr.-Nice-Guy routine should have skipped Molina. She *needed* him. He was the one with Amelia's case file. Only he knew what he had and hadn't found. And now there was no way he was going to help her.

Kate rested her head down on the rough-hewn tabletop, then turned to look around the brick-walled kitchen, with its European cabinetry, polished stone, and stainless fixtures. Kate never cooked, and yet the huge appliances would not have been out of place in a small restaurant. She'd bought all of that for Amelia. Amelia, who didn't have a dad and hadn't had enough of a mother. Kate had figured she could at least have the very best of everything else. So stupid. What had Amelia needed with a four-thousand-dollar stove? And now Kate would have to stare at it as she ate takeout alone in that kitchen for the rest of her life. Right on cue, she felt that acid in her throat.

Kate swallowed hard as she pushed herself up and headed back for the stairs and Amelia's room. She had a job to finish, and she was going to do it. She owed that much to her daughter.

Upstairs, Kate took a deep breath as she pushed open Amelia's bedroom door. When she stepped inside and flipped on the light, the air smelled stale. Like death. Like Amelia had died right there, in that room, and her body had been left there to rot.

This time Kate felt sure she was going to vomit. She rushed across the room and shoved open a window, sticking her head out and gasping for fresh air.

She was imagining the smell. The rational part of Kate realized this, but knowing it didn't help. It still took about a dozen deep breaths of fresh air for the nausea to ebb. When it finally did, Kate turned and lowered herself onto the windowsill, the sharp November air rushing in on either side, slicing at her arms.

It was even worse being in Amelia's room than Kate had imagined. Sitting there, she missed her daughter so much it made everything ache—her legs, her hands, her eyelids. Her flesh felt covered in bruises as her eyes moved over the crammed bookcases lining almost every wall in Amelia's room.

Amelia had learned to read when she was four, and after that a book was forever in her hands. She read in the bath, while walking down the sidewalk, in the dark at night with a flashlight. Even those many shelves had not been enough for Amelia's library, and the overflow sat in tall stacks along each wall. Kate had sometimes worried that Amelia's obsession with books was a sign of loneliness. That if she'd had a sibling or even a dad—if Kate hadn't been working all the time—that Amelia might have been more fixated on real people instead of made-up ones.

Now it seemed such a stupid thing to worry about, especially when Kate looked away from the books and over to the one wall without shelves. It was covered with photographs—Amelia as a little girl with Leelah, with her teammates and camp friends. With Kate. There was a large one of Amelia and Sylvia on the sixth-grade field trip to DC that Kate had chaperoned. It had been one of the few times over the years that Kate had been able to sneak away from work for that kind of school commitment. And it had been perfect, except for the lingering sense Kate had had afterward that almost every other parent there—even the full-time working ones—had come along on that kind of trip many times before.

What mattered now, though, was that Amelia had been happy in the photographs. Every single one. Their small family might not have been the one Kate had planned on, but Amelia had never cared. At least not until a couple of weeks before she'd died, when she'd suddenly started asking about her father.

"You seriously *never* told him about me?" Amelia had demanded, waking Kate up early one Saturday morning. "I mean, did you ever even try to find him?"

"Find who?"

"Hello, my *dad*." Amelia had crossed her arms. "You know, the hippie with the guitar on his way to Africa? The one that you supposedly met one dark and stormy night at a dive bar up by Columbia? Did they even have bars in that neighborhood back then? Wasn't it like a war zone up there?"

Kate blinked at the clock, then at Amelia, then back at the clock. Seven fifteen a.m. on a Saturday. She didn't want this to be happening. She didn't want Amelia to be asking these questions, not now. She'd known that someday, when Amelia was old enough, the sketchy story Kate had told her about her father would require elaboration. But it was too soon. She hadn't yet worked out what to say. The truth still felt out of the question. But a vague lie to a child perpetuated over the years by silence was different from a brand-new one straight to her teenage daughter's face.

"What are you even doing awake, Amelia?" Kate asked, trying to buy time. "Let's talk about this later. I'm really exhausted, and you must be, too."

"Later, sure." Amelia sounded angry, but there was something else in her eyes—fear, worry. It made Kate's stomach churn.

"Amelia, what's wrong?" Kate asked, pushing herself up in bed. "Did something happen?"

"No," Amelia said, crossing her arms. She looked away from Kate with a pout, her eyes fixed on the far corner of the bedroom. Kate kept staring at her daughter, hoping the weight would make Amelia confess whatever had brought her there, demanding answers at the crack of dawn. "Nothing happened. I mean, except for me getting tired of waiting for you to tell me the truth."

But it was more, Kate could tell. Did she want to know what? No, that was the honest truth. Kate did not.

"Amelia, I don't know what you think—"

"Mom, come on," Amelia said, her voice cracking. She turned to look out Kate's bedroom windows. Anywhere, it seemed, but at Kate. "You, alone, in a bar? Hooking up with some random guy? Some accident that was the 'best thing that ever happened to you'?" Amelia shook her head, then finally looked at Kate. Her eyes were glassy. "No way, Mom. I'm not buying it. It's not you."

Kate stared at Amelia for a minute, then dropped back down onto the bed. She turned over and pressed the side of her face into the pillow so that her daughter wouldn't be able to look into her own damp eyes.

"I never said it *was* me, Amelia. That's kind of the whole point. I also never said I was perfect. Back then I was doing a lot of things that weren't exactly well thought out," she said quietly, careful to make sure she didn't suggest that Amelia had been a mistake. "Anyway, if you have questions about your dad, you can ask them. I've always told you that you can ask me anything you want, Amelia."

"And you'll tell me the truth?"

"Yes, Amelia," Kate said, her little liar's heart pounding hard in her chest. "I'll tell you the truth."

And in that moment, Kate had decided that she would. She would tell her daughter everything about how she had been conceived, about the mistakes Kate had made and the things she had done to cover them up. Because Amelia deserved the truth. She was entitled to her history, whatever the cost. Just not at that precise moment. Kate needed time, to prepare.

"I want to meet him," Amelia said.

Kate had blinked at her daughter, trying to hold her face still.

"Okay," she'd said finally. And then she'd decided to lie some more. "Then we can try to do that. But I just . . . I can't make any promises that we'll find him."

Four days later, Amelia was dead. Kate didn't think that Amelia's questions about her dad were related to her death. And not knowing her dad would never have been a reason for Amelia to kill herself. But it was strange, the timing of Amelia's suddenly suspecting something. Worse yet was the possibility that Amelia had died thinking Kate had lied to her.

Kate forced herself off the windowsill and over to the bookshelves. She ran her hand down the well-worn spines—*The Odyssey*, *The Sound and the Fury*, *Lolita*, and, of course, all those books by Virginia Woolf. Virginia Woolf—suicide committer extraordinaire—was her daughter's favorite author. The coincidence hadn't been lost on Kate. But Amelia would have found copying her literary hero in that way to be a pathetic cliché, of that Kate felt sure.

She backed up and sat down hard on Amelia's bed, then dropped her face into her hands. She was still slumped over when she heard Amelia's door creak open. For a second she thought it was the wind—until she saw a big hand reaching inside to push the door open. She should hide, dive under the bed, run for the window—

But she was frozen.

"Who's there!" she screamed as loud as she could. "Get the fuck out of my house!"

"You're not armed, are you?" a voice called from behind the door. Seth's voice.

"Holy shit, Seth, *what* are you doing sneaking up on me?!"

Slowly, Seth's face peeked around the door. His eyes were wide, and he had his hands raised in the air.

"I rang the doorbell," he answered sheepishly. He shuffled into the room in his khakis and muted button-down—the modest, nondescript uniform he'd always favored, even now that he had a high-profile job as senior legal adviser to Senator Schumer. It was the kind of outfit that probably gave Thomas—Seth's handsome and supremely fashionable husband—hives. "No one answered, and your front door was unlocked. You know, you really should lock your front door. Any lunatic could just wander in off the street."

"I can see that," Kate said sharply. Her heart was still pounding.

"Well, I'm not sure that was necessary."

"I'm sorry," Kate mumbled as she dropped her face back into her hands.

She shouldn't snap at Seth. He'd been so good to her, and it wasn't as though she had friends to spare, at least not in the city. Between the hours she worked and the time she spent with Amelia, she hadn't made many new friends over the years. All of Kate's close friends—apart from Seth—were ones she'd made years ago in college or high school. And none of them lived nearby. Kate looked up at Seth and patted the bed next to her. He came over and sat down. He looked around Amelia's room, his face stiffening as he seemed to realize, finally, where they were.

"Maybe we should go downstairs," he said anxiously. "Get you some fresh air."

"I got a text today about Amelia, two actually," Kate said, ignoring his attempt to get her out of the room. "They said she didn't jump."

"Really?" Seth's eyes widened momentarily, then thinned suspiciously. "Wait, texts from who?"

"I don't know. They were anonymous."

His eyebrows lifted. "Anony—"

"Don't you start, too," Kate said quietly, looking Seth straight in the eye. "Please?"

He stared back at her hard for a minute before his face finally softened.

"Okay." He wrapped an arm around Kate's narrow shoulders. His chin rested on the top of her head as he squeezed. "Okay."

"Maybe it's a good thing," Kate said. "Deep down, I never really believed Amelia killed herself. But I knew that would just look like denial."

"Yeah, and didn't the police—"

"Police make mistakes," Kate snapped. "Why not this time?"

"Okay," Seth said again, holding up his palms.

He was humoring her. It was obvious. But Kate didn't even care. She looked around the room. It was one thing to go through Amelia's things, but it would be nice not to have to do it in that room, so filled with her daughter's memories and the smell of death.

"The first thing I need to do is make sure the police didn't miss anything in here."

"Like what?" Seth asked. "What do you think really happened, Kate?"

She shrugged. "I don't know." She took a deep breath, trying not to let her imagination start rolling out even more awful possibilities. "But I need to find out. Do you think you could look around up here, through her desk, her drawers, and see if there's anything? I was going to take her book bag downstairs. I just . . . I'd rather not be in here anymore."

"Of course," Seth said, though he didn't exactly look thrilled. "But what am I looking for?"

"Something that proves that Amelia didn't kill herself," Kate said quietly. "Or something, I guess, that proves that she did."

Kate headed downstairs with Amelia's worn messenger bag. Far away from her daughter's room, she found she could handle looking through Amelia's phone and computer. But sitting at the kitchen table with the bag on her lap, Kate was still worried that some critical trace of Amelia would fly out as soon as she opened it.

Finally, she managed to get herself to flip open the top of the bag. Inside were a couple of notebooks, Amelia's small laptop, a granola bar, ChapStick, some gum, her iPhone, and her wallet. Kate lifted each out of the bag and rested them gently on the tabletop. The ordinary things of a living, breathing girl. Now, the precious artifacts of a dead one.

Kate picked up Amelia's iPhone first. It, too, was dead—the grim irony of which made Kate wince. Once she'd found the charger in an outside pocket of Amelia's bag, Kate quickly discovered that the phone was also password protected. Kate could have sworn that Molina had specifically told her he'd gone through Amelia's phone. But without the password—which even Kate didn't know—that was impossible. It took Kate two tries to come up with the right combination of numbers: Amelia's birthday and her own. It brought tears to Kate's eyes.

When Kate finally made her way to Amelia's text messages, she couldn't believe what she was seeing. There were hundreds and hundreds of saved messages, from scores of different people—some were named, some were just phone numbers, many were listed as unknown or blocked numbers. Some were from Kate. Some texts were long threads of conversations. Others were a single message. How had Amelia—with her courses and extracurriculars and her sports—had the time to send so many texts? More important, shouldn't Kate have known?

Maybe she should even have been reading them all along. Some mothers of teenagers did that, read all their kids' electronic traffic— texts, e-mails, Facebook pages. Kate was plugged in enough to the world of mothering—mostly through other women at work who had kids—to know that some mothers put their kids on notice that they'd be checking periodically; others seized the opportunity of a child's un-attended smartphone to do their snooping undetected.

Kate had done neither. She'd opted, instead, to trust Amelia.

Or at least that was what she'd told herself she'd been doing. Be-cause sitting there staring at all those many, many messages, not mon-itoring suddenly felt less like a deliberate parenting philosophy and more like a consequence of Kate's compressed schedule. Certainly, it had been neglectful, and so very, very stupid. Amelia had been *fifteen* years old. Even if she had been trying to stay away from trouble, it had been Kate's job to make sure she'd succeed.

Kate held her breath as she began to scroll randomly through the text messages. Most of them were meaningless teenage exchanges about lunch, or sports practice, or homework. Then there was one near the end, the day before Amelia had died. It was a back and forth with an unnamed phone number that turned out to be a boy named Ben.

AMELIA

Who is this?

UNKNOWN NUMBER

Ben, it's my brother's phone

AMELIA

Oh hi, I almost didn't answer.

UNKNOWN NUMBER

Did you ask about Paris?

AMELIA

Yep. No go.

UNKNOWN NUMBER

Maybe she'll change her mind?

AMELIA

I don't think so. Other ideas?

UNKNOWN NUMBER

Not really. She's your mom.

AMELIA

I know. She's all mine. Lucky me.

Kate closed her eyes and bent over, a sudden ache in her belly. To be mad at your parents was the birthright of every teenager. Kate knew that. She was still mad at her own parents. But for good reason. They were cold and distant and limited. Kate had truly believed that she was a much better mother than Gretchen had ever been, not that she'd set the bar very high. But what if her relationship with Amelia hadn't been as good as she'd believed? What if Kate really hadn't known Amelia that well after all?

Kate pressed the phone to her chest and squeezed her eyes tighter shut, as if that alone could keep her from crying. It didn't. And so she let herself go. Her spine collapsed as her cheeks grew wet, and she cried on until she could cry no more.

Finally, Kate sniffled hard and dragged a hand across her wet nose and mouth. She placed Amelia's phone gently back down on the table. She knew she'd have to wade through all those text messages eventually. She'd have to swim down the tangled tributaries of Amelia's chatter and hope that she didn't stumble across too much else that hurt her feelings. But not right now. For now, it was enough to know that there were things there she'd need to take a closer look at.

Kate grabbed some tissues to dry her face, then picked up Amelia's notebooks and started paging through them. She ran her fingers over Amelia's jaggedy scrawl, tracing the impressions she'd left in the paper. She tried to imagine Amelia putting them there. As Kate flipped the English notebook closed, some stapled pages slid to the floor. She bent to pick them up.

Representations of Time: To the Lighthouse, by Amelia Baron. It was the paper Amelia had supposedly cheated on. This could be Kate's chance to clear her daughter's name. Not Kate specifically, of course. She could examine each and every page and still have had no idea whether Amelia had copied portions of it. But in Kate's mind, the part of Amelia's story that suggested she had cheated had always been the most far-fetched. Amelia had known everything there was to know about Virginia Woolf. She'd read *To the Lighthouse* many, many times and had always received her very best grades in English, which was saying a lot, given how great her grades were generally. Amelia wouldn't have *needed* to plagiarize anything. Add to that the fact that Amelia had never been a liar. That she was, in fact, a compulsive rule follower and that she absolutely worshipped her English teacher, Liv, and none of it made any sense. Knowing Amelia hadn't cheated and proving it, though, were two very different things.

Kate put the term paper down on the table and pulled Amelia's laptop out of her bag. Soon she had it on and was scanning her way through the extremely well-organized files. The Word documents were separated into folders labeled with class names and the corresponding semester. There were only four loose files, each titled *gRaCe FULLY* and labeled with a different date. Kate picked one at random and opened it. The document had a glossy layout—professional border, colored banner, elaborate font—that made it look like an official school newsletter.

gRaCeFULLY

Because there are 176 definitions for the word *loser* on urbandictionary.com. Don't Be a Statistic

---

Hey bitches!
Yes, it's us again, with all the shit that's not fit to print . . .

Lots of news to report today. First of all, we hear that a certain chemistry professor is getting a whole bunch of his questions for his first year Chem Lab from the California Standards Exam. And those, ladies and gents, are available ONLINE. I mean, how fucking lazy can you be? The guy can't even make up his own test questions? . . . It's not our fault he's a lazy shit. So, I say, have at it—here's a link to the exam: caedu/ standardtests/chemistry.com.

Apparently, there was another rainbow party in the 6th grade this past weekend. Will somebody please tell those kids that that is so 2008. And totally gross BTW.

And will someone else tell Tempest Bain to wear underwear? I mean, we know the chick's a dancer and she has a fly body and all, but do we seriously need to see her cha-cha?

And word is that Bethany Kane is ready and willing. Oh wait, sorry, that's OLD news. She's already screwed half the varsity lettermen.

Sylvia Golde is also getting her ticket punched again these days. Don't know who the lucky boy is yet, but Sylvia was on the gymnastics team when she was little, so no doubt—whoever he is—he's getting his money's worth.

And the Maggies started tapping this week, people, so the other clubs

can't be far behind. If you didn't get your invite yet, maybe you still will.
But most of you losers shouldn't hold your fucking breath.

A rainbow party? And in the *sixth* grade? Kate had heard the term once, from Beatrice, who'd seen something about it on *Oprah*. But she'd quietly assumed it was something exaggerated for ratings, if not made up entirely. And this *gRaCeFULLY* thing had effectively called Amelia's best friend a slut. Could that be true? Suddenly, the fact that Amelia had *never* talked about boys seemed suspicious. Somebody who went to that much trouble *not* to talk about something probably had too much to say.

Kate opened and quickly closed two more of the *gRaCeFULLY* files. One had another dig about Sylvia—something about her being on the Pill—and there was no question why the last *gRaCeFULLY* had been saved.

Amelia Baron has arrived, ladies and gentlemen. That's right, as of two nights ago, she's officially a woman. So for all of you out there who'd hoped to hook that brass ring, too bad so sad— somebody beat you to the punch. And you'll never believe who the lucky winner is. But you won't hear it here. Some things even I know better than to put in writing.

Staring at the screen, Kate's throat started to burn again. She wasn't upset that Amelia might have had sex—or maybe she was a little upset about that—but she was more hurt that her daughter hadn't told her. She'd always imagined that she and Amelia would talk about it beforehand. For years, Kate had been preparing speeches about love and safety and trust. About being true to yourself while connecting with another person. About choosing carefully when and how much to give over to anyone. Kate had planned to tell Amelia all those things, things she should have known much better herself. And so why hadn't she? What had she been waiting for?

"Hey."

Kate startled and looked up toward the steps. Seth was slowly lowering himself into the kitchen. He looked as if he were hoping something would stop him from making it all the way there.

"You found something," Kate said.

She could tell from the look on Seth's face that he had. And whatever it was, it wasn't good.

Seth nodded as he came over to sit down across from Kate. He pulled out a folded piece of paper that he had tucked into his shirt pocket. He put it on the table and slid it toward Kate but didn't lift his fingers.

"I found it in her desk drawer." Kate tried to slide the note free, but Seth pressed his fingers harder against it. "Are you sure you should be doing this? What if you find out things that you'd be better off not knowing?"

"If it happened to Amelia, I need to know it. I need to know everything, Seth."

He nodded finally, lifting his fingers. Kate unfolded the square of paper.

I HATE YOU!!!

The three little words screamed out from the center of the torn square of lined notebook paper. Kate's chest tightened. Somebody had written that to *Amelia*? The letters looked so angry, too—jaggedy and thick, as if someone had leaned their full weight against the pencil.

It didn't make any sense. Amelia wasn't the kind of girl people hated. She was smart and pretty and athletic. A girl people might have been jealous of, if she hadn't been so fundamentally modest. She didn't go around trying to draw attention to herself the way Sylvia did. How could someone possibly hate her?

"I don't understand," Kate said more to herself than to Seth. "Who would have written something like this to Amelia?"

Seth's mouth turned down as he stared at the tabletop. Finally, he shook his head and reached into his back pocket. He pulled out a stack of two dozen more similarly folded squares of paper. When he opened his hands, they rained down on the tabletop into an awful, lopsided pile.

"They all say the same thing." His voice was sad, but angry, too. "All twenty-two of them. I think they're from different people. The handwriting's not the same."

Kate's hands hovered over the pile, her fingers moving in disbelief.

"Oh my God," she whispered, unable to pull her eyes away from the notes.

"I know," Seth said. "It's bad. But maybe it's not what it looks like."

"Some kind of gang was harassing Amelia." Kate turned to look at him, her eyes so wide they'd begun to burn. "What else could it be?"

Seth shook his head and looked down. "I don't know," he said. "I don't have any fucking idea. To be honest, all I can think about right now is heading down to that school and slapping some kids upside the head. I can't imagine how you feel."

"Neither can I," Kate said, pressing her hands to her chest to see if her heart was still beating. "I can't feel anything."

"I didn't find a note from Amelia or anything. Nothing else really except a box under her bed with a bunch of your old journals and photo albums in it."

"Mine?" Kate had kept a journal religiously from middle school all the way up until she graduated from law school, when the demands of raising a baby and having a career made the prospect of having thoughts about her life—much less jotting them down at the end of the day—an absurd impossibility. She hadn't seen the journals in years. "Under her bed?"

"I'm pretty sure. Some of them are those black moleskin ones you were always carrying around in law school. I didn't look in them or anything, but your name was on the front of one."

"What was she doing with my journals?" Kate asked.

Maybe Amelia had never again asked about her dad because she'd gone and found all the answers herself. And what else was in there that Kate would not have wanted Amelia to read? Her agonizing over whether to keep Amelia? How she'd decided to keep her initially only to later turn up at the door of a clinic no fewer than four times, each time intent on *not* keeping her? Had she also read the part where Kate's doubts about whether she should keep her baby had briefly ripened after her birth into regret that she had. Because those regrets had so quickly been overshadowed by love for her daughter. Deep, heartwrenching, life-changing love. But would Amelia have kept reading long enough to get to that part?

"I don't know what she was doing with them," Seth said. "But I know that nothing Amelia could have read would have changed how much she loved you. And she did, Kate. She really loved you."

"Then why do I feel even worse?"

Seth reached forward and put his hand over Kate's. "Because she's still gone."

After Seth had reluctantly agreed that he should be heading home, Kate picked up Amelia's phone again and went to her list of contacts. There were 367 names and numbers saved in her daughter's phone. Kate had maybe a couple dozen in her own phone, including every living relative, all of her and Amelia's doctors and dentists, and their last three cleaning women. How could Amelia have known so many people?

Kate's eyes rolled down the list of unfamiliar names. Many were girls, maybe even most. But there were lots of boys' names, too: Adam, Aikin, Aiden, Arden—or maybe that was a girl. Kate recognized only a few of them. Bennett Weiss was someone Amelia had played soccer with back when she'd been young enough to be on a coed team. George McDonnell was another name Amelia had mentioned once or twice before, same, too, for Carter Rose.

But then there were so very many others. The phone numbers were mostly local with a couple of Manhattan ones sprinkled in. Others, though, had area codes that Kate didn't recognize. She scrolled up, checking the Bs for a Ben, and there he was, at the top: 518-555-0119.

Kate was still staring at the list of names when somebody knocked hard on the kitchen windows. She jumped, cracking her knee against the leg of the table.

"Sorry!" called the voice of a woman through the windows.

In the dark outside, she was hard to make out beyond long dark hair. The woman pointed toward the door before her face disappeared from the windows.

Kate made her way over to the ground floor kitchen door slowly. She was not in the mood to talk to anyone. But the way the woman had pointed toward the door with such confidence made Kate suspect she wouldn't leave just because she was ignored, at least not quickly. Kate took a deep breath before she slowly pulled open the door.

The woman was standing the couple of steps up from the recessed kitchen floor, lit in the glow from the streetlight. With her long black hair, enormous black eyes, and delicate pale face, she was extremely beautiful, almost in a disconcerting way. She held out a perfectly manicured hand.

"I'm so sorry to have startled you," she said with a smile. Her lipstick was deep red, and flawless, too. She motioned toward the front steps above, leading to the upstairs door off the living room. "I rang the bell upstairs. I don't think it's working by the way. Then I saw the lights on down here. And now you'd probably like for me to identify myself and tell you what I'm doing lurking around your home. I'm Adele Goodwin, I'm with Grace Hall's PTA."

"Hi," Kate said. As she reached to shake her hand, Kate noticed the huge diamond ring and matching band on the woman's wedding finger, and the sparkling tennis bracelet on her wrist. Adele shuddered then, rubbing her hands up and down her arms. It was the first truly cold night of the year. "I'm sorry, come in," Kate said reluctantly. "It's freezing out there."

"Oh, are you sure? I don't want to intrude. I'm realizing now that I should have called first. I hate unannounced visitors myself."

No, I'm not sure, Kate wanted to say. Because if Kate was

uncomfortable around Grace Hall's general parenting population, what she'd glimpsed of the PTA at back-to-school nights made its members some of the last people she would have wanted in her house. These were not the PTA moms of her childhood either, with bad jeans and plates of cookies and loads of free time to sew homemade Halloween costumes. Most of the women were creative types, architects or designers or writers, sometimes with flexible careers, but always with extremely lucrative ones. They were fashionably dressed and decidedly unwelcoming. Grown-up cheerleaders with impressive résumés and enormous bank accounts.

"Oh no, that's okay," Kate said unconvincingly as she turned back toward the kitchen table and glimpsed all those awful little notes still piled up in the center. She rushed ahead, scooped them up, and dumped them in a nearby drawer. It was awkward and suspicious, but there was no alternative. Kate avoided eye contact and pointed toward the table. "Please have a seat. I was just . . . Can I get you something to drink?"

"No, thank you, I've already imposed enough," Adele said. Her coat was open now, revealing a pretty emerald wrap dress underneath and very tall fashionable heels. She had several heavy necklaces wrapped elegantly around her throat and she was looking around the kitchen, openly appraising it, though the conclusion she'd reached was unreadable. "I really don't want to take up too much of your time. We just wanted to talk to you about some events the PTA would like to organize in Amelia's honor. We didn't want to go ahead without speaking with you first."

"Events?" Kate did not like the sound of that.

Events meant parties. Parties she might be expected to attend. Kate wrote modest but not embarrassing checks to Grace Hall when asked to make contributions, but she'd always avoided events whenever possible. As an outsider to the school's clubby parenting network, she would have felt too much like the odd man out. Attending now, when she was no longer a parent at all, was unthinkable.

Adele waved a hand and shook her head, grimacing. "Events, I'm sorry, that sounded terrible," she said, and she did look embarrassed.

But there was something else, too, in her voice, a deliberateness that Kate found unsettling. "You'll have to forgive me, it's been a long day. I had back-to-back meetings, and my brain has liquefied." Adele smiled again. This time it was a harder smile. "We'd like to honor Amelia at the auction by dedicating a memorial."

"Oh," Kate said, even though she wanted to say no. Wanted to say: *Please leave.* "I'm afraid I probably won't be of much help. My job . . . I work really long hours. It's always been hard for me to make it to school events like the auction."

It was as good an excuse as any. Familiar, socially acceptable.

"All we'd need from you would be some childhood photos and your permission, of course," Adele said, her smile more relaxed now, warmer. Maybe she'd been nervous, uncomfortable having to talk with Kate about this. "And believe me, I understand completely about the work issue. You're a lawyer, right? A partner at a firm?"

"Yes," Kate said, wondering if that was part of the narrative now surrounding Amelia's death: *her mother, the lawyer.*

"I am, too—a lawyer, I mean. I'm in-house now, at Time Warner. But back in the day I was an associate in the corporate department at Dechter, Weiss." Adele shook her head, as a stiffness set over her face. "My job's not exactly as challenging as being a partner in a big firm, but at least the hours are human. Especially having Zadie. I don't know how you ever balanced—"

Adele fell silent abruptly, seeming to realize the faux pas she'd been about to make. Because Kate evidently hadn't balanced it all. Her daughter was dead, which hardly marked her parenting as a rousing success. Adele knit her fingers together on her lap, then shifted in her chair.

"Anyway," she said. She looked desperate to change the subject. "Which firm are you at?"

"Slone, Thayer," Kate said, racking her brain for an excuse that would get Adele to leave, immediately. *We don't have to do this*, Kate wanted to say to her. *You can just go.* She willed her phone to ring, for the fire alarm to go off. "I'm a litigation partner."

"Ah, Slone, Thayer. Yes, that's quite a place. It must be . . . interesting working there." Adele grimaced. The firm did have a reputation of being especially cutthroat. "I knew a few people who went there straight out of law school. Seems as if it has quite an intense culture. I still know a few lawyers there, in fact. Maybe you know them?"

"It's a huge place," Kate said. She had even less interest in playing the name game with Adele than she had in enduring more small talk. "There are hundreds of us in the New York office. If they're outside of litigation, I'd never know them."

"Of course," Adele smiled and fluttered her lashes. She'd gotten the message. "Anyway, I should be getting out of your way here. You can just send along the pictures when you have time. Oh, but there was one other thing. We don't want to overreach, of course, but several children have indicated an interest in sponsoring a suicide awareness benefit in Amelia's honor as well. They want to raise money for a national hotline. It seems like it might be an important part of the healing process for them. We were hoping that—"

"No," Kate snapped. Her voice had been too loud, almost like a bark.

"No?" Adele looked startled, then confused, then a little annoyed. "I'm afraid I don't understand."

"I'm sorry, I didn't mean to— I just . . ." Kate hesitated. What was there to say now, but the truth. "I'm not sure that Amelia killed herself."

"What?" Adele wrapped her fingers protectively around her throat. She looked frightened.

"No, no." Kate waved her hands. She should never have said anything. The last thing she wanted was for her suspicions to get back to the PTA. It wouldn't garner her any more goodwill with the police to have a jittery horde of Grace Hall parents pounding on the police station door. "I mean, it might have been an accident or something. There are still questions, that's all. If you could hold off on a suicide benefit, at least one in Amelia's honor, until I can get them answered, I would appreciate it."

"What kind of questions?" Adele's eyes had popped wide open. She wasn't getting tossed off the scent that easily.

"Really, I can't . . . the police . . . I'm sure you understand," she said, hoping that Adele wouldn't press her for more. But her eyes were still locked on Kate's. Adele wasn't budging without at least getting tossed a bone. "Something happened today. It might be nothing, but it—"

"Might be something," Adele said quietly. Her eyes were glassy now as they scanned back and forth across the tabletop, as if she was studying something written there. "Of course, yes, I see."

"Then you understand?" Kate was having a hard time believing that Adele wasn't pressing her for more details. "You'll wait on the suicide benefit?"

"Oh, yes, yes. Of course. You just let us know when we can proceed." Adele stood abruptly, then strode for the door. "And thank you for your time, Ms. Baron," she said as she pulled it open. When she turned back, she reached out to shake Kate's hand, flashing a smooth smile. "Your daughter was a lovely girl, Ms. Baron. I met her at the beginning of the year when she volunteered for the Harvest Festival. She was so polite and dedicated. You must have been very proud. The most exquisite, unusual eyes, too. That's a family trait? Two different colors like that?"

"No, it was a genetic disorder," Kate said, trying to figure out how they'd veered off into this conversation when she'd been so close to getting Adele to leave. "Waardenburg syndrome. There's no family history of it, but it can just happen randomly sometimes."

"Oh, I see, how unusual," Adele said, staring at Kate in an odd, unsettling way. Finally, she turned on a heel and started down the sidewalk, raising one hand in a wave. "Well, they were lovely. Just lovely."

gRaCeFULLY

SEPTEMBER 26TH

Because there are 176 definitions for the word *loser* on urbandictionary.com.
Don't Be a Statistic

Hey bitches!

Word is out that Charlie Kugler is one of the new Magpies, too, but a little birdie told us her Yalie boyfriend is trying to get her to bail. I guess he likes his heiresses to wear underwear and whatnot.

Oh, and on bobblehead watch: word on the street is that Tempest Bain has an appointment at Renfrew. Proving once again that no one is actually almost six feet tall and a hundred pounds without an eating disorder.

Looks like George McDonnell is on the wagon again. My guess is it's because he got locked up by the boys in blue over the weekend for smoking weed on the street down by the Old Stone House. Hey George, note to self, your parents are potheads, too . . . smoke the stuff at HOME.

One final bit of faculty news, Liv was stood up AGAIN this weekend. Can you believe it? I don't swing that way, but if I did, I'd never stand you up, Livy. You got to start meeting a better class of men, Liv. You should check out some of the dads. Trust me, they are all checking you out.

facebook

SEPTEMBER 30

Amelia Baron
is hoping she doesn't get caught

> **Chloe Frankel** and **2 others** like this
>
> Sylvia Golde   doing what? Sucking up too much?

Amelia

DYLAN

hiya

AMELIA

what's up

DYLAN

did you scope out Zaritski?

AMELIA

yeah, I think it will be ok

DYLAN

u sound so cool about it

AMELIA

really?

DYLAN

usually people are freaked

AMELIA

maybe I should be

DYLAN

nah I like you cool; c u ltr

AMELIA

gnite

SEPTEMBER 30, 10:14 PM

AMELIA

you awake?

BEN

yep

AMELIA

Dylan just texted me

BEN

really??? What she say?

AMELIA

nothing really

BEN

sounds awesome

AMELIA

ugh, never mind then

BEN

come on, she must have said something

AMELIA

just hi or whatever

BEN

more games?

AMELIA

what's with the third degree?

BEN

don't want to c u get stung by the queen B

AMELIA

come on

BEN

seriously, do u just want to b her friend because you don't know if she
wants to b yours?

AMELIA

don't psychoanalyze me tonite. I'm stressed.

BEN

oh yeah project lock-up 2morrow?

AMELIA

yeah

BEN

don't get caught, my good girl gone bad

AMELIA

gee thanks. I've g2g

OCTOBER 1, 7:18 AM

BEN

sorry, didn't mean to ride u last nite about being friends with Dylan

AMELIA

its okay

BEN

don't want to c you get hurt. I worry about that girl

AMELIA

me too

BEN

that makes me feel better; b sure to b careful

OCTOBER 1, 7:37 AM

BLOCKED NUMBER

where, oh where, has your little daddy gone?

Amelia

Mr. Woodhouse was still staring down at the note from Mr. Zaritski. He'd made me bring it with me to the headmaster's office like some kind of disclaimer on an unwanted package. Or maybe that was just standard practice. What did I know? I'd never been sent down to the headmaster's office before. And I was kind of nervous being there, but kind of relieved, too. Never doing anything wrong was a crapload of pressure sometimes.

Woodhouse had his cheek resting against one hand, his eyelids low as he read. Old wasn't my thing, but he was cute. Cuter than average even, with his arty black glasses and his grayish-black hair that was just shaggy enough to be kind of downtown. He had a thing about him, too, like that brooding, intense kind of thing. I should have liked that thing in guys. I liked it in books. And in poetry and photographs. I even liked the idea of it in boys. But in real life: nothing.

I was pretty much alone in that. Most of the girls at Grace Hall had a crush on Mr. Woodhouse. There were even bets about who he'd sleep with first. Not *if*, but when. Dylan was on the list. No one could figure out who she was sleeping with, so why not Woodhouse? Zadie was a candidate, too, and if anyone had the balls to close the deal with Woodhouse, it would probably be her. I'd even heard Sylvia's name thrown around, which made me feel kind of bad for her because it

was only on account of how many other people she'd slept with. I felt
a little bad for Woodhouse, too. He was a disaster waiting to happen.

"Is this right, what it says here?" Mr. Woodhouse asked, looking up
from the paper finally. His face was still resting on his hand.

"I don't know," I said. "The note was addressed to you. I didn't
violate your privacy by reading it or anything."

It had come out way more smart-ass than I'd planned. I was supposed to be sticking with the facts and saying as little as possible. That
was Phase I of the Magpie avoid-getting-punished-if-you-get-caught
strategy. For sure what the Maggies really cared about was us fledg-
lings not saying anything about them if we got nabbed. I knew that.
I wasn't stupid. The main thing they cared about was no one finding
out who they were. We weren't even allowed to program their names
and numbers into our phones in case someone tried to identify them
from their texts. And they used Maggie #1 (Zadie), Maggie #2 (Dylan),
and so on instead of their names to refer to one another. It all seemed
a little paranoid, but it did work. So far, no one seemed to know who
they were. Of course, I'd already broken the rules a little by putting
Dylan's name in my contact list. I wasn't even sure why. I also didn't
make Ben use the Maggie numbers to talk about anybody. He would
have made fun of me if I had.

"It says that you zip-tied Mr. Zaritski's bag to his desk," Mr. Woodhouse said. "Did you, Amelia?"

"Did I what?" Answer all questions with a question.

Woodhouse stared at me for a long time, then took a deep, tired
breath.

"Listen, Amelia, I know we don't know each other very well, and
there's a reason for that. I looked through your file before you got
down here, and it's basically flawless—outstanding grades, two varsity
letters, head of the French club, four honors classes. You've never even
been marked late. And now this? Why?"

I thought for a second about the morning a couple of weeks earlier when Sylvia had been telling me about Ian Greene and I'd gotten
that first invitation from the Maggies. I'd definitely been late that

day. Will had taken my name down and everything. But somebody in the office must have decided not to write it in my file. Sylvia had been right. When you were a smart kid, a good kid, Grace Hall cleaned up after you.

"Does that mean I get first-offense leniency?" I asked. I made myself smile, but I could tell I wasn't really pulling it off. Pretending wouldn't turn me into a kid who did bad stuff, got caught, then made jokes. "Also, I have a calculus quiz in ten minutes that I don't want to miss. Can I go?"

"No," Mr. Woodhouse said. "You can't *go*, Amelia. This isn't just going away. Not until you explain to me what's going on. Mr. Zaritski's note says that he threw his back out tugging on his bag. Apparently, he already has three bulging discs."

"Of course he does," I said, rolling my eyes.

Who was this person I kept on sounding like? Zadie maybe? Her whole f-you thing was kind of contagious, and there was a little part of me that wanted to be like her, or at least to be treated the way she was. Teachers, the administration, everyone gave Zadie a wide berth, overlooked little lapses, and not because they thought she couldn't possibly do anything wrong. They were afraid of her. No one was ever afraid of me.

"Amelia, Mr. Zaritski may not be the easiest person," Mr. Woodhouse said. He didn't like Mr. Zaritski. He was trying to hide it, but I could tell. "But he is still a person, and you zip-tied his bag to the leg of his desk. Why now and why him? You've had only one evaluation in his class so far, and it was excellent."

I shrugged. The zip ties had been the Maggies' idea, not mine. It was the first of the three hazing pranks I had to do before I officially became a Magpie. I'd pulled my assignments out of a hat at the last meeting. The meetings were twice a week and once on weekends, always at a different time and a different place. It wasn't easy making up that many excuses about where I had to be for Sylvia and my mom, but it was also kind of fun having a secret. And the meetings weren't bad either; they weren't quite like parties, but almost. Someone usually brought a bottle of wine, and people were constantly headed outside to smoke cigarettes. Occasionally, there was a joint that got passed around, which I still hadn't taken when it came my way. But I'd come close. I was still on the fence about becoming a full-fledged Maggie, but so far I kept on finding myself going to the meetings and doing what I was told. Partly, I was worried about what Zadie would do if I stopped. Partly, I liked getting to spend more time with Dylan.

Dylan and I were actually becoming pretty close. And I liked having a new friend who was separate from Sylvia. She would have thought it was ridiculous, my liking Dylan, but it wasn't because Dylan was beautiful or popular. Or at least that wasn't the whole reason. Maybe it was a tiny part of it—a part I wasn't proud of—but I also just really liked being around her. Dylan had this mysterious energy. Maybe it was because she was an actress or something, but one minute you'd be talking to her, and then it was like she'd just disappear into some private world. She'd always reappear just when you thought maybe you'd lost her for good. It made the time you had with her feel, I don't know, precious or something.

Plus, Dylan and I had things in common, not in what we liked so much as the way we liked it. I was obsessed with books and writing. For Dylan it was numbers. It was definitely not what you'd expect, given how pretty she was, but Dylan was insanely good at math. She loved it, too. Anytime I would have stuck my head in a novel, she'd be doing these little books of math puzzles and expert sudoku. We were kindred geek spirits, Dylan and I. She was just a lot more stealth about her geekiness than me. I'd never known someone like me in that way before. And I wanted to keep on knowing her, something I was pretty sure wouldn't happen if I got booted from the Maggies for not following orders.

And zip-tying a teacher's bag wasn't a major deal anyway, definitely not when it was my biology teacher, Mr. Zaritski. He was supposedly some genius, and so parents loved him, but as far as the other kids and I were concerned he was just a big mass of unsmiling meanness. Zaritski pretty much seemed like he hated kids, and he was an annoying complainer, too—the weather, the pollen, his sinuses, his knees, the bad parking spot it took him forty-five minutes to find. He never shut up about all the bad crap in his life. Like anybody was going to care about the feelings of a guy who spent his weekends taking down signs advertising stoop sales and trying to get double strollers banned from sidewalks. I'd picked Mr. Zaritski to get his bag zip-tied because he deserved to get picked on.

The next prank—Vaseline on a doorknob—was supposed to be on an administrator. I already had a plan for the who and the when on that. And Mrs. Pearl deserved to get her hand gummed up as much as Zaritski deserved to get his bag zip-tied.

But the third and last trial . . . I wasn't sure I'd be able to go through with it. I was supposed to find some real dorky kid—the kind who was all pale because he spent so much time in his apartment alone playing Xbox—and pretend online that I was a girl who liked him. It was a whole drawn-out thing, which was supposed to end with my getting him to text me naked pictures of himself. I didn't know how I was going to get out of it without Zadie beating me up, but I felt like I had way too much in common with those pasty boys to do a thing like that.

Then again, I'd have sworn I'd never do something like I'd already done to Zaritski. It had been pretty easy, too, both consciencewise and executionwise. I'd seen him going into the bathroom with his crossword puzzle. His morning constitutional, everybody joked, always at the exact same time every day and always for at least ten minutes. It had been the second lunch period, so the hallways had been empty. But someone, somewhere must have seen me. It hadn't taken Zaritski long to pin the whole thing on me.

Woodhouse was still staring at me, waiting for me to say something. According to the Magpies, I was supposed to move on to Phase II of Project Avoid Getting Punished If You Get Caught—crying hysterically—only if keeping my mouth shut totally bombed. From the way Mr. Woodhouse's eyebrows were up by his hairline, it didn't look like Phase I was exactly a big win. But I was pretty sure I wouldn't be able to pull off the hysterics. I just didn't feel upset. Even though a couple of weeks earlier I'd have sworn I'd have been bawling sitting there in the headmaster's office.

"What proof is there anyway that I even did it?" I asked, channeling my mom. "Don't you need evidence or something?"

"Let me ask you something, Amelia," Woodhouse said, eyeing my messenger bag. "If I look in there, am I going to find zip ties?"

Why hadn't I thrown them out? I kept thinking I might need them for something else. I was such a total idiot. Now my life of crime was going to be finished before it ever got started.

"No," I said, gripping my bag tighter, trying to figure out what the hell I'd do when he tried to grab it to take a look.

"Listen, Amelia, regardless of what I think is fair under the circumstances, Mr. Zaritski isn't just going to let this drop." Woodhouse shifted his chin to the opposite hand. He looked sure that I was going to tell him everything he wanted to know. That it was only a matter of time. "We're going to have to figure out a way for you to make it up to him. And it's going to have to start with your coming clean."

Phase III: fall on your sword, take full responsibility, and accept punishment. And never, ever mention the Magpies. Doing so, we'd learned, would be grounds for expulsion from the club, which seemed to mean something a lot worse than just not being in the club anymore.

"Then fine, I'll tell Zaritski I'm sorry or whatever," I said.

"That's a start," Mr. Woodhouse said, like he hadn't even heard the part about my taking the blame. "But, Amelia, this isn't you. You didn't come up with this on your own. I know you didn't."

I did not like where this conversation was headed.

"Oh yeah?"

"Yeah," Woodhouse said. "And I'm not asking you to betray any confidences. I understand how hard that could be. But I want you to think about whether the girls who put you up to this are actually your friends. Whether they really have your best interests at heart."

"Sure," I said, keeping it short. I didn't want to confirm the existence of the Maggies by accident. "Okay."

Woodhouse was looking at me like he was a therapist all of a sudden. Like I was some kid on the brink. That's life as a good kid. First they don't believe you'd ever do something wrong; then when they figure out you did, they think you're having a nervous breakdown.

"Listen, I understand that you spend a lot of time on your own, that your mom has to work a lot, and that it's just the two of you," Woodhouse said. "These groups, they pick on people who are looking for something, knowing they'll be easier to manipulate."

"I'm not looking for anything," I said. And that was true, except, for some reason, it felt like a total lie.

Woodhouse frowned, nodding as he looked down. "Okay, Amelia," he said finally. He almost looked kind of sad. "But I've taught in a lot of schools, in a lot of different places, and it's always the same. The odds are stacked against a good kid like you staying good. That's true, even at a place like Grace Hall."

Now I was getting annoyed. I didn't need Woodhouse trying to get all inside my head. I wanted to tell him to back off, but agreeing was the fastest way to wrap it up and get out of that office.

"Sure, whatever, I guess." I shrugged.

"Anyway, I just wanted to say that the Magpies are not the answer. Some of those girls—" Woodhouse hesitated. He lifted his hands like he was surrendering, then his face softened. "They are all nice girls individually. Most of them are, at least. But collectively, their judgment is"—he paused like he was trying to find the right word—"clouded. I want to be sure you see that before it's too late."

Woodhouse had been playing dumb. Turned out, he knew all about the Magpies. It even sounded like he knew who was in the group. It felt like a trap.

"I've really got to be getting back to class for real now. I mean, don't I? I can apologize to Mr. Zaritski—I'll do the time or the punishment or whatever—but I don't know what else there is I can do."

"Okay, Amelia, you can go," Woodhouse said, looking beaten down. It was my window. I had to get out of there before he changed his mind. I jumped to my feet. "I'll talk to Zaritski. An apology might not go all the way, but it will certainly be a good start. And we'll keep it off the record this time. Next time, Amelia, it will be a different story."

"Thanks, Mr. Woodhouse," I said, rushing to the door before he changed his mind.

"And, Amelia," he called after me. "I'm serious about being careful. Sometimes it's hard to tell how fast the current's moving until you're headed over a waterfall."

After school, I was sitting in a sticky booth in the mostly empty Roma Pizza, waiting for Sylvia to come back with our slices. I was still feeling a little amped from the thing with Zaritski, especially after sailing out of Woodhouse's office, all mission accomplished and whatnot. All those years of keeping my nose jammed down into books really had given me some kind of Grace Hall–ified force field.

My phone vibrated with a text as Sylvia was on her way back to the booth with our two slices. I jerked it out of my bag, trying to read it before she got there. It was from a blocked number, which meant one of the Maggies.

Party, @ Maggie 2. Put pizza down, dump harlot. We're about to pop your cherry.

It was from Zadie, I could tell even though the number was blocked. She'd called Sylvia a harlot before. Holy crap, how did Zadie know I was a virgin? But no, wait, she couldn't. She didn't. She probably meant my first coed party. I needed to calm down. She'd told us we'd get to go to a Magpie–Wolf's Gate party after all of us newbies had pulled off our first deed. And Maggie 2 was Dylan. A party at Dylan's house was not something I wanted to miss. I shoved my phone back in my bag.

"Why do they always have to make it so hot?" Sylvia said, tossing the two greasy paper plates onto the table and shaking out her hands. "It's totally the best pizza in the hood, but you say 'not-so-hot' and they, like, make it *extra* hot."

Luckily, Sylvia hadn't seemed to notice I'd been looking at my phone. And now that she'd sat down, she was focused on using her electric blue nails to organize the little cheese-covered squares she still had them cutting her slices into like she was a three-year-old. I looked past Sylvia through the flowers painted on Roma's front windows to the Yogo Monster and the liquor store on the other side of Seventh Avenue. I expected to see Zadie over there, watching me. But there was just a big pack of moms with strollers and little kids.

"So I know that Ian saying he wants to hang out isn't the same as him saying he wants to be, like, my *boyfriend* or whatever," Sylvia said, picking up on her Ian monologue pretty much exactly where she'd left off when she'd gotten up to get our slices. She popped another square of pizza into her mouth, then checked her own phone for texts. From the disappointed look on her face, she didn't seem to have any. "But he did say once that he never hooks up more than once with girls who go to his school. So him hooking up with me a bunch of times has to mean *something*, right?"

I snapped my eyes down from the window when I felt her looking at me.

"Um, yeah," I said. From the way Sylvia's face balled up I knew it hadn't been enthusiastic enough. And Ian Greene did seem totally into Sylvia. Of course, that wildness of hers that all the boys loved hadn't yet taken its turn into full-on wacko. "I mean, yes, totally. Absolutely."

Her face relaxed a little. "You *really* think so?"

"Definitely. Nobody hooks up more than once with somebody they go to school with unless they think it could be a real thing," I said, as though all my information on this kind of thing didn't actually come from *gRaCeFULLY*. "It's too messy. Especially for somebody like Ian. Why would he bother? He could totally meet girls anywhere."

Sylvia nodded, but she looked kind of worried. My phone vibrated then with another text. I tried to be subtle about checking, but Sylvia was looking right at me.

Don't be late, it said.

"Who's that? Your BFF Ben?" Sylvia asked, rolling her eyes. "I'm telling you, that kid has way too much free time to be texting you. Can you say *loser*?"

"I have time to text him back," I said. "Am I a loser, too?"

Sylvia shrugged. "If the shoe fits," she said. I scowled at her. "Listen, don't blame me. You're the one who's settling for cybersex."

I wanted so badly to shove my phone in her face. I wanted to tell her that it was *she* who was the loser, not me. Because *I*'d been tapped by the Maggies, and the Maggies didn't tap losers. Except, of course, I couldn't tell Sylvia anything about the Maggies. I felt bad about that. I even felt bad for bragging about the Maggies in my head. And Sylvia was Sylvia, too. When she felt bad about herself, she picked on me. It was just the way she was, which reminded me of those stupid texts about my dad that I was almost 100 percent sure she'd sent as some kind of joke.

"By the way, what's up with the texts about my dad?" I asked. I felt more pissed off once I'd brought it up. It was a seriously messed-up joke. "Why would you ever think that was funny?"

"What are you talking about?" She was trying to play all innocent, and she was doing a pretty good job.

"Sylvia, come on. I know it was you."

"Let me see it." She held out her hand for my phone. "Because I so did not send you any text about your dad."

Right away, I dropped my phone back into my bag, then played like it was too much of a pain to dig for it. There was no possible way I could let her get her hands on my phone. What if another text from Zadie came through?

"I'm not making it up," I said.

"I didn't say you were."

"The last one said, 'Your dad isn't who you think he is.'"

"And it was from *my* number?"

"No, it was blocked."

"But you still thought *I* sent it to you?" Sylvia looked all offended. "Thanks."

"I guess I was hoping it was you." Which was more true than I'd realized.

But it definitely wasn't Sylvia. That was for sure. Because she was a terrible liar. If she hadn't been telling the truth, I'd have totally known it. It could have been from Zadie or someone else in the Maggies. It wasn't a secret that I didn't live with my dad, but the fact that I'd never even met him kind of was. Sylvia was pretty much the only person who knew that.

"What did your mom say?"

"About what?"

"Um, the *text*?" Sylvia asked, looking at me like I had to be playing dumb on purpose.

"I didn't tell her," I said, feeling a little guilty.

"Why not?"

I'd thought about it, obviously, but I wanted to figure out who they were from first. If the messages had come from Sylvia, my mom probably would have wanted to have some humiliating sit-down with her mom. And if they *hadn't* come from Sylvia, my mom would have called the school to tell them someone was stalking me. It wouldn't be long before she ended up talking to Woodhouse, and he would tell her all about the Maggies.

"I didn't tell my mom because I thought it was from *you*."

"Oh yeah, I forgot. Nice."

"Anyway, that last text was from my coach," I said. "I left my cleats back at the field. I have to go get them."

Sylvia looked a little wounded. "You're coming back, though, right?"

I looked down at the time on my phone. "I've got a bio test tomorrow. Probably not."

"Oh, okay, I guess," Sylvia said. "But before you go, can you at least—just bottom line, you don't think I should call Ian again, do you? I mean, I should wait for him to text me back?"

Dylan lived up on Second Street near the park, in a brownstone that looked a lot like ours except it was white stone instead of red, and there was a kind-of-cool, kind-of-creepy sculpture out in front of a small tree with hands at the end of the branches instead of leaves. I was standing at the bottom of the steps staring at it when the door flew open. At the top was Dylan, barefoot in a loose dress and a bunch of necklaces. She had a cigarette in her hand, which she looked weird holding. Like it was a stage prop.

"Come on, come on," she said, waving me up. "You're one of the guests of honor."

When I got to the top of the steps, she crushed the cigarette out on the stoop, linked her arm through mine, and guided me inside. Her living room was packed with furniture and tchotchkes and bodies—boys and girls piled on couches and stretched across the floor. It was filled with smoke, too. Pot, cigarettes; most people had a beer in their hand. I must have stopped walking because Dylan tugged me gently forward, toward the kitchen.

"You look like you've never seen a party before," she laughed as she headed to the refrigerator and pulled out a Brooklyn Lager.

I had been to parties before—slumber parties, movie parties, birthday parties, even some boy-girl parties. Never a party like this.

Dylan snapped off the cap and handed me the beer like she was handing me a stick of gum. I took it. Or I must have, because there the bottle was, in my hand. It felt cold and slimy and heavier than I would have expected. I gripped it tight so I wouldn't accidentally drop it. I'd had wine at Christmas, and Sylvia and I had once done a shot of her father's disgusting whiskey. But I'd never had a beer before, definitely not one of my own at a party full of cool kids. I was staring down at the bottle when Zadie came pounding into the kitchen. She seemed drunk already, or maybe just more angry than usual.

"Ugh," she said when she saw me, shielding her eyes like I was hard to look at. "If it isn't Crazy Eyes. Delightful."

"Be nice, Zadie," Dylan said, without bothering to look at her. "You said that you would be."

Zadie grabbed two beers from the refrigerator and slammed it shut with her hip. Dylan tensed at the noise but didn't turn around.

"Nice?" Zadie growled, still glaring at me.

I took a long swallow of beer and tried not to gag.

"Yes, nice," Dylan said. "You promised."

"We never said 'nice,' we said 'not mean.'" Zadie came around to stand next to Dylan. She leaned over to whisper in her ear, but Dylan kept pulling her head away. "And considering what I *really* think about Crazy Eyes here, I think I'm being charming as all fuck."

Crazy Eyes? Zadie seriously hated me, but why? We didn't even know each other. But with each meeting of the Magpies, how much she despised me became way more obvious. It was only when Dylan started being extra nice to make up for it that I had decided to stay. She even said I reminded her of herself when she was a sophomore. It might have just been a thing to say, but it still felt good thinking Dylan saw what we had in common.

I took another gulp of beer, holding my breath so I wouldn't have to taste it.

"I don't exactly love your badass ballerina, you know," Dylan mumbled, crossing her arms. She looked upset now. "But I'm not taking it out on her."

Your badass ballerina. Did that mean I was *her* Crazy Eyes? Because I had been wondering who could have possibly picked me to be in the Maggies in the first place.

Zadie was still hanging near Dylan. She reached out slowly, pushing a few strands of Dylan's hair gently behind her ear.

"Don't touch me," Dylan snapped, knocking Zadie's hand away.

"Temper, temper," Zadie said, with a mean smile. Then she held up her hands—a beer in each one—before sashaying toward the door. "Be careful, Crazy Eyes, that one bites."

Carter appeared in the doorway to the kitchen then, looking disoriented and nervous. It was a relief to see a friendly face, but he didn't even look in my direction before Zadie charged at him.

"There you are!" she said, pressing her hips against him, then her mouth hard over his. Carter looked woozy when Zadie came up for air. She grabbed his hand and jerked him toward the living room, smiling back at us over her shoulder. "Catch you later, ladies."

"She's not as bad as she seems," Dylan said when she was gone. But she didn't sound convinced. "You have to really know her. She's my best friend. A lot of the time, it's felt like she was my only friend."

"What do you mean?" I laughed a little, even though it definitely didn't seem like she was making a joke. "You have a million friends."

"Not ones who know the real me," Dylan said, her eyes turning glassy. "Not like Zadie knows me."

"I'd like to know the real you," I said, feeling my cheeks flush, but I was glad I'd said it all the same.

"Come on," Dylan said, smiling as she linked her arm through mine. "I want to show you something upstairs."

I followed her back through the smoky, antique-filled living room toward the creaky, dark staircase. Her house, laid out so much like mine, couldn't have looked more different. Stuffy and overstuffed, but not in a totally bad way. Like a set for a Jane Austen movie. I looked over my shoulder as I started up the stairs. That's when I caught a glimpse of Ian Greene sitting on the couch. But who was that sitting with him? It had been a girl, definitely. And I could have sworn it was Zadie. I thought I recognized her pointy boots and her little plaid skirt. Was that Ian's hand on Zadie's leg? But she'd just been with Carter in the kitchen. She couldn't have traded up that quickly. It was too late, though, to go back and check as Dylan pulled me up the steps and out of sight.

"Come on," Dylan said, half playfully, half losing patience. "Hurry up."

When I looked back, Ian was gone, disappeared along with the rest of the living room.

"Are all the guys here in Wolf's Gate?" I asked when we were at the top of the steps. I tried to sound nonchalant.

"Yeah. Most of them are okay. Some of them are assholes." She sounded bored as she pointed to a doorway halfway down the hall. "We're going in there."

We turned inside a small office, with a big mahogany desk and a formal leather chair. The walls were lined with books, the old, leather kind with fancy gold trim and thin crinkly pages. And not just new books made to look old either. These were old, old books.

"Wow," I said, stepping closer. The classics were all there—*Odyssey*, *Moby-Dick*, Dante's *Inferno*. "This is amazing."

"Nobody reads them," Dylan said, like she didn't want me getting the wrong idea. "My dad just collects them. Original ones, too." She pulled one book down, which was displayed alone on a little shelf. "Like this one."

I took the book reluctantly, afraid I'd spill what was left of my beer on top of it. It was a first edition of *The Sun Also Rises*.

"Wow," I said again. I could hear myself sounding totally stupid, but I couldn't help it. The book was pretty amazing.

"Anyway, I thought maybe they'd be your kind of thing," Dylan said, grabbing *The Sun Also Rises* from me and shoving it back on the shelf. She'd cooled suddenly, that warm smile that had guided me up the stairs had vanished. I'd offended her somehow, but I had no idea when. "Actually, I've gotta go," Dylan said, turning fast for the door. "You can stay and look around if you want, but I've gotta go do something. I'll see you back downstairs in a couple of minutes."

Then she was gone. And there I stood, alone in Dylan's library, a nearly empty beer in one hand and a bunch of questions in my head. I had no idea what had just happened, much less how to fix it. It wasn't easy when I didn't really understand what was going on between Dylan and me in the first place.

I texted Ben as soon as I got home:

AMELIA
I went to the first coed party today

BEN
Was it debauch?

AMELIA
Pretty much

BEN
Sex, drugs

AMELIA

Pretty much

BEN

But I'm guessing not for you

AMELIA

Not really; Dylan was really nice to me though

BEN

That's good

AMELIA

Then she turned off all of a sudden

BEN

Not good. Why?

AMELIA

IDK, I'm asking you

BEN

What do I know about girls? I think you're all crazy. That's why I stick with boys

AMELIA

U r useless

BEN

:)

I dropped my phone, rolled over in bed, and picked up *To the Lighthouse*. It wasn't like I needed to read it again to write my English paper. I practically knew the whole thing by heart. Virginia Woolf was kind of my hero. Not because she walked into a river with rocks in her pockets—though as far as ways to kill yourself went, that did have a certain style—but because she was crazy talented and had been who she'd wanted to be, despite the world telling her to be someone different.

How inconspicuous she felt herself by Paul's side! He, glowing, burning; she, aloof, satirical; he, bound for adventure; she, moored to the shore . . .

I put the book down and looked at the clock. It was close to ten. I'd gotten a text from my mom at a little past eight telling me that she was on her way home soon, but that I should go ahead and eat. I'd ordered enough sushi for her. If I didn't order her dinner, she'd go to bed without eating at all.

With Leelah not around anymore, I ate alone a lot, usually three or four times a week—Japanese, Chinese, Thai. Never Indian. It would have made me miss Leelah's cooking too much. Most of the time, it wasn't so bad. The takeout people knew my address by heart and said things like "For you, anything."

I didn't blame my mom for having to work. She had a job, and she had to do it well. Most of the time I was proud of her for that. It was still lonely sometimes, though. But that didn't mean I was "looking for something" like Woodhouse had said. I was fine just the way I was.

Besides, we had our Friday night dinner dates, which neither of us was allowed to cancel, ever. And we tried for brunch together on Saturdays, and we'd always curl up on a couch together for a movie on Sunday nights. We did other things on weekends, too, depending on my homework and field hockey schedule and how much work my mom had to do. And now my Maggie meetings. We went to museums or got our nails done together. Once we went on a cupcake walking tour in Manhattan. In summer, we always spent a week somewhere at the beach together—Fire Island, Block Island, Nantucket. And I knew my mom would have spent even more time with me if she could have.

I heard the front door open downstairs a few minutes later. Then my mom was on the stairs, creeping up, probably afraid she might wake me. When she finally pushed open my bedroom door and poked her head inside, her dark blond hair was pulled back in a low ponytail and she was wearing her tortoiseshell glasses, the ones that I thought were cool in a mom kind of way. She looked beat, with big dark shadows under her blue eyes. But still pretty. My mom was always pretty. Not in a MILF sort of way, that would have been humiliating. My mom was just a regular mom, but a pretty one.

I waved a hand back and forth, my head still down on the pillow, so she'd know I was awake.

"Oh hi." She smiled, looking pleasantly surprised. "I didn't wake you, did I?"

"Nah." I pushed myself up in bed and put my book down on the nightstand. "I was just reading."

"Haven't you already read *To the Lighthouse* a bunch of times?"

And that was my mom. She could have been around a lot more and noticed a lot less. Maybe we weren't all *Leave It to Beaver* or whatever, but what we had worked for us.

"Yeah, like ten times. But we're supposed to write a paper on it for English. I was just looking at it again to decide what I was going to do it on."

"Should you be in a different English class?" my mom asked. "I know we thought that another honors class would be too much. But being bored isn't good either." She looked concerned. "We pay a lot of money for that school. They should be able to accommodate your needs."

"Mom, the class is fine, seriously. Liv's, like, my favorite teacher." I shrugged. My mom got like this—all intense about stuff that wasn't that important. It was because she felt guilty for not being around. She was always itching to go to bat for me, on everything. Even things I didn't need help with. "Besides, I've got some ideas about how I can make the paper more interesting."

"You promise to tell me if it ends up *not* being okay?" she asked seriously. "I mean, with classes or anything else."

I thought then about my dad. I didn't think whoever had sent those stupid texts really knew anything about him, or me. But the texts had gotten me wondering about who, and where, my dad really was.

He was supposedly some guy my mom had met one night fifteen years ago. "A boy in a bar," my mom called him, who was a do-gooder on his way to Africa when they crossed paths. That was awesome and everything, to think of my dad being that person, except he didn't sound *at all* like the kind of guy my mom would ever go for. Seth was my mom's type—supernice, and smart and buttoned-up—except not gay like Seth was now. Actually, the whole setup didn't make any sense. My mom didn't go to bars, ever. She hardly ever drank. I don't know when I stopped believing the story. It was kind of gradually, over time, and I'd never really cared before about finding out the truth. I'd figured that if my dad had been worth finding, he would have tracked me down a long time ago.

And then came the texts.

As much as I wanted not to care about them, they were bugging me. *It* was bugging me. I wanted to tell my mom that she didn't have to protect me anymore, that I could handle knowing the truth about my dad. But looking at her tired eyes, that way she was smiling at me like she was trying to make me feel her love through her teeth, I just couldn't do it. I couldn't rip the whole thing open. I didn't want my mom to think she wasn't enough for me. Also, I was a little afraid that what she'd tell me might make me mad. At her.

Besides, there were other, more important things I needed to talk to her about. I needed some advice. I couldn't go into any secret club nonsense obviously. My mom would have charged down to Grace Hall in the middle of the night and taken the place apart brick by brick. She'd also definitely hire Leelah back on the spot. And that would be the end of the Magpies, and Dylan. Instead, I'd have to get my questions in through the back door.

"Did you belong to a sorority in college?" I asked her instead.

Sorority, secret club. It was a safe way to get in most of my questions.

"A sorority?" My mom looked confused for a second, then kind of embarrassed. "Yes, I'm afraid to say I did. In my defense, pretty much everybody at Duke belonged to one. It didn't feel like there was much of a choice."

"Was it fun?" I asked. "I mean, were you glad you did it?"

"Glad?" She wrinkled her forehead and tapped a finger to her lips. "I don't think *glad* would be the word I'd use. I survived it, let's put it that way."

It was funny imagining my mom at something like a Maggie meeting. If I was a Goody Two-shoes, my mom was a saint.

"What kinds of hazing stuff did you have to do?" I asked, feeling this weird secret bond with her.

"Wait, what's with all the questions about sororities, Amelia?" My mom narrowed her eyes at me. "You're not planning on running off to college early, are you?"

"No," I said, scrambling to think of an excuse. "I'm writing a paper on sororities, for my Moral Controversy in America class."

Wow, where had I pulled that out from? I was getting better and better at this lying thing.

"Moral Controversy in America? Have I heard about this class before?"

"Yes, you were there when I picked it."

"I was?" She looked confused. "Do you still take regular classes, too, like math?"

I rolled my eyes. "Mom, come on."

"Well, if it's for a paper, then my honest answer is that I think sororities are bad. I think they're terrible, actually. I think they make girls feel awful about themselves under the guise of sisterhood."

That didn't sound good. And she wasn't even playing it up on purpose to talk me out of something. That was her real unbiased opinion. But then again, a secret club wasn't *exactly* the same thing as a sorority. Not at all. Actually, they were really, really different. High school and college were totally different.

"But for the record, should you end up in a sorority, I won't hold it against you." She put a hand on my forehead. "Are you sure you're okay? You look pale."

"I'm fine," I said, pulling my head away. "And how old were you when you first went out with boys?"

My mom blew some air out of her cheeks. "Wanted to?" she asked. "Or actually did? Because I always spent more time thinking about boys than actually being with them. As you know, romance has never been my forte."

"When did you start *liking* boys?"

I'd been wondering lately if my late blooming might be genetic.

"Before I answer this, are you *already* dating somebody? Because our agreement was fifteen, but only *after* we talked about it. I won't be mad, though, I promise. You can always tell me the truth, no matter what."

"I'm not dating anyone, Mom," I said, making sure to look her in the eyes. "I would tell you, I swear. It's just research, for the same paper."

"The same paper?" she asked, her eyebrows scrunched low.

It had been a bad lie. It didn't even really make sense.

"Yeah, it's a two-parter."

She looked skeptical still.

"Uh-huh. Okay, let's see, I guess I was thirteen maybe," she said, wiggling her hand around like it might have been even younger. "It's hard to remember exactly. But I am sure that I never kissed anyone until I was fifteen, *at least*. Maybe even twenty."

She looked at me like she was trying to drive her point home, but then she smiled. One of the things that was great about my mom, as a mom, was that she always knew when she was being kind of ridiculous.

"Oh, okay," I said, suddenly feeling kind of lonely. Thirteen was younger than fifteen. Only by two years, but they felt like big years. Maybe there was something wrong with me. Not that I could really expect my mom to make me feel better when I wasn't even telling her what we were really talking about. "Thanks. That was all I needed to know."

She leaned forward to give me a hug, talking into my hair.

"I'm sorry I didn't make it home for dinner, Amelia. I was trying to get out the door, and then I got stuck on the phone and—"

"It's okay, Mom," I said. "It's not like you want to stay at work, I know."

And I did know that, even though sometimes it sucked anyway. My mom's eyes were glassy when she leaned back to smile at me. When she got really tired, she was a total crier. She ran a hand down my cheek.

"You are one sweet girl, Amelia."

She kissed me on the forehead, then pushed herself off the bed and headed for the door. My mom was almost there when I realized that I *really* didn't want her to go. I needed to talk to her more. I needed to tell her everything.

"Mom," I called after her.

She turned around in the doorway. "What, honey?"

"I got tapped by—"

Her phone rang then, and she patted her coat pockets looking for it. When she finally pulled it out, she looked aggravated when she saw who was calling.

"Ugh, sorry," she said, turning to answer it. "Hello, yes, hold on just one second." Then she turned back to me, her hand muffling the phone. "Victor is in Tokyo, and he apparently thinks the world revolves around his time zone. But I should probably take it. He's called me four times today. Can it wait, Amelia?"

I stared at the phone in her hand and her trying-so-hard face. If I'd told my mom that I needed her to hang up the phone right then, she would have. I knew that. I also knew that she would do anything to make sure I didn't get hurt by the Maggies or Dylan. And I knew that I could trust her with everything. But maybe I just wasn't ready to, after all. Not yet. Not until I understood what there was to tell.

"It can wait," I said.

"Are you sure?" she asked. "This is your time, not theirs."

"I know, Mom," I said, and it meant a lot that she'd said that. It meant everything. "I'm sure."

Kate

Three weeks, four days, and five hours. That's how long it's been since Amelia was born.

I feel like it should be getting easier. But it isn't.

The first few days were the toughest, though. In the hospital, all by myself, trying to figure out how to breast-feed in the middle of the night. I had a hard time just getting out of bed. Everything hurt. And then there was picking her up out of the little plastic bassinette.

She's so small and soft. Like her bones are made of sponge. It's a sick joke that nature made them so damageable.

At least the baby nurse Gretchen is paying for comes today. I'll be grateful when she's here, even if the only reason my mom paid for her is so that she could rush out of town after three short nights at the Essex House. Gretchen still had the nerve to get teary when she was leaving, though. Surely tears of disappointment.

Mothers. I am one now. That's the craziest part. Me: a mother. To an actual, real live person.

The nurses in the hospital kept telling me that I should have Amelia sent to the nursery so that I could get some rest. They promised to bring her back in for feedings. I know they kept offering because I was alone. My roommate, whose husband was there to help with her baby all day long, didn't send her baby away.

So I didn't either. Amelia's not going to get less because it's just me. Not yet. Not ever.

Kate

JUNE 30, 1997

He called me up to his office today to tell me that my memo of collateral estoppel was the best he'd ever read by a summer associate. That's like having the president come out of the Oval Office to give you a pat on the back. It never happens.

I can already tell that the best way to get over Seth won't be another boy; it'll be by being the best summer associate Slone, Thayer has ever seen.

Kate

Kate was standing in the kitchen, finger poised over the coffeemaker, when there was a knock at the kitchen door. It was barely light, only a few minutes past seven a.m. She hit Start and made her way over to the windows. When Kate peered out, there was her next-door neighbor Kelsey, bouncing foot to foot in running pants and a bright yellow Nike shell, a knit cap pulled low over her short pixie hair.

Kelsey had six-year-old twins, whom she stayed home with full-time, and a gorgeous Brazilian husband, who was as visibly devoted to her as she was to her children. Kelsey's idealized image of motherhood had always made Kate feel inadequate. Not because of anything Kelsey did, but because of how unconflicted she seemed. She wanted to be a full-time mother, and so she was. There was no push and pull, no wobbly balancing act in which someone was forever the loser— Amelia, Kate, her job.

In the weeks since Kate's friends had gone home, Kelsey had been a lifesaver. She'd dropped off casseroles, bought groceries, and done laundry for Kate, all without being asked and without the expectation of a thank-you. She'd almost seemed disappointed when Kate had told her that she'd be going back to work and would no longer be in need of her help.

"Are you locked out?" Kate asked when she opened the door.

"No, no, I'm fine," Kelsey said, waving a hand. She was still bouncing back and forth on her toned legs. "I just wanted to check in and see how your first day back was."

"Oh, yeah, it was—" Kate hesitated, suddenly unable to recall anything that had happened at the office.

Ever since she'd gotten that text about Amelia's not jumping, everything had been fuzzy and hard to keep track of. It didn't help that she'd stayed up half the night reading Amelia's texts. She'd started with the ones between Amelia and Sylvia, because they'd seemed least likely to be too upsetting. She'd marveled at the intricate minutiae in their conversations. A rogue pimple, someone's poor choice of shoes, an accidental hallway brush against a particular boy, the details of the strange dream one of them had had the night before—all of them topics worthy of dissection in the seemingly nonstop stream of messages that passed between the two girls. There were so many texts that it was hard to believe the girls were ever physically in the same room. But they had been, almost until the very end.

Make a run for it, I'll cover you, was the last text Sylvia had sent Amelia when she'd been in Mr. Woodhouse's office.

Sylvia had admitted to Molina that she'd helped Amelia sneak out of the headmaster's office minutes before she died. But when Sylvia had ducked into the bathroom afterward, Amelia had disappeared. Like everyone else, Sylvia had had no idea what could have driven Amelia to the roof, or off it.

"Are you okay, Kate?" Kelsey asked. She'd stopped bouncing and was staring at her, concerned.

"Yes, I'm sorry. I'm just distracted." Kate shook her head hard. "I was making coffee. Do you want to come in and have some?"

The invitation was an impulse, an unfamiliar one. As helpful as Kelsey had been recently, the two women had never sat down alone over coffee. But Kate wanted to now. She wanted to sit with Kelsey and pretend the two of them were close friends.

"Oh sure," Kelsey said, looking taken aback. She checked her watch. "But I should probably make it quick. Gabriel's with the boys, and he'll need to leave for work in a few minutes."

Kate went to get the coffee as Kelsey sat down at the kitchen table. When she came back, she placed a mug down in front of each of them, the whole time telling herself that this was the way this kind of thing was done. An impromptu invitation, a casual conversation. This was how spouseless, childless people survived being completely alone. Maybe she was supposed to offer muffins or cookies or something, too. She had neither. Kate could feel Kelsey staring at her.

"I'm sorry, I know I'm acting strangely—"

"No, no, not at all," Kelsey said, quickly and unconvincingly. "I'm the one who knocked on your door at seven a.m."

Kate smiled down into her coffee cup and tried not to cry. Kelsey was so sweet and generous. She was the kind of person who was meant to be a mother, not someone like Kate, who'd been too distracted by her own ambition. If Kate had been less busy, if she'd paid closer attention, maybe she'd have been able to prevent whatever had happened to Amelia.

"I got an anonymous text yesterday saying that Amelia didn't jump. It has me, I don't know, rattled."

"Oh my God!" Kelsey gasped, cupping a hand over her mouth. "That's awful. Who would do something like that?"

"I don't know." Kate shook her head. "But I think whoever it is might actually be telling the truth."

"Really? I thought the police—" Kelsey stopped herself. "Oh, I guess I don't know any of the details. But I didn't realize there was ever any question."

"There wasn't." Kate took a sip of coffee. "At least, not according to the police. But I never had that much confidence in the detective who did the investigating. He seemed in such a hurry to get on to a more exciting case or something." Kate hated the way she sounded, defensive, accusatory, desperate. "Deep down, I also never believed that Amelia would kill herself. And now, with this text. Last night,

I found some suspicious notes in her room, too." Kate shrugged. "All of it together—it seems like maybe there was something going on in Amelia's life that I didn't know about. That I probably should have. Something not good."

"Oh," Kelsey said. She looked down at the tabletop, shifting uncomfortably on the bench. "Listen, I didn't tell you this before because there didn't seem to be any point. But now, I don't know."

Kate's stomach clenched. "What?"

Kelsey took a deep breath, then wrapped her hands tight around her mug.

"I saw Amelia with a boy a week or so before she died. Here, going into the house."

"Really?" Kate's heart picked up speed. "A boy, here?"

Going into the house to fool around, surely. It didn't have to be that, but how blind was Kate going to be? How long was she going to let herself believe that having good grades and being a star athlete equaled *not* having sex? Amelia had asked Kate outright just weeks before she'd died about when she had first started liking boys. Kate had taken Amelia's "academic research" excuse at face value. It wasn't so much that she'd *actually* believed it at the time; the question had set off alarm bells. Maybe she'd allowed herself to believe it because it was easier that way.

"He could have been just a friend. I don't know," Kelsey said, but it was obvious she didn't really think that. She paused, looked down, took another deep breath. "I only saw them on the steps, on their way inside and again when they were leaving."

"Amelia hanging out after school with a boy in our empty house doesn't exactly sound like friends to me," Kate said. "It's embarrassing how naive I've been. But Amelia was such a good kid. I got lulled into a false sense of—"

"It wasn't after school, Kate."

"What? What do you mean?"

"It was in the middle of a school day," Kelsey said quietly. "I'm sorry. I don't mean to belabor the point. Maybe it's not even important, but it feels like it could be."

"The middle of the day?" Kate asked, sounding angrier than she'd intended.

Amelia skipping school? She wouldn't have believed that any more than she believed Amelia had cheated, if Kelsey hadn't seen it with her own eyes.

"I'm sorry I didn't say something about it before . . . I just . . ." Kelsey's voice was wobbly. She looked sick with worry. "I didn't want to tell you anything upsetting if it didn't matter. But now that you're saying that you think maybe Amelia didn't kill herself. And there was something about that boy. I don't know, he made me uncomfortable."

"He made you *uncomfortable*?"

"Not him so much as the way Amelia seemed with him. She was nervous or sad or something. I only saw them together for a few seconds, so it was hard to tell. But her body language was off."

"You saw Amelia cutting school and going into our empty house with a boy that made her, and you, uncomfortable, and you didn't think you should tell me?"

"I figured I'd ask Amelia about it when she babysat the next time. Encourage her to tell you. But then there was no next time. I was afraid if I said something to you directly that you might feel like I was judging your parenting. I'm so sorry, Kate." Kelsey's voice cracked, then her eyes got wide. "Oh my God, what if that boy had something to do with what happened to Amelia?"

When Kate got off the F train at Bryant Park, it was misting and dark, as if the sun had never fully risen. As she crossed the street and headed west on Forty-second Street, the rain picked up from a mist to a drizzle. Kate heard her phone alert with a new message as she stepped up onto the far sidewalk. She paused out of the rain to read it, bracing herself for another message about Amelia.

I know your little secret. Soon everybody else will, too.

Kate's hands were still shaking when she got into work and found her way to the IT Department. She'd never actually been there before. When she had a problem with her computer, the IT Department came to her. As it turned out, all of Slone, Thayer's very many critical IT functions were tucked into an unimpressive cubby, down on the second floor near the copy center.

Kate knocked on the door open halfway, but no one answered. She waited another minute before knocking a second time, then pushed it the rest of the way open. Sure enough, there was Duncan, Bose headphones on, facing the window as he played air drums with wild abandon. Kate watched him for a second, but he didn't notice her. She had no choice but to step up and tap on his shoulder.

"What the fuck!" he shouted, jumping up so fast that he banged his thighs on his desk. "Ouch!"

"Oh, I'm so sorry," Kate breathed. "I didn't mean to scare you."

"Dude, that's okay," Duncan said, his usual stoner tone, high and wired. "Just don't do that again, like, seriously. It'll permanently mess with my chi. We don't get a whole lot of visitors down here. You can't, like, sneak up on us, ever."

He closed his eyes and took a few deep breaths in through his nose. Finally, he opened his eyes and exhaled deeply. And just like that he was back to the relaxed surfer dude Kate had always known him to be.

She held out her phone. "I got another text like the one Beatrice asked you to trace for me before. You really can't tell me who's sending them?"

Duncan took the phone and looked down at the message.

"That's seriously messed up," he said after he'd read it.

"Yeah, thanks," Kate said. "I can see that. I was hoping you could help me with the who's-it-from part."

"Oh yeah, right." He clicked a couple of buttons on the phone and frowned. "They used the phone company site again to route the message."

"So that's it? Do you think the police could do something more?"

He shrugged. "In general, I try to steer clear of the po-po. I can't say what they've got up their sleeve, like, policewise. But the phone company would have a record of who logged on from where to send this message, so maybe the police could subpoena it. I guess they'd need probable cause or whatever. I can say that technologywise, with just this phone, the police aren't going to be able to do anything different than me." He handed it back to Kate. "Sorry."

"Thanks anyway," she said. "Do you think you could maybe help with some other things, like getting everything off my daughter's laptop, and the texts printed off her phone?"

"Definitely," Duncan said more quietly. His mouth turned down sadly as Kate dumped Amelia's phone and computer and assorted wires and chargers onto his desk. "But you sure you want *everything*, like her Facebook page and Twitter and all that? Some of it might be easier to look at online."

Facebook. Kate had planned never to look at Amelia's Facebook page. Her daughter would still be so alive on there. Amelia's friends, she already knew, had been using the page as a makeshift memorial, going on there to leave I-miss-you messages for her. The thought of seeing them was completely unbearable.

"I don't think Amelia had a Twitter account. She never mentioned it."

"You sure?" Duncan asked. "Most kids in high school are on Twitter at least sometimes, and they're texting all the time. Then there's Facebook. E-mail's like the new snail mail. Don't know if she'd bother to mention Twitter. It's all second nature to them. Like, of course they have it."

Kate was staring at him. It was too much. There were so very many places where terrible things about her daughter's life could be tucked. Kate thought again about that text she'd seen to some boy named Ben. Lucky me, Amelia had written sarcastically about having Kate for a mom. Reading that had been awful, and it could get much, much worse.

"What do you say we slice it this way?" Duncan piped up, rescuing Kate from her choked silence. "I'll print out all the Word docs and anything else on her hard drive, and I'll get you her browser history. On the other accounts like Facebook, I'll set you up with the passwords. That way you can, you know, take a quick peek," Duncan said, resting one hand on Amelia's computer. "Because you don't want to like get into the deets of your kid's Facebook page. I mean, I'm twenty-four, and I'm a pretty scrubbed-up guy and whatevs, but my 'rents would stroke out if they saw my whole page. You've gotta filter it for ma and pa. I mean, who wants to see their kid doing body shots, like, ever?"

"Body shots?"

"Come on, dude, you're not that old." Duncan rolled his eyes. "Facebook just wasn't around back when you were letting the good times roll."

"How long will this all take?"

Duncan looked at the clock. "Couple hours, max. I'll shoot you a text when I have everything."

Kate was on her way up to her office when her cell phone rang. It came up as a blocked number. She paused in a quiet stretch of hallway off the elevator bank, feeling queasy as she answered.

"Hello?"

"This is Lieutenant Lewis Thompson with the Seventy-eighth Precinct." The voice had the same thick Brooklyn twang as Molina's but was extremely careful and polite. "Is this Ms. Kate Baron?"

"Yes?"

"I've been assigned your daughter's case and—"

"What happened to Detective Molina?" Kate asked, then immediately wished she hadn't. It wasn't as though she wanted Molina back. She would take this Lieutenant Thompson person, whoever he was. She would take anybody over Molina.

"He's not with the department anymore."

"He got fired?" It was one thing to suspect Molina was incompetent, but to be *that* right would have been almost frightening.

"Voluntary departure. Took a job in private security. His last day was yesterday."

"Oh, I see," Kate said, even though she did not see. She did not see at all. He'd called her only the day before.

"But we got the results of the handwriting analysis—"

"Wait, you did one?"

"This case got kicked back to me based on the results."

"How could they test the handwriting if they didn't even have a sample from Amelia?"

Kate was already bracing to be told that the *sorry* written on that wall was definitively her daughter's. And she was done accepting at face value that the police were doing their job with the proper thoroughness.

"They did have a sample from your daughter, or at least from somebody. I've got it right here in my hand. It's a note directed to a Jeremy, thanking him for providing a reference. It's signed 'Amelia.' That ring any bells?"

Jeremy, of course. Amelia had sent him a thank-you note for writing her a recommendation to Princeton's summer journalism program. Jeremy was an alumnus, and when he'd heard that Amelia was applying, he'd generously offered to support her application to the prestigious program for high-school students without Kate's even having to ask. Apparently, Jeremy had done more than just call the police commissioner, he'd pushed the handwriting analysis through.

"If you think there's a chance this note isn't your daughter's," the lieutenant went on, "let's run the test again with a sample you provide. I want to be one hundred percent sure we get it right this time."

"So the handwriting matches?" Kate asked, still preparing for the bad news. "Amelia wrote 'sorry' on that wall?"

"Can you answer my question first, ma'am?" Lieutenant Thompson asked, not impatiently, exactly, but firm. "Is that note from your daughter?"

"Yes, it's from Amelia."

"Then it looks like whoever wrote on that wall, it wasn't your daughter."

"The handwriting's not Amelia's?"

"Not even close."

Kate raced back to her office to grab her things and let Beatrice know that she'd be out for the rest of the day. She'd told Lieutenant Thompson that she'd meet him out in Park Slope, at Dizzy's, in an hour. And she had a stop to make before she headed out.

She darted down the internal stairs two flights, then around the corner to Jeremy's huge office. When she jerked to a stop at his open door, he had his chair swiveled in the opposite direction, probably to hide the fact that he was reading the sports section of the *New York Post*.

Jeremy startled when Kate knocked.

"I just wanted to say thank you," she said as he turned around. "For speaking to the police commissioner and for arranging the handwriting analysis. It's amazing that you kept that note."

"It was a nice note," he said. "Was the handwriting a match?"

Kate shook her head. "No."

"Really?" Jeremy looked stunned. "Wow."

"I know. I didn't think Amelia wrote it, but to get confirmation . . . It's still shocking. Anyway, they've assigned somebody new to the case, too. I'm on my way out to meet him."

"I'm glad to hear they're taking the whole thing seriously," Jeremy said. "Maybe now you can get some real answers."

"I hope so," Kate said, staring at him. She thought for a second about saying something more, but she already knew that she wouldn't. "Anyway, thanks for your help."

"Absolutely. If there's anything else I can do, please let me know," Jeremy said. "Will you keep me posted, too? Let me know what you find out?"

"Definitely," Kate said as she turned for the door.

"Oh, and one last thing," Jeremy called after her. "I know this isn't on your radar right now—and it shouldn't be—but I wanted to let you know that I've pulled Daniel off Associated. You'll be the only partner on the case when you're back. No rush at all. I mean it. Between the senior associates and me, we'll be fine whenever you come back. But it was something I needed to move forward with. Daniel made a lucky call on the subpoena, and he wrote a good brief for the Second Circuit. It'll go down as a win in his column, but you've logged six years on that case. It's yours, and it should stay yours. I may work you all to death, but I believe in loyalty. It should count for something. That's a message the other junior partners in the firm need to hear. When you come back I'm going to pull out, too."

Jeremy was the senior partner on virtually every major litigation matter the firm had. Directly or indirectly, he'd brought in most of those clients, so they remained his, even if he didn't do any of the work. It was a ceremonial thing as well as a billable thing.

"What do you mean?"

"I mean, it's your case—the billables, the profit, the client." Jeremy had an eager look on his face, like he was bestowing a precious gift on Kate, one that he had labored over with his own hands. "It'll be like you brought them in yourself. Victor's fully on board, too. In fact, he seemed delighted to see me go."

Kate had heard rumors of Jeremy "giving cases" to partners over the years, cases that then went on to define the future of their careers. Having an enormous client like Associated Mutual Bank considered *hers* would do just that for Kate. It was the kind of opportunity she would have relished before Amelia died. Now it made her feel vaguely sick. But she didn't want to disappoint Jeremy. He was trying to help her in the only way he knew how: by pushing her career ahead.

"Thank you," Kate said, because she was supposed to, and because she meant it. "For everything you've done."

Dizzy's was mostly empty when Kate stepped inside. She looked over the worn red booths and hodgepodge of eclectic pictures on the walls until she finally spotted a slight man in his mid-sixties with curly gray hair seated at the far back. He had on a suit jacket and tie, and he was talking to a cute waitress with a nose ring and a red bandana tied around her head. Kate watched as he said something else and the waitress tipped her head back and laughed hard. Finally, Kate moved toward his table. He was the only person seated alone. Though he hardly looked the part, Kate figured he must be Lieutenant Lewis Thompson.

"Lieutenant Thompson?" Kate asked tentatively, once she'd made her way over to him.

"You can call me Lew, as in Lewis." He held out his hand. Up close he was even smaller, with pale blue eyes behind thin, wire-rimmed glasses. "Have a seat."

"I'm sorry that I'm late," Kate said, trying not to feel defeated by the way he looked. But it was hard to imagine him chasing after bad guys, much less catching one of them.

The lieutenant looked past Kate and motioned for the waitress. "You know what you want to eat? Sorry, I couldn't wait."

He motioned to his food: fruit, a vegetable omelet, whole-wheat toast. Even his meal was not coplike. Then again, it wasn't as if Molina, the seemingly quintessential cop, had gotten her anywhere.

"What can I get you, hon?" the waitress asked Lew, who in turn pointed to Kate.

"Just coffee is fine," she said, even though she was actually hungry.

"You sure?" Lew asked, once the waitress had disappeared. "Nothing is more important than eating right."

"What department did you say you were from?" Kate asked, afraid that he might say something like traffic enforcement. "I think you said it on the phone, but I missed it."

"Seventy-eighth Precinct, Homicide," he said, taking another careful bite.

"Homicide?"

"Homicide, as in a dead body," he said, reading Kate's mind. "I don't have any new evidence on your daughter's case yet, apart from the handwriting analysis. I'm here to listen, not to talk. So, why don't you tell me why you think your daughter didn't kill herself."

Over two cups of coffee, Kate talked. She talked about the kind of student and daughter Amelia had been. She talked about not believing Amelia would cheat. Not believing that she'd killed herself. All the while, Kate kept telling herself that it wasn't just her denial talking, that it wasn't just that she couldn't live with the thought that her child had taken her own life. But a tiny part of her was afraid that her denial was the reason she was sitting there, across from this small lieutenant. But she pressed on, describing the mystery boy whom Kelsey had seen and all those little "I hate you" notes. And she told Lieutenant Thompson about the texts she'd gotten, three of them now.

"So what's the secret this person thinks you have?"

"I have no idea," Kate said, over that little voice inside her screaming *Maybe I do! Maybe I do!* "Honestly, I don't."

"And you have no idea who might be sending the texts."

Kate shook her head. "I had the IT Department at my firm check it. The texts came from the same phone company site, but that's all they could tell me. They're also going to pull all the text messages and e-mails off Amelia's phone and laptop. I'm not sure Molina went through all of that the first time." Kate resisted the urge to say that Molina had outright lied, but there didn't seem any harm in hinting at as much. "He said he did, but he didn't have the password to her phone, so I don't know how he could have. He missed those little notes in Amelia's room, too."

"Hmm. Okay, we'll get our guys on the texts. They're not the fastest, but they might be able to get some more specifics. We can subpoena the phone company, too. But they're not exactly lightning quick either," Lew said. "I did go back through your daughter's file, though."

"And?"

"It's maybe a little thin."

"Maybe?"

"Listen, a decent cop doing a decent job can look a lot of different ways. There's a range." He measured the distance with his hands. "But in a case like this, you would expect more witness interviews, more detailed notes. There were some of each, but probably not enough, and then there's the autopsy report."

Kate had never seen the report. She hadn't asked, and it hadn't been offered.

"What about it?"

"First off, it wasn't in the investigation file," he said. "I went into Manhattan to track down a copy, and all they had at the main OCME office were the photographs. I'm no expert at analyzing autopsy photos, but there's at least one thing that doesn't seem to go with someone falling on purpose."

This was it, what Kate had wanted: real proof that Amelia hadn't killed herself. And yet, suddenly, she felt panicked.

"What do you mean?"

"There were scratches on Amelia's forearms, long ones. Like maybe they were put there with someone's fingernails." He paused when Kate winced. "Are you sure you want to hear this? This level of detail probably isn't necessary."

"I want to know," she said, trying to get herself to breathe. "I have to. Keep going."

"The body positioning, too. It doesn't rule out suicide, the way, say, landing far out from the building might. But it raises questions. Questions someone should have gotten answers to."

"Can we call Molina and ask?"

"I already did." Lew rearranged his knife and fork so that they lined up straight on either side of his plate. "At the moment, he's apparently unreachable, out on a fishing boat somewhere in the Florida Keys. He's not due back for another week."

"Did you say he's going to be a *security* guard?" Kate asked, because that sounded like someone being demoted, not someone who'd have the money to take a big fishing trip.

"Not like an eight-bucks-an-hour security guard at Best Buy or something. He's working at Carmon Industries, corporate security. They hire cops, FBI, that kind of thing. From what I hear, it's a plum deal, if you like that sort of thing."

"Doesn't this all seem awfully convenient? The missing autopsy report, Molina's leaving the police force right as I start asking questions."

"The timing's off, no question."

"Off?" Kate asked. Now she was getting irritated. Was he seriously going to be as oblivious as Molina? "That's it? That's all you're going to say, that it's off?"

Lew took one last sip of coffee and nodded. "For now."

"So we're just going to sit here and wait for Molina to get back from vacation?" It came out even louder and angrier than Kate had intended.

She could feel the waitress and a busboy turn in her direction. Kate didn't care. She'd had enough. She'd been pushed off, quieted down, and disregarded once. She'd been made to accept something she did not believe. She wasn't going to sit there and let it happen again.

"No," Lew said calmly. He stood and carefully flattened several dollars, placing them under the salt and pepper shakers. "We're going to start again at ground zero, retrace Molina's steps. Cut a new trail where we have to. Your daughter is dead, and we've got the word 'sorry' written on a wall near where it happened by somebody other than her. We've got some questionable medical findings and an anonymous message that says she didn't kill herself. That's more than enough for me to reopen the investigation."

"Oh," Kate said, feeling relieved and a little spooked that there had been some threshold they'd hurdled over without her even realizing there'd been one to cross. "Okay, good."

"So, we've got questions. Who do you think is going to have the answers?"

"I don't know," Kate said, her voice cracking. "I honestly don't."

"Sure you do," Lew said, waving her out the door with him. "You know a lot more than you think."

It was Kate's idea to go talk to Sylvia first. Molina had interviewed her last time. But it had always seemed to Kate that Sylvia should know something more. And Lew had agreed she was as good a place to start as any.

Sylvia's mom, Julia, swung open the door wearing narrow-legged pants that billowed out at the hips, a slim tank top, and red ballet flats. It was the kind of blatantly unflattering outfit Kate could never have pulled off. But on Julia it looked positively lovely. It helped that she was effortlessly beautiful, with a lean, toned figure and an exotic bone structure. With her hair back in a messy ponytail, she looked much younger than she could possibly be, given her children's ages. Her older son was a sophomore at Stanford.

"Oh hi," Julia said, her slight Dutch accent more prominent than usual. She looked surprised and confused, her eyes moving from Kate to Lew and back again. Before Kate could explain why they were there, a little terrier came zooming around the edge of the door barking wildly. "Beeper, no!" Julia scolded the little dog, using a foot to slide him gently across the polished wood floor. "Sorry, let me just put the dog out back."

A few seconds later she returned from placing the dog outside on the deck off the kitchen.

"Come in, come in," Julia said, waving them inside. "What a nice surprise."

She was trying to sound pleased to see Kate, but it was obvious that she wasn't. Kate didn't blame her. Julia was the mother of a girl whose best friend had just committed suicide. She wanted to forget, not spend time with that dead child's mother.

"This is Lieutenant Thompson," Kate said. "He's been helping me look into what happened to Amelia."

Julia held out her hand, which Lew shook firmly. He seemed somewhat larger now, though not much.

"It's nice to meet you, Lieutenant," Julia said, but she looked tense.

"Does the police being involved again mean there's been some new development?"

"We're just following up on initial interviews," Lew said nonchalantly. "To confirm nothing was missed."

"I think that's a good idea. Personally, I've never believed it was a suicide," Julia said.

"Why not?" Lew asked.

"Amelia was like a surrogate daughter," Julia said firmly. "She was always so grounded, in a way that I could only hope my own kids would be." It wasn't easy hearing Julia talk about Amelia this way, like she had her own claim to her. The worst part was that she did, given how much time Amelia had spent at their house, and with Julia a stay-at-home mom. "Call it a mother's instinct. That's not very scientific, I suppose, but that doesn't make it any less accurate."

"Thank you for saying that," Kate said, feeling a mix of relief and jealousy. "And for caring so much about Amelia. She thought about this as a second home."

Julia stared back at Kate, her eyes getting shiny. She looked for a moment as if she might say something else, but then she seemed to think the better of it.

"We have a couple of questions for your daughter," Lew said from behind them. "It won't take long."

"Oh, I see," Julia said, sounding surprised. Though it seemed unlikely that she could have thought they were there just to talk to her. "Um, okay. Come this way."

She turned and led them tentatively deeper into the brownstone, which was a happy mix of top-grade appliances and adolescent-related detritus. But the clutter was pleasant somehow, comforting.

"Have a seat," Julia said, when they were out in the living room, a bright space with a high ceiling and puffy white couches. An arrangement of orange tulips was on the heavy wooden coffee table. "I'll just— I'll go get Sylvia from upstairs," Julia said, looking warily toward the steps. "I do have to warn you, she hasn't been herself since what happened to Amelia. I think she feels responsible. Maybe that's part of why I don't believe it was a suicide. I don't want her to feel guilty anymore."

Lew and Kate sat in silence for what felt like a long time, waiting for Julia to come back down the stairs. Finally, they creaked under the sound of heavy footsteps, and a moment later Julia emerged, smiling stiffly. Behind her was Sylvia, pale and gaunt in skinny jeans and a shapeless black T-shirt, so big that it easily could have been a dress. Her dark hair was in a ponytail like her mother's, but much messier. Sylvia had always cared so much about the way she looked. It was part of what defined her. Now she looked just awful. It was heartbreaking.

"Come on, honey," Julia said, her voice warbled and high. "Have a seat on the couch here. Kate and the police officer need to ask you some questions."

Julia sat down herself and patted the couch next to her, then looked over at her daughter.

Sylvia didn't move.

"Mom, stop talking to me like I'm some kind of head case."

Julia smiled at Kate, partly embarrassed and partly, it seemed, sad for everyone involved.

"Sylvia, we just have a few questions about Amelia, then we can get right out of your hair," Lew said calmly. "But you're going to have to bear with us here because these are probably questions you've answered before.

"Okay, I guess, whatever." Sylvia rolled her eyes. "I mean, I don't have a choice, right?"

"No, I guess you don't," Lew said. "You and Amelia were best friends?"

"Yeah. I mean, supposedly, since, like, kindergarten."

"Was Amelia depressed or upset about anything?" Lew asked.

"We're teenagers," Sylvia said. "We're *all* depressed."

Kate smiled. It was the kind of thing Amelia would have said.

"But nothing out of the ordinary?" Lew pressed on, ignoring her sarcasm.

"She was kind of wanting to know who her dad was lately, I guess," Sylvia said. "She'd gotten some weird texts about it. Like a Who's-your-daddy? kind of thing. I don't know exactly because she wouldn't show them to me. And I think the number was blocked. But she wasn't upset, like, kill-yourself upset about it." Sylvia's eyes flicked in Kate's direction, then at the ground. "But she said she didn't believe anymore what you'd told her about her dad. She talked about finding out the truth on her own if she had to."

Texts about her dad? Now it made sense, Amelia's sudden questions. But why hadn't she told Kate? And who had sent them?

"Do you know if she made any progress finding him?" Lew asked.

Sylvia shook her head. "She said that she knew where her mom's old journals were, that she was going to look through them."

"Did she?" Kate braced herself.

"I don't know," Sylvia said. "She never talked about it again. I was going to ask her, but then, you know, everything happened."

"What about any intimate relationships?" Lew asked. "Like a boy perhaps?"

"There *definitely* wasn't any boy," Sylvia said.

"My neighbor saw Amelia going into our house in the middle of the day with some boy a few days before she died," Kate said. "You didn't know anything about that?"

"Maybe it was that Ben kid," Sylvia said. She seemed nervous suddenly. "Their whole thing was really weird. Amelia lied to me about it, too, so who knows?"

"Yeah, I saw some text from a Ben," Kate said, her stomach balling up as she remembered it again: lucky you. "Does he go to school with you?"

"No, he applied to that same Dorks-R-Us summer thing at Princeton," Sylvia said. She sounded disgusted, or maybe jealous. It was hard to tell with her. "They were always texting back and forth, and Amelia was always, like, 'He's gay and he lives up in Albany; he's lonely.' Except the whole thing seemed way creepy to me."

Lew was jotting down notes. "Amelia wrote to him?"

"She said he got her e-mail from somebody at Princeton." She shrugged. "Like I said, the whole thing was weird. He was even supposed to be coming here on the day she died. You know that, right? Amelia was always sketchy with the details about him. She was embarrassed, I think, which she totally should have been."

"So you don't have any idea where we could find Ben, a phone number, last name, e-mail?" Lew asked. "Maybe a school name?"

Sylvia shook her head. "But it's got to be on her phone; she was, like, constantly texting with him."

"It is," Kate said. "I saw it."

"Okay, good. Any disagreements, problems with anybody else?" Lew asked. "Maybe some girls she had a problem with?"

"Nope."

"Sylvia, I found all these little notes in her room," Kate said, still feeling like Sylvia was holding out. "They all said 'I hate you.' It looked like they were written by different people. Do you know what that could be about?"

Sylvia made a face and shook her head. "Nobody writes, like, actual notes anymore. You sure they weren't just Amelia's? She was always working on one crazy project or another."

"That's true." Kate smiled, thinking of the time when Amelia was seven and she'd cut apart one of her two copies of *The Giving Tree* to make a mobile out of the phrases.

But Sylvia had seemed weirdly unsurprised by the "I hate you" notes. Kate had been shocked. She would have thought that Sylvia would have been, too. Or at least would have been a lot more curious. Unless, of course, she already knew all about the notes.

"What about this school newsletter?" Lew asked.

"Yeah, *gRaCeFully*, that's what it's called," Kate said. "Do you know who writes it, Sylvia?"

Sylvia stared down at her hands, shaking her head.

"What are they talking about?" Julia leaned into Sylvia, trying to make eye contact with her daughter. "Why do you look bothered suddenly?"

"I'm not *bothered*, Mom."

"It's this gossip blog or newsletter or something," Kate said. "It was— The things in it were pretty harsh."

"Harsh?" Julia asked. "Why have I never heard about this before?"

"Because it's stupid," Sylvia said. "And it's only been around, like, a couple years."

Kate wished now that they hadn't brought it up. It probably wasn't that important, and she didn't want Julia searching out *gRaCeFULLY* and seeing what had been written there about Sylvia. She wouldn't wish that on anybody.

"Who puts this *gRaCeFULLY* thing out?" Lew asked.

Sylvia shrugged. "Somebody stupid who has nothing better to do."

"Was Amelia upset about things written about her there?" Lew asked. "Some of it was pretty personal."

"Wait a second," Julia said. "I'm sorry to interrupt, but a mean-spirited gossip blob about students is being posted up somewhere at the school?"

"It's a *blog*, Mom. Not a *blob*. It's on a *computer*," Sylvia huffed. "And I don't see why we're talking about this. Amelia offed herself. End of conversation."

"Sylvia!" Julia scolded. "I know this isn't easy for you, but think about Kate's feelings, for goodness' sake! She's just trying to make sure they understand exactly what happened to Amelia."

"She jumped off a roof." Sylvia drew out the words viciously. "What else is there to know?"

"Why," Kate said, trying not to let Sylvia upset her. Sylvia was upset, too—Kate understood that. "I want to know *why*. I want to know what happened in Amelia's life to put her in that place. Because I don't believe it. I don't think she would have done it."

"What about this paper the school says she cheated on?" Lew asked. "They say that's why she jumped. She was upset about getting caught. Did Amelia talk to you about this paper, Sylvia?"

"Pff," Sylvia huffed. "Amelia was way too smart to ever have to cheat on anything. And if she *was* ever going to cheat on something, it *definitely* wouldn't haven been an *English* paper. She could have taught that class." Sylvia said. "She was upset about them saying she did it and whatever. But she knew she didn't. The truth would have come out."

"So if it wasn't boys or drugs and it wasn't getting caught cheating," Lew said, "then why do you think she would have done it?"

"Because she was stupid," Sylvia said angrily. She crossed her thin arms over her huge T-shirt so that it collapsed down over the tiny frame hidden inside. She turned back toward the steps. "And selfish, and I wish I'd never met her."

gRaCeFULLY

Because there are 176 definitions for the word *loser* on urbandictionary.com.
Don't Be a Statistic

Hey bitches!

Oh, you silly, silly boys. Word is, a bunch of underclassmen were conned into sending photos of their "junk" to various Maggie pledges who were pretending to be secret admirers. Said junk photos were then texted out to all girls in their homerooms. Word of advice, fellas: if you get a text from a girl who says she wants to see your stuff, IT'S A LIE! No girl ever wants to get a picture of your wiener.

Looks like our dear, unfortunately named Jessica DEALER is about to get booted for passing out pills to the bored and beautiful of Grace Hall. Three private schools in three months, Jessica? You know, your unfortunate last name does not have to be your destiny.

Word is that the filthy rich (poorly credentialed) stepfather of one—how shall I put it?—academically challenged senior is on a campaign to get her into the Ivy League. And when I say campaign, I mean, hell hath no fury like a board member with a big, fat checkbook and street connections. Word is, he's planning on wiretapping the admissions office or, alternatively, breaking some kneecaps.

The entire lacrosse team was thrown out of Kale's Tavern this past weekend, not because they were underage and wasted but because one of those idiots PISSED ON THE FLOOR! Yo idiots, if someone is stupid enough to serve you, the least you can do is have the courtesy to locate the commode.

Amelia

AMELIA

more weirdness

BEN

uh-oh, what happened?

AMELIA

she's so up and down and weird. sometimes I feel like she doesn't want to be friends with me

BEN

sorry but you girls are all crazy; did you finish up the Maggie to do's

AMELIA

yes

BEN

even . . .

AMELIA

yes

BEN

I thought

AMELIA

I know, I said I wasn't going to do it; but it's not like I had any choice

BEN

uh-huh, sure

AMELIA

don't judge. it's mean

BEN

whatever; does the kid know the thing was a scam?

AMELIA

tomorrow

BEN

oh, man

AMELIA

I know, I suck; c/u g2g

OCTOBER 5, 11:41 PM

SYLVIA

does my butt look better in my black James jeans or that vintage dress I got in the West Village?

AMELIA

trick question?

SYLVIA

haha

AMELIA

vintage

SYLVIA

I knew it! ty!!! Xoxo

OCTOBER 5, 11:47 PM

DYLAN

I was just thinking about you

AMELIA

me too

DYLAN

good thoughts?

AMELIA

definitely

DYLAN

   excellent; c/u 2morrow

AMELIA

   byee

OCTOBER 5, 11:52 PM

CARTER

   dude what was biology homework?

AMELIA

   127-47; plus lab

CARTER

   fuck; thx. You going to Chloe's party Friday?

AMELIA

   idk

CARTER

   come; it'll be cool

AMELIA

   maybe c/u

OCTOBER 6, 1:02 AM

BLOCKED NUMBER

   ur mom's lying to you. are you just going to let her do that?

facebook

OCTOBER 6

Amelia Baron
is ready to be amazed

Carter Rose	I'm @ 322 Garfield; come anytime
Sylvia Golde	yack, on both of you

Amelia

Sylvia and I were sitting at a random table in the Tea Lounge doing our homework. The tattooed baristas had some indie band blasting on the radio, and the place was packed—writers, college students, and moms talking to their friends while they ignored their noisy rug rats. The Tea Lounge was always packed and the mismatched, garage-sale furniture kind of beaten down, but it was still awesome. Whenever we could, Sylvia and I went there after school to do our homework. She would order an espresso she could barely choke down and me a chai latte, and we'd pretend we were in college.

"'What is done out of love always takes place beyond good and evil,'" Sylvia recited from the book she was reading.

"Oh yeah?" I asked, only half listening. "Dope."

I had my eyes on my laptop. I was finishing up the *To the Lighthouse* paper. At first, I'd been kind of annoyed by the topics Liv had given us. It wasn't like I was some crazy genius or whatever, but they were all way too easy. Like stupid easy. But she'd pulled me aside after class and said that I could write about anything I wanted to, and I'd finally come up with an idea that was totally interesting. I thought Liv would be impressed, too. I wanted her to be.

I liked Liv, and not just because she was young and pretty and wore funky jewelry and had this mysterious tattoo that you could see a little bit of when she wore her hair in a ponytail. Liv was also the most into-it teacher I'd ever had. And she was a writer, too, like me. She'd even shown me a couple of the short stories she'd published in some small literary mags, and they were pretty good. I mean, not like *New Yorker* good, but not half bad.

Liv was crazy supportive of my fiction writing, too. She kept trying to get me to do something with it, like submit some stories to a writing fellowship. But it was one thing to do that summer journalism program at Princeton. Articles about *things* weren't the same thing as stories I'd made up. Those I wasn't ready for the world to pick apart, not yet.

"Who would have thought that good old Nietzsche was such a romantic?" Sylvia asked. I could feel her staring at me, waiting for me to be interested. I wasn't. "You wouldn't know this, Amelia. But when you're in love, that's what it's like—*beyond good and evil.*" She was only half joking with all the Shakespearean high drama. Everything with boys was like that for Sylvia—all life and death and up and down and way too much sleeping potion. "I know I've *liked* other guys before"—Sylvia was dead serious now—"but with Ian, it's the real deal. I liked him at the beginning just because he was cute and had that sweet little accent and everything—and also because I thought maybe I could someday end up a duchess—but now it's like, I don't know, he's just such an amazing person. He's really opened my eyes."

She was looking at me like I was supposed to have all these questions about this love of hers. I didn't. It would have been easier to come up with something if Sylvia hadn't said pretty much the exact same thing about three different guys. And the really crazy thing was, she wasn't even lying. Sylvia believed what she was saying. But that was part of what made Sylvia so great, too. She had this ginormous, out-of-control heart that gobbled up everything in its path. It was nice to be near it, especially because sometimes I could barely feel my own heart beating beneath the weight of my hyperactive brain.

Also, who knows, maybe this time with Ian was finally the real deal. Unlikely, but not totally impossible.

"Oh crap," I said, remembering the time. "I'm late. I'm babysitting for Kelsey this afternoon."

I had only ten minutes to get out of the Tea Lounge and to the Maggie meeting at Zadie's house, which was way over on Eighth Street. And I couldn't be late. Zadie supposedly had some big announcement for the three of us about the last thing we had to do before we became full-fledged Magpies. Which, by the way, I still wasn't even sure I wanted. But I was sure I'd do whatever it took to stay friends with Dylan.

"You're not even listening to me, are you?" Sylvia asked, flipping absentmindedly through her *Introduction to Philosophy* textbook. Then she stopped and squinted at me suspiciously. "What *is* going on with you these days anyway? You're never around, and when you are you act like a freak. And all the spacey, bad-poetry Facebook status updates? 'Amelia Baron is ready to be amazed.' You know that's a pet peeve of mine—people trying to be all arty on Facebook. It's like you're in love with somebody or something."

My eyes snapped up from my homework. I couldn't help it.

"Holy shit, you *are*!" she shrieked, smacking her book down on the table so loud that the scraggly screenwriter behind us looked as if he were about to backhand her.

"Shut up," I hissed. "You're going to get us kicked out of here."

"OMG, who is he?" Sylvia was grinning, her eyes aglow. "Amelia Baron, you finally fall in love with a boy and you don't even *bother* to tell me? I'm your *best* friend. You have a moral obligation to tell me this stuff." But she seemed more excited than mad. "I demand you start at the beginning and tell me absolutely *everything*. Then maybe I'll forgive you. He's older, isn't he? OMG, he's not bald, is he?"

And this was why Sylvia was still my best friend. She seemed like she would have wanted nothing more than for me to be in love. She had her head up her own butt 90 percent of the time, but in that last 10 percent she was an awesome friend.

"There you are, hon!" came an accented voice behind us before I had to say anything.

Sylvia's face lit up as she turned to see Ian Greene weaving his way in our direction through the tattered sea of Tea Lounge chairs. He was wearing tight jeans and a fitted black T-shirt, his sandy-blond hair pushed up into a deconstructed fauxhawk. He was wearing some weird European sneakers, too, which looked like bowling shoes. The whole look was very I-don't-fucking-care English rock star, or total loser. It could go either way. On Ian, it cut a good way. I took in his obvious cuteness, waiting to feel my own twinge. Nothing. I could see that he was hot, anybody could. But I didn't *feel* it.

Ian and I had crossed paths at another coed party the weekend before. This one had been at one of the boys' houses and had been a whole lot crazier—I hadn't gotten home until close to two a.m. with, luckily, my mom sound asleep. There'd been a lot of much harder drugs, and people were practically having sex in the halls. Ian and I hadn't talked at that party either. I'd seen him with Zadie at one point, but as far as I could tell, he'd been trying to get away from her. We didn't talk about the party afterward either. Actually, we hadn't spoken about our respective club affiliations at all. Instead, it was a secret we'd silently agreed to keep between us, and from Sylvia. And so there it sat, this weird ball of tension. And I hated knowing something about Sylvia's boyfriend that she didn't know. It probably worked in her favor that I was there to keep an eye on him, especially with Zadie buzzing around, but it still felt like a betrayal. One that I was pretty sure Sylvia would never have forgiven me for.

Ian hooked an arm around Sylvia's neck as he kissed her. Even his casual gestures like that seemed edgy. When they separated, Sylvia beamed at him so hard it was like she might burst into flames.

"I've been looking all over for you," Ian said to Sylvia. He gave a manly nod to the grumpy screenwriter next to us, stole his free chair without asking, and sat on it backward. "I thought we were headed up to the park to take some snaps this afternoon."

Sylvia grinned at me. "He likes to take pictures of me," she said with put-on modesty. "How adorable is that?" She turned back to Ian. "I thought you had crew practice until four? I was going to text you in a few minutes. Amelia has to leave anyway."

"Are you certain?" Ian asked, his voice lifting respectfully. "I was only teasing Sylvia here. I don't want to bugger up your plans. She and I can arrange a meet-up later."

He was trying to stay on my good side. I hoped for Sylvia's sake that wasn't because he thought I already had something on him.

"No, Sylvia's right," I said, looking at my watch. I stood and gathered my things, then motioned for Ian to take my seat. "I have to be somewhere at four o'clock."

Sylvia tilted her head coquettishly to the side as Ian sat down close to her. One of her crossed legs was swinging back and forth. The whole rest of her body looked rubbery. Ian couldn't take his eyes off her either. Looking at them, I felt better about their whole thing. I'd never seen Ian look at Zadie or any other girl that way. Sylvia would be okay. Their affection was totally mutual.

"Okay, see you later, then," I said even though neither of them was listening.

I waited a second more, then turned to go. I was almost at the door when Sylvia finally called after me.

"Hey, BFF!" When I turned, she and Ian had their hands clasped together. "BTW, you are *so* not off the hook. I know you're keeping secrets. You're going to have to spill the four-one-one eventually."

When I left the Tea Lounge, I headed up Union toward Seventh Avenue. It had gotten kind of cold while we'd been in there, the sun covered now by a heavy layer of steel-colored clouds. The wind had picked up, too. It was the first week in October, and it finally really felt like fall. I zipped up my sweatshirt and pulled my hood over my head. But as I turned south onto Seventh Avenue, the wind was even stronger, cutting straight through, and I hunched up my shoulders and kept my face down, hoping the gummed-up Seventh Avenue seas would magically part.

No dice. After school in Park Slope, the sidewalks were always jammed with tons of schoolkids and moms and all these other random, writer/artist types—not quite cool, not quite homeless—who were always bumming around the hood while all the real grown-ups were at work.

I walked on past the Ace Supermarket, where the Grace Hall kids shoplifted candy bars, and La Bagel Delight, which served its bagels hot out of the oven. I walked past PS 321, that clown car of a school. Looking at its jammed playground, I could never figure out how that little building could ever fit all those kids.

When I walked past Pino's, there was a crowd of Grace Hall middle-school kids still hanging out inside, and a couple of blocks up, there were some more sitting on a bench in front of the Cocoa Bar, which was too nice, and quiet, a place inside for the after-school kids. Across the street from the Cocoa Bar was John Jay High School, but by that hour the cops had already herded most of those students toward home.

For the rest of the dozen or so blocks, I kept my face down, out of the wind. That way I wouldn't have to worry about running into someone like our neighbor Kelsey or Sylvia's mom, Julia. I liked them both. They were always nice to me. But they'd have questions I didn't want to answer.

And I thought about Sylvia thinking I was in love. I wondered what it meant that it sort of felt like it was true.

By the time I was finally at Eighth Street, I was shivering like crazy. I made a quick left toward Zadie's house, hoping the wind might let up if I was walking in another direction. But it only got worse. I tucked my chin in and hugged my arms tight around myself.

I'd taken only a couple of steps when I got knocked off-balance, hard. Then someone's hand was on my arm. I looked down and saw it there, touching me. A man's big hand. *Holy shit, holy shit, holy shit, I'm getting mugged. Or raped.* I had to move, run, get away. Yell.

"Let go of me, you asshole!" I screamed as loud as I could, trying to twist my arm out of his hand. "Let go!"

"Amelia, it's me!" He knew my name. How the hell did he know my name? "Sorry, I'm so, so sorry. I wasn't thinking. I didn't mean to scare you."

I jerked my arm hard again, but his hand wasn't even on me any-more. When I fell back a couple of feet and looked up, there was Mr. Woodhouse, in running pants, sneakers, and a windbreaker. He had on a black knit hat that made him look like he should have been riding a skateboard. And he looked totally freaked-out.

"I am so sorry, Amelia." He raised his hands, eyes wide as he looked around the sidewalk. He took another step back, probably in case any-one was thinking of calling the cops. "I called your name a couple of times. I guess you didn't hear me with your hood up. I shouldn't have touched you like that. I truly apologize."

My heart was beating so hard I could feel it in my fingertips.

"Yeah, you shouldn't have," I said, trying to catch my breath. "I'm not real good with, like, random men grabbing me."

"God, I think I've been teaching too many years in upstate Con-necticut," he said. "You forget in a city, people are on guard."

"I probably wouldn't go around grabbing girls, pretty much any-where."

"Good point," he said with a smile. Then he looked up and down the block, confused. "You don't live around here, do you?"

Woodhouse was starting to creep me out a little. Had he, like, mem-orized my file or something? Not to mention that I wasn't psyched about his knowing even the general vicinity that I was heading in. I felt stressed enough that I'd taken the risk of programming Dylan's name into my phone. Tipping off the headmaster about the location of a Maggie meeting would probably have gotten my finger chopped off.

"I'm visiting my aunt. She lives over here."

Why hadn't I said friend? I didn't even have an aunt. Woodhouse probably knew that, too.

"That must be nice to have her so nearby," he said. I couldn't tell if it was a jab at my lying or not.

Then he was quiet for this long, awkward time. And he was nod-ding a little like he was working over in his head something he wanted to say. Finally, he squinted into the sinking sun.

"It'll be dark before long. Be careful on your way home. You never know when some fool is going to jump out and grab you." He smiled, then pointed his chin in the direction I was headed. "And tell Zadie and the rest of the girls that they'd better behave themselves."

Zadie snapped open the big steel door before I'd even rung her bell. I was just praying she hadn't seen me talking to Mr. Woodhouse.

"You're late," she barked, looking over my head to the sidewalk like she was checking to see if I'd been followed. Then she yanked my sweatshirt, dragging me inside. "Jesus, don't stand out there like a fucking asshole."

I'd thought Zadie had been letting me into her building, not her house. But it was one big open space inside with floor-to-ceiling windows on one side and exposed brick on the other. The floors looked like a sidewalk, except polished, and the little bit of furniture was superlow, cold, and modern. Except for a bookshelf full of photographs and a couple of expensive-looking vases, the place looked more like a furniture store than a house where people actually lived.

"Christ, come on." Zadie brushed past me toward a set of suspended steel stairs. "Everyone's already downstairs."

I followed her down the steps into a finished basement. At the front was a small room with empty bookshelves and a set of reading chairs. Next to that was a hallway covered with a modern, patterned carpet— blues and reds and greens spiraling together down the length of the long hallway.

Zadie had said everyone was already there, hadn't she? It was so weirdly quiet down there, though. Silent actually. What if there wasn't anyone else there? What if the whole meeting had been some kind of setup? Zadie *really* hated me. I might not have known why, but I knew that much for sure. And now there I was, trapped down in her quiet basement, locked away from the world where no one would ever hear me scream.

"What are you waiting for?" Zadie asked, flapping a hand at me.

"It's so quiet down here," I said. Like an idiot.

"Um, that's because it's soundproofed, you freak," Zadie said, like everyone had soundproofed rooms in their houses. She was glaring at me, too. "My stepdad's media room is down here, and he likes it quiet. Now, do you want all the specs on the house before you get your ass moving?"

"Why do you hate me so much?" I heard myself ask. Part of me was glad that I had. The other, smarter part of me wanted to throttle that first part. "Tell me what I'm doing and I'll try to stop, I swear."

Zadie's eyes thinned to blue gashes as she pushed her face into mine. I could smell cigarettes on her hair. I could see that white stripe up close, too. The hair was so completely colorless in that one perfectly geometric spot. Like she'd painted bleach on with a ruler.

"Can you stop being *you*?" Zadie asked quietly. Her face was so close now. Close enough that we could have kissed. "I mean, if you *can*, that would be awesome. Otherwise, I guess we'll have to stick with me hating you."

Dylan bounded into the room then from down the long hallway.

"There you are!" She smiled. My heart skipped, thinking she was talking to me. But she turned to Zadie instead. "Everybody's getting tired of waiting, Zad. A couple of the girls told their parents they'd be home."

"Okay," Zadie said without taking her eyes off me. "I'm coming. But make sure Crazy Eyes sits far away from me. The stench of her perfection makes me sick."

Zadie spun around and pounded off down the hall. I kept my eyes on the ground as I moved to follow her. I was afraid if I looked at Dylan, I might start to cry. I couldn't do this anymore. I couldn't deal with Zadie hating me that much just so I could hang out with Dylan.

"Sorry I was late," I muttered to Dylan as I walked past her. "I didn't mean to keep everyone waiting. I ran into someone outside and—"

"Shh," Dylan whispered, holding a finger to her lips. She leaned over like she was checking to see if Zadie had really gone.

"Why did she let me in the club if she hates me so much?" I asked. "I seriously don't get it."

"Let you in?" Dylan asked quietly. She looked confused. "Zadie picked you."

"Picked me? What are you talking about?"

"Dylan!" Zadie screamed from down the hall. "Get the fuck down here already!"

Dylan looked up at me and smiled—calmly, sweetly. "We could ignore her." Her grin turned mischievous. "But I think today, she might actually kill somebody."

"Let's not risk it." I shook my head and looked down the long hallway, which felt like it led to an electric chair. I wasn't buying this whole idea that Zadie had been the one to tap me, but now wasn't the time to press for details. "I'm pretty sure I'd be the first to go."

Dylan smiled playfully. "Probably."

And then she just stood there for a long time, smiling at me. With her smooth skin and arched cheekbones and thick, auburn curls, Dylan was the most perfect person I had ever seen. Flawless. Without flaw. It was hard to look at her, like she—like I—might shatter if I kept my eyes on her for too long.

Dylan smiled at me one last time then turned, headed the way Zadie had gone. I watched her go, feeling the wind getting sucked from me. But Dylan had taken only a couple of steps when she came back and linked her fingers tightly through mine.

I couldn't take my eyes off our interlocked hands as Dylan tugged me onward down the long, dark hallway. I could hear voices now, far at the other end. There was light spilling back, too, and I could sense the distant movement of assembled bodies. I wanted that hallway to go on forever. I wanted to keep Dylan's fingers knitted through mine. I wanted never to let her go.

Dylan froze on the edge of the rectangle of light reflected back on the hallway carpet from that far room. She dropped my hand. Her back was to me, her arms outstretched in a low cross when I bumped into her.

"So, the game," I heard Zadie saying.

"What are you waiting for?" I whispered in Dylan's ear. Zadie was going to lose it when she finally noticed I *still* wasn't in the room.

Dylan didn't answer. Instead, she slowly turned around. Her face was only inches from mine. I could feel her breath on my face. I could feel the beating of my own heart. I was sure Dylan could feel it, too. But the only sound was Zadie's voice, floating up and away.

"And this game isn't for uptight people or hung-up people or whatever," Zadie was saying. "So speak now or you lame asses should hit the road."

Then Dylan's mouth was on mine. Her lips were so small and soft and delicate when I finally started kissing her back. Nothing like the rough saltiness of that lifeguard in Chatham I'd kissed two summers ago.

As our mouths pressed together, Dylan held a hand against my face. And in that second, I was sure. I didn't just want to be her friend. I didn't just want to be like her. I wanted to be kissing her.

Then, all of a sudden, with a gasp and a tug, Dylan was gone. And there I stood, alone in the darkness, on the edge of that small rectangle of light.

It took me a second to catch my breath. My heart was still banging as I slid into the room where everyone was gathered. I kept my eyes down, hoping my cheeks weren't as red as they felt. I pressed the back of my hands to my lips, but stopped short of wiping. Instead, I pressed my fingers to my mouth, trying to hold the kiss inside.

I glanced up once to see if anyone was watching me. But the girls—some sprawled over leather, movie-theater-style chairs, others leaning against the walls or seated cross-legged on the floor—all had their eyes on Zadie, who was standing at the front of the room, behind her some sleek electronic equipment and a huge flat-screen TV.

I looked around for Dylan as I slid down against the nearest wall. I was terrified that she was gone, that she'd somehow slipped away and disappeared. But when I finally looked at Zadie, there was Dylan, sitting on a chair to her right. And she was staring back at me, not frowning exactly, but not smiling either. She looked more surprised and maybe confused.

But she kissed me, I reminded myself, recalling how absurd it had sounded when Sylvia hadn't been sure if that had been the case with Ian. *Didn't she? Why is she surprised?*

"We've got a blog—*Birds of a Feather*, it's called." Zadie looked proud of herself. "I came up with that. Anyway, everybody's got a page with pictures of themselves up. The object of the game is to get as many people as you can to, you know, 'like' your pictures." She went on and on about the pictures and how to get more people to "like" you. I wasn't really listening. All I could think about was that kiss, and how exactly right it had felt. There was a pain in my foot a second later. It took me a minute to realize that Zadie was stepping on my toes. "Are you fucking listening, bitch?"

"Um, uh, yeah," came out of my mouth in a blubbery stutter. I could feel the other girls looking at me, too. "I'm listening."

Zadie crossed her arms and smiled, scarily. She was closer now, looming over me.

"You in?"

Did I have to be *in* anymore? After what had just happened with Dylan, maybe I didn't. I hadn't really been listening, but what I had heard of this game—blog, pictures, strangers—I didn't like. I didn't want any part of it.

I tried to see past Zadie to Dylan, to see if she'd give me some kind of sign. But she was leaning over, talking to Bethany. It didn't seem like she'd noticed, much less cared, that Zadie was in my face. She'd completely disappeared, again.

If Dylan could get bored with me that quickly, how would I ever keep her attention once I wasn't even a Maggie anymore? Once we weren't seeing each other all the time at meetings and parties. Maybe Dylan would pretend she didn't know me anymore. Maybe she'd take it as some kind of insult that I hadn't stayed in the club for her. Maybe she'd be mad. If she'd just look at me, then I'd know. I thought of the kiss again, of the way that Dylan's soft hand had cradled my face.

"So?" Zadie nudged at my leg again with her foot. "What's it gonna be, Crazy Eyes? You ready to pack it in?"

I looked over at Dylan one last time. She wasn't talking to Bethany anymore. She was staring at the ground, not looking very happy. What if Dylan secretly wanted me to go? No, that couldn't be. It wouldn't make any sense. She'd just kissed me. Hadn't she?

"I want to stay," I kind of squeaked, then cleared my throat. I forced myself to hold Zadie's mean stare. "I'll play."

Zadie glared at me for a minute more, as if she were trying to make me change my mind.

"I'm staying," I repeated, but my voice was shaky.

"Zadie, enough!" Dylan finally shouted from across the room. She'd stood up. Her arms were crossed, her hips pushed to the side in a bring-it-on kind of way that I'd never seen before. "Seriously, just leave her the fuck alone!"

It was the first time I'd ever heard Dylan sound like that—mad, and kind of tough. And it was all because she was defending me. My heart felt like it might burst. The kiss had meant something after all. Now I was sure of it.

On our way out twenty minutes later—after a bunch of way-too-vague "details" about this supposed "game" had been laid out—we ran into Zadie's stepdad in the kitchen. He was tall and athletic-looking, with a thick head of dark hair. He had on a flashy European suit and a big tacky ring on one finger. He'd spent a lot of money on his clothes. You could see that. But he was still a supercheesy guy, not like the other dads in Park Slope, who were once in a while cool, but were mostly preppy and kind of dorky. They were never Eurotrash. Not even the ones who were actually from Europe.

There was a bottle of scotch open on the counter and a mostly empty bar glass next to it. Zadie's stepdad was clicking through his iPhone as he stood there. He had a BlackBerry in his other hand.

There was a woman in the corner, older, with graying blond hair swept up in a loose bun and faded black pants under an apron. She was fluffing the pillows on the couch. For a second I thought she must be Zadie's mother, until I noticed that she was fluffing like her life depended on it. We had a housecleaner—most people in Park Slope did—but she looked like a full-on maid, maybe even an indentured servant.

"Hey!" Zadie's stepdad called with a big, booming voice. "Look at what we have here! It's the Maggies flapping up from their secret lair."

He was smiling in a kind of drunk way that was sort of charming and also kind of gross.

"Ugh, shut up, Frank," Zadie said, but playfully, as she swanned up next to him and scooped his drink out of his hand. She took one sip, then another. "Mmm," she said. "You are always breaking out the good stuff when you think no one else is home."

Her stepdad snatched the glass back when she tried to take another sip. "Your mom is going to kill me if she smells whiskey on you when she gets home. Now come on, introduce me to your friends here."

I was at the front of the pack. I'd been trying to get out of the house as fast as possible, and now I was right there, on full display. Zadie rolled her eyes and leaned forward, her elbows on the granite countertop.

"Ugh," she said, taking his iPhone out of his hands and tapping through screens. "They're not my friends."

"Come on now," her stepdad said, wrapping an arm around her shoulder. He turned back to us. "I hope Zadie's been a good host to all of you. As far as I'm concerned, you're welcome in our home anytime. I like this whole club business. I was in something like that once. Best thing ever. Those guys are still my best friends. Clubs keep life, you know, better organized."

"I don't think a gang counts as a club, Frank." Zadie smiled back at us. She was showing off. "Frank here grew up on the wrong side of Brooklyn. He thinks the Skull and Bones society is about killing people."

Frank's eyes flashed once at her, then his face took back its easy smile. He shrugged.

"Maybe so," he said. "But a brotherhood is a brotherhood. And I was also a cop, remember? That's the club to end all damn clubs, trust me."

"Oh right, it seems so impossible that anyone let you carry a gun that I hardly ever remember." Zadie motioned to the door. "Anyway, they were just going."

"Good, so you can go get to work on those college essays," he said. "Because I finally made the bet with that asshole Teddy—you get into two Ivies, and that shit owes me five thousand dollars."

"And who gets to keep the money if I get in?"

"You can take the money and flush it down the toilet for all I care. I just want to be able to tell that stuck-up piece of shit to go fuck himself, excuse my French."

"Behold, ladies," Zadie said with a dramatic wave of her hand. "A dad who places bets on whether you're going to get into college. This is what you get when your mom marries a guy from the wrong side of Brooklyn."

"Yeah, that's right," her stepdad said, as he tossed some of the newly fluffed pillows to the floor so he could sit down on the couch, then rested his feet up on the pricey-looking coffee table. "You get a boat-load of free cash *and* a kick-ass good time."

Kate

Kate and Lew were sitting on her couch in front of the two now-open boxes, which a messenger had delivered shortly after they'd gotten back from Sylvia's. Each was packed with pages and pages of documents. Duncan had rubber-banded them together—each a couple of inches or more high—and labeled them: E-MAIL, TEXTS, WORD DOCS.

"There's so much," Kate whispered, as Lew pulled out the note Duncan had sent along with them.

"Sounds like there's more, too, he's got some passwords listed here—Facebook, Twitter," Lew said. "Looks like there was a blog she was posting to also. We'll have to take a look at that. Hard to say yet what the primary mode of communication is for these kids. Gchat, Facebook, texting—it's different in every school, you know."

At sixty-odd years old, Lew sounded much better versed in teenage modes of communication than Kate. She barely understood the point of Twitter, much less had any idea how to follow anyone.

"So you've dealt with this kind of electronic history on cases before?"

"On cases, no." Lew smiled and shook his head. "But I've got six grandkids. They manage to get me on Facebook more than once a day, sending me pictures and messages and all sorts of stuff."

"Six grandkids?" Kate repeated quietly, trying not to let herself think of all the grandchildren she'd never have.

"And only half of our kids have started their own families, God help me once they all get going," he said, trying to sound annoyed, even though he obviously wasn't. He motioned to the boxes. "I think we should divide and conquer here."

"Can you look at her Facebook and Twitter accounts and that blog?" Kate asked. "There's a desktop computer on the second floor, in my office."

Lew nodded in the direction of the stacks of pages. "You'll be okay down here with all that?"

"No," Kate said, taking a deep breath, "probably not."

Once Lew had disappeared up the steps, Kate pulled out the first stack of papers, Amelia's Word documents. They seemed the least likely to plummet her into hysterics, though she knew that the real dirt and, thus, anything useful, would likely be in Amelia's texts. But she wasn't yet ready to dive headlong into those. Luckily, aside from the *gRaCeFULLY* posts that Kate had already seen, the Word documents were all school papers or stories that Amelia had written. Kate was almost done flipping through what was left of the stack when she came to a paper titled *To the Lighthouse: Friendship and Feminism*, by Amelia Baron. It was the paper Amelia had supposedly plagiarized. Except the title didn't sound the same as the one that had fallen out of Amelia's notebook.

Kate took the paper downstairs to the kitchen, to the drawer where she'd dumped all those mean little notes when Adele had shown up at her door. She'd slid Amelia's paper into that same drawer. She tugged it out now and looked at the title page: *Representations of Time: To The Lighthouse*, by Amelia Baron. Not the same, not even close.

Kate turned to the kitchen table, setting the papers out side by side. She flipped through the pages, skimming. The papers had nothing in common as far as she could see. Why would Amelia have two different papers on the exact same book? Kate stared down at them, tracing her fingers over the titles. It was proof Amelia didn't cheat. Kate felt sure of it, even if she couldn't explain how.

Kate left the papers on the table and headed back up to the living room, where the seemingly endless stacks of documents remained. She pulled the e-mails out first; a Post-it on top read: "Only printed out last 4 months. You want more let me know." All those messages in four months.

The first e-mail was from George McDonnell. You going to Chloe's party this weekend? Heard somebody's bringing E. E? As in ecstasy? Was George McDonnell the mystery boy whom Amelia had gone into the house with? Kate was still trying to accept the whole sex thing, and now there were drugs involved, too?

Kate ripped the stack of e-mails apart, praying Duncan would have thought to include Amelia's outgoing messages. Sure enough, about three quarters of the way through there was a flag and a note: "Sent File." Kate raced through Amelia's messages until she laid her hands on her daughter's reply.

E? What are you like a drug addict all of a sudden or something? Amelia had written. Not cool, bro. Anyway, I can't go, I've got an early practice Sunday a.m.

Kate closed her eyes and clutched the e-mail to her chest. Thank God. Maybe she was right about some things after all. Kate looked at Amelia's next sent e-mail, and it was to her lacrosse coach, Ms. Bing. Is the training camp going to be over spring break again this year?

Maybe it wasn't all lies and bad surprises. But then, about a dozen pages in, Kate got to an e-mail that stopped her cold.

I'm sorry, Amelia. I was out of line. Can we talk about it? Please.
—Phillip

Whoever this Phillip was, something had happened between Amelia and him. Some kind of fight. Kate looked up at the e-mail address: p_woodhouse@gracehall.edu.

Phillip Woodhouse, the headmaster of Grace Hall? Kate blinked at the e-mail, then looked again at the address. What was Phillip Woodhouse doing e-mailing Amelia with that kind of tone: *I'm sorry? I was out of line*? When did a headmaster ever apologize to a student? And what kind of line, exactly, had he drifted across?

Kate startled when she heard Lew on the stairs. When she turned up, he was ashen.

"What's wrong?" Kate asked. First the e-mail from Woodhouse and now that awful look on Lew's face: it was too much. The adrenaline was making her hands shake. "What did you find?"

She waited for Lew's expression to lift, but instead he just paused some distance away and gripped the back of the armchair.

"I think you should come up and see for yourself," he said finally.

"What—no. Why? Upstairs?" Kate felt queasy as she looked toward the steps. "Just tell me what you found. Something on her Facebook account?"

He shook his head. "Like I said, you need to see it."

Kate felt light-headed as she looked back down at the e-mails on her lap.

"But I found another paper," she said finally, trying to buy herself time. "Two different papers for the same assignment. The one they said Amelia cheated on."

"Huh," Lew said, not sounding very interested. "That bears looking into."

"And I found this." She stood up and held out the e-mail to him.

He glanced down at it.

"Who's Phillip Woodhouse?" he asked. "We think he could be our mystery boyfriend?"

"He's the headmaster at Grace Hall."

Lew frowned, then looked back down at the e-mail.

"Let's not panic yet," he said. "We'll follow up, see what it's about. There could be a reasonable explanation. It doesn't say anything specifically inappropriate."

Kate stared at Lew in silence until he looked up. He nodded.

"Fair enough," he said. "I agree, it needs explaining."

———

Upstairs in her small office, Kate took a seat in the desk chair in front
of the sleeping computer screen.

"Okay," she said, waving for Lew to proceed. She was nauseated.
"Let's get this over with."

Lew moved the mouse until the screen clicked to life. And there
was Amelia wearing nothing but pink lace underwear and a matching
push-up bra. She was leaning suggestively over the desk chair in her
bedroom, rear end toward the camera.

"Oh my God!" Kate gasped, shielding her eyes with a hand. She
thought for a second about looking again, making sure of what she'd
seen. But she couldn't possibly. That sexy girl vamping for the camera
had been Amelia. There was no question about it. Kate shuddered
hard, trying to dislodge the image from her mind. "Turn it off! Please,
turn it off!"

Lew reached forward and switched off the monitor.

"What was that?" Kate shouted.

"The blog she was posting to," Lew said glumly. He seemed mor-
tified.

"Amelia took a picture like that and posted it where anybody could
see it?!" Kate shouted, as if it had been Lew who'd told Amelia to do it.

"Not anyone," Lew said gently. "Someone would have to know
Amelia's alias to find her."

Kate was going to throw up, right there on the keyboard. Was her
daughter a secret prostitute or something? An exhibitionist? What on
earth would possess her to take half-naked pictures of herself, much
less post them *online*? It was the kind of thing that— No, it was not
the kind of thing that anyone did.

"How many people saw this? Can you tell?"

Because maybe it wasn't as awful as it seemed. Ten, fifteen—these
were the numbers jumping around Kate's head. That wouldn't be great,
but it wasn't the same as working at an escort service. This could just
be what kids did these days, too—saw one another in their underwear.
Maybe it was the new safe sex: get naked on the Internet so you didn't

have to in real life. Not that Kate really believed that. There was nothing healthy about those pictures that were now burned into her memory.

"There are one thousand two hundred and eighty-eight notes."

"What?" Kate had forgotten what they had been talking about.

"You asked how many people had seen this," Lew said reluctantly. "That's how many people 'liked' her picture. Some wrote comments."

"More than a thousand people saw these pictures?" Kate asked, her eyes so wide they were burning.

"This—whatever it is—was bigger than just Amelia," Lew said, ignoring her question, probably because the answer was that even more than that had. "There are more than two dozen girls in this group."

"Group?"

"Birds of a Feather. From what I can tell, there was some sort of ranking system in place, almost like a game."

"A game? With pictures like this? Oh my God, that's sick." Suddenly Kate was furious. "We have to find these girls. We have to tell their parents exactly what they're doing. This isn't right. This wasn't Amelia's idea. Somebody put her up to it."

"Agreed, but I expect all the names on here are aliases. Do you have some kind of yearbook or something we could cross-reference to get the girls' real names?"

"There's a meet book, with all the students' pictures. It's online."

As Kate went to her bedroom to get her laptop to compare the pictures side by side, all she could think about was the possibility that Amelia really had killed herself after all. If she'd gotten mixed up with something like this, posing half naked, maybe she'd felt so guilty and embarrassed she couldn't live with it anymore.

When Kate came back into her office, Lew was on the phone.

"Yeah, okay," he said quietly, rubbing his forehead. "I'll be there as soon as I can."

His jaw was clenched as he hung up.

"What's wrong?" Kate asked.

She'd been bracing herself for him to get a call, pulling him off the case, telling him his time could be better spent elsewhere. But not now. Not after seeing those pictures. Lew took a deep breath, his hand still on his forehead.

"If you give me the site and password for that meet book, I can do the cross-checking myself tonight," he said. "You'd probably be better off not seeing the rest of the pictures anyway."

"Where are you going?"

"Home. This past summer my wife had a stroke," Lew said quietly. He shook his head as he stared at the ground. When he looked up at Kate, his eyes were watery. "When she has a bad day, I'm the only one she'll listen to. Half the time, I'm not even sure she knows who I am, but she listens anyway. That was her home-care nurse. Sounds like today was a really bad day."

Kate blinked at him. She wished she was the kind of person who'd put a stroke victim ahead of her own anxiety. But all she wanted to do was grab onto Lew's pant leg and beg him to stay, to not leave her side until she knew all the awfulness about Amelia there was left to discover.

"Okay," she managed to get out. "Yes, I mean, of course. Do you know maybe when you'll be back?"

"First thing in the morning," Lew said. He paused in front of Kate in the doorway, looking her straight in the eye. His face softened then in a way Kate hadn't seen it before. She could imagine it was the way he looked at his own grown children, firmness overlaid with warmth. It made her want to cry. "Try not to worry. We're going to figure out what happened to her."

After Lew had gone, Kate resisted the temptation to go back on the *Birds of a Feather* blog. It wasn't hard. She couldn't possibly stomach seeing those pictures of Amelia again, not ever.

Kate returned instead to her boxes. She needed to finish looking through Amelia's e-mails. Specifically, she wanted to see whether there were any more from Woodhouse. There could be an innocent explanation for one such e-mail. Perhaps. But not for more than one.

By the time Kate had gone through all of the messages, the sun had gone down. The living room was dark except for the pale circle of light from the standing lamp next to the couch. It cast a fuzzy halo over the coffee table where Kate had put all the e-mails she'd found from Woodhouse.

There were seventeen in all.

Kate had spread them out over her coffee table like some kind of terrible patchwork quilt, then crossed her arms and stared down at them. Most of the messages were brief, a sentence or two, asking Amelia to meet with Woodhouse, to think about what he'd said or to think about what she was doing. But in one, he almost seemed to be threatening her. Think about your future, Amelia. This could cost you.

Amelia had responded, by e-mail, only two times, with almost as few words: Okay and What time.

Could there have been something between Amelia and Woodhouse—an affair, sexual harassment, something? Kate had met him the day Amelia died. Apparently, they'd had a whole conversation that Kate had absolutely no recollection of. He'd been at the funeral, too. Kate did remember that much, but everything that day had been a blur. She closed her eyes and tried to picture Woodhouse. He'd been young, hadn't he? Attractive even? Kate had a flash of hipster glasses and shaggy, art-house hair. *If* she was even picturing the right person. For sure, Woodhouse had an impressive background—a Fulbright scholarship and a master's degree from Harvard in public policy and education, which he'd gotten around the same time as Kate had gotten her law degree. She remembered reading about him in the bulletin Grace Hall had sent around when he became headmaster. But who said a guy with a great résumé couldn't also be a pedophile?

There was a knock at the front door then, once, then three times much harder. It was impatient, aggressive almost. Kate stood up from the couch and, with her arms wrapped tight around her, walked hesitantly through the darkness to the door. She didn't turn on the light. She wasn't ready yet to announce that she was home.

Bam! Bam! Bam! The knocking came again when she was almost at the door.

Kate's stomach was tight as she leaned to look through the peephole. There, on the stoop, was Seth, arms crossed, jaw clenched. When Kate swung open the door, his hand was raised as if he were about to pound again. He looked relieved for a second, then angry.

"No. Not allowed, not these days," he scolded, striding inside past her. "Do you know how many times I've called you today?"

"No, I've—"

"Twelve," Seth snapped. "I left you *twelve* messages. But do you bother to call me back? No, of course not. I had to make Thomas leave work at six thirty to go meet the nanny so I could come *here* to check on you. Do you know how early six thirty is at McCann Erikson? It's like taking a half day. Let's just say that Thomas is pissed at me for impinging on his workaholic persona and, by extension, he is also pissed at you. Now, what could possibly be your excuse for not calling me back?" Seth looked around the room. "And why are you sitting here in the dark? I've told you before that'll depress you. There are actual studies that—"

Seth fell silent as Kate's face began to melt. A second later she was sobbing.

"Oh my," Seth said, stepping forward and wrapping his arms around her. "Okay, okay. You can sit in the dark if you want to, honey. And screw Thomas. Lola's his daughter, too. He can climb down from his ivory tower to pick her up for once. Come on now, what you need is a drink."

Twenty minutes later, wineglasses in hand—and with Seth up to speed on everything—they were staring down at the pages covering Kate's coffee table.

"It is a tad *Lolita*," Seth said. "What are you going to do?"

Kate shook her head. "Find out why he sent them, I guess."

"Are you sure it matters?" Seth asked.

"What do you mean? Of course it matters."

"Listen, Kate, you know I love you, right?"

Kate glared at him for a second, knowing he was about to say something she didn't want to hear. "I guess so."

"And you know I loved Amelia."

She nodded.

"I get wanting to know that Amelia's death wasn't a suicide," he said. "But if you already know it, why do you have to prove it? And to whom?"

Kate could tell Seth still thought that Amelia's death had been a suicide, though. That he thought all of this searching was just part of Kate's healing process. Necessary, perhaps, but ultimately futile.

"She was my *daughter*. The only one I will ever have and—"

"Listen, I know what that means, with Lola now, especially. But—"

"You think I should let it drop. That if somebody *killed* Amelia, I should just let them off the hook?"

Seth shook his head and frowned. His usually snappy demeanor was muted now, almost completely.

"I'm saying that you should let yourself off the hook," he said quietly. "None of this is going to bring Amelia back, and it might drive you right off the edge. What if you learn something about her and this Woodhouse character that is creepy and terrible, but doesn't have anything to do with why she died? Then what? I'm just saying that Amelia would want you to take care of you, too. *I* want you to take care of you."

He was right, of course, about her learning awful things. She had already learned things she wished she could purge from her memory. Kate's cell phone vibrated on the coffee table then, making a loud hollow sound against the wood. She and Seth both turned to look at it, then back at each other. Kate didn't move.

Without her asking him to, Seth got up to check her phone. "It's just a voice mail," he said, handing it to her.

It was from Daniel.

"I just want to make sure you're not worried about the whole Associated thing," Daniel's recorded voice said. He was trying to sound cheerful. He didn't. He sounded wound up, if not exactly angry. "I saw the writing on the wall a long time ago. I'm never going to win Jeremy over. That's why I'm headed to Meyers, Jenkins in a few weeks. They offered me this insane equity partnership deal, too. So I'm all good, trust me. In the meantime, I'm headed to Scotland to go golfing, if you can believe it. I haven't taken a vacation in two years. Anyway, I'm sure I'll see you around. Take care, Kate, and congratulations. You deserve it."

Kate kept the phone up against her ear for a minute after the message had ended. Daniel gone to another firm after all these years trying to claw his way to the top of Slone, Thayer? Out of her life, just like that. She was relieved, but something else, too. Unsettled. *Deserve it.* That was the part of what Daniel had said that she didn't like. He didn't think anyone deserved anything good but him.

"Who was it?" Seth asked, not falling for Kate's phone-to-the-ear routine. "Jeremy want you to come in so you can scrape gum off his shoe?" He lifted his hands in the air and waved them around. "Oh Kate! Help me! Help me! I can't touch my shoes with my lily-white hands."

"Are you done?" Kate asked.

Seth took a sip of his wine and sighed. "I suppose."

"Anyway, it was Daniel, not Jeremy."

"Oh boy," Seth said. "Even better. What did Captain Corporate Crusader have to say for himself today? Did he climb over some old ladies to get to a bag of cash? Or maybe he threw some puppies into the river in exchange for a chance to first chair a trial."

"I thought you were done?"

Seth shrugged. "Daniel deserves it. You know, I ran into him at an alumni event last year and he said he was considering a class action to stop Human Rights Watch from soliciting donations on his block."

"I'm sure he was joking," Kate said.

Seth raised an eyebrow. "That makes one of us. You know, I've heard rumors that his ex-wife, Gail, had to seek inpatient treatment after their divorce."

"Now you're just making things up."

"Maybe, but come on. Daniel definitely exploits people. You know that better than anyone. He's been taking liberties with you ever since you and he—"

"Can you please not remind me?"

"Sorry," Seth said, looking chastised.

Kate's phone vibrated again, in her hand.

"Daniel is not calling you *again*, is he?"

"It's not a voice mail, it's a text," she said, though she'd only glanced at her phone. "Will you read it, please?"

She handed the phone back to Seth. He snatched it from her and looked down, as if he were going to sort this nonsense out once and for all. But as he read, his face slowly sank.

"Read it," Kate said.

"Kate, I don't think— It's only two words. Who knows what it—"

"Seth, please." He took a breath and fidgeted in his chair, like he was trying to buy time.

"Okay, okay, fine," he said quietly, lifting the phone up to read. He took another short, loud breath. " *'Fucking whore.'* "

gRaCeFULLY
OCTOBER 10TH

Because there are 176 definitions for the word *loser* on urbandictionary.com.
Don't Be a Statistic

So, there's dissension in the ranks of the chess club, everyone . . .

We know, we know, who wants to hear about those dorks right? But wait, this is seriously good. Apparently, a certain young lady on the team known for her aggressive style of, um, gamesmanship (okay, it's Ainsley Brown) turned up late for her match at Horace Mann last Saturday because she was otherwise occupied in the lavatory with a certain male opponent from Stuyvesant. Word is that the opponent was more than happy to throw the match in exchange for services rendered.

School administration officials claim they are narrowing in on the sticky-fingered cad who lifted two of the school's new iPads. It's either those lame asses from Wolf's Gate or the Gamblers Anonymous chemistry prof, Mr. Hale. In which case I hope they fire his ass, ideally before he grades my last test.

And the Maggies are at it again. This time there's pictures and a blog involved. I don't have the deets, but I bet they are sweet.

Also, looks like both Ian Greene and Dylan Crosby have wandering eyes. We knew, poor Sylvia, that your hours were numbered. And Dylan seems to be wandering to somebody at LONG last. Details will follow.

Check me back later, people. I'll have more mad scoop.

Amelia

DYLAN

u free 2morrow

AMELIA

def what time?

DYLAN

after schl

AMELIA

what d u want to do?

DYLAN

hang out; park maybe; movies

AMELIA

like a date

DYLAN

sure, I guess

AMELIA

sounds good c/u ltr

OCTOBER 13, 9:03 PM

BEN

what's up?

AMELIA

nada how r u?

BEN

fine; u talk to your mom?

AMELIA

not yet; still on fence

BEN

why?

AMELIA

did u tell your parents right away?

BEN

pretty much

AMELIA

and they were cool?

BEN

dad came around faster than mom

AMELIA

my mom wld be cool, but its still weird; like a bad sex talk

BEN

yeah, but u will feel better after, trust me

AMELIA

maybe; I've g2g. ltr xo

OCTOBER 13, 9:11 PM

SYLVIA

did you see the last gracefully?

AMELIA

Not yet, why?

SYLVIA

I just read it and it said that Ian's eyes are wandering WTF!!!

AMELIA

100 percent of the crap on there is a total lie . . .

SYLVIA

I hope u r rite

facebook

Amelia Baron

"They became part of that unreal but penetrating and exciting universe which is the world seen through the eyes of love." Virginia Woolf, To the Lighthouse

Sylvia Golde   Ick enough with the pretentious literary references

George McDonnell   yeah seriously stfu

Chloe Frankel   I thought it was lovely, Amelia. I love that book

Amelia

I woke up with the sun in my eyes. It was low in the sky, just over the top of the brownstones across the street. I squinted and held a hand up to block it as I checked the clock on my nightstand. It was already almost five p.m. and I was babysitting for Kelsey at six thirty. So much for my movie date with Dylan. Not that I really cared. I mean, assuming Dylan wasn't avoiding going out in public on purpose.

"Have you seriously read all of these?" Dylan asked.

When I rolled over in bed, she was at the edge of my room, staring up at all the books on my packed shelves. She was wearing only her tank top and underwear, her hair tied in a thick knot at her neck with some of it falling in loose tendrils around her face. She looked like a princess.

"I mean, it's like a full-on library in here." Her voice was a blend of awe and freaked-out-ness. "I've never seen this many books in someone's house."

"What about the library in your house."

"My dad collects books," Dylan said. "He doesn't actually *read* them. They might as well be, like, commemorative plates, or guns. You've read these, right?"

I looked up and down the long, crammed shelves. It did seem kind of freakish now that I was seeing it the way Dylan must be. Though it wasn't as if her carrying around black-belt sudoku puzzles like they were a security blanket was exactly normal either.

"Not *all* of them," I lied. "That would be crazy. Anyway, some of them might be my mom's, I think."

Lying made me feel kind of sad. After all the hiding and sneaking around and pretending I'd done so I could be in the Maggies and stay close to Dylan, it would have been nice to be able to be myself 100 percent when I was alone with her. But I kind of felt like she was always about to slip through my fingers, and I didn't know which of my quirks wasn't cutting it. It didn't help that Dylan was also pretty paranoid that people would find out about us. Like that would be a fate worse than death. I didn't want to run around Brooklyn declaring our love or marching in the pride parade or anything, at least not yet. But I also didn't care who found out. The only thing I cared about was Dylan. The one time I'd asked if she was embarrassed about us hadn't gone well.

"No," Dylan had said, all way testy. We'd been in my bedroom, as usual. "I just don't like anyone at school knowing anything about my personal life, okay?"

Personal life. It had rolled off her tongue like it was this major thing she was used to hiding. It made me wonder how many boys had kept Dylan's secrets before me. There could have been other girls, too, for all I knew. That was a question I'd been keeping myself from asking for weeks. I was afraid of the answer. Either way, there'd be drawbacks. But I did keep hoping Dylan would change her mind about keeping us a secret. Because I didn't know if I was in love with her, but she was all I thought about. And when we were together, I felt connected to something bigger and better than myself. That felt like love to me.

I wanted Dylan to stay, to order dinner and pretend we were an old married couple. I could even call and tell Kelsey I was sick. I never did that. It was irresponsible, but I would do that for Dylan. I already knew she'd never stay anyway, though. Dylan only ever came over for a couple of hours after school. Then she'd always say she needed to get home for dinner, to do her homework, because her mom needed to talk to her. Maybe that was all true. But it always felt like they were excuses.

Dylan was still staring up at my shelves.

"It's okay if they are all your books or whatever," she said. I'd always been a bad liar. "I think it's cool that you love to read." She backed up and sat down on the edge of the bed next to me. "I think other people picture things in their heads when they read. They imagine whole worlds. For me, there's only words on a page, that's it."

"You seriously don't picture *anything*?" I asked. "That's so weird."

I watched Dylan's mouth turn down. *Weird*. Why had I said it like that? Like there was something wrong with her.

"That's cool, that's what I mean," I added, but it was too late.

"Yeah, whatever, it's totally not. But I'm not like you, Amelia. I'm not like anyone." Dylan jerked up from the bed then and grabbed her jeans. Her face was empty as she wriggled into them. Once she got that faraway look on her face, I knew our date was over. "I've got to go. My mom's big episode is on tonight. She's having friends over to watch it. I have to help her get ready."

She sounded like a robot.

"Sure, okay." I sat up in bed and pulled my own shirt back on. Then there they were, pressing up against the insides of my lips again. The questions that had no good answers. But this time I couldn't stop myself. "Am I the first girl you've been with?"

"What difference does it make?" At least she didn't seem freaked-out by the question. I'd figured it would have sent her jetting for the door. "I'm with you now, aren't I?"

Dylan pulled her jacket on and picked up her bag, then untwisted her hair from the knot it had been dangling in. She'd told me once that her mom hated it when she wore her hair up. She said it made Dylan's jaw look too wide.

"It doesn't matter, I guess. But are you *with* me with me?" I felt kind of sick to my stomach. This was a mistake, trying to make her talk to me about this stuff. I should have just been happy with what

I was getting from her. But I couldn't get myself to shut up. "Because sometimes it feels like maybe you don't want to be."

Dylan smiled then, the brightness rushing back to her face. She came over and bounced down onto the bed next to me. Her hip was pressed against my leg as she smoothed some hair out from in front of my face and tucked it behind my ear.

"I like you, Amelia," she said. "But I want what we have to be about us and not proving some point or whatever to everybody at Grace Hall or in the Maggies. This isn't anybody's business but ours."

She hadn't answered my question, I knew that. But putting how she felt that way was romantic. Like it was us against the world. I was a stupid jerk, messing with the good thing we had. Why did I need so bad for people to know about us? Because I was a freak, that's why. I couldn't just let things be. That was what happened when you spent as much time alone as I did. You got weird and clingy.

I nodded. "I'm sorry, I just—"

"It's okay. I get it." Dylan smiled, as she leaned forward to kiss me. "You're a little needy. Most of the time, it's pretty cute."

Dylan hadn't been gone ten minutes when I heard a weird noise downstairs. I was at my desk finishing my biology homework. I froze and listened again. But I had to be hearing things. I should have turned on some stupid lights downstairs because already it was practically dark outside. And now, I was stuck way up in my bedroom in a house that was getting dark fast. It was a total rookie mistake. The kind I didn't usually make because I was such an expert at being on my own.

I held my breath and listened for the same noise. For a second there was nothing. I was about to take a deep breath when there it came again. A quiet thump, thump, then a louder thud. Like someone was banging into stuff in the dark because they didn't know their way around. Holy crap, could there seriously be someone *in* my house?

I grabbed up my cell phone and dialed 911, but I didn't press Send. What if the noise turned out to be nothing—which I was totally sure was the case—and my mom found out I'd called the police? She'd be totally freaked that *I'd* been that freaked. Then she'd feel all guilty that I was home alone and scared. One way or another I'd end up getting Leelah back. And Leelah would mean the end of the Maggies. And Dylan.

I kept my finger over the Send key on my phone as I crept toward the door. I poked my head out of my bedroom and looked down the steps. It was dark down there except for a teeny glow coming up from the ground floor. Someone must have turned on a light in the kitchen, a small one, over the stove, maybe, or in the bathroom. There was a chance I'd left it on, or maybe my mom had before she left for work. But I didn't think so.

I couldn't just sit there and wait to see if there was someone downstairs waiting for the chance to, I don't know, murder me or something. I was much better off heading down to check it out. If I got trapped up in my room, there'd be no escape. I started down the stairs, my back sliding down the wall. My finger still on Send. I could hear the cabinets opening and closing now. Drawers sliding open and shut. There was definitely someone down there searching for something. Someone who didn't know where to look.

I couldn't risk waiting much longer to make that 911 call. Once I saw who it was—and they saw me—it'd be way too late. I was halfway down the second set of steps, the ones to the kitchen, when I hit Send. Then I held my breath.

"Nine-one-one, what's your emergency?" an operator asked. But whoever was down there in the kitchen would hear me if I answered. "*Hello?* Nine-one-one, is this an emergency?"

"Yes," I whispered finally. "There's someone in my house and—" Then out of the corner of my eye, I saw someone there, at the bottom of the steps. "Holy shit!"

I turned, scrambling back up the steps. When I did, the phone slipped from my hands and bounced down, far out of reach.

"Amelia! Oh my God, what are you doing?"

I was all the way at the top of the steps before I realized that it had been my mom's voice. When I turned to look, she was standing at the bottom looking freaked, holding my phone. She put it to her ear.

"Hello? Yes, no," she said to the 911 operator, who must have thought I was getting beaten to death. "That was my daughter. She thought I was an intruder. Yes. No. Sure, hold on." She looked seriously bugged out as she held the phone up in the air. "She wants to talk to you, to be sure you're okay. *Are* you okay, Amelia?"

It took a lot of convincing before the 911 operator believed that I was actually okay and that it was really my mom she'd been talking to.

"Mom, why didn't you tell me you were coming home?!" I yelled at her when I was off the phone. "You can't just show up ten hours earlier than you *ever* do!"

Between all the stuff with Zadie and the creepy texts about my dad and all that, I was extra jumpy these days.

"I'm so sorry, Amelia. I didn't mean to scare you," my mom said, putting a hand on my back. "I should have texted, you're right. I was just so excited about sneaking away early. I wanted to surprise you."

"Mission accomplished," I said.

I was being a jerk, but I couldn't help it. My whole life felt so beyond ridiculous all of a sudden. I mean, I was home alone *all* the time. And whatever if it had been my decision not to have Leelah come anymore. It wasn't really fair that my choice was to be treated like a baby or to live in solitary confinement. I definitely would have been more normal with Dylan if my mom was around more. Maybe I'd have even told her about Dylan and the Maggies and everything, which would have been nice because I *really* wanted somebody to know. My mom looked down at her shoes for a while, then up to the ceiling. She closed her eyes and shook her head.

"You're right, Amelia. I should never surprise you when you're home alone," she said. "I don't know what to say. I wasn't thinking."

She looked so tired. So totally exhausted. All of a sudden my throat started tightening up. I went around day after day pretending it didn't matter that she wasn't there. Most of the time it didn't. But right now, it kind of did.

"It's fine, Mom, whatever," I said, because it would be easier on both of us just to pretend that was true.

"Listen, can we at least try to salvage the night?" She smiled even though she still looked sad. "Hey, maybe we could have a Friday date night on a Tuesday. We could even go to Ginza and have hibachi. Your favorite."

"Okay," I said, feeling bad for her. And it did sound fun. Besides, maybe this was my chance. Maybe I could finally talk to her while we were having dinner, about Dylan, the Maggies, even the texts about my dad. All of it. "Yeah, Ginza would be good."

"Great," my mom said, wrapping an arm around my shoulders and squeezing too hard. "Let's go now, because I'm starving."

I was feeling giddy as I got my coat. This was all actually working out pretty well. I hated having secrets from my mom. It was going to be good to tell her everything finally. And if she had a secret or two from me—like about my dad—this could be her chance to come clean, too. Lately, I'd started even wondering if there was a chance that Uncle Seth could be my dad. He and my mom—as crazy as it was—had been dating around the time I was born. And if there was a genetic part to me liking Dylan and being a late bloomer on that front, Seth had been that way, too. It would make sense. I kind of liked the idea actually. Seth was funny and interesting and supersmart. I could be totally into having him as a dad. And I'd get a half or step or something little sister as a bonus, too.

There was a knock at the door then. "Who's that?" my mom asked.

"I don't know," I said, feeling a little worried it might be Dylan.

Telling my mom about her would be one thing, but I wasn't ready for the two of them to meet.

"Oh hi," my mom said, in her trying-to-be-social voice. "How are you?"

When she opened the door all the way, there was Kelsey standing out on our front stoop wearing a cute red cocktail dress and a full face of makeup.

"Hi," she said, looking confused. "Amelia, I thought you were babysitting the boys tonight? Did I mix something up?"

I got a text from Heather the next day, in the middle of school. Photog. Ur house 1 hour. I'd totally forgotten about agreeing to play Zadie's stupid game.

"Who's that from?" Sylvia asked, trying to look over my shoulder at the message.

We were sitting in the school courtyard eating the Yogo Monster we'd bought for lunch down on Seventh Avenue. It was sunny, and we were both wearing sunglasses and light jackets, trying to pretend it was still warm enough to be sitting outside eating frozen yogurt. I dropped my phone in my bag so she couldn't read the message.

"My mom."

"In the middle of a workday?" Sylvia asked, her eyes big and shocked. "Be still my heart. If she keeps this up, she'll win Mother of the Year."

"Stop it, Sylvia," I said. "I'm not in the mood."

And I was feeling punchy about my mom after we'd never gotten the chance to talk the night before. She was passed out in bed when I got home from babysitting, glasses still on, a *New York* magazine gripped in her hands. I didn't have the heart to wake her.

Then after sleeping on it, I'd decided in the morning that I wasn't ready yet to tell her about Dylan after all. I would. Just not yet. I loved my mom, and we were close, but just thinking about the time she'd told me about where babies came from still gave me the willies. She'd done the best she could to make it casual and normal, but it had still been all kinds of icky. And this was *me* having sex. Even if I left out the actual sex part, it was still me with a *girl*. Maybe it should have been the same as me telling her that I was seeing a guy, but it felt a lot more complicated.

Sylvia shrugged. "Whatever, just trying to help."

I looked around the courtyard.

"Where's Ian today?"

I didn't feel like talking to her anymore, and Ian was always a sure-fire distraction.

"Where *is* Ian?" Sylvia growled. "That's a *very*, very good question. One that *I* don't have an answer to because I haven't heard from that asshole *all* day."

"Asshole?" I asked. Sylvia never talked about Ian that way. Not even as a joke. "What's that about?"

"Hello? I texted you about it. Do you even read my messages anymore?"

"Oh right, the *gRaCeFULLY* thing? Come on, Sylvia. You're going to believe that stupid thing? It's all made up."

"Not all of it," she said. "There's been plenty of stuff on there about me that I wish wasn't true but totally is."

"Whatever, I don't believe it," I said. "Ian's crazy about you."

And I really didn't believe it. I'd seen Ian at a lot of Maggie parties. He'd had lots of chances to cheat, especially with Zadie, who was still hanging on him every chance she got. But as far as I knew, he hadn't taken her up on it. I hadn't seen him take anybody up on anything. Sylvia looked down into her plain, nonfat Yogo Monster mixed with Chips Ahoy! cookies, and jabbed at it with her spoon. She shook her head.

"Well, he's been MIA *a lot* lately, and he's got all these lame excuses, like his dad having a last-minute gallery show or his kid sister's doctor's appointment. His mom getting him an interview with some art agent? I mean, is there even such a thing as an art agent?"

"If there is," I said, "I feel like Ian would have one."

Sylvia rolled her eyes, then stared off. I watched her face slowly sinking. Sylvia being mad was bad. Sylvia sad was terrible. She always got all shrunken, like a wrinkled balloon.

"I know what cheating feels like," Sylvia said quietly. When she looked at me, her eyes were glassy. "It feels like this. And it seriously fucking sucks."

"Maybe he just needs some space or whatever."

But Sylvia was right. She did usually have good instincts about this stuff. I thought about Zadie again. With a girl like her, maybe it was only a matter of time.

"Space, right." Sylvia laughed, but not like it was funny. "To find a new ho."

"That's not what I meant."

"Thanks for the pep talk, Amelia. But—and no offense—like, seriously, what do you know? You've kissed one guy your whole life. And I'm not sure a drunk lifeguard even counts." She stared at me for a minute. I waited for her to remember our conversation from the Tea Lounge, the one about the relationship she'd guessed I was having. But it was like it had never even happened. It was a relief and a letdown that Sylvia had never brought it up again. "It's kind of hard to take relationship advice from somebody who's never been in a relationship. And texting with some freak up in Albany doesn't count."

"Ben's not a freak," I said, kind of halfheartedly.

He had been acting kind of different lately. At first, he'd been really supportive about Dylan and everything, but then he'd turned weirdly judgmental all of a sudden. He'd started talking to me like he was my big brother or something, telling me that I should watch out for Dylan because a girl like her wasn't a girl I could count on. As if he even knew her. I'd started thinking he was kind of jealous or maybe just tired of listening to me talk about her.

"I love you, so I'm going to tell it to you straight," Sylvia said. "Ben is *definitely* a freak. Any guy who just wants to *talk* to some girl all the time is a freak."

"Ben's gay, Sylvia," I said. "I've told you that, like, a million times. And I'm his friend. I don't know why you don't believe me."

"Right, sure. Because you can totally believe everything some guy you've never met says. For all you know, he's not even a guy. And even if everything he's told you is true, somebody who spends more time on their computer than with real live people is weird, period."

"Whatever." I shrugged.

But maybe Sylvia was right. Maybe I should ratchet things down with Ben for a while. Between Sylvia and Dylan I had enough to juggle without worrying about what was going on with him. I'd been thinking a lot about telling Sylvia about Dylan, too. It was too much pressure keeping that a secret on top of the Magpies. I didn't think Sylvia would be that freaked-out about the girl part either. She'd be surprised, sure. I was still surprised. Sometimes I still wasn't even 100 percent sure it was true. There was a chance she'd be mad I hadn't told her about Dylan sooner—not that I really could have when I was still figuring it out myself—but she was definitely going to be way more pissed off about the Maggies.

But what if I was wrong? What if Sylvia did care about the me-with-a-girl thing? I mean, we *had* been naked together, like, hundreds of times. We'd shared a bed almost as often. Sylvia had shown me how a tampon worked. And had explained—with diagrams—what it was like when a guy went down on you. We'd shared all our secrets up until now. What if nothing was ever the same after I told her?

"Ms. Golde?" someone called from across the courtyard before I could work myself up to opening my mouth about Dylan. When we looked up, there was spooky Dr. Lipton, the school counselor. With her pale skin and high-collared black dress, she looked, as usual, like a vampire. "We had an appointment. Ms. Golde."

"Oh, craptastic," Sylvia said, loud enough for Dr. Lipton to hear.

"Did something happen?" I asked.

Sylvia had had some problems at the end of freshman year. Her mom had caught her cutting herself a couple of times. It wasn't as big a deal as it sounded, at least according to Sylvia. But her mom totally lost it. She sent Sylvia to, like, ten different therapists all at the same time and had Dr. Lipton's head permanently implanted way up Sylvia's butt. So far, this year, Sylvia had been totally fine. At least, as far as I knew.

"Nothing happened," Sylvia said. "My mom's being a bitch. Same old."

"Sylvia, seriously. Are you sure you're okay?" I did feel bad that

I'd kind of missed the whole boat on the cutting thing the first time around. I wasn't going to let that happen again. "I mean, with all this stuff with Ian and everything."

"Jesus, yes. You people," Sylvia hissed, then sauntered off toward Dr. Lipton. "For somebody having an affair with a pretend gay kid, I think you should be a little more worried about yourself and a little less worried about me."

It was great for me that Dr. Lipton had turned up because I'd had no idea how I was going to ditch Sylvia in time to get back to my house in time for the "photog." I still wanted to bag out of the stupid game, but I hadn't figured out a way to do it without maybe offending Dylan. And things were going so well with her, I didn't want to screw it up.

I headed back inside along with the wave of people coming back from lunch, then made a hard right through the atrium toward the side door. I'd learned from the Maggies that the fire stairs were the best way to duck out of school. On that side there were no administration offices and no classrooms. I'd slipped out in the middle of the day that way at least five times now, no problem. It was a left, then another left, and through a set of doors to the staircase and then—

"Oh hi," Liv said, slamming her laptop closed.

She was hunched over it on the steps. From the look on her face, I'd have thought I busted her surfing porn. I felt busted, too. For a second, I even thought about diving back the way I'd come, but it was too late. And I couldn't think of anything I could have been doing that would have put me out in that stairwell, except sneaking out.

"Hi," I said, still hoping that a good excuse for being out there was going to come to me.

"So we're both kind of busted, huh?" Liv said, reading my mind. She looked pretty, as usual, in a fluttery blouse and big, chunky necklace. "I'm supposed to be at a faculty meeting, and you've caught me hiding out here instead, working on a story."

"What's it about?" I asked. Talking about Liv's story was a better option than explaining what I was doing there.

"What's what about?" Now Liv was the one acting weird.

"The, um, story?"

"Oh you know, a boy, a girl, tragedy ensues. It's a work in progress," she said, smiling. "And speaking of stories, Amelia, I'm glad I ran into you. There's something I need to tell you."

"What?"

"You look nervous. Don't worry, it's nothing bad, it's . . . I ended up submitting your story to that fellowship."

"What?" I'd told her I didn't want to apply. What kind of teacher did that?

"I know, I took the risk and overruled you, and I've been feeling guilty ever since." She shook her head. "I think you're such a talented storyteller, and I was trying to support you. But just because I'd personally like a creative writing fellowship doesn't mean you do. I think I've been so wrapped up with my own frustrations in getting work published that I . . . Anyway, it wasn't my place to make that decision for you, and I'm sorry. That's all I can say."

I stared down at my shoes feeling weirdly exposed and kind of mad, until it occurred to me that I was looking at this all wrong. It was annoying that Liv had done that, but if she felt bad about the fellowship, I could maybe use it to my advantage to get out of that side door and home in time.

"It's okay, I guess," I said. "But I do kind of have to go. I have an, um, dentist appointment. And my mom forgot to write me a note, and so—"

"Oh," Liv said quietly. I couldn't tell if she believed me. Actually, I could kind of tell she didn't. "The dentist, huh?"

"I have a cavity."

She nodded slowly, biting down on her lower lip.

"Then we'll call it even for now." She smiled. "You go to the dentist and I won't say anything, if you promise to forgive me for sending your story. And also not tell anyone I skipped out on a faculty meeting to work on a story."

"It's a deal," I said, pushing open the door. When I turned back, I felt good, safe. Looked after. "Thanks, Liv."

I ran through the side yard and away from the school without looking back. From there, I jetted down Prospect Park West toward First Street, sure at any second that Mrs. Pearl or somebody was going to yell out my name. As I rounded the corner, I looked back over my shoulder to make sure no one was watching. I was turning around when something cracked against my forehead and sent me bouncing back.

"Ouch!" I shouted.

"Oh, my bad," came a voice. "You all right, luv?"

My head was vibrating when I looked up.

"I am *such* a prat," Ian Greene said. "I shouldn't have been texting and walking. I'm so sorry."

"I'm okay," I said, even though my eye was killing me. I must have collided with his shoulder or something. "Don't worry about it. And I'm actually kind of late, so . . ."

I started to step around him, trying to navigate with my one good eye.

"Yes, well," he said, "I believe I might be the one you're late for."

Ian held up his camera kind of bashfully.

"It's apparently one of my hazing responsibilities." He shrugged sheepishly. "To be honest, this whole business has made me regret getting involved with this club nonsense in the first place. Perhaps Sylvia was right. They are quite mad."

Ian being a great photographer was obviously not the reason Zadie had sent him to take the photographs. Zadie was trying to create problems between Sylvia and me. Or, who knows, maybe Sylvia and Ian.

"Yeah, the stuff with the clubs can get kind of crazy," I said. I sounded awkward and nervous and guilty. It was one thing for me to keep from Sylvia what I did with the Maggies, but for any of those secrets to include Ian? But so far my guilt wasn't driving me to call the whole thing off. I was still more worried about Dylan, and myself. "Do you even know what the pictures are supposed to be like? They didn't tell us anything."

"Well, to add to the cloak-and-dagger nonsense," Ian said, "they've sent me here with a sealed envelope, which apparently contains the instructions for this little photo shoot. I'm not supposed to open it until you and I are alone inside."

"Seriously?"

"I'm afraid so."

Now this was officially getting stupid. And the longer I let it go, the further I was sliding into Zadie's trap. But what choice did I have? Zadie was probably betting I'd call off the photo shoot. That was probably the whole point. It would finally give her a reason to throw me out of the Maggies and away from Dylan. I took a deep breath.

"Okay, well, I guess we should get to my house then," I said. "Before someone sees us standing here or whatever."

Ian smiled. He looked relieved to be moving on, too. He rolled out an arm and bowed his head like nobility. "After you, madam."

When we were inside, I dropped my bags on the living room couch.

"You can hang out down here or whatever," I said. "I'm just going to run upstairs and change my clothes."

I figured I should at least make an effort to look halfway decent. Dylan would be seeing the pictures.

"Shall we check out our marching orders first?"

"Oh right, sure. Do the honors."

Ian ripped open the envelope. "Check out *Birds of a Feather* blog," he read. "Take same kind of pictures." He looked up at me, forehead creased. "A treasure hunt. Lovely. Got a computer?"

I led Ian upstairs to my bedroom, which was a lot messier than I'd remembered leaving it. I hoped it hadn't been that gross when Dylan was over the night before. I stepped over a pile of clothes and sat down at my computer and started combing through the many search results for a *Birds of a Feather* blog. Finally, I clicked on one and a picture of Heather popped up next to the name Honey Baxter. It was just a shot of her face. There was a small paragraph next to the photo, which included her home city (New York), her age (a lie that she was eighteen), and one sentence about her "likes" (chocolate) and "dislikes" (losers).

And then I clicked on the photo, which led me to several more shots. In the first, Heather was in a lace push-up bra and matching panties, bent over, legs spread. The next was her leaning in, hands on her boobs and another with a finger hooked in her mouth. There were twelve pictures, all of them pretty much the same: porn.

"Holy crap," I said.

"Yes, crap indeed," Ian said, his eyes wide.

Once I'd found my way back to the blog's home page, I could see that there was a page of photos for every girl in the Maggies, with pretty much the same kinds of pictures. They'd each been "liked" by hundreds, sometimes thousands of people. Zadie had the most "likes." I clicked on one picture of her, and several others flashed up on the screen. They were especially flattering, I had to give her credit for that. Black-and-white, with shadowy, dramatic lighting, they were almost artistic. And Zadie looked to be completely naked in each one, covered only by her hands, a scarf, a shadow.

"What's the point of all this?" Ian asked.

At least he hadn't seemed particularly interested in the photos of Zadie. I took it as a sign, proof even, that nothing had happened between them.

"I have no idea," I said. "I didn't know they were doing . . . well, nothing like this."

"What'll they do to you?"

"What do you mean?"

"When you say no?" he asked, then his brow furrowed even deeper. "Because you cannot possibly be contemplating participating in this nonsense."

"No. I mean, I don't think so."

"You don't *think* so? I'd assume you'd be uncomfortable with this kind of thing. I mean, given your situation."

"Situation?"

"Just that you're a . . ." He looked uncomfortable. "I don't know, more modest than some of these other girls. Quite honestly, I mean that as a compliment."

Sylvia had told Ian Greene I was a virgin. Ugh, it was beyond humiliating. Not to mention, not even true anymore.

I turned away from Ian and looked back at the computer screen. I held my breath as I clicked on Dylan's profile. She was beautiful in the shots, of course. But there was something else, too, that made them stand out. A sadness, which made them hard to look at, and impossible to turn away from. She didn't want to be playing the game any more than I did. It was Zadie who'd made her do it.

"You headed back to school?" Ian asked. He was gathering up his stuff. "Personally, I haven't worked out how to get back in without anyone noticing. Perhaps you could lend a hand."

As he moved toward the door with his big camera in his hand, I felt something slipping through my fingers. *Uptight, uptight Crazy Eyes*. Even if Zadie didn't throw me out of the Maggies—a big if—Dylan might feel judged if I didn't post my pictures, too. What if she didn't want to be with me anymore because of it?

"Wait," I said when Ian was almost at my bedroom door. He paused but didn't turn around. "I want to do it."

He turned around slowly.

"You don't need these girls, Amelia," he said quietly. He looked disappointed. "Sylvia is right. It's all bollocks, this rubbish with the clubs."

I shrugged. "I'm not doing it for them."

"And what about Sylvia?" he asked. "I don't expect she'd be chuffed about me seeing her best pal in her knickers."

"Hmm, yeah," I said, considering. He was, of course, right. "She already thinks you're cheating on her, too. You know that, right?"

"Yes." Ian Greene nodded, holding my stare. "I know."

Not: *No way!* or *Isn't that absurd!* Just: *I know*. He might as well have told me whom he was sleeping with. But it wasn't Zadie. I felt sure of that after seeing his uninterest in her photos, unless he was uninterested because he'd already seen the real thing. But Ian Greene had to have better taste than that. Zadie was so obvious.

Why, oh why, had I even said that to him? It was bad enough that I'd known Ian was in Wolf's Gate, now I knew something about him—at least maybe—that I *really* did not want to know. I'd just been so sure he wasn't actually cheating on Sylvia that it had seemed such a harmless thing to say. I'd figured he and I would have a good laugh about how silly Sylvia was. And that would be that. I'd never thought in a million years that he'd basically confirm it.

It was one more reason to call off the whole nonsense with the pictures. Except with each passing minute, I felt more like I couldn't. None of the reasons I needed to do it had changed.

"Sylvia won't care about you taking the pictures," I said. My biggest lie yet. She would definitely care if she found out. I was just banking on the fact that she never would. "I'm gay, Ian. I don't even like guys."

Gay. I felt a little light-headed. It was the first time I'd said it out loud, to anyone. Even Dylan and I—we were doing what we were doing, but we didn't talk about it. Not that way.

"Oh." Ian pulled his head back a little, then smiled kind of awkwardly. "Right. I mean, good. Great for you."

And there it was, out in the world. I'd told someone—Ian Greene no less—and the world had not fallen apart. My head had not exploded, and Ian had not disappeared in a puff of smoke. It was amazing. I felt like I could fly.

"Sylvia doesn't know yet, so please don't tell her." Who knows, maybe she really wouldn't care about the pictures once she knew I was gay. It was possible. "I'm planning to tell her myself as soon as I find the right time."

"Yes," he said. "Yes, of course."

"Please, Ian, I need to do this," I said, trying to push Sylvia as far out of my head as I could. Because not only was I doing this thing with Sylvia's boyfriend, I was also asking him to lie to her about it. But if the situation were reversed, Sylvia probably would have done the same to me. She would do anything she had to, to keep a boy she really cared about. That didn't make it right, but it did make it feel a little less wrong. "And I can't without your help."

Ian took a deep breath and exhaled with puffed-up cheeks, then shook his head as he stared at the carpet. Apparently, even Ian the philanderer had a line he didn't much want to cross.

"Okay," he said finally. Not that he looked happy about it. "But you owe me."

Amelia

AMELIA

hi! how r U?!

BEN

that's how u r going 2 play it? . . .

AMELIA

u r mad. What did I do?

BEN

nothing

AMELIA

is this the silent tretmnt?

BEN

listen, you're busy. I get that. You have a girlfriend now. But no one likes to be dumped by the side of the rd

AMELIA

u r right, sorry. I didn't mean to hurt your feelings. Friends again?

BEN

okay. Friends always

OCTOBER 18, 12:16 AM

AMELIA

forgot to ask. What about that kid on soccer team?

BEN

thx for asking. turns out he has a girlfriend at "boarding school."

AMELIA

closet case?

BEN

definitely; you tell Sylvia yet?

AMELIA

told her I needed to talk, but then she ditched me 4 Ian.

BEN

you tell your mom?

AMELIA

not yet; she wasn't home till late again

BEN

you've got 2 tell somebody; you'll feel better if u do

AMELIA

when am I going to see u? I thought you were coming to NYC? I really really need to see you soon! we have to meet! if we don't, I'm going to start to wonder if u r avoiding me on purpose ;(

BEN

still working on it; u'll be 1st to know; xoxo

AMELIA

xoxoxo

Kate

When I woke up this morning, I had myself convinced I'd dreamed the whole thing. That I'd made it up. Because there was no way I'd done a thing like that. Not me.

But it was me. This me I hate. So I called in sick to the office and stayed in bed all day. I may never go back to work. They can give me a cold offer or no offer. I don't even care anymore.

I deserve to be unemployed for the rest of my life.

JULY 22, 1997

To: Kate Baron
From: Daniel Moore
Subject: ?

Where are you? You missed an awesome summer associate event last night, and you know I think most of them are crap. It was an after-hours, private tour of the New York Stock Exchange. Seriously badass. Then dinner at Cipriani. I'm telling you, Kate, it was not the one to miss.

Feel better,
D

Kate

Through her living room windows, Kate watched the sun rise, turning the world a dull gray, then a muted pink. She'd stayed up all night. For a long time after Seth left, she sat huddled on her couch staring at her phone, wedged into the cushion of the armchair where she'd thrown it after he'd read aloud that last awful text message to her.

By dawn, Kate had finally made her way through almost all of the files that Duncan had sent her, except Amelia's text messages, which she'd been putting off until the end. Kate had been planning to read the texts when she felt ready. Until finally she realized she never would be.

Kate first wanted to see the texts Amelia had received about her dad. The fact that they were both getting anonymous texts about whom Kate had slept with didn't seem like a coincidence. But finding those particular messages was easier said than done. The Unknown and Blocked Number sections of Amelia's texts were huge. It took twenty minutes of paging through before Kate finally found what she was looking for.

Your mommy was a home wrecker. And your daddy is a whore.

My God. Sylvia hadn't said anything that prepared her for something that awful. What Amelia must have felt when reading that

Kate could only imagine. Shame, surely. Shame that wasn't even rightfully hers.

Kate paged through more of the Blocked Number and Unknown messages, trying to shake the awful empty burn in her stomach. They were a hodgepodge of junk texts, reminders from school, ordinary messages from friends who had blocked numbers. There were some weird references to Maggie, usually with a number, but there was no Maggie in Amelia's contact list. Kate couldn't remember Amelia ever mentioning one either. Eventually, reading so many meaningless messages, Kate's eyes began to glaze over. She'd hardly made a dent in the Blocked Number messages, but she needed a break.

Kate turned instead to the texts to and from Ben. There were a lot of those, too, and Kate soon found herself haphazardly picking her way through them—reading some, skimming others, skipping a handful altogether. This less-than-methodical way of reviewing Amelia's texts was bound to leave things overlooked. Maybe a small part of Kate wanted it that way. She was still afraid to know everything, at least all at once. There were also so many texts it would have taken her days to read through each and every one; she had no choice but to pick and choose.

At least the messages between Amelia and Ben were sweet and warm and supportive. Reading them, Kate couldn't help but fall a little bit in love with this boy named Ben, whoever he was. The strangeness in how Amelia had met him soon seemed to matter much less than the fact that he had been such a genuinely good friend to her. Even compared to Sylvia. Because while it was obvious that the girls had loved each other, their relationship had tilted hard in favor of Sylvia. With Ben, it seemed that Amelia had shared more secrets, especially about the boy named Dylan whom Amelia liked or might like. It was a relief, too, the way Amelia talked about Dylan—nervous and a little embarrassed, giddy. Young. Not at all like some hardened girl who was hawking her wares on the Internet.

Kate moved on from Ben's texts to read some of those between Amelia and the boy named Dylan, trying to follow the crooked trail of her daughter's life. Of course, none of it was as clearly spelled out as Kate had hoped. Actually, it wasn't spelled out at all. Including the many references in Dylan's texts to Maggie #1, Maggie #2, and so on. They were code names, Kate had figured out, though she didn't know to whom they were referring or why they were being used. What Kate was sure of was that there had been something romantic between Dylan and Amelia, how serious it was wasn't clear. The two of them did make plans to meet at least once in the middle of a school day, which meant he could have been the boy who Kelsey had seen. It was possible: that was all Kate could say for sure. Of course, the more she looked into Amelia's life, the more she was beginning to feel like anything was possible.

"I don't want this to become the focus here," Kate said, handing Lew her cell phone when he finally got to her house a couple of hours later. "But could you add this text to the others that your people are trying to trace? The messages seem to be getting more hostile. Also, I found one of the ones that Amelia got about her dad. It would be good to know who sent that one, too."

Lew stared down at Kate's phone, nodding slowly. Standing there in the living room, with a freshly showered Lew, Kate suddenly realized how strung out she must look: exhausted and unwashed and in the same clothes. She hadn't even brushed her teeth yet.

"I'll have the IT guys take a look," Lew said. "I'll also check in about their progress on the earlier texts. They've been moving a hell of a lot slower than I would like. But then our IT Department is pretty much a single guy with an old PC who works this stuff out for all the Brooklyn precincts. I'll try to expedite the subpoena on the phone company, too." He took a deep breath. "Now, given this new message, I think it's time you tell me about Amelia's dad."

Lew—with his six grandkids, and the ailing wife he cared for so attentively—was such an upstanding person. He'd probably never slept with the wrong person. He certainly would have never lied to his own children. Kate stared at him for a moment, wondering whether she could wriggle away from her dirty little secret any longer. But she already knew that the answer was no. That it should have been no a long time ago.

"Okay," Kate said finally, dropping down onto the couch and staring at her hands. Seth was the only other person who knew. Kate had known that she'd probably have to tell Lew eventually, but that wasn't making it any easier. "His name is Daniel Moore," she finally managed to say. "We went to law school together, and he works—or worked—at my firm. He's not a very nice person."

"Does he know about Amelia?"

"No," Kate said. Her voice was high and tight. It was a liar's voice. "I mean, yes. He knows about Amelia, but he doesn't know that she was his."

"He never suspected?"

"He must have, I guess. But he didn't ask. To be honest, I would have lied if he had." Kate couldn't even bring herself to look at Lew. "We'd broken off whatever it was between us before I ever found out I was pregnant. Daniel kept his distance for a long time after Amelia was born. Maybe he was afraid I'd change my mind and come asking for something."

"And you never told Amelia about him?" Lew asked.

Kate shook her head. "I know how it must seem. But Daniel's not a good— We weren't— He's not the kind of man I wanted for Amelia's father. So I guess I just made it so he wasn't. I'm not proud of what I did, but we were never in a relationship. It was sex between two people who didn't even really like each other. We couldn't have a baby together. But *I* wanted her. And I didn't want Daniel trying to convince me not to have her, which, knowing him, he definitely would have done. Then he got married a couple of years after Amelia was born, and it wouldn't have been fair to tell him then. He's divorced now, but it's not like I can tell him about Amelia when she's already dead."

"Well, we can leave it alone for now, I suppose. But if it starts looking like Amelia had contact with him, we're going to have to talk to him."

"Oh my God, you don't think . . ."

Lew shook his head. "I think it's a lot more likely that Amelia's death had something to do with this." He held up his red folder. "I matched up the girls in the Birds of a Feather group with the school meet book." Lew opened his folder and pulled out a single page. On it was a pristine chart—girls' names, addresses, and parents' names. "They're all students at Grace Hall, mostly upperclassman. There are twenty-two of them."

"Same number as the notes," Kate said. "I think maybe Amelia refers to all these girls as Maggie in her texts. The name, with a bunch of different numbers, comes up again and again."

"Could be," Lew said. "Either way, I think it's time we ask the school."

Inside Grace Hall's cool stone vestibule, there was a guard seated behind a computer at a big wooden desk. He was older and droopy-eyed. His loose, fleshy face had a bluish cast from the computer screen. His name tag read WILL FINKLE.

"Can I help you?" he asked lazily, keeping his eyes on the computer.

"We'd like to see the headmaster." Lew flashed his badge, making him seem more like an actual police officer than he had since Kate first met him. "It's about the girl who died here a few weeks ago."

"You don't say," the guard said drily, like he'd gotten bored waiting for someone to show up asking questions about her. He met eyes with Kate. He recognized her, she was sure of it. But he was having no problem pretending that he didn't. "Gonna need some ID first." Kate dug out her driver's license as Lew handed over his badge. The guard eyed them, hunting and pecking his way through recording their information in his computer. "Sign here," he said when he was finally done, pointing to a small, electronic signature box. Seconds later, two visitor passes were spit out of a small printer.

"A lot of high-tech security for a school," Lew said, nodding in the direction of the computer.

"When you've got more money than you know what to do with," the guard said, "you find something to do with it."

"Is it new?"

"Maybe three weeks ago for the computer . . . last week they added this." The guard hooked his finger back toward a box to swipe key cards. "You know how many kids forget those damn cards? I must be up and out of this chair fifty, sixty times every morning unlocking the damn door."

"What inspired it?"

"You tell me," the guard said. "You're the ones here about a dead girl."

The heavily floral air of the main lobby brought on Kate's nausea as they headed toward the main office. Two grand wood staircases curved up in front of a pretty, antique chest of drawers—old-looking, without been precious—with an enormous flower arrangement on top of it. Above was a painting that could have been an actual Picasso. On the opposite wall was a huge black-and-white photograph of a scantily clad, voluptuous dancer sitting in a filthy dressing room.

Lew and Kate stood shoulder to shoulder in front of the photograph, staring at it and the little plaque beneath that read DIANE ARBUS, BURLESQUE COMEDIENNE IN HER DRESSING ROOM, ATLANTIC CITY, NJ, 1963. A GIFT OF THE GREENE FAMILY. It was new. Kate may not have been at the school often, but a picture like that was the kind of thing she would have remembered. On the one hand, the edgy photograph's bold placement dovetailed nicely with Grace Hall's progressive streak; on the other, it seemed totally inappropriate. Especially now.

"Do you think the new security means something?" Kate asked.

Lew frowned. "Hard to say." He was still staring at the picture. It wasn't sitting well with him either. "Seems like they're hiding something. Could just be a guilty conscience."

"Ms. Baron!" someone called from down the hall then. The voice was high, shrill.

When Kate and Lew turned, there was an older woman marching quickly down the hall; her graying hair was pinned up, and she was wearing a tailored tweed suit. Mrs. Pearl. Kate might not have been able to picture Woodhouse very clearly, but Mrs. Pearl had left an indelible impression. And not a particularly good one.

"If we'd known you were coming, we'd have had someone come out to meet you," Mrs. Pearl said, staring pointedly at Kate before reaching out a crinkled hand to Lew. "I'm Mrs. Pearl, the dean of students at Grace Hall."

"Lieutenant Lew Thompson," he said, shaking her hand firmly.

Mrs. Pearl stared at them for a moment longer, as if she was expecting an explanation for their surprise visit. When none was offered, she smiled, but not very pleasantly. "I'm afraid Mr. Woodhouse isn't even here. He's at an independent schools conference in Boston. He'll be back tomorrow. If you'd like, I can schedule an appointment for you to come back—"

"It can't wait," Kate said, reaching out for the folder Lew was holding.

He relinquished it, reluctantly. He had made it clear that he was supposed to do the talking. But seeing Mrs. Pearl again, Kate was suddenly too angry to stay quiet. She held the folder out toward Mrs. Pearl.

"I'm sorry, what is that?" Mrs. Pearl asked, blinking down at the folder but not moving to take it.

"It's a list of girls who were in some kind of club with Amelia," Kate said, pressing the folder closer to Mrs. Pearl so that the corner was almost sticking into her breastbone. She sounded angry, too. In fact, she was much angrier at the school administration than she'd even realized. What had they been doing to stop kids from banding together into some kind of porn ring? It wasn't as if they were short on resources. "They posted half-naked pictures of themselves on a blog."

Mrs. Pearl took a step back, raising her hands in front of her chest, which Kate had apparently begun poking the folder into.

"That certainly sounds like upsetting information to have come across," Mrs. Pearl said smoothly. "But as you can imagine, Grace Hall can't control—practically or legally—what the children do off of school grounds."

"Off of school grounds? This is something they're doing *online*," Kate snapped. "It's not *happening* anywhere. And I think the girls were bullying Amelia, too. I found hate notes in her room, and I've only started sorting through her texts. God knows what else I'm going to find. Bullying has to be against the rules, no matter where it happens."

Kate was aware that using the term *bullying* instantly transformed the conversation into a hot-button one. But she was glad. She wanted them to listen up. She was going to make it impossible for them not to listen this time.

"Bullied?" Mrs. Pearl asked, looking a little surprised and a lot skeptical. "That is an extremely serious allegation, Ms. Baron. I assume you have proof?"

"Amelia's dead," Kate said. "That seems like pretty good proof to me."

"Lieutenant." Mrs. Pearl's eyelashes fluttered as she turned her attention from Kate to Lew, as though she were in search of a voice of reason. "I thought the police had ruled Amelia's death a suicide. In fact, we're planning to have a huge suicide awareness benefit a week from now in Amelia's honor. It's to raise money for a national hotline. Are you telling me now that she didn't kill herself?"

"There are questions," Lew said. "Substantial ones."

"Suicide awareness benefit?" Kate asked. "I asked someone with the PTA to wait before doing that."

Mrs. Pearl frowned. "Well, I can't speak to that, but the benefit is scheduled for next Friday. If you have further questions, I suggest you talk to the PTA. In terms of discussing this supposed harassment, I'm afraid you'll have to wait for Mr. Woodhouse."

Kate was about to snap at her when Lew's hand came down hard on her arm, cutting her off before she even got started.

"That's fine," he said to Mrs. Pearl. "We can wait. In the meantime, we'd also like to speak with Amelia's English teacher."

Mrs. Pearl crossed her arms and narrowed her eyes as if she was calculating how much it would cost her to refuse this request, too.

"I suppose that's fine," she said finally. "*If* she's available."

Ten minutes later, their three sets of feet were echoing loudly down the stone hallway as Mrs. Pearl led them toward a waiting area near Liv's office.

"Wait here," she said, pointing to the small cluster of furniture, which included two wing-back armchairs and a couple of small tables. "Liv should be out shortly. Now, if there's nothing else, I really do need to be getting back to work."

She turned toward her office without waiting for a response.

"Actually, there is one other thing, Mrs. Pearl," Lew called after her.

She spun back on a heel, her mouth pulled flat. "Yes, Lieutenant."

"The new security out front, was that in response to Amelia's death?

"Not in *response*, Lieutenant, no," Mrs. Pearl said coolly. She could see where Lew was headed. "But as you can imagine, any child's death, even a suicide, reminds all parents of their own children's vulnerability. As to whether there was a stronger causal link than that, you'd have to ask the school board yourself, Lieutenant. They arranged for the new security measures."

"I'd be happy to speak with them," Lew said. "I'll just need their names."

Mrs. Pearl came back and picked up a school catalogue from the stack that lay on a nearby side table. She held it out to Lew.

"Their names are right in there, at the back," she said. "The office can help you with their phone numbers. Now, if you have further questions, I suggest you direct them to Mr. Woodhouse. And that you make an appointment."

As Mrs. Pearl strode away, Lew sat down and opened the school catalogue across his lap, along with his chart of the girls in Birds of a Feather. His finger traced down the list of names as his head moved back and forth. He stopped about halfway down and looked up.

"What is it?" Kate asked.

"One of the girls, Zadie Goodwin"—Lew handed her the list— "look at the last name of her father or, rather, her stepfather, I guess."

Kate took the page and scanned down the names. Zadie. Had Amelia mentioned her? Had she read her name in Amelia's texts? Kate didn't think so, and yet she'd heard the name somewhere before. Finally, there she was at the bottom of the list: Zadie Goodwin. Father: *Frank S. Carmon.*

"That's the name of the place where Molina went to work, isn't it?" Kate asked. "Do you think this Frank Carmon is *that* Carmon? Carmon Industries?"

"I know he is."

"Are you serious?"

"Frank Carmon used to be a cop," Lew said. "He had a reputation, and not exactly a good one. Anyway, he left to start Carmon Industries more than a decade back."

"Do you think it's a coincidence that that's where Molina went to work?"

"No," Lew said, meeting eyes with Kate. "I don't."

Kate looked back down at the chart, her eyes moving over to Zadie's mother's name: Adele Goodwin.

"Oh my God," she whispered. That was where she'd heard Zadie's name before. "Her mother came to my house. She's the one trying to push through this suicide awareness benefit."

There was a click then, followed by a beep, and the door to the west wing of the school opened. A pretty woman in her late twenties with elfin bone structure and pin-straight, long blond hair leaned out. She was wearing tall leather boots and a short kind of Mod Squad dress. She leaned back against the door, holding it open, card key in one hand.

"Ms. Baron?" she asked, smiling tentatively.

"Yes." Kate jumped to her feet as if she'd just been caught cheating herself.

"I'm Liv." The young woman held out her free hand. "I'm so sorry to leave you waiting out here. We're still trying to get used to all these locked doors."

"That's okay. This is Lieutenant Lew Thompson," Kate said. "He's been helping me look into Amelia's death."

"Oh, I didn't realize the police were involved again," Liv said, looking taken aback. "Mrs. Pearl didn't mention that."

"Is that okay?" Kate asked, not knowing what she'd do if Liv said no. "Do you mind if Lew comes along?"

"Oh no, of course not," Liv said, looking embarrassed as she reached out to shake Lew's hand. "I was just startled, that's all. It's nice to meet you, Lieutenant. Please, come this way."

Liv's office was a sliver of space, with only enough room for a desk, one narrow guest chair, and four stacks of books. Two unmounted shelves were leaning against one wall. Another was covered in framed photographs, neatly arranged in a pleasing, slightly off-kilter pattern. Liv was in most of them—hiking and biking, traveling—with friends, some maybe boyfriends, young men with artful sideburns and copious plaid.

"I know. They're too much." Liv said, gesturing to the pictures. "The kids make fun of me. They're always saying I'm trying to act like I'm a kid myself." She shrugged, looking up at the pictures. "Maybe I am. But you can't help who you are."

Why Amelia had liked Liv so much was already obvious.

"No," Kate said, "you can't."

"And I'm sorry about the accommodations." She motioned to Lew who, with no place to sit, was leaning against the wall. "Offices are given out based on seniority. As you can see from this closet I've been in for the past four years, there isn't a lot of teacher turnover at Grace Hall."

"No, it's fine," Kate said. "Thank you for agreeing to meet with us."

"Anything I can do," Liv said. "Amelia was one of my favorite students of all time—creative and funny, and so insightful. It was hard to keep up with her sometimes." She laughed lightly for a second, then shook her head and frowned, as if she'd just remembered that

Amelia was dead. She was teary when she looked up at Kate. "I'm sorry." She wiped at her eyes. "I'm sure you didn't come here for me to get upset."

And it was true. Liv wasn't allowed to *cry*. Not when she was so young and pretty and destined to make lots of babies of her own someday. Not when the only child Kate would likely ever have was dead. As Liv sniffled loudly and dabbed at her eyes with a tissue, all Kate could do was stare at her. She closed her mouth, afraid something unfortunate might fly out. Something like: *If you hadn't turned my daughter in for cheating, none of this ever would have happened.* Kate didn't really believe that, or at least not entirely. Still, it would have felt good to say.

"Maybe we could start first with this paper Amelia was accused of plagiarizing," Lew said. He opened his red folder and pulled out the two papers Kate had found. "One of these papers, the one with your notations, was found in Amelia's bag. The other was on her computer."

Liv took the two papers and set them side by side on her desk. Her eyebrows were drawn low as she flipped through them. Her eyes were wide when she finally looked up.

"The one with my comments is the paper I received from Amelia, the one that had the sections that were copied," Liv said, her voice rushed and a little desperate. Like she'd been sure she was right, except now she was panicking that she wasn't. "And I want to be clear, this wasn't a case of overparaphrasing, or one copied sentence. I never would have turned a student like Amelia in for something like that. But most of her paper was lifted straight from an academic treatise on Virginia Woolf. I had no choice."

"And this other paper?" Lew asked. "You haven't seen it before?"

"No," Liv said emphatically, flipping through the second paper. "I wish that I had. It looks like a good paper. I mean, I can't tell if it's copied just by looking at it—there are thousands of sources on Virginia Woolf. But it certainly looks original and creative, exactly the kind of thing Amelia would write."

"Did you actually see Amelia hand in that other paper?" Kate asked. "Is there a chance there was some kind of mix-up?"

"Students submit all their papers online at Grace Hall," Liv said. "They use a secure e-mail system, so I don't see how there could have been an error."

"And then you print them out?" Lew asked.

"Yes, well, actually my student assistant opens them and prints them out for me. I run the plagiarism program after I've read the hard copy. I'm required these days to check, but I considered it an afterthought. It never occurred to me that it would actually flag something," Liv said. "And why wouldn't Amelia have just said it wasn't her paper? She refused to give me any explanation when I asked her about the copied sections. Believe me, I asked and asked. I practically begged her."

"I don't know why Amelia didn't explain," Lew said. "But I think we should at least speak with your assistant."

"Oh, okay," Liv said, looking nervous. "Her name is Bethany— actually, before I give you her last name, may I just check with Delia, Mrs. Pearl, first? These days, Grace Hall has such crazy restrictions about giving out student information and such draconian punishments for running afoul of them."

"These days?" Lew asked.

"Let's just say they've reiterated several times recently what they claim were always the policies about student confidentiality," Liv said. "Anyway, I can't do something that will get me fired. I complain about this office and some of the school's rules, but I'm not ready to be a starving novelist just yet."

"Not a problem." Lew handed her his card. At the same time he handed Kate the Birds of a Feather list, his finger indicating Bethany Kane's name. "You can reach me here once you've spoken to Mrs. Pearl. And we'll need you to do it quickly, for obvious reasons."

Bethany Kane was in the Birds of a Feather group. She'd switched Amelia's papers online, then printed out the new one before giving it to Liv. The Birds of a Feather had set it up to make it look as if Amelia were cheating. Did it even matter anymore what had happened up there on the roof? Even if it had turned out that Amelia had jumped on her own—though that was still not what Kate believed—she knew now that her daughter had been bullied to death. The only thing Kate still didn't know was why. *Why* had those girls hated Amelia so much, and so suddenly?

"Yes." Liv stared down at the card. "Of course, I'll speak to her as soon as possible."

"Can I ask you something else?" Kate's voice was gravelly and hoarse.

"Of course," Liv said.

"We found a bunch of notes in Amelia's drawer at home that all said 'I hate you.' Written by twenty-two different people," Kate said, not wanting to say the rest, but knowing that she needed to. "And it looks like Amelia was involved with a group of girls who posted revealing pictures of themselves up on the Internet."

"Revealing pictures?" Liv looked as horrified as Kate felt, which was both disquieting and comforting. "*Amelia?* I find that so hard to believe. I mean, there are a lot of kids at Grace Hall who don't exactly have their heads screwed on straight, but Amelia was never one of them."

"So you don't have any idea what it's about?" Kate asked. "The group online was called Birds of a Feather. It seems like they had meetings after school and things like that. Like they were in some kind of club."

Liv crossed her arms and looked down. She shook her head as she stared at her desk. Kate waited for her to say she had no idea.

"I'm sorry, but I can't," she said instead, looking as if she was in pain.

"You can't?" Lew asked, sounding more annoyed than Kate had heard him before.

"Like I said before, Grace Hall really restricts—"

"Wait a second," Kate said. She could feel her composure slipping through her fingers. "Amelia is dead and this—whatever it is—might have had something to do with it, and you're telling me that you know something, but that you can't talk about it?"

"I'm sorry, but I'll lose my job," Liv said quietly. She looked again as if she might cry. "But you're asking the right questions. I can say that much. You should keep asking them. Talk to Phillip Woodhouse. I know he would— Well, he'd want to tell you. There's this whole thing between him and the school board and lawyers." She shook her head and looked down. "I'm sorry, but I've already said more than I'm supposed to."

"Oh my God." Kate stared at Liv, wide-eyed. "You're actually serious."

Lew put his hand on Kate's forearm again. It was an order. And as much as she hated it, Kate knew he was right. Getting angry with Liv wasn't going to get them anywhere.

"We understand," Lew said. "We're not trying to get anyone fired. We'll talk with the administration, but we'll be back afterward to ask you more questions."

"Yes, of course," Liv said, looking heartbroken. "I do truly want to help, I swear."

"What about this school gossip blog, what was it called, grace-something?" Lew asked.

"Yeah, *gRaCeFULLY.*" Liv rolled her eyes and shook her head. "Luckily, it's stopped, at least for now."

"Why didn't the administration shut it down earlier?" Lew asked.

"They were never able to find out who was behind it. They tried to trace where the posts were coming from, but I guess whoever is doing it has covered their tracks pretty well. I had heard that they were hiring a computer security expert to help. But now that it's down anyway, I'm not sure where that stands." Liv's phone pinged then with what sounded like a text. She reached for it and read, then made an exasperated noise. "God, I'm really sorry to do this, but apparently there's a department meeting that I completely forgot about. Is there anything else I can tell you before I rush off? I'm happy to meet again, too, if that's helpful."

Liv was gathering her things—a pad of paper, her phone.

"Did Amelia ever talk to you about a boy named Dylan?" Kate asked. It seemed like a safe question, one that she should be allowed—as a mother—to ask. "It seems like maybe he and Amelia were seeing each other."

Liv froze, looking from Kate to Lew and back to Kate again. She looked uncomfortable.

"I did hear that Amelia was dating Dylan. Not from her, so I don't know for sure that it was true or if dating is even the right word for it. Involved might be a better way of putting it," Liv said quietly. "But Dylan Crosby is not a boy, Ms. Baron. She's a girl."

Amelia

OCTOBER 19, 9:52 PM

DYLAN

what's up?

AMELIA

not much; what's up with you?

DYLAN

bad mood

AMELIA

why?

DYLAN

idk

AMELIA

lets do something fun 2morrow

DYLAN

fun sounds good; you got ideas?

AMELIA

doing anything w/you would qualify

DYLAN

:) c/u 2morrow

AMELIA

ok c/u xo

OCTOBER 19, 9:59 PM

SYLVIA

   she's one of the Maggies

AMELIA

   who is?

SYLVIA

   the girl Ian's fucking

AMELIA

   no way

SYLVIA

   yeah, one of those Maggie bitches is all over him

AMELIA

   who?

SYLVIA

   don't know; but I am going 2 find out.

OCTOBER 19, 10:05 PM

CHLOE

   party, my place, Friday night 9

OCTOBER 19, 10:12 PM

AMELIA

   when can I c u??? If you keep avoiding me, I'm going to start thinking
   you're a serial killer or something

BEN

   Gee, thx

AMELIA

   I'm joking, sort of. But come on, when r u coming?

BEN

   maybe Thursday, I'm working on it.

AMELIA

yeah! Now I don't need to start blocking your calls ;)

OCTOBER 19, 10:25 PM

COACH BING

correction: bus leaves for sat game at 7:30 am; NOT 8:30 am; do not B
late

OCTOBER 19, 10:32 PM

DYLAN

Sometimes I hate this place. Want 2 run away?

AMELIA

I'm in; when do we leave?

facebook

Amelia Baron

"I thought how unpleasant it is to be locked out; and I thought how it is worse perhaps to be locked in." Virginia Woolf, A Room of One's Own

Sylvia Golde	I totally mean this in the nicest way possible, but you are seriously starting to seem like a freak
George McDonnell	Starting???
Carter Rose	Dude I think that ship has sailed

Amelia

" 'A piece of knowledge is never false or true—but only more or less biologically and evolutionary useful. All dogmatic creeds are approximations: these approximations form a humus from which better approximations grow,' " Sylvia read from her philosophy textbook with dramatic flourish. "In case you were wondering who said that—"

"I wasn't," I said without looking up.

It was our free period, and we were in Grace Hall's brand-new state-of-the-art library, complete with walls of glass, high-tech computer equipment, and old-school touches—antique light fixtures, stained glass, and rough-hewn, refurbished desks. It had been renamed the Rose Library, after the Rose family (Carter, Bennett, and Cole included), who had financed the renovations. My eyes were on my biology lab work, but I was having a hard time concentrating, even without Sylvia talking.

I was supposed to meet Dylan after school. She'd said she had something to tell me. After her text the night before about running away together, I was pretty sure it was going to be something good. Maybe even that she was ready for us to see each other out in the open.

"Ernst Mach, that's who said that," Sylvia went on because, as usual, she didn't care if I wanted to listen or not. "And you want to know what I say? I say, Fuck you, Ernst. I don't even think that's English. And what kind of name is Ernst anyway? It's, like, missing a vowel or something."

"Why did you take Intro to Philosophy in the first place?" I looked up at her. I was annoyed. Sometimes the stuff Sylvia did was so stupid, and she never owned any of it. "Everyone knows that's one of the hardest classes in the whole school. No one told you to sign up for it."

"I like to be challenged as much as the next guy," Sylvia said sheepishly. "You're not the only intellectually curious person around here, you know."

I narrowed my eyes at her. "Oh wait, now I remember. Brian Porter's in that class, isn't he?"

Sylvia shifted in her chair. Brian was the boy she'd been chasing around last spring during registration. Her pre-Ian crush. She'd caught Brian eventually, but he'd wriggled away by midsummer, right on schedule.

"The worst part is that he dropped out, like, the second day," she admitted finally. She shook her head.

"You could have dropped out, too, you know."

"And have Brian *know* I was only in the class because of him? Come on, I still have a *little* pride."

"I hope for your sake that Ian doesn't sign up for Comparative Literature or something next semester," I said. "That one's supposed to be the real killer."

"Whatever, I don't care *what* Ian does anymore." Sylvia was trying to sound tough, but her face got all quivery as she looked out over the crowded library. "You seriously don't read my texts, do you? Hello, I think he's cheating on me."

"Oh, right. I forgot," I said. I hated that we were talking about Ian. Ever since he'd basically admitted to me that he *was* cheating, I'd been trying to avoid discussing their relationship. But if they didn't break up soon, I was going to have to tell Sylvia. And I really, really did not want to do that. "Whatever, then, he's a total idiot."

"See, even you're not saying I'm crazy anymore. You think something's up with him, too." Sylvia looked sad as she went back to scanning the library, probably for Ian. "Whatever, boys suck."

I needed to change the subject away from Ian before Sylvia went off the deep end. And I had been wanting to tell her about Dylan, especially now that Ian knew. The perfect time was never going to come.

"I'm with somebody," I blurted out while Sylvia was still looking around. "I mean, I think. Anyway, you were right when you thought so before."

"Holy shit, I knew it!" Sylvia swatted at me playfully. "For how long? Who is it? You have to tell me *everything*. OMG, I am so excited!"

Sylvia still managed to really surprise me sometimes. I didn't think I'd be able to get her focused on me instead of Ian, not even for a second.

"I guess it's been, like, two weeks or something."

"Two weeks!" Sylvia yelled. The librarian shushed us loudly from the circulation desk. Sylvia flapped an annoyed hand in her direction. "I thought you were going to say a day or two. Two weeks and you didn't tell me? Oh wait, please, please, please tell me you are *not* dating creepy Ben."

"I'm not dating Ben," I said. "And he's also not creepy."

"Not gay, very creepy," Sylvia said. "But that's fine, we can agree to disagree on that. I don't want to talk about stupid Ben right now anyway. I want to talk about this hottie who finally got Amelia Baron laid. *Who* is it? Carter, George McDonnell—I swear those boys have been *dying* to get up your skirt for *years*."

I took a deep breath and stared at Sylvia. This was it. I was about to tell my best friend I was dating a girl.

"I probably should have told you this earlier," I started. It was going to be okay. Sylvia would be cool with it. I knew that she would be. She had to be. "Not that it matters, like, between us or whatever, but—"

"Holy crap," Sylvia said suddenly, ducking her head down. She leaned for a second to peek around me, then ducked back again. "Is that Ian over there? With a *girl*?"

"What are you talking about?" I asked, turning around. Sure enough, there was Ian on the other side of the library, near the reference section and the big wooden globe. He was with a girl, but she bent down behind something before I could make out who she was.

"Isn't that Susan Dolan?" Sylvia hissed. "OMG, she is such a ho."

I'd seen her for only a second, but she could have been Susan Dolan. And if Ian was flirting out in the open with her, it wasn't good. Susan slept around, a lot. Selfishly, I was relieved it wasn't Zadie. At least Susan Dolan wasn't a Maggie. The secret I shared with Ian had nothing to do with his being with her.

"I'm gay, Sylvia," I said, pressing on despite the surprise Ian drama.

Because it was true, and it was time to start coming clean, about everything. And all of a sudden, it felt like now or never.

Sylvia was still totally focused on trying to peek around me subtly. It was like she hadn't even heard what I'd said. Then, suddenly, her eyes snapped over to me.

"Wait, *what* did you just say?"

"I think, maybe, I'm gay."

"No, you're not," Sylvia said dismissively, going back to her surveillance. "Gay is not, like, a maybe thing."

I'd imagined Sylvia surprised, or sad, or even a little freaked-out. But I'd never thought she wouldn't believe me.

"I don't mean maybe," I said. "I mean, I *know*. I know I'm gay."

Sylvia huffed all dramatically. "Okay, you do know gay people have sex, right? Being gay isn't like a backdoor way to be abstinent because— Oh my God." Sylvia ducked down again. "Is that his *hand* on her *butt*? I can't look. You do it. You do it. Turn around and check."

I was trying not to get pissed off. Ian out in public with another girl—especially a girl like Susan Dolan—was big. But after the bomb I'd just dropped? I mean, a few minutes focused on me and my personal drama would have been nice. Then again, I did feel bad for Sylvia, too. Getting blown off like that, in front of everybody—it sucked.

I tossed my pencil to the ground, giving me an excuse to turn and look in Ian's direction. I didn't see him at first as I groped around the floor trying to pick it up. But then he finally stood up from where he'd been crouched behind a bookshelf. A second later, Susan Dolan popped up next to him. I hung there for a second watching them smile at each other as they bumped shoulders playfully. Oh, it was bad. *Really* bad.

"Looking for this?" someone asked.

Next to my hand were a man's trendy brown lace-ups. When I leaned back, there was Mr. Woodhouse, holding my pencil up in the air.

"Yeah, thanks," I said, reaching out to take it.

"Yeah, thanks for that," Sylvia said, shooing Woodhouse away with her hand. "But we're kind of trying to, you know, *study* here."

Sylvia didn't like Woodhouse because he kept threatening her with academic probation. Woodhouse was kind of a hard-ass about academics that way. Mostly kids either hated him or wanted to sleep with him. There wasn't a lot of in-between. Woodhouse looked back at Sylvia for a second like he was trying hard not to hate her back. It kind of made me like him more.

"Can you stop by my office after school today, Amelia?" he asked, turning to me. "There's something we need to discuss."

"What? Why?" I sounded way too nervous. These days, I had such a guilty conscience. "I mean, because I have field hockey after school."

"I already spoke to Ms. Bing," Woodhouse said. "It won't take long." Then he turned to Sylvia. "And Ms. Golde, I'm glad to see you're studying. I got a call today from your Spanish teacher. Wherever your focus has been the past few weeks, it's time to turn it back to your schoolwork. You can't afford to be on academic probation again."

Sylvia was ignoring him, doodling in her notebook.

"Sure thing, *head*master," she said finally, still not looking up.

"Terrific, Ms. Golde," he said, looking bummed-out. "Just terrific, Anyway, Amelia, I'll see you later."

As Woodhouse walked away, Sylvia waved at him like she was trying to physically remove him from her line of sight. Then she started looking around the library in every possible direction. But Ian and Susan Dolan were already gone.

"Great, thanks, Mr. Fucking Woodhouse."

I got a text from Dylan in the middle of AP biology. Your house, free period?

We wouldn't have long, twenty minutes after travel time, which made the whole thing kind of risky. But kind of exciting, too.

I jetted out of school as soon as biology ended. When I turned the last corner, I could see Dylan sitting on my stoop. Her face was resting on a hand, her head turned the other way, as if she were trying to shield it from the wind. And it was kind of cold out, even with the bright fall sun that was making her hair look like it was on fire.

I was a few houses away when Dylan finally turned in my direction. Her face lit up as she grinned. Seeing her look at me that way, I knew she felt the same way about me as I did about her. I was finally sure of it. I was sure of something else, too. I wasn't just into Dylan. I didn't just have a crush on her. I was in love with her. Completely and totally, like, head over heels.

In a way, it was kind of a relief. Because there was no turning back now, not anymore. There was no more being careful. And after being so weird and flighty for so long, it finally felt like something had

changed for Dylan, too. I could see it in the way she was looking at me.
I smiled back at her, my footsteps coming faster now.

"Come inside," I said, grabbing her hand and racing up the steps.
All I wanted to do was kiss her right there, on the street. But two teenage girls making out on the sidewalk in the middle of the school day
was a thing people would notice. Maybe even something they'd see fit
to mention to my mom. "I have something to tell you."

We were still inside the vestibule, the door barely closed, when
Dylan started kissing me, her hands moving to peel off layers of my
clothes. In the rush of hands and skin and mouths, it felt like the words
I'd been about to say, all the important ones, had already been said.
Dylan knew how I felt. And I knew how she felt, too.

Afterward, we lay together naked on my living room couch, our legs
pretzled together.

"I love that your mother is never home," Dylan said, curling against
me and resting her head on my chest. She traced a finger down the
length of my arm. "It must be great just being left alone."

"Sometimes," I said. "But I like hanging out with my mom. It
would be nice if she could be here a *little* more."

I remembered how angry I'd been the time I'd woken her up super-
early to yell at her about whoever my dad was. I'd just gotten another
one of those texts about my dad the night before, and all of sudden I'd
been super pissed off about it, so mad that I hadn't cared anymore if it
hurt my mom's feelings. I'd even dug up all her old journals from the
basement with this plan that I was going to read all of them to find out
what had happened for myself.

I'd started reading some of them, too—a few pages here, a few
pages there—but I hadn't gotten that far. I read a couple of entries
from when my mom first found out she was pregnant and from right
after I was born. It didn't say who my dad was. Mostly, reading it just
made me feel bad for her. My mom had been so alone and scared back
then. I wasn't mad at her feeling that not-so-good way about me as a
baby either, but that didn't mean I wanted to read a whole lot about it.

Plus, it felt wrong. My mom didn't go around reading my private stuff, at least as far as I knew.

And what if my mom had been protecting me from my dad for a reason? She loved me. She would do that. She would let me be really mad at her if that's what it took to keep me safe. And my mom was all I had—all I'd ever had—and I loved her. I didn't want to find out anything that would change that. I could live my whole life with a hole where my dad was supposed to go, as long as my mom would be there to fill it.

"My mom is *always* around," Dylan said. "It's a drag."

I'd met Dylan's mom once, but otherwise I didn't know much about her except that she was an actress who'd once thought she'd be the next Marilyn Monroe—and she was definitely glamorous, like Dylan—but had had to settle for a bunch of guest spots on all the different *Law & Order*s. She was intense with Dylan, too, pushing her to be an actress even though Dylan hated it, wanting her to wear her hair this way or that, always telling her to lose weight even though she was already crazy skinny. Like Dylan was a dress-up doll instead of an actual person. Dylan didn't seem to mind, but a lot of what she told me about her mom gave me the creeps. It also made me glad I had my mom—even if I didn't always have her around as much as I would have liked.

"I thought you and your mom were really close," I said.

"We are. My mom and I are best friends," Dylan said, as if she had it memorized. "Her and Zadie and my dad, they're the only people who know the real me." I tried not to take it personally that I hadn't made the short list. I hadn't known Dylan that long. "Anyway, I'm glad your mom's not here. It gives us a place to be alone."

"Me too," I said, a fluttery feeling rushing into my chest. "You know, I almost told Sylvia about us today."

"Almost?" Dylan sounded surprised and a little nervous.

"Don't worry, I only got to the part about me liking a girl," I said. "Not which girl."

"But that's the most important part." Dylan smiled up at me playfully, her blue eyes shining.

I let go of the breath I hadn't known I'd been holding. I'd been worried that Dylan would be mad at me for even telling Sylvia that much.

"You are *definitely* the most important part," I said, grinning back at her. "The funny thing is that Sylvia didn't believe me anyway. She thinks I'm confused about being gay."

Dylan lay back down and stared up at the ceiling.

"Are you confused?" she asked.

"No," I said, wishing she would look at me. "Are you?"

"I don't trust people," she said, as if that answered the question. She also didn't sound as if she thought this was a bad thing, just a fact I should be aware of. "All they want to do is to put a label on you. Call you this or that. Then that's all you are, forever."

I got the sense that she was talking about more than just us. Like her whole life she'd been trying to outrun people putting a label on her.

"No one gets to decide who I am but me," I said. And, wow, did I mean it. I was actually kind of impressed with myself. I looked over at Dylan, waiting for her to turn toward me, proud of me, too. But she kept her eyes on the ceiling. "I don't care what other people think. I only care about you."

Dylan was quiet then for a long time, so long that it started getting hard to breathe. Finally, she looked at me.

"Okay," she said quietly. More like she was trying to agree with me than that she actually did. But it was a start. "Me too."

"Can I ask you something else?" I knew it was a dangerous question, but I had to know. Especially now. "Were you and Zadie ever, like, together?"

"Zadie? Are you serious?" Dylan laughed hard. "That's so gross. We're like sisters. We've known each other since we were five. Zadie's the only person besides my parents who knows everything about me. She's always been there for me, too, especially when I *really* needed someone, which sometimes feels like it's all the time."

"Oh," I said, not feeling nearly as relieved as I'd hoped to. I wanted to ask Dylan what she meant about needing someone all the time. I sort of understood a friendship like that because of the one Sylvia and I had. Except I felt like Dylan was talking about something different. "That's cool."

"Anyway, Zadie's into guys," Dylan went on. "She and I are just best friends, okay? She watches out for me, but that's it."

"Okay," I said, smiling. Because even if I still didn't totally believe her, I really wanted to. "Good."

We hugged then, and I closed my eyes and breathed in the sweet smell of Dylan's wild hair. Then I had the one bad thought I'd been trying not to think about for days.

"Ugh," I said.

"What?"

"I just remembered that those pictures of me are supposed to go up on that stupid blog tomorrow," I said. I'd been having major second thoughts ever since Ian had taken the pictures. And if I had Dylan now—for real—what did I even need the Maggies for? "I'm not psyched about gross old fat guys with sticky fingers sitting around in their underwear liking pictures of me."

"Yum," Dylan laughed. "You make it sound so delicious."

"I'm serious," I said, but I was laughing, too, making Dylan's head rock back and forth on my chest. "Doesn't it make you uncomfortable having that out there?"

When I looked at the side of Dylan's face, her smile was fading.

"I guess," she said. She shrugged. "But pretty much everything makes me uncomfortable."

"Half-naked pictures on the Internet probably should."

Dylan was silent. Her pictures were already up there. I'd probably insulted her.

"Well, anyway," I said in a lame try at changing the subject, without really changing it at all. "I'm going to tell Zadie I don't want to play anymore. That I changed my mind."

"But she'll kick you out of the Maggies," Dylan said, jerking up to look at me. Her eyes were all jumpy and scared. "I mean, she *definitely* will."

"You're the only part of the Maggies I care about."

Dylan lay back down and was quiet for an even longer time. It kind of sucked. I'd been hoping she'd say something like "Yeah, screw Zadie, we don't need her!" But she hadn't. She hadn't said anything. We were still lying there, bodies threaded together, when I heard the front door open.

"Holy shit," I whispered. "It's my mom."

We were both naked. Our clothes were all the way over in the vestibule. It was one thing to tell my mom about Dylan, but it would be totally different for her to walk in on us like that. I grabbed the throw from the back of the couch and tossed it on top of Dylan. Then I crossed my arms over my naked chest and bent forward, hoping to hide as much of myself as possible. I squeezed my eyes shut like a little kid willing myself to disappear.

"Well, well," someone said. The voice was not my mom's. "Isn't this romantic?"

When I opened my eyes, Zadie was standing there in my living room. In one hand she held our clothes. In the other, she had her iPhone out. She was filming us.

"How did you get in here?!" I yelled. "You can't just come into my house!"

"The door *was* unlocked," Zadie said smugly, moving around like she was trying to get a better shot with her phone. Dylan pulled up the throw so that her breasts were covered and turned her face away. "You guys must have been in quite a rush because I don't even think the door was really closed."

I wanted to get up and grab my clothes from Zadie, but I didn't want her filming me, walking across the room naked.

"What are you, like, a stalker or something? How did you even know we were here?!" I yelled at her. "You can't be here! This is my house."

"Stalker? That's a bit harsh, don't you think?" Zadie smirked. "But, if you must know, I did follow you. And then I waited and waited and waited outside, *forever*." She pulled the phone away for a second, staring straight at Dylan, who wouldn't look at her. "I have to give you two credit. You have stamina. But then I guess it's different for girls."

I waited for Dylan to scream at Zadie. To turn back into that girl I'd seen in Zadie's basement that day. But she was just sitting there, dissolving into the couch.

"Get out!" I yelled even louder. "Get the fuck out of my house!"

Zadie let out a bored sigh as she turned the camera back on me.

"You know, this isn't going to make a very good movie unless you guys do something, you know, interesting." She walked closer, until the camera was only a couple of feet from my face. "You don't get two million hits on YouTube just for being two half-naked girls. It's totally been done. We need action. How about a kiss? Or somebody could maybe grab a boob or something?"

Then something in me snapped. I jumped up and lunged at the clothes under Zadie's arm. She dropped them instantly, springing away so that she and her phone were safely out of reach. She kept filming the whole time, though, as I scooped my clothes off the floor and pulled on my T-shirt and jeans. When I was dressed, I spun around and shoved my face right up into hers.

"Get the fuck out of my house or I'm calling the police."

"That's cute." She leaned in closer. "You're defending her honor." Then she shook her head with disappointment. "Tsk, tsk, Crazy Eyes, I thought you were supposed to be *extra* smart. Do you think Dylan actually gives a shit about you? You think you *mean* something to her? You don't even know her. You're *nothing*. And by tomorrow, you'll be forgotten, like the stale skanky ho you are."

"If you don't leave"—my fingernails were digging into my palms inside my clenched fists—"I am going to make you get out."

"Ooh, how very butch of you." Zadie whistled, then leaned in to hold her camera up in my face. "Is that your thing? You wear the pants? I like it. It's hot."

"You fucking bitch—"

"Stop!" Dylan shouted suddenly from the other side of the room.

When I turned, she was fully dressed, pushing her feet back into her boots. She looked ready to cry. "Please, just stop."

"What are you doing, Dylan?" My voice squeaked, like a panicked little kid. "Where are you going? You don't have to leave. Zadie's going, right now."

"Oh yes, sweetheart," Zadie said, smiling viciously. Dylan was already shuffling toward the door. "I am leaving. And your girlfriend's coming with me."

I got back to school somehow. I wanted to find Dylan before she forgot what we had. I didn't remember leaving the house, but the next thing I knew I was sitting in Liv's class. She was standing at the front of the room talking. I could see her mouth moving, but the words were all garbled and faraway.

I realized she was talking to me only when I saw everyone staring.

"Amelia? I know that *you* know the answer to this," Liv said. "Please enlighten the rest of the class."

When I turned toward the sound of Liv's voice, my head felt filled with wet sand. Like it might snap free of my neck and thud lifeless to the ground.

"Amelia? Are you okay?" Liv sounded worried. "You don't look very good."

Finally, my eyes focused on her. When they did, they filled with tears. Liv was still staring at me when the bell rang and all the other kids moved at once, the room a rush of color and flesh and sound. Except for me. I couldn't move.

Instead, I sat there replaying it over and over in my head—Dylan lumbering like a zombie out of my house. She hadn't even turned back to say good-bye. Then there was that look on Zadie's face, so fucking pleased. The whole thing had turned out exactly as she'd planned.

"Do you need to go to the nurse, Amelia?" The classroom was empty, but Liv was at my desk now. She looked freaked. "You're as white as a sheet. I could walk you down."

I tried to shake my head, but it wouldn't budge.

"Okay," Liv said, sounding unconvinced. "But there is something wrong. I can see that. Do you want to talk about it?"

Did I want to talk about it? Did I want to tell my nice English teacher that the first girl I'd ever loved had just sliced open my chest and plucked out my heart?

"I just got my period," I said instead. "I have cramps."

"Oh," Liv said, looking embarrassed that she'd pushed for details. "Are you still up for stopping by Mr. Woodhouse's office? He asked me to send you down after class. But if you're not feeling well enough—"

"No, it's okay," I said, because it was a thing to do, a place to be. A direction to move in. And maybe a tiny part of me hoped Woodhouse would do something to make Zadie disappear. "I can go."

I sat in Woodhouse's office waiting for him to get off the phone. I could see my legs against the seat of the chair, could see the armrests under my hands. But I couldn't feel any of it. I couldn't feel anything.

"Sorry," he said when he'd hung up. He shook his head. "Alumnae can be insistent. Don't be that way years from now. It's . . . well, anyway, I don't think you ever would be."

I stared at him. I couldn't even pretend to do anything else.

"Are you okay, Amelia?"

Fix it, I screamed silently. *Throw her out of school. Have her arrested.* "I have a headache. A migraine."

"Oh, okay, well then, I won't keep you."

He grabbed an envelope off his desk and held it out to me. I stared down at it.

"It's yours," he said quickly. "Open it."

I stared at it a little longer before finally reaching for it. Everything was moving in slow motion. I felt the weight of the envelope in my hands, saw Woodhouse staring at me as if he'd just given me a present. I felt sure that inside was going to be an eight-by-ten glossy of Dylan and me rolled up together.

"Come on, I already know what's in it. They called me," Wood-house said. He sounded giddy now. "Open it."

My fingers were clumsy and thick as I tried to tear the envelope open. Inside was regular paper, nothing glossy like a photograph. I sucked in a little air as I tugged out a letter addressed to me, in care of the school. My eyes fell on the second paragraph: "This fellowship will cover the full cost of the conference, and an excerpt of your piece, *Today, I Am*, will be published in the accompanying anthology."

"Liv feels badly because she submitted the piece over your objections," Woodhouse said. "She didn't want you to feel pressured to take it, so she decided not to be here."

"Oh," I said, staring down and trying to process that I'd won some fellowship I hadn't even applied for.

But given what a huge mound of shit the rest of my life had become, it did make me a little happy. Not *happy* happy, but less dead, maybe. It was a good reminder that there had been a me before I'd ever heard of the Maggies, or Dylan.

"You should celebrate," Woodhouse said. "You're the first Mittle-branch winner Grace Hall has ever had. It's a testament to your talent, Amelia. Really." Then he took a deep, tired breath. "But Amelia, the fellowship is contingent on my writing a recommendation for you. And to be able to do that in good conscience, I need to know you're out of the club. That you're not a Maggie any longer. I'm also going to need for you to give me the names of the other girls who are members. I've been overlooking a lot, Amelia. You've left school grounds unauthorized at least five times in the past three weeks. I can't write that recommendation unless you help me, now."

"You're *blackmailing* me?"

"Amelia, you know that's not what I mean." Woodhouse frowned. "But these girls are going to hurt someone. I know they will. Maybe not you, not yet, but it will happen eventually. Asking you to do the right thing isn't blackmail. If I can get their names from you, maybe I can protect them from themselves."

"And what happens when they find out it was me who gave them up?" Not that there was any way I was telling Woodhouse anything, not with Zadie holding that video of Dylan and me. "What then?"

"That won't happen, Amelia," Woodhouse said. "I promise."

"Sure you do." I stood up. "Can I go?"

"Yes, Amelia, you may go," Woodhouse said. He looked more than disappointed. Sad almost. "But think about what I said. These girls aren't worth your future."

gRaCeFULLY

Because there are 176 definitions for the word *loser* on urbandictionary.com.
Don't Be a Statistic

Hey people,

So Dylan Crosby is indeed in love. That's the word on the street. Who she's in love with is another question. I know we were all hoping it would be Mr. Woodhouse. I mean, I feel like he deserves a hot, nubile, young thing. But it's not Phillip, as far as we can tell.

A bunch of the senior class—the membership of Devonkill, sources tell me—got picked up by their parents at the 78th Precinct last night. Seems like they mistook a stoop for a nightclub on the wrong block. Come on, people, everybody knows that you don't party on Montgomery Place. That little block is like the nicest in the whole hood. And John Turturro suffers stoop sitters for no man.

But lucky for those idiots, one of their dads is a councilman. So faster than you can say expunged, they were all bounced. One of them did get her sweet seventeen at the Standard Hotel kiboshed. Don't worry, though, sunshine, I've heard that place won't even let you wear tiaras.

We're still a few months off from early decision notices going out, but Zadie Goodwin seems really confident about her early admission chances. Part of me thinks that's because her stepdaddy's been greasing some serious wheels. Then again, maybe she's been greasing them herself, down on her knees.

Kate

Called in sick to work for third straight day. I promised myself it was the last. I'll go back tomorrow. Seems stupid to ruin my whole entire life just because I screwed up a part of it.

Last night, I decided to go drown my sorrows at a bar by myself. And I drank a lot of beer. I don't even drink beer.

But that was what Rowan was drinking. And you want to know who Rowan is? He's the completely cute boy I ended up talking with all night long about his passion for teaching and mine for helping people as a lawyer, which was when I remembered that that was what I'd gone to law school to do: to help people. I was going to be a public defender or help homeless people. Instead, I ended up in the Slone, Thayer pit of corporate greed.

I blame Gretchen. The worst part is that I fit right in. They love me there. I blame her for that, too.

Rowan would never fit in. He's funny and principled and smart, with this great shaggy beard and the warmest eyes. I felt as if I'd known him my whole life, and that was even before beer number three, when I got pretty drunk.

And so by the time he dropped the bomb that he was on his way to Africa, where he was going to build schools and then teach whole villages how to read and probably purify all their water in his free time, I had already completely fallen for him.

We exchanged e-mail addresses. But come on, three years? One night? I give us two e-mails back and forth.

The only really good choice I made was not sleeping with him. At least then it doesn't really count as another failed romance. The kiss was amazing, though. And I needed it. I was pretty much convinced that I was never going to be able kiss anyone again, at least not without feeling like a whore.

Kate

JULY 24, 1997

Jeremy: Are you okay?

Kate: I'm fine

Jeremy: Are you sure? You were out for three days.

Kate: The flu. I'm fine.

Jeremy: I can make an excuse for you. You don't have to be at the meeting. I have your memo.

Kate: No, I'll be there. I'm fine. Really.

JULY 25, 1997

Daniel: Are you coming tonight?

Kate: No

Daniel: Why? You know you're doing the exact opposite of what you're supposed to do as a summer associate. You're supposed to NOT do any work and party nonstop on their dime.

Kate: You do know these firm chats are monitored, right?

Daniel: Slone, Thayer knows the deal as well as I do.
Come. It's a catered picnic for the philharmonic in
the park. Free champagne. A bunch of us are going out
afterward too.

Kate: Ok; I'll come

Daniel: Seriously?

Kate: Seriously.

Kate

To: Kate Baron
From: rowan627@aol.com
Subject: Sorry!

Katie! I just saw your e-mail! I know you sent it about two weeks ago. And I'm so glad you did. How has your summer been? I've thought so much about you since I got here. I really did feel a connection with you, Katie. I wasn't just saying that. And I hope you e-mailing means you felt the same way.

Do I sound crazy? Probably. That's the problem with e-mail. There's nothing to stop me from running my mouth . . .

Anyway, Ghana is cool. Weird and scary and beautiful. And they seem to like my guitar playing, which is a bonus. I wish you were here to see it with me. And I know we don't even know each other. But I still mean it.

Anyway, write with news of the U.S., more importantly, of you. Have you thought any more about bagging the corporate gig . . . ? If you do, we could always use an extra set of hands down here. I'll have access to Internet for the next few weeks, but then I'll be out of touch for six months, I know. Six months. Six months and we only knew each other like six hours.

Then again, things that are meant to work out, usually do.

Everyone has beacons. Lights that guide them home.

peace,
Rowan

Kate

A girl. Amelia was in love with a girl. After Lew had dropped Kate back home, she'd sat on her living room couch, coat still on, repeating the words to herself over and over again. My daughter was in love with a *girl*. My daughter was in love with a *girl*. Her interest in boys hadn't been late blooming; it had been dead on the vine.

Kate wasn't upset that Amelia had been gay, but she was hurt and shaken that she'd had absolutely no idea. None. *I'm sure you had a feeling, deep down*, her friends would have said if they knew. Because in some magical, cosmic way, mothers were supposed to know every important thing about their children. Kate had worried from the start that she might lack this special motherly intuition, but she'd always believed her genuine closeness with Amelia would overcome any shortfall. She'd been so very wrong. That was obvious now.

Suddenly, all those little "I hate you" notes had taken on an even more sinister meaning, too. Was that what the Birds of a Feather group had objected to, that Amelia was gay? It seemed a stretch that being gay would be such an offense to a bunch of teenagers in a neighborhood as progressive as Park Slope. But maybe it had been an affair between two of their members that had been the real problem. Because Dylan had been on the list, too. Lew had pointed out her name after they'd left Liv's office. It had taken every ounce of Kate's self-control not to race straight to her computer when she got home and pull up Dylan's *Birds of a Feather* pictures. But seeing her daughter's girlfriend posing half naked for the camera was, Kate knew, more than she could possibly handle.

She dug her phone out of her bag and texted Seth instead.

Amelia was gay.

In under a minute, he called. As she knew he would.

"What do you mean she was gay?" were the first words out of his mouth.

"I just found out she had a girlfriend."

"Huh." There was a long silence as Kate waited for Seth to say something more.

"'Huh'? That's it?" she snapped. "That's all you're going to say? I mean, did you *know*?"

"How would I know?" Seth asked, sounding defensive. "It's not like we all emit some secret frequency that only other gays can hear."

"But you don't exactly seem surprised."

Seth took a noisy breath. "I thought maybe Amelia was figuring some stuff out. I mean, she was gorgeous and a teenager and without a boy in sight? It raised some flags. But I'm sure none of that was lost on you."

Except that it had been, completely and totally, lost on her.

"Why didn't she tell me?" Kate asked. Her voice was thin, rough. "We were close. Why didn't she think she could come to me?"

"Listen, my parents are lovely people. They love me unconditionally, and we've always been close, too. I knew that my having feelings for other boys would never change that. And look how long it took for me to come out, even to myself. *I* wasn't ready. That was the bottom line. It didn't have anything to do with my parents."

"Then why do I feel so awful?"

"Listen, Lola's only five, and even I know that being a parent is awful ninety-five percent of the time," Seth said. "As far as I can tell, it's that last five percent that keeps the human race from dying out. Four parts blinding terror, one part perfection. It's like mainlining heroin. One taste of life on that edge and you're hooked."

"Yeah, great," Kate said. "You're not exactly making me feel better."

"You were a good mother, Kate," Seth said, turning serious. "You loved Amelia, and she loved you back. You did the best you could. You tried your ass off. How it ends up is a crapshoot. All you can do is be thankful for every minute the whole thing doesn't fall to shit."

"And when it does?"

"You find a good friend with a big shoulder to cry on. I can come over now, if you want. Maybe you shouldn't be alone."

"No, no," Kate said, not wanting the pressure of having to act cheered up. "Thanks, but I think I'm going to take a bath."

"That's an excellent idea," Seth said, even though it was only mid-morning. "Just no maudlin music or candles or anything, okay? I don't want you burning your house down, too."

"Flame-free, peppy sound track. Yes, will do."

As Kate headed upstairs toward the bathroom, her home phone rang. She turned and went downstairs to answer it, only because she thought it might be Lew. He'd had to go back to his office to file an update. He wanted all the T's crossed and I's dotted on the investigation this time. But the number on the caller ID wasn't Lew's. It was a New York 917 cell phone number that Kate didn't recognize.

"Hello?" she answered. Her voice sounded rough, like she'd been asleep or crying or both.

"Mrs. Baron?" the man on the other end asked tentatively. "Am I calling at a bad time?"

"That depends, who are you?"

"Oh right, it would be helpful if I identified myself." He sounded nervous. "This is Phillip Woodhouse, Grace Hall's headmaster. I'm sorry I wasn't there when you came by. I'm at a private-school confer-ence up in Boston."

"Yes, that's what Mrs. Pearl told us. Is it fun?"

Kate could hear herself sounding like a sarcastic bitch. But between his inappropriate e-mails and his role in covering up whatever sick club Amelia had been part of, Phillip Woodhouse wasn't entitled to politeness. He should be counting himself lucky that Kate wasn't screaming at him.

"Um, well, no, not exactly." He sounded confused. "Anyway, I wanted to be sure you'd gotten everything you needed."

"Well, let's see, my daughter was a part of some club at Grace Hall that had her taking half-naked pictures of herself and posting them online. That same group ended up turning on her and sending her hate mail. And apparently, Grace Hall knew about all of this. But I can't get anyone to tell me anything because of rules the school has put in place. *Your* school, Mr. Woodhouse." Kate's voice shook as it rose. "So no, I didn't get everything I needed. But you must already know that. You've circled the wagons quite nicely, Mr. Woodhouse."

There was a long silence, then the sound of Woodhouse exhaling. "I can imagine your frustration Mrs. Baron, but—"

"My *frustration*?" Kate shouted. "My daughter is dead, Mr. Woodhouse. You do realize that, right? Trust me, you don't feel *frustrated* when your only child is killed."

"Killed?"

"Yes, killed," Kate said. "Because Amelia didn't jump. We—and that's the police and I, by the way—know that she didn't. Now it's just a matter of figuring out which of your students—or faculty—pushed her."

"Well, that's— I didn't know there was new information." He sounded genuinely sad or regretful or concerned. Or maybe he was just good at pretending that he was. "I wish that changed what I'm at liberty to discuss with you. Regardless of how I feel personally, I can't tell you anything about that blog or anything in relation to it either. I'm contractually prohibited from doing so. But I assure you, no one is more upset about that than me."

"Try me!" Kate yelled so loud that it burned her throat. She needed to calm down, though. She needed to pull herself together enough to get at least some of her questions answered. "But I guess you're not contractually prohibited from pursuing a relationship with a student?"

"A relationship?" Woodhouse asked. "I'm afraid I don't know what you're talking about."

"I've seen the e-mails you sent Amelia, Mr. Woodhouse. All of them," Kate said. "I don't know what you think you were doing, but I know all about it. And if you don't tell me what I want to know about this group of girls, I'm going to go public with the e-mails you sent my daughter as proof you were harassing her sexually."

"Harassing her?" Woodhouse sounded stunned. "What are you talking about? I never harassed Amelia. Maybe I pushed too hard near the end and I regret that, but I was trying to help her."

"Is that what you people are calling it these days? Some of that special, after-school guidance, the kind you tell a girl like Amelia to keep a secret."

Kate wasn't even sure she believed what she was saying, but she didn't care. She was going to use whatever ammunition she had to get the answers she wanted.

"Mrs. Baron, you have every right to be upset, but I didn't make any kind of inappropriate overtures toward Amelia." He sounded heartbroken. "She was a promising student, an extraordinary one, and I was trying to keep her on the right track. I'd rather you didn't take my e-mails out of context. I'm sure you're right about how they will be perceived if you distribute them. I promise you that we are on the same side here. If you could just be patient. I'm working on getting—"

"I'm done being patient, Mr. Woodhouse," Kate said calmly. "You have twenty-four hours to tell me everything about this club Amelia was in, or I will forward your e-mails to every single Grace Hall parent. And if that doesn't work, I'll pursue a civil action. Maybe even a criminal one. I'm a partner at a very large law firm with substantial resources and I have plenty of time on my hands. So that's not a threat, Mr. Woodhouse, it's a promise."

Kate hung up before Woodhouse could say anything else and stared down breathlessly at the phone in her hand. She'd never threatened someone like that in her entire life. Certainly, she'd never leveraged her position at Slone, Thayer in that way. She really had no actual proof that Woodhouse had harassed Amelia either. The e-mails were suggestive of something, but they weren't in and of themselves inappropriate. Kate had found no mention of Woodhouse anywhere else in the texts she'd gotten through either, not even in Amelia's conversations with Ben. Lew had checked Woodhouse's background, too, and it was pristine.

Of course, that didn't prove he *hadn't* done something this time. And there were still many more texts for Kate to go through. She hadn't even read all of those between Amelia and Ben. Still, Kate had her doubts. She just had to hope that Woodhouse came around before she had to make good on her threat.

Kate was still holding the home phone in her hand when her cell phone rang. This had to be Lew, she thought as she rushed over. But it was Jeremy. He never called her on her cell phone unless there was some kind of work emergency.

"Is everything okay?" she answered, without saying hello.

"Yes, yes, absolutely," Jeremy said, attempting his usual breeziness. But there was something tight in his voice.

"Is it Victor?" Kate asked. "You don't have to protect me. I can handle it." Not that she'd necessarily rush back to the office to help. Her days of compromising Amelia for her job were over. "Is he angry that I'm unavailable? I can't say that I'm surprised. Maybe you really should have given the case to Daniel. Honestly, I think you—"

"No, I shouldn't have," Jeremy said matter-of-factly. "And I'm not calling about Associated anyway. Something's come up, something personal."

"Personal for whom?" Kate asked.

"For us," Jeremy said.

"What do you mean for—" As the words were coming out of Kate's mouth, a hole opened up in the bottom of her stomach. "Oh."

She'd pushed the memory so far from her mind that there were times it ceased to exist. Almost. She and Jeremy had certainly never spoken of it again, and for years that had been enough to erase what had happened. Until now.

"It's terrible timing, I know," Jeremy said, sounding uncharacteristically troubled. Disturbingly so. "But I just didn't— I think you have to know."

"Know what?" Kate felt sick.

"I think we should talk, in person," Jeremy said. "Maybe we could meet somewhere for drinks in your neighborhood around six p.m."

"Jeremy, I'd really rather if you told me now," Kate said. "I'm not sure I can handle waiting for more bad news."

"I know, Kate, and I'm sorry." His voice was somber, almost unrecognizable. It was that tone more than anything that made Kate stop arguing. "But I really think it's best."

"Okay," she said. "Let's meet at the Thistle Tavern at six p.m."

"Sounds good. I'll see you there," Jeremy said. "And Kate, I'm sorry."

"For what?"

"For everything."

It was late afternoon by the time Lew came back, after three p.m. when Lew and Kate were on the way up the steps to Dylan's front door.

"You're sure you're going to be okay in here?" Lew asked, pausing halfway up. "Because the closer we get to the people who were actually involved in what happened to Amelia, the more worried they're going to be about protecting themselves. No one's going to be watching out for your feelings."

Kate tried to hold her face perfectly still. "I know," she said. "I'll be okay. I promise."

Of course, the real answer was no. No, Kate would not be okay. Was not okay. Because she'd already read through every text between Dylan and Amelia. She knew that her daughter had loved this girl and had been desperate to keep her. That Dylan had broken Amelia's heart, though the bits and pieces she'd gathered hadn't explained why.

Lew looked at Kate sternly, waiting for her to crack. When she didn't, he took an exasperated breath and turned back to ring the bell.

An attractive woman with high cheekbones and long auburn hair answered. She was older than Kate, late forties maybe, but striking and meticulously maintained. She looked familiar, too, though Kate couldn't place her.

"Can I help you?" she asked, with a large frozen smile.

Lew flashed his badge, which only served to stiffen her more.

"I'm Lieutenant Lew Thompson, and this is Kate Baron. We'd like to ask your daughter a few questions about the student who died at Grace Hall a few weeks ago. Amelia Baron? Kate is her mother."

"Oh my goodness," she said, with a big, dramatic sigh, then reached out two hands and clasped them around Kate's forearms, pulling her closer. "*What* a horrific tragedy. Unspeakable, really. Come in, come in. I'm Celeste, Dylan's mother."

Inside, the brownstone was full of dark, polished woods, lots of ornate Victorian furniture, and heavy brocades. All of the original details of the home were intact, including pocket doors, stained glass windows, and a tin ceiling. There were lots of small decorative items, too—a collection of snuffboxes in a glass case, small vases, old pictures in heavy frames—covering every available surface. All of it was nicely arranged, but the sheer volume was overwhelming.

They were still standing in the foyer, which felt claustrophobic with an overweighted coatrack and a tall mirrored armoire. But Celeste—who'd dropped Kate's arms just as suddenly as she'd grasped them—didn't look like she had any intention of inviting them any farther inside.

"So you were saying, you came to speak to Dylan about Amelia?"

Celeste's voice was odd. Not an accent as much as overly precise dic-
tion. "I must say, such a exquisite girl. To be that bright and that beautiful. And with those unique eyes of hers? Just extraordinary. Truly. I
told her that she should have been an actress. The camera would have
loved her. And I would know, I'm an actress," she said, with over-
played modesty. "Perhaps, you've seen me on *Law & Order SVU*. I'm a
series regular. I play an attorney."

"I don't watch much TV," Kate said, trying to process this stranger
talking about her daughter as though the two had been good friends.

"Oh, I see, how unusual," Celeste said, as though Kate had just
confessed membership in some strange cult. She smiled forcefully once
again. "Well, then, I guess you wouldn't have seen me."

"How did you know Amelia?" Kate asked, bracing to learn that
Amelia had shared details of her sexual awakening with her girlfriend's mother.

"She was a friend of Dylan's, of course. That's why you're here, isn't
it? But I wouldn't say I knew her." Celeste waved a hand. "I only met
her once."

"We think your daughter might have some information relevant to
Amelia's death," Lew said, trying to steer the conversation back to the
reason they were there.

Celeste put one hand to the back of her neck. "I thought— I didn't
realize there was anything to be investigating."

"There are always more facts to confirm," Lew said noncommit-
tally. He was being careful, maybe because he suspected Dylan was
more involved in what had happened than he had let on, even to Kate.
"Is your daughter home, ma'am? I can promise it won't take long."

Celeste looked from Lew to Kate, then back to Lew, as if she were
calculating the path of least resistance.

"Of course," she said finally, with another fake smile. "I'll go get her."

When she came down the steps a minute later, Dylan was behind
her. She was a beautiful girl, with a head of wild reddish curls like her
mother's and the kind of dramatic bone structure usually reserved for
adults. She was tall and willowy, too, even in her ripped, boyish jeans

and plain white T-shirt. And there she was: the girl who had broken Amelia's heart. *Who gave you the right?* Kate thought. *When there's no way you deserved her.* Kate was glad that she'd agreed to stay quiet. She couldn't imagine the things she might say.

"Hi, Dylan, I'm Lieutenant Lew Thompson," he said, then turned to Celeste as he motioned to the crowded living room. "Mind if we have a seat?"

"Please," Celeste said with a grand gesture. "Make yourselves right at home."

Dylan shuffled in behind them, setting herself down stiffly next to her mother on the edge of the hard tufted couch. She hadn't made eye contact with anyone, and her body language was tight and closed. She was nervous, maybe, but it seemed to Kate like something more.

"Dylan, some of the things I have to ask you about may be sensitive," Lew said. His manner was light, as though he was talking to a much younger girl. "Do you want to take a minute first and get your mom up to speed here about this Birds of a Feather group?"

Kate watched for worry to cloud Celeste's face. Instead, she smiled easily.

"Oh, don't worry. My daughter and I don't have any secrets, Lieutenant," Celeste said.

"As parents we'd all like to think that," Lew began gently. "But in this particular situation—"

"I know about the pictures, if that's what this is about," Celeste said.

"You knew?" Kate asked in disbelief.

Celeste should have said something to the school, to the other parents, to somebody. For the sake of the other girls, if not her own. What kind of mother was she?

"I wouldn't say I'm pleased Dylan participated, but I don't believe in hovering. She has the right to make her own choices, which includes the right to make poor ones."

Dylan leaned her head against her mother's shoulder then, and Celeste wrapped an arm around her head. It might have been a sweet

expression of mother-child affection, if it hadn't been so disconcert-
ingly childlike. As Celeste ran a hand over her daughter's hair, it was
as if she were comforting an overwhelmed toddler.

"In that case, we'll just get down to it," Lew said, his mouth pulled
flat. "So you're in this Birds of a Feather group, Dylan?"

Dylan looked to her mom, who nodded for her to continue.

"Yeah," she said, numbly. "The Magpies—that's what they're called."

Magpies. Maggie #1, Maggie #2. They were definitely aliases for
the girls in the Birds of a Feather group.

"It's some kind of club?" Lew asked.

Dylan nodded. She was staring at the floor and pulling her
sleeves down over her hands and popping them back out over and
over again.

"A secret club," she said, without looking up. Now she was thread-
ing her fingers together and pulling them apart, over and over. "With
secret invitations and secret rules and secret secrets."

"The clubs have a long history at Grace Hall, long before even my
days as a student there," Celeste said smoothly. "I was a Grace Hall
lifer, just like Dylan. The idea of the clubs is actually quite charming.
You know . . . the camaraderie, the sisterhood. They were abolished
because of an incident right before I came to the Upper School. A
tragedy, no doubt, but an isolated one. It was a shame for all the students who came afterward, myself included, that they issued such a
blanket prohibition."

Kate saw Lew's face visibly tighten. Celeste was getting under his
skin. It was her preening, maybe, or her utter obliviousness to what
had been at stake for the girls. It was hard to say what was bothering
him the most. There were so many options.

"And Amelia was in this Magpie club, too?" Lew asked, forcing his
attention back to Dylan.

"For a little while."

"Long enough to get her pictures posted."

Dylan shrugged. "I guess."

"And what was the point of the pictures?"

"It was a game," Dylan said. Her voice was mechanical. "The person with the most 'likes' wins."

"A *game*?" Kate asked in disbelief. She just couldn't stay quiet any longer. "What could you girls possibly have been . . ."

But getting outraged certainly wasn't going to make Dylan be any more forthcoming. It would offend Celeste, too, who'd already made clear she thought the whole thing was good fun.

"Whose idea was this game?" Lew asked.

Dylan gripped the couch on either side of her, then began tapping her fingers in a quick, almost playful rhythm that was completely at odds with the somber conversation they were having.

Finally, Dylan shook her head, then shrugged. "I don't remember."

But it was obvious she was lying, covering up for someone.

"What would happen if someone refused to play?"

"I don't know," Dylan mumbled, staring at her shoes. Suddenly, her fingers froze. "No one ever said no."

"Not even Amelia?" Lew asked.

Dylan shook her head, shifting around on the couch uneasily.

"You and Amelia were close, weren't you?" Kate asked.

She shouldn't be asking about their relationship. It was for Lew to do. They'd discussed it specifically. But it was too much with Dylan sitting right there, holding all the answers.

Dylan looked up at her mom, as if she was trying to tell her something with her eyes. Celeste put a hand over her daughter's and squeezed.

"Dylan and Amelia did have a close friendship, if that's what you're asking, Kate," Celeste said calmly.

"It was more than a friendship," Kate said, willing herself to stay calm, too.

Celeste waved a hand with theatric flourish. "They're teenagers. These things between them, they're ephemeral, and the lines are much blurrier than they were in our day. Wouldn't you agree?" Celeste waited for Kate to nod. She didn't. "Personally, I don't think teenagers understand what their relationships are half the time, much less why they end."

A warning had risen up in Celeste's eyes, too. She didn't like where the conversation was headed, and she was fully prepared to push back and push back hard if necessary.

"I've read Amelia's texts," Kate said, forcing herself to stay seated, even though all she wanted was to jump up, grab Dylan, and shake her until she admitted what those girls had done to Amelia and why. "Honestly, there didn't seem to be anything blurry about it. Amelia was in love with Dylan."

Celeste smiled stiffly and crossed her arms.

"Perhaps we should back up for a minute," she said. "Why exactly are you here, now, all these weeks later? We were told that Amelia had cheated and that it had led to her suicide. Impulsive suicide—that was what they called it. We were even given instructions about what to look out for in our own children."

"Who told you that?" Kate asked.

"At the school's assembly for parents," Celeste said.

"Assembly?"

"Right after Amelia . . . right after. Parents had questions. They wanted to understand. The school counselor was there and an outside expert, I think." Celeste turned to look at Dylan, who'd sunk deeper into the couch, her hands returned to their tapping, this time even faster. "I'm sorry, but my daughter has— This kind of situation can be stressful for her." She looked from Lew to Kate, seeming aggravated that what she'd given them so far hadn't been enough. "If you must know, Dylan sometimes has difficulty processing social situations." She squeezed her daughter's hand. "It's an extremely mild condition, *extremely*. Frankly, I think this discussion would be stressful for anyone. Regardless, you'll need to finish up your questions, *now*."

A condition? There were the tics with her hands, the way Dylan hadn't made eye contact with them, the distance that had taken over her face. Kate didn't know exactly what condition Celeste was referring to, but a difficulty processing social situations could have explained why Amelia had found Dylan's behavior confusing.

"Did Amelia know?" Kate asked, turning to Dylan for an answer. "About your condition?"

"Grace Hall doesn't even know," Celeste said, jumping in to answer on Dylan's behalf. "Only a very select group of trusted family and friends do. We've never wanted Dylan labeled unnecessarily."

"Zadie knows," Dylan said robotically. "Zadie knows everything."

The way she said it made the hair on Kate's arms stand on end.

"As I said, we consider Dylan's situation a private family matter." Celeste rose abruptly. And it was clear that by *private* she meant *secret*. It was also clear that she regretted mentioning it. "We've tried to be as helpful as we can. I ask that you respect our privacy by not mentioning Dylan's situation to anyone at Grace Hall. College applications are on the horizon. We wouldn't want to confuse the issue."

"Yeah, sure," Kate said quietly.

She was still staring at Dylan. Couldn't take her eyes off the girl. Kate had been so sure that Dylan was the villain. Now it was hard not to feel sorry for her, too. She didn't know what it was like for Dylan to function within her limitations, much less what it was like for her to pretend—at her mother's request—that she didn't have them. Kate had felt the terrible weight of her own daughter's secrets. And they were enough to break her heart.

"Now, if you wouldn't mind," Celeste said, motioning toward the door.

"One last thing," Lew said as he stood. "Dylan, Amelia was asked to leave the club, wasn't she?" He pulled out one of the "I hate you" notes from his back pocket and put it on the table. Dylan nodded as she looked down at the piece of paper but didn't reach for it. "What was she kicked out for?"

There was a long silence. It filled the room, pressing out hard on the windowpanes.

"Because she liked me, and I liked her back," she whispered finally, still staring down at the notes. When she looked up at Kate, there were tears in her eyes. "But Zadie invited Amelia into the club because of you."

They walked in silence for a few blocks after they'd left Dylan's house. Kate felt shell-shocked. It didn't help that she had even more questions now. Celeste had whisked Dylan away before they could get her to explain how Kate could possibly have been the reason Amelia had been invited into the Magpies.

"Before I go," Lew said when they reached Kate's house. His hands were pushed deep in his pockets, eyes to the ground. "You're going to need to tell me."

"Tell you what?" Kate asked.

"What Dylan meant when she said that Zadie tapped Amelia because of you." His voice was calm but serious.

"I honestly have no idea." Kate felt guilty even though she had nothing to hide. But she knew how it looked. If she were Lew, she would have wondered, too. "I've never met that girl in my entire life. I don't even know what she looks like."

"But you did meet her mother," Lew said. "She came by your house, didn't she?"

"To ask about that suicide awareness benefit the PTA wants to do in Amelia's honor. I did ask her not to do it, which apparently they've decided to ignore, because they're going ahead with it. But I did mention that there had been some new developments." Kate pressed a hand flat against her hollow stomach. God, why had she told Adele anything? "But that can't have had anything to do with it. Amelia was invited into the Magpies months before I ever met her mother."

"Then it's something else," Lew said. "But Dylan wasn't making that part up. It was too far-fetched, not to mention unnecessary."

Kate stared at the ground, racking her brain. "I just— I don't know what it could be."

Lew looked her straight in the eye for a minute, then nodded, like he'd come to some conclusion.

"Then we'll just have to ask Zadie," he said, starting to back away. "But tomorrow. You need some time off."

"I don't. I could—"

"You do," Lew said firmly. "And don't bother arguing. I've got five kids, remember? I've got a lot of practice sticking on no."

Everything ached as Kate sat down hard in her desk chair and reached to turn on the lamp. As she did, she noticed the picture of Amelia up on the shelf. Age seven, she was propped on her toes at the edge of the waves on one of their many trips to Coney Island. Arms outstretched, she was kissing the air. It had always been Kate's favorite picture of Amelia. To her, it was proof that they had had a happy life together. That they had been a family with their own history and traditions. A tiny family, but one that had worked. Kate had made a lot of mistakes in her life, too many. She certainly hadn't been a perfect mother either, but she had built something for her daughter that mattered.

"Why did you have to pick *that* girl, Amelia?" Kate heard herself say out loud. The worst part was how familiar her daughter's choice had been, so similar to so many of her own. "She's beautiful, I get that part. But she's so, I don't know, troubled. It's not her fault—look at her mother. But didn't you see it? I would have thought you'd see that."

Kate hadn't allowed herself to do this since Amelia died, talk out loud to her dead daughter. The thought of doing so had always made her feel unhinged. For some reason, it was a comfort now. Perhaps because she was already so undone.

"Whoever broke up with who or why, she was lucky to have you," Kate said. "Anybody would have been. I hope you know that."

Kate paused then, staring again at the picture. She wasn't waiting for an answer, at least not exactly.

"You could have told me about her, too. You loving her would never have made me love you any less."

Kate was still staring up at the picture when her phone rang. DAD

CELL read the caller ID. Her father calling her? If it had been her mother, she would certainly have let it go to voice mail. But her father never called, certainly not from the cell phone he hardly ever used.

"Dad, what's wrong?" Kate asked. Her parents were reasonably healthy, but they weren't exactly young anymore. There was some staticky noise on the other end, but nothing else. Kate wondered for a minute whether her dad had dialed her number by accident. "Dad, are you there?"

"Oh, yes," he said finally, clearing his throat. "I was momentarily distracted, apologies. I was taking a walk down to the lake, and I could have sworn I just saw a White-crested Elaenia. Of course, that's not possible because that's a South American bird, but—" His voice was filled with childlike wonder. Kate could hear him breathing harder, too, as though he was walking faster. "Let me circle back here and check. Bear with me for a moment."

"Dad?" Kate asked, even though it sounded like he'd pulled the phone away from his ear again. "Dad?"

"Oh yes, sorry," he said, returning to the phone finally. The awe in his voice was gone. "I must have been seeing things. I'm afraid birding might be a young man's game, not that you'd suspect it from the demographic of that Galapagos cruise I was just on." He cleared his throat. "In any event, your mother asked that I call and check in on you."

"Mom asked that you call me?" Kate suspected her dad was making that up in order to keep some emotional distance. "I find that hard to believe."

"The truth often is," he said. "But yes, she asked that I make sure you were okay. She seems upset about the last conversation the two of you had. I didn't press for details. You know I don't like to get into the middle of things. But I did say I would call. Are you okay, Kate?"

"No," she said, resisting the temptation to tell him what he wanted to hear, but having no real interest in sharing any details. She knew he didn't really want details anyway. "I'm not sure I am."

"Yes, well," he said quietly. "I suppose some things never do get any better."

It was the first time he had ever just let her bad feelings be. She'd thought for sure she'd heard him wrong.

"No, they don't," Kate said, her voice wavering.

"You know, your mother means well," her father said more stiffly. He was treading into uncharted emotional waters, and his discomfort was obvious. "She doesn't always know how to . . . Remember when we first came to New York to meet Amelia right after she was born? Did you know your mother cried all the way back to the airport because she was so worried about you?"

"I don't think that's why—"

"It is," he said. "She didn't cry again, that's not your mother's way. But on that day . . ." He took a deep breath. "So will you be okay? Can I tell your mother that?"

Her father was many things, but he wasn't a liar. Kate wasn't entirely sure that she believed this story about Gretchen racked with motherly concern, but at this very late date, she also wasn't sure that it mattered.

"To be honest, I don't know if I will be okay, Dad," Kate said, her eyes filling with tears. She was so overwhelmed suddenly by sadness and regret, coming from infinite directions. "But you can . . . You should tell Mom that I will be."

The Thistle Tavern was much busier at six p.m. on a weekday than Kate would have expected, but then she'd never actually been inside. It was just one of the many grown-up neighborhood spots she'd always wanted to visit but had never had the time to.

Inside, the tavern didn't disappoint. It was filled with dark woods and muted brass, the menu etched on a big chalkboard above the bar, and servers who—with their peekaboo tattoos and scruffy facial hair—looked as if they'd just walked off the set of an independent film. She saw Jeremy sitting at the short, crowded bar, his back to the door. He was nursing a beer and chatting with the sideburned bartender like the two were old college buddies, slipping effortlessly, as usual, into some stranger's skin.

"Hi," Kate said, interrupting them.

Jeremy turned and smiled brightly. He jumped off his stool and gallantly offered it to Kate. She took it only because it would have been more awkward not to. The bartender seemed disappointed, not so much that they were being interrupted, but that it was Kate who'd done the interrupting. Like he'd had higher expectations for whoever it was Jeremy had been waiting for. Kate looked down at her clothes, an old sweater, jeans, and overly practical weekend clogs. Her hair was pulled back, too, and she had no makeup on. Someone like Jeremy did deserve better, but it wasn't as though it were a date. And Kate, as she was at the moment, was the best she could do.

"What can I get you?" the bartender asked, a little begrudgingly.

"A glass of white wine," Kate said, not that she felt like having a drink.

"I'll get you a list."

"Oh, I don't need a list," Kate said. "You can pick it."

"The most expensive one it is," the bartender said, winking at Jeremy.

The stool next to Kate opened up, and Jeremy took a seat as the bartender was bringing Kate's wine. They sat in silence until he was gone again.

"Did you not go into the office today?" Kate asked, motioning to Jeremy's jeans and fashionably casual button-down.

"I ended up leaving early." He shook his head and took a long sip of beer. "I needed some space. Some time to think."

"About what?"

"Oh, lots of things," he said, staring down into his drink as he worked his way up to saying something. "Listen, I know this is late in coming, but I wanted to apologize, Kate, for what happened between us, you know, back then. It was totally inappropriate for me to have that kind of relationship with you."

Kate felt a flash of anger. She could not believe Jeremy was doing this now.

"You cannot be serious."

Jeremy looked confused. "What do you mean?"

"You called me out here in the middle of everything else I'm going through to talk about you regretting the *one* night—no, one *hour*—we spent more than a *decade* ago?"

Jeremy looked wounded. He truly believed he was always at the front of everyone's mind.

"I just wanted to be sure that you know I take full responsibility," he said. "Especially now, I feel like— It's important to me that you know that it wasn't your fault."

"My *fault*?" Kate laughed a little crazily. But then the situation was crazy. "Fine, I know it. Now, can I go?"

Jeremy frowned, then pulled a folded piece of paper out of his shirt pocket. He held it out to Kate.

She didn't take it. "What is that?"

"It was on inside-the-law dot com this morning," he said, as Kate reluctantly took it from him. "I'm having someone try to figure out who's responsible, but that's easier said than done."

Kate looked down and read: "Slone, Thayer's Jeremy Firth Beds Them Down Then Boosts Them Up." Kate closed her eyes without reading any more.

"It doesn't mention you by name," he went on. "Luckily, it doesn't mention anybody by name except me. And a lot of the details aren't true. There's all sorts of nonsense about sex in conference rooms and elevators and that it went on for years. But I think there could be enough in there that people might guess that some of it is about you."

"Oh my God," Kate said, tears rushing to her eyes. "What about Vera?"

"She hasn't read it." Jeremy shook his head. "At least not yet. Somebody will probably tell her eventually, though I'm not sure who'd want to be the messenger."

He turned to look at Kate, then back down into his beer.

"I feel so—" She cupped a hand over her mouth. "Poor Vera. She's going to hate me."

"That's not Vera's style. She'll definitely hate me, but not you," he said quietly. Then he took a deep breath. "You should also know that the post mentions other women, too. They're wrong on the details, but they're not wrong that there were other women. I wish I could say otherwise."

"I knew there were other women," Kate said, feeling ashamed hearing herself admit it and annoyed with Jeremy for thinking she'd been naive enough to believe she was the only one. "Even back then I knew it."

Knowing that Jeremy had slept with—was sleeping with—other female associates around the time they'd slept together had actually made Kate feel better. Somehow, it had made her less accountable.

"I'm not proud of the person I was," Jeremy said. "But I'm different now. I've been different for a long time. I've been one hundred percent faithful to Vera for the past decade. I wasn't always, but I'm a good husband now."

Kate stared at him, her body rocking ever so slightly from the force of her pounding heart. What was it he wanted from her? Absolution? She had none to give. And she had more important things to worry about than Jeremy's misdirected conscience. She needed to get out of that bar and away from him.

"I have to go," she finally managed, shoving herself off the stool.

"Wait, where are you going?" Jeremy asked, jumping to his feet. "There's something else we need to talk about, Kate."

"No, there isn't," Kate said, brushing past him toward the door. "And I'm not angry, Jeremy, or upset, or whatever it is you think I am. But I never want to talk about any of this, ever again."

Kate tried to breathe as she rushed away from the Thistle Tavern toward her house, but the burning in her lungs only pushed her closer to the edge of tears. She looked over her shoulder once to make sure that Jeremy wasn't following her. When she turned back, the sidewalk blurred as she started to cry. She cried hard as she walked down crowded Seventh Avenue, a hand clamped over her grimace, tears streaming down her face as she wove past all the people staring at her. Her phone vibrated then in her pocket. Jeremy had sent a text instead of following. Of course he had. *I'm sorry, come back. I need you to understand*, was what Kate braced herself to read. Not that what it said would matter. She was done talking to him, at least for now.

Kate dug her phone out of her pocket and looked down at the message:

What's he going to give you this time, slut?

Amelia

BEN

  any word?

AMELIA

BEN

  give it time; she'll come around

AMELIA

  u don't believe that

BEN

  if she doesn't then she's stupid

AMELIA

  thx

BEN

  I mean it

AMELIA

  I know; g2g not in mood to talk

BEN

  ok c/u

OCTOBER 21, 9:18 PM

SYLVIA

dude, what is up?

AMELIA

nothing

SYLVIA

you looked seriously out of it at school

AMELIA

I have my period

SYLVIA

oh, bummer; I stalked Susan Dolan today

AMELIA

oh geez

SYLVIA

you know she goes and buys a big ass BAG of twizzlers at the rite aid
after school and eats them ALL on the way home

AMELIA

gross

SYLVIA

she must barf them up too that skinny bitch

AMELIA

g2g; I don't feel good

SYLVIA

ok; c/u ltr; get yourself some midol or some shit

OCTOBER 22, 2:01 AM

BLOCKED NUMBER

bitch

OCTOBER 22, 2:02 AM

BLOCKED NUMBER

slut

OCTOBER 22, 2:03 AM

BLOCKED NUMBER
  whore

OCTOBER 22, 2:04 AM

BLOCKED NUMBER
  dyke

OCTOBER 22, 2:05 AM

BLOCKED NUMBER
  bitch bitch bitch bitch

OCTOBER 22, 2:10 AM

BLOCKED NUMBER
  die bitch die

OCTOBER 22, 2:11 AM

BLOCKED NUMBER
  loser slut

OCTOBER 22, 2:12 AM

BLOCKED NUMBER
  nasty skank

OCTOBER 22, 2:13 AM

BLOCKED NUMBER
  whore

OCTOBER 22, 2:14 AM

BLOCKED NUMBER
carpet muncher

OCTOBER 22, 2:15 AM

BLOCKED NUMBER
cunt, cunt, cunt

OCTOBER 22, 2:20 AM

BLOCKED NUMBER
queer

OCTOBER 22, 2:21 AM

BLOCKED NUMBER
lesbo bitch cunt

OCTOBER 22, 2:22 AM

BLOCKED NUMBER
homo

OCTOBER 22, 2:23 AM

BLOCKED NUMBER
dyke, dyke, dyke, die

OCTOBER 22, 2:24 AM

BLOCKED NUMBER
ho bag

OCTOBER 22, 2:25 AM

BLOCKED NUMBER
  dirty skanky tramp

OCTOBER 22, 2:30 AM

BLOCKED NUMBER
  fucking bitch I hope you die

OCTOBER 22, 2:31 AM

BLOCKED NUMBER
  pussy lover

OCTOBER 22, 2:32 AM

BLOCKED NUMBER
  lying whore

OCTOBER 22, 2:33 AM

BLOCKED NUMBER
  we

OCTOBER 22, 2:34 AM

BLOCKED NUMBER
  know

OCTOBER 22, 2:35 AM

BLOCKED NUMBER
  where

OCTOBER 22, 2:36 AM

BLOCKED NUMBER

you

OCTOBER 22, 2:37 AM

BLOCKED NUMBER

live

OCTOBER 22, 2:38 AM

BLOCKED NUMBER

and

OCTOBER 22, 2:39 AM

BLOCKED NUMBER

we're

OCTOBER 22, 2:40 AM

BLOCKED NUMBER

coming

OCTOBER 22, 2:41 AM

BLOCKED NUMBER

for

OCTOBER 22, 2:42 AM

BLOCKED NUMBER

you

facebook

Amelia Baron

"The eyes of others our prisons; their thoughts our cages." Virginia Woolf,
Monday or Tuesday

Carter Rose	that is one depressed chick
Ainsley Brown	I think it's beautiful
Carter Rose	maybe that means you're one depressed chick too

Amelia

The texts started coming in the middle of the night. Attached to each was a shot of me in my underwear. I read every single one and looked at each picture. I probably shouldn't have, but I couldn't help it. It was like I couldn't believe it was really happening. After I looked, I deleted each message right away. Because it was one thing to make myself look at them once. After that, they needed to disappear.

The very last text I got was different from the rest. It was about Sylvia. Talk to Woodhouse or anybody else and Sylvia will pay. That slut will never live down what we'll broadcast about her.

It was smart. Because even if I decided I could live with the Maggies humiliating me, I knew that Sylvia would never survive it. If things going south with Ian hadn't sent her reaching for sharp objects again, the Maggies going after her surely would. And she was the only person who was totally innocent in the whole entire situation.

When I got to school the morning after the texts, I saw Dylan in the hall. But she wouldn't even look at me, and she turned fast in the opposite direction when I headed toward her. It wouldn't have been so bad if I hadn't been counting the minutes until I could forgive her. But it's a lot harder to forgive someone who's not looking to apologize.

It wasn't just Dylan ignoring me either. All the Maggies were whispering and laughing, making sure I knew they were talking about me whenever I walked past. After lunch, somebody wrote the word *lesbo* on my locker in red lipstick. At least that's what I'd thought it was until I tried to wipe it away, hoping the whole time that the other kids in the crowded hall hadn't noticed what it said. It wasn't until it was smeared all over my palm and my locker that I realized it was nail polish, not lipstick.

When I came back to my locker after French, it had been emptied out—the books, notebooks, my field hockey stuff, all gone. In its place were twenty-two little notes that all said "I hate you"—one for each Maggie—and six live crickets. I clamped a hand over my mouth and tried not to scream when one of the crickets jumped out at me. I found my books and notebooks in a garbage can nearby. But it wasn't until practice was halfway over that I finally found my field hockey stuff. It was spread out on a bench in the gym, with the contents of a sanitary napkin can dumped on top of it.

That night the texts came again, starting and stopping the way they had before, but this time with enough space in between that I'd start to fall asleep, only to get jerked awake a few minutes later by another text. Like the first night, the texts were all insults or threats or whatever with a picture attached. The last one, which came at 3:53 a.m., was for sure from Zadie. Attached was the video she'd shot when she'd walked in on Dylan and me. In it I looked so angry it was kind of scary, even to me.

Zadie had managed to keep Dylan's face out of every shot. She'd protected her best friend. The video showed only the legs and body of a naked girl, not which girl. I realized now that Zadie had been biding her time for when she'd call a stop to us. She'd known from the start that Dylan would walk out the door whenever she finally said the word. I should have known it, too. I had one of those way-too-close, way-old friendships all of my own. Sylvia got me to do things I'd never have done otherwise. With her it was small things, but I understood how it could happen. And the way Dylan talked about Zadie, their friendship was in a whole other league. From the beginning, I should have known I could never compete.

When I finally got downstairs the next morning, my mom was fully dressed, bag over her shoulder, BlackBerry in hand.

"Hey there," she said, as she rushed around the kitchen getting her stuff together. She looked stressed. "Good morning."

I watched her for a second, not saying anything. I wanted to tell her what was going on. I needed to. But where was I going to start? With the Maggies, with Dylan, with Zadie walking in on us? It was all too much. And no one wanted to start up a sex talk with her mom on purpose. That was a thing you avoided. Instead, I stood there trying to figure out how I could tell her some of it, but not all. That was easier said than done. It was such a tangled mess.

I watched my mom grab a banana from the counter and shove her folders into her bag, then her keys.

"Tonight's going to be a *really* late one. I'm sorry. I know this is ridiculous, but it's going to end soon. And I was thinking maybe we could go somewhere for the long weekend over Thanksgiving. Someplace like Bermuda or something, maybe," she said as she rushed over to give me a kiss, then a hard hug.

"What?" I sounded mad. I was. How could she not notice that something was so totally wrong. "Are you serious?"

My whole life, I'd figured that it was okay that my mom wasn't home all the time, because when I *really* needed her, she'd know it. And she would be there. But now, here I was, really needing her, and she hadn't even noticed a thing.

"Okay, not exactly the 'Yeah, Mom!' I was hoping for, but maybe we can talk about it this weekend."

She was going to leave any second, I could tell. "Mom, can't you just stay and listen to me for *one* minute right now?"

My mom took a deep breath and exhaled. "Yes, Amelia, I can listen, for a minute. I'm always here to listen."

"I want to spend next semester in Paris," I said.

Paris was Ben's idea. I didn't have all the details worked out, but the plan was basically to leave school for a semester. When I came back in the fall, Zadie and Heather and Rachel and a lot of the other Maggies would have already graduated. Not Dylan, she'd have another year. I left that part out when I was talking to Ben. I didn't want to give him the wrong idea that I was still thinking about her. Even if I was.

Part of me was really asking to go to Paris as, like, an actual legitimate solution to my problems. Part of me was hoping that if I started talking about wanting to be in another *country* for a semester, my mom might, I don't know, get the hint that something was seriously wrong.

If my mom didn't agree to the semester away—which I didn't think she would—my next move was going to be to say that I wanted to change schools. I didn't want to leave Grace Hall. I'd miss Liv and Sylvia and my field hockey team. But I'd go if I had to.

"Paris?" My mom was looking at me like I was crazy. She looked stressed, too. She was worried about being late for work, I could tell. I'd use that, too, if I had to. She said yes to a lot of stuff when she was late for work. "For a whole *semester*? And Paris is so far away."

"What does it even matter?" I snapped. *Ask what's wrong. Ask what's wrong.* "You're never here anyway."

"Amelia, come on, that's not fair," my mom said, looking kind of hurt. "And a semester abroad is for college, not high school."

"It'll be educational."

I was leaving out the part about the semester abroad not even being through Grace Hall. It wouldn't help my case.

"Amelia, I wish I could just blow off my meeting and stay to talk this out. But I honestly can't. Can we please talk more about it tonight, when I get home?" she asked.

I tried to swallow back the tears bubbling up in my throat. Why wasn't she asking me what was wrong?

"Just say yes, Mom!" I yelled at her. Because maybe that would work. "It's really easy, listen: yes. Just like that."

She blinked a few times, looking all hurt and kind of shocked.

"Amelia, come on," she said quietly. "I'm not saying no, necessarily. You know I'll hear you out. I always do." She was headed for the front door now. "But I can't do that right this second. Once I know more about the program, maybe I'll feel differently. That means we need *time* to talk about it."

"They need an answer today, Mom."

She turned back at the door. "If they need an answer today, then the answer will have to be no."

"Great, awesome," I mumbled. "That's totally helpful."

She took a deep breath and stared up at the ceiling.

"Are you okay, Amelia?" She asked, her hand on the doorknob. "Because I am stressed about work, and it would be good if I could get there. But I can stay if you need me to. You know that, right?"

I wasn't actually sure I knew anything anymore. I'd been standing there all mad because my mom wasn't asking me what was wrong, but now that she had, I didn't want to tell her anything. Because what could she do to fix it? Nothing. Anything she did would only make it worse. That I was sure about. All I wanted to do was cry. Alone.

"No, whatever, it's okay," I said. "School's just really annoying right now."

My mom came back across the room and wrapped her arms around me. She squeezed me so tight like she was trying to crush me. Or maybe that was the way I was holding on to her.

Finally, she let me go and headed for the door. She turned back as she opened it.

"Everything will get easier, I promise," she said. "It always does."

Dr. Lipton was sitting in a chair in the corner of her office when I knocked on her door. She had a folder open on her lap and was reading the papers inside. Sun was streaming in the window behind her, making her skin look see-through. She twitched up when I knocked. Made me jump, too.

"Sorry," I said, already having second thoughts about this. I'd never gone to see a guidance counselor, ever. But I needed to talk to somebody, somebody who would keep what I told her a secret. "I just, um . . . Do you want me to come back later?"

"No, no," she said. But she was looking at me like a stranger who'd just asked for a bite of her sandwich. "Come in. Have a seat."

She closed her folder and set it delicately on the table next to her.

"What can I do for you?" she asked, reaching behind her for her appointment book. "We didn't have a session scheduled, did we?" She ran her finger up and down the page. "Amy, is it?"

"Amelia. No, I didn't have an appointment. Should I make one?" This was a mistake, definitely. "I could come back."

Dr. Lipton stared at me for a long time, completely motionless, like some kind of lizard. I kept waiting for her tongue to shoot out of her mouth and stick to my cheek.

"Well, you're here now," she said finally. "And you certainly seem agitated, that much I can see."

"Is what we talk about here confidential?" I asked, staying in the doorway.

"Yes," she said, seeming curious now, "it is. Why don't you come in and tell me what brings you here, Amelia."

Finally, I shuffled inside her office. It was pretty and bright, with comfy-looking couches. Too comfy. Like you'd be sucked down into some kind of head-shrinker vortex the second you sat on them.

"Close the door before you sit," she said, and I did, even though I hated the idea of being locked in there. Finally, I made myself sit. My hands felt ice cold when I folded them in my lap.

"Now, what's going on?"

I was quiet for a while, until it got so uncomfortable in there I started to feel kind of sick.

"Someone kind of broke up with me, I guess."

"Kind of?"

"Well, she left, and now she's not talking to me."

"Rejection is always difficult," Dr. Lipton said calmly. She hadn't batted an eye when I'd said *she* instead of *he*. It had kind of been a test.

"Yeah," I said.

As I stared at her, the back of my throat started to burn. I really didn't want to cry in there. Who knew what happened when you cried?

"Do you know *why* she ended the relationship?"

I shook my head again, swallowing over the big ball stuck at the back of my throat.

"She has this best friend who hates me," I finally got out. "But I don't even know if that's what it was. It's complicated."

"Relationships often are," she said. "And uncertainty is never helpful. It allows for too much . . . rumination. Does that make sense?"

I shrugged. "I guess."

"Open questions impede the healing process."

Healing process. That made it sound like it really was over with Dylan. That I might just have to move on.

"And now a bunch of other kids are messing with me also."

"This has something to do with this relationship?"

I thought about the question for a minute. It did suck that Dylan wasn't standing up for me. That she'd walked out of my house when I'd been screaming her name. That she hadn't tried to contact me since. But Dylan hadn't sent me any of the texts, at least I was pretty sure she hadn't. She hadn't written on my locker or put a bunch of bugs inside it. There was no way. Zadie was responsible for those things. And I knew better than anybody that it wasn't fair to hold somebody responsible for the things her best friend did.

"It's separate, and it's not separate. Some of the people messing with me are her friends, I guess. They're all in a club together."

"Ah, a club," Dr. Lipton said. "Let me guess, the Magpies?"

"Yeah, I was in it for a while," I said. It was a relief to tell someone finally.

"This is largely the point of the club, to make outsiders feel badly and to constantly threaten insiders with losing their special status. These dynamics are always fraught with danger. I'm not surprised to hear it has gotten out of hand again."

I shook my head as my eyes filled with tears. "But what they're doing—it's so much worse than I ever thought it would be."

"Harassment is prohibited by the code of conduct, you know," Dr. Lipton said. "If what these girls are doing rises to that level and they're doing it on school grounds, they could be expelled. In fact, I'd be obligated to report it to the headmaster."

I thought about the pictures and the texts and my field hockey uniform covered in blood-soaked waste. I thought about the whispers and the crickets. How the word *dyke* kept popping up everywhere. But did I want them all thrown out of school, if "them all" ended up including Dylan? And what about Sylvia? How would she survive what they'd do to her?

I looked at Dr. Lipton, my heart beating fast. "But you said this was all confidential."

She narrowed her eyes at me. "It is." She held up a finger. "Provided no one is in danger."

She looked at me hard. Danger. She was worried I was going to kill myself or something. The thought had never occurred to me.

"I'm not going to kill myself, if that's what you mean. I just wouldn't—that's not the kind of thing I'd ever do," I said. "But if that changes, I'll for sure let you know."

"Have you told your parents?"

"It's just my mom," I said. It was a reflex. "But no, I haven't told her."

I hated that I'd turned into such a teenage cliché. I would have sworn six weeks earlier that I would definitely have told my mom everything. That I would have told her at the beginning. But six weeks ago, my life had been a whole lot less complicated.

"You should tell her," Dr. Lipton said firmly. "Your mom loves you. She's there to help you."

"That's what I'm afraid of. My mom trying to help and making a bigger mess out of everything."

"At a minimum, you need to confide in someone," Dr. Lipton said. "Bullies thrive on shame and alienation. You need to reach out to at least one friend, tell her about what's going on. You need a support network," Dr. Lipton said. "Can you do that?"

I nodded, even though I was beyond dreading it. Sylvia was, of course, that friend I'd have to go to, and she was going to be seriously pissed off when she found out about the Maggies. Not to mention that I was totally embarrassed. This was exactly why she—and I—had thought that the clubs sucked in the first place. Their whole purpose was to make people's lives hell.

"Then I want you to write this girl a letter, an e-mail, with all the questions you want to ask her," Dr. Lipton went on. "Everything you want to know about what happened. Everything you're afraid to know. But *do not* send it. I want you to imagine the answers."

"Imagine them?" That sounded so totally dumb.

"Yes, imagine them. *Do not* send it," she repeated firmly. "This exercise is designed to give you control over the situation and your feelings. I think you will find that you already have all the answers you need."

"Okay," I said, even though the whole thing still sounded stupid.

"Agreed?" Dr. Lipton asked. She was staring at me, waiting for an answer.

"Oh yeah, okay. Sure."

"Good then." She walked over and opened her office door. "Then make an appointment to come back to see me next week. I'll want an update. We can talk more then about your confiding in your mother."

When I finally found Sylvia at lunchtime, she was in the courtyard with Ian. They were sitting at a table, knees touching as they talked. A few days earlier they'd been practically broken up. They hadn't, but things between them still didn't look good. Ian kept looking around, then pulling back like he was searching for a pocket of air or a place to hide.

Poor Sylvia. Her heart on the verge of being broken again. But there was a little part of me that was glad she was about to need me as much as I needed her. Brokenhearted Sylvia was a lot more generous than in-love Sylvia. At the moment, though, she was so wrapped up in Ian that she didn't even notice me until I was standing right next to her.

"Oh hi," she said, finally looking up. She looked kind of pissed that I was interrupting. "What's up?"

Ian looked thrilled that I'd arrived.

"Oh here," he said, jumping up. "Take my seat. I need to be going anyway."

"Going where?" Sylvia asked him. "We didn't even talk about this weekend. The concert?"

"Oh right, at the Living Room." Ian rubbed a hand across his forehead and sucked some air in through his teeth. "About that. Turns out I won't be able to make it after all. But you should go on, have a great time, luv. We can catch up later in the weekend."

My stomach tightened as I watched Sylvia's face falling. Telling her about my crap would have to wait. I had to help her salvage this conversation. She needed to see it through, for better or worse. I was actually kind of hoping for worse, that she'd put some more pressure on Ian and he'd end up breaking up with her once and for all. Because these half measures were like watching some mostly squashed squirrel trying to drag himself out of the middle of the road.

"No, you should stay, Ian," I said, stepping back. "I just wanted to say hi. I'll catch you later, Sylvia."

I spun around before Ian could stop me and rushed back across the courtyard. When I looked back, Ian and Sylvia were still there together, still not talking. Ian was kicking at the ground with one fashionable European sneaker. Sylvia was watching him, waiting.

The whole rest of the day went by without anything else bad happening—nothing was taken from my locker, nothing written on it. I could hardly believe it. I didn't even get any more texts. By the time I was back home that night, e-mailing the final version of my Virginia Woolf paper to Liv, I was almost feeling relaxed. I figured Zadie had gotten bored with making my life a living hell.

I'd just managed to get myself to fall asleep when the first text came. And when my phone pinged with that first message—skank—it scared the shit out of me. My heart was pounding as I sat up in bed, staring at my phone. It had been smart of them to hold off all day. Thinking it was over made it so much worse when it started up again.

After the first one, the messages came—over and over and over. Each more sick than the last, each with the same picture attached, one that I had never seen. It was me kissing Dylan. Except you couldn't tell that it was Dylan. Only that it was me—definitely me, definitely kissing some girl.

"Can we bag first period?" I asked Sylvia when I met her at the corner the next morning. We were still four blocks away from school. Far enough that we could duck out of the flow without anyone asking questions. "We could go get a muffin or something."

"Did Amelia Baron seriously just suggest that we *skip* school?" Sylvia batted her eyes, pressed a hand to her chest, and pretended to choke. "What's next, the stripper pole?"

"I'm serious, Sylvia. I just—" I turned to look at the school. "I can't deal right now. Besides, I'll only be missing art. That doesn't even count as skipping school."

"I'd be missing Spanish, but considering the fact that I can't understand a goddamn thing anyone is saying in that stupid class, I don't think that counts as skipping either." She linked her arm through mine. "Now, this isn't some ploy to get me alone so you can try to make out with me, is it?" She rolled her eyes as we ducked back down the street, heading for Seventh Avenue. "Considering you are a *lesbian* and all."

"You seriously still don't believe me?" I asked when we were halfway down the block.

Sylvia had texted me a couple of times after I'd told her I was gay with a WTF!! But I'd been avoiding getting into it with her. It wasn't hard. She was so obsessed with Ian that she kept forgetting to ask me about it when we were actually together.

"I believe that *you* believe it," Sylvia said, checking over her shoulder to see if anyone was following us. There were truant officers in the neighborhood, but they tended to be a little racist. They probably wouldn't bother two young white girls whose parents might be more pissed that their kids had been hassled than about their skipping school. "Just because you can't be normal around guys doesn't mean you don't like them. Maybe you're not gay, you're just a freak."

"Wow, thanks."

Without talking about it, we both headed in the same direction, toward the Connecticut Muffin across the street from PS 321. We always went there whenever we were out of school and the public schools weren't. We liked sitting there, watching all those little public-school kids floating by in that huge nutso sea of people. There was something nice about how big and messy it all was. By comparison, it made the morning insanity at our school seem like nothing.

"So what is up with Ian?" I asked once we'd each gotten a muffin— lemon poppy for me, blueberry for Sylvia—and were sitting on the high stools facing the window. I'd get to Dylan and the Maggies, but I needed to warm up first.

"I don't know." Sylvia shrugged. "I finally accept that Susan Dolan has a boyfriend. I saw her kissing him, and she seemed really into him. Ian says everything is fine between us, but he's still acting weird. There's somebody else—not Susan, but somebody."

I didn't doubt anymore that she was right.

"Any idea who?"

Sylvia shrugged. "I'm starting to think it doesn't even matter." Finally, she swiveled in my direction. "But what about *you*? Supposedly playing for the other team is *way* more interesting than Ian."

I held my breath for a second. This was my chance. I needed to come clean, about everything. I needed an ally, like Dr. Lipton had said, and Sylvia was my best option, my only option, really. She was going to be mad about the Maggies, and my lies, for sure. The only way to find out how mad was to tell her.

"I did something stupid," I started finally. "And you're going to be mad at me."

"I don't care if you really are a lesbo, you know," she said. "It's just less competition for me."

I laughed, hard. A real laugh, too. Only Sylvia could have made me laugh at a moment like that. Because only she would have seen me liking girls as a chance for her to get more boys. She was a lot of things, but judgmental had never been one of them. This was going to be okay. All of it. I took another deep breath and sank down on my stool, leaning against the thin strip of counter that ran along Connecticut Muffin's window. Getting the worst part out of the way first was the only way to go.

"I got tapped by a club."

"What?" Sylvia blinked at me.

"I got tapped."

"What?" She asked again, louder this time. Her eyes were even wider. "What club?"

"The Maggies."

"Holy— And you didn't *tell* me?" she asked, looking more floored than mad. "I bet no one has ever told them no. The Maggies, man, they must have been pissed. You have to tell me the whole story."

I took a deep breath and stared down at my half-eaten muffin.

"I didn't tell them no."

Sylvia's face froze for a second, then crunched up into seriously pissed off.

"*You* joined the *Maggies*? When?"

I sucked in a breath.

"At the beginning of the year," I said quietly.

"You're lying!" Sylvia shouted, jumping off her stool. "There's no way you would have been in a club this whole time and never told me!" I could feel the guy behind the counter watching us, trying to decide whether to throw us out. "And what about our pact? You decided to forget all about that?"

Sylvia was right. I was a complete asshole.

"I don't know what happened." It was a beyond-lame excuse, but it was totally the truth for a change. "They invited me to join, and I guess—you always have a boyfriend and my mom's never around or whatever. Sometimes I feel like I don't have anyone."

"Oh please." Sylvia's voice was cold. "Cry me a fucking river."

When I looked up at her, her face was still all pinched up, but her eyes had filled with tears.

"I'm sorry, Sylvia," I said. She was right, it had been a totally selfish, disloyal, mean thing to do. "And I know sorry's not enough, but I don't know what else to say."

Sylvia moved her jaw back and forth, and with each slide of it some of her anger seemed to leak out. Finally, she pulled a hand up to her face, halfway covering her mouth.

"God, I am so fucking stupid," she said, her voice a little muffled. "Here I was, feeling bad because I was spending so much time with Ian, and the whole time you were out with all your new secret friends. I have to hand it to you, Baron, you are one good fucking liar."

She was right. I had told so many lies. They were piled up, smothering me.

"It just kind of happened, and then I didn't know how to get out," I said. When I glanced over in Sylvia's direction, she was still glaring at me. But at least she hadn't stormed out; that had to count for something. "And then I, like, fell for somebody in the club, too, and I was worried I would lose her if I dropped out. You know what that's like, doing something because of someone you like. It's not always so well thought out."

"Is that like a reverse gay panic defense or something?" she snapped. "You get to lie to your best friend and be a total dickhead *because* you're gay?" Putting it that way, it did sound really stupid. I hung my head and shrugged. "I do a lot of crappy stuff, Amelia. Maybe I'm all about me sometimes and kind of slutty and I make bad choices for guys I like. But I have never, ever lied, not to you."

And it was true. Sylvia was always honest, even when it would be easier on both of us if she wasn't.

I was out of excuses. I turned to look at her. Sylvia was staring out the windows now, face a little less angry, a lot more hurt. I sat there, staring at this girl who had been my best friend for almost ten years, who'd stuck by me through third-grade teasing, and a sometimes MIA mom, and a broken ankle in the middle of the summer, and bad haircuts, and ugly sweaters. This friend who had never, ever judged me or asked for me to be anything other than who I was. And all I could do was hate myself. How could I have picked anyone over being honest with her?

"I'm sorry, Sylvia. I really, really am."

I'd expected her to tell me to go to hell then. To say she never wanted to talk to me again. But she just kept on looking out the window. Finally, she took a huffy breath and climbed back up onto her stool.

"Okay, so spill it," she said, still not looking at me. "Because now you definitely owe me every disgusting triple-X detail. First off, who is she?"

I was so relieved, I almost started to cry.

"Dylan Crosby," I said, praying that nothing I said now would make Sylvia turn on me again.

"Seriously?" Sylvia whipped her head in my direction. "I thought she was sleeping with Woodhouse."

I shook my head. "I'm pretty sure she was just sleeping with me."

"Wow, I did not see that one coming." Sylvia nodded then. "She is hot, I'll give you that. If you were going to pick some other chick over me, I'm glad she was at least good-looking. But the *Maggies?*" She stuck a finger down her throat and made a gagging sound. "I mean, I seriously can't be your friend anymore if you turn into one of those bobbleheaded bitches."

"You don't have to worry," I said. "They already kicked me out. And Dylan dumped me, too."

"Ew, bitches." Sylvia looked offended on my behalf. "What happened?"

"I don't know exactly," I said. "Zadie hates me, and she has this weird possessive thing with Dylan."

"Ooh, Zadie, yikes," Sylvia said. *"She's* gay, too?"

"No," I said. "Which makes the whole thing even weirder."

Sylvia blew out some air. "That chick is seriously coco loco. You should steer way clear of her."

"It's way too late for that," I said. "Anyway, I decided last night that I want to send Dylan an e-mail. I was hoping you could help me."

I had heard what Dr. Lipton had said about not sending it. But I was going to have to agree to disagree on that point. It wasn't like I'd made up what Dylan and I had had together. And I needed her to tell me how she could just throw that away. Besides, maybe she was just waiting for me to change her mind.

"An e-mail? Um, you sure that's such a good idea?" Sylvia asked. "Because it sounds like a seriously shit plan to me. If Dylan won't talk to you it's because *she* doesn't want to. At least not bad enough. Take it from me, it's good to listen to people when they tell you something like that."

As if Sylvia had not sent literally hundreds of the exact same e-mail, in the face of much worse rejection. I stared at her for a long time, waiting for the same thing to occur to her. Finally, she shrugged.

"Okay, fair enough," she said, holding up her hands. "I'll come over after school, and we can write it together. But just because I've *sent* a whole lot of e-mails like that doesn't mean any of them ever worked. At least, not in the way I wanted them to."

"Well," I said, smiling, "there's always a first time for everything."

gRaCeFULLY
OCTOBER 24TH

**Because there are 176 definitions for the word *loser* on urbandictionary.com.
Don't Be a Statistic**

---

*We finally have proof that Dylan Crosby isn't a secret Jesus freak! And we
heard it straight from the man himself, who says they went full-on* Animal
Kingdom *in Prospect Park. Her idea. He—okay, George McDonnell—
asked me to keep his name out of it, but a fella ought to get credit. Anyway, doesn't sound real virginal to me. Wherever Dylan has been getting
around, it might not have been in these parts, but it sure as hell sounds like
it was somewhere.*

*Okay, anybody out there able to tell me why one of the clubs is picking
on one poor little honor roll sophomore? And this is like old-school, fire-and-
brimstone crap. What gives? Come on, ladies, the kid can't be that bad.*

*And to that poor little sophomore who just WON'T see the writing on
the wall: just because he has a nice accent doesn't make the lies coming out
of his mouth any more true. Come on now, a little self-respect, please. This
is getting hard to watch.*

*And speaking of self-respect—or lack thereof—looks like Bethany
Kane is making good on her promise to have sex with the whole soccer
team. She's only got three guys left, and two of them boys might be gay. Be
gentle with them, Beth.*

Later, peeps.

Kate

AUGUST 22, 1997

Daniel: Tonight? It's our last night as summer
    associates . . .

Kate: Can't

Daniel: Why?

Kate: Not in the mood

Daniel: I find that hard to believe

Kate: Fuck you

Daniel: Testy, testy

AUGUST 28, 1997, 10:25 PM

To: rowan627@aol.com
From: Kate Baron
Re: Sorry!

Did I miss my window? Have you gone off into the wilds of no Internet access
yet? Hope things are still going well for you. I just wanted to say that you
didn't imagine it. I felt it, too. Maybe it's easy to make more out of things
once they're already over. Or maybe not.

Anyway, I like the idea of a beacon. I could really use some light right now.

Xo,
Katie

SEPTEMBER 2, 1997, 2:19 AM

To: Kate Baron
From: rowan627@aol.com
Re: Sorry!

Totally did not miss me! Awesome to hear from you. Can't write tonight,
there's Kobine on—it's a big local festival . . . I'll write more in the a.m.

peace,
Rowan

Amelia

AMELIA

   you're still coming tmrw right?

BEN

   I think so.

AMELIA

   I HAVE to c u. things have been so bad; cld use a good friend.

BEN

   things are still bad?

AMELIA

   yeah, but going 2 get bettr; Sylvia's helping me write to Dylan

BEN

   write what?

AMELIA

   e-mail asking ?'s

BEN

   like why she's a bitch?

AMELIA

   come on, don't b mean

BEN

   mean? she's the 1 treating u like crap. there's a fine line between devoted
   and doormat

AMELIA

okay, okay, big brother. where are we going to meet tomorrow?

BEN

totally up to u; but like I said I'll have to confirm tmrw

AMELIA

will u come to Grace Hall? maybe I can show u some of these people

after school lets out. promise me you'll come; don't bail on me like

absolutely everyone else.

BEN

I'll do the best I can.

OCTOBER 23, 6:42 PM

SYLVIA

sorry, late. on way to write lesbian love letter

AMELIA

u just like saying lesbian

SYLVIA

I do; L is so good for sexy alliteration; lusty, loose, lips

AMELIA

u are grossing me out.

SYLVIA

then my work here is done; b there soon

Kate

It was still dark, barely past five, when Kate went downstairs to find her phone. There was a new text, this one from Duncan overnight:

> Finally traced Gracefully; almost stumped me; can c why school cldn't; address is 891 Hoyt in Bklyn. Home of a chick named Liv Britton. If you end up talking to her, tell her there's a computer dude in Manhattan sending her mad respect. And if she's cute, do me a favor and throw her my digits.

Liv? The devoted teacher who had supposedly cared so much about Amelia, who had supported her writing and had thought it inconceivable that she would have killed herself, had written all those awful things about all those students, those *children*. She'd written things about Amelia, too. What was wrong with her? She was supposed to be one of the people they could trust.

But she was a liar. A liar who'd accused Amelia of cheating.

Kate was going to see to it that Liv got fired, maybe even sued—defamation, abuse of authority. It didn't matter. One way or another, everyone was going to know what she'd done. Kate was going to see to it.

Lew was scheduled to pick up Kate shortly before eight a.m., but if she had to wait any longer to finally confront Woodhouse and Liv, she was going to wear a hole in her living room floor. Kate's heart leaped when there was a knock at her door a little before seven thirty. She was praying it was Lew arriving early.

"Hi," Kelsey said when Kate swung open the door. She looked tired and unkempt in her baggy sweatpants. Her short blond hair was sprouting up at the back like she'd just rolled out of bed. She held up the meet book that Kate had given her. "I found him."

"You did?" Kate had asked Kelsey to look for the boy she'd seen going into the house with Amelia, but she'd written off the possibility of actually finding him.

"Sorry it took me so long," Kelsey said, flipping open the book to the page her finger was stuck in. "But he's not in the yearbook, and I missed the pages of new students at the back of the meet book. I was paging through it again this morning when I noticed them for the first time."

Kelsey pointed to one of the photos. Kate looked at the name beneath the picture.

"Ian Greene," she said quietly. She recognized the name from some of Amelia's texts. He was Sylvia's on-again, off-again boyfriend.

"That's him," Kelsey said. "It's definitely him."

Okay, but DO NOT talk to ANYONE until I get there, Lew had written in response to Kate's text that she couldn't wait at home anymore and planned to head over to Grace Hall and meet him there. Kate didn't respond to Lew's warning. She wasn't going to make any promises she couldn't keep.

She figured making her way to the school slowly was a decent compromise. When she was finally on Prospect Park West, there was already a steady flow of arriving students. They were shouting and swearing and jostling and laughing. The crush of bodies was awful—claustrophobic and almost frightening. Kate couldn't believe Amelia had never complained. As she marched along inside the mass, she felt the whole time like a bloody riot might break out. Kate couldn't catch a real breath until she jumped to the side of the rush up near the school's front steps.

Standing on the edge of the sidewalk, sucking in fresh air, Kate caught sight of him: Ian Greene. She recognized him instantly from his photo in the meet book. Handsome and sure of himself, he was sauntering toward school with his arm looped over the shoulders of a pretty blond girl. Kate watched his easy smile and confident stride, walking as if he didn't have a care in the world.

The sight of him filled Kate with such sudden rage—uncontrollable, devouring, blind. Someone should *pay* for what had happened to Amelia—Liv, Woodhouse, Dylan, the Magpies. Ian Greene.

Kate lurched forward and back into the crowd. Amelia was gay, and Ian Greene had been involved with her best friend. What possible reason would they have had to be together in an empty house in the middle of the day? Unless *he* hadn't known that she was gay. Maybe when Ian Greene had found out, he'd gotten angry at Amelia. Maybe the next time he hadn't wanted to take no for an answer.

Maybe, maybe, Kate thought as she threaded her way through the pack of students until she was walking right behind Ian. Kate could feel kids staring at her. She heard them wondering aloud what she was doing cutting in front of them, walking in their midst. Who was the creepy lady all by herself? they wanted to know. Before someone official could ask that same question, Kate reached forward and tapped Ian's shoulder.

"Excuse me," she said. "Are you Ian Greene?"

He turned around with such a casual, unbothered expression on his face, like a famous person accustomed to being approached by strangers.

"Yes, I'm Ian," he said, with a proper English accent. Then he narrowed his eyes like he was trying to place Kate. "Sorry, but do I know you?"

"I'm Amelia Baron's mother," she said, hoping he'd flinch. He didn't. "Can I talk to you for a minute?"

"Oh," Ian said, finally looking a little nervous, though not nearly enough, as far as Kate was concerned. "Afraid I can't be late for school."

"Yeah, and we have a chemistry test," the girl chimed in, moving her finger in a rude circle in front of Kate's face. "So, you know, maybe another time."

Kate clenched her jaw to keep from grabbing the girl's finger. "Please, Ian," she said more gently, shifting tactics and hoping to win him over instead on sympathy grounds. "It will only take a minute, I promise."

"Yeah, except a minute's too long, and—" The girl fell silent when Ian turned to blink at her, seeming appalled by her rudeness. "Sorry," she said obediently.

"I'll meet you in class, Susan," he said, dismissing her. "Tell Mr. Hale I got boxed up for a moment."

"What is it I can do for you, Mrs. Baron?" Ian asked when Susan was gone. He pushed his hands deep into his front pockets.

It was a boyish gesture, one at odds with how mature he otherwise seemed. Like maybe he was trying on purpose to make himself seem more vulnerable.

"What were you and Amelia doing at our house in the middle of the school day?"

"Middle of the school day?" Ian asked. He was doing his best to play dumb. It was not the least bit convincing. "At Amelia's house?"

"My neighbor saw you," Kate said. "I just want to know what happened. Why the two of you were together."

"What happened?" Ian's eyes were wide now. "You don't mean, like—"

"I don't think you two were having sex. But I don't understand what you were doing together at our house in the middle of the day," Kate said. Drugs had, of course, crossed her mind. Almost anything seemed possible now. And Ian certainly looked like the sophisticated type who could be into God only knows what. "Whatever it is, I won't tell anyone. I just want to . . . I need to know what happened to my daughter. I need to know what she was doing."

Ian closed his eyes for a second, then looked off over Kate's shoulder, debating. Finally, he looked down and kicked at the ground with one shoe.

"I was on the hook for it to my club, and Amelia was on the hook to it for hers. To be quite honest, I didn't want to do it. She insisted."

"Didn't want to do what?" Kate asked. Her heart was pounding.

"Take the photographs," he said, more casually now.

"The ones posted on that blog?" Kate asked. She tried to stop herself, but all she could picture was her sweet little girl taking off her clothes and lifting her ass in the air for this smug, shaggy-haired, high-school heartthrob. What possible difference could it make that her daughter was gay, if he wasn't? "*You* took those pictures of Amelia?"

Looking at Ian Greene and the cocky, slouched way he was standing there, Kate thought about every boy who'd ever treated her as if she was worth what *they'd* decided. Every man she'd let believe that was true. All she could think about was how much better she'd wanted for Amelia.

"But like I said, it wasn't anything seedy." Ian smiled, oblivious to the fury that must have overtaken Kate's face. Because she could feel it now, coming out of her pores. "I actually think the shots are quite lovely. How could they not be, I suppose. Amelia was such a fit girl. You certainly didn't have to be another girl to appreciate that."

It took Kate a minute to realize that she'd slapped him. Hard and more than once. There was the stunned look on Ian Greene's face, the bright red mark on his cheek and her own throbbing hand. But as soon as she'd pieced it together, all she wanted to do was hit him again. She wanted to keep on hitting him until some part of her felt better. She might have, too, if the big, round security guard hadn't come rushing over and grabbed her arm.

"Whoa, lady!" he shouted, looking stunned. "What the hell you think you're doing?"

"She slapped a student," Mrs. Pearl said to Lew. "Unprovoked and in full view of dozens of witnesses."

They were seated in the headmaster's office, Mrs. Pearl behind the enormous mahogany desk, peering down on Lew and Kate in the guest chairs on the other side. Kate was slumped back in hers, feeling like a surly high-school student, with Lew playing the role of disappointed but protective dad. His elbows were on his knees, and he was crouched forward in a thoughtful listening pose.

"Yes, I understand that," he said gently. "And it certainly would be better if that hadn't happened. But I'm sure that Kate would be more than willing to apologize to Ian, and—"

"*Apologize?*" Mrs. Pearl hissed. "You are joking, Lieutenant. She *assaulted* Ian Greene. A minor, I might add. If I'm not mistaken, *that* is a crime, and *you* are a police officer. I'm wondering why you haven't arrested her yet."

Lew nodded for a long minute, staring down at the floor.

"Fair enough," he said finally, as if he wouldn't mind doing just that. "Of course, that would mean a trial. And at a trial, Ms. Baron would naturally put forth the affirmative defense of diminished mental capacity." He shook his head like he was working through the implications. "And you know what that would mean."

Mrs. Pearl rolled her eyes. "No, Lieutenant Thompson, I do not." She tapped her pencil against her desk three times. "Please, by all means, enlighten me."

"Ms. Baron here would have to lay out everything she knows about those secret clubs, including those half-naked pictures." He paused, then twirled his fingers forward like wheels turning. "And then her lawyer would have to get into how Amelia and Mr. Greene cut school for their own little photo shoot. I can't imagine that boy's parents wanting any of that made public. They might even think their kid deserved to get slapped. What I am one hundred percent sure of is that Grace Hall's parents don't want the school they've paid all this money to going from being a golden ticket to the Ivy League to being known as Porn U." Lew paused, then looked Mrs. Pearl dead in the eye. "Oh, and then there'd be the reporters. School like this, a sexy scandal like that? The *Post* will go nuts."

Kate would have grabbed Lew and hugged him if he hadn't been so palpably disappointed in her.

"Fine." Mrs. Pearl tapped the desk three more times before standing. "But she needs to leave campus immediately. Before she does any more damage. And she needs not to return, ever."

"I need to see Mr. Woodhouse first," Kate said, panicking. She was pushing her luck, she knew. But she couldn't possibly leave Grace Hall without meeting with him. She needed to look in his eyes to know whether he was telling the truth. And she needed answers from Liv, *now*. "When I spoke with him by phone, he said that I could come by anytime. There's something else I need to speak with Liv about, too."

Mrs. Pearl let out a disgusted laugh. "You are joking, right?"

"No, I'm not," Kate said quietly. "I understand what I did was wrong, but it doesn't make all the questions I have about Amelia go away."

"Perhaps it should make *you* go away, though, Ms. Baron," Mrs. Pearl said. "I'm willing to assume your outrageous conduct is a result of what you've been through, but you have exceeded the bounds of my goodwill."

Kate looked around. "Is Mr. Woodhouse even here?" Presumably, he'd be there in his office if he were. "He's not, is he? Is he *ever* here?"

Mrs. Pearl looked at Lew. "Lieutenant Thompson, I'm going to say this one last time: *she* needs to leave school property, immediately."

Lew put his hand on Kate's elbow and tugged her up from her chair. "Come on," he said. "Let's get you some air."

"No!" Kate shouted, jerking her arm away. "I'm not leaving until I get answers!"

"Look at me," Lew said, leaning over and staring her dead in the eye. His voice was an unexpectedly scary growl. "Get up, and get out that door. Now."

Kate stormed down the front steps in front of Lew and charged halfway down the block before she whipped around.

"So that's it!" she shouted. "You're letting them off the hook! Just like that!"

Lew came to a stop in front of Kate and took a deep, tired breath. He crossed his arms, his expression somewhere between aggravation and pity.

"I didn't even have a chance to tell you that Liv writes that *gRaCe-FULLY* blog," Kate went on. "Duncan finally traced it. A teacher wrote all those awful things about the *children* she teaches. She wrote things about Amelia. She's a liar. She lied right to our faces. Maybe she lied about Amelia's paper, too."

"That's certainly a thing she'll need to answer for."

"Good, then can we go back and talk to her?" Kate stepped toward the school.

Lew put a hand on her arm. "No, not you," he said. "You've done enough damage. If we're lucky, that boy's parents won't end up calling the police. If they do, I won't be able to keep them from arresting you."

"But—"

"No," Lew said firmly. "I'll go back to talk to the teacher. I'll press her on the blog and Amelia's paper. But you are going home. Get some rest. Try to get your head right. I'll come by to let you know what I've found once I'm done." He moved toward the school, then paused. He pulled a piece of paper out of his pocket and handed it to Kate. "Almost forgot. We're going to have to wait for a response from the phone company subpoena on the anonymous texts to you and Amelia, but the IT guys tracked down an address for Ben. He doesn't live in Albany."

Kate looked down at the address on the page: 968 Fifth Avenue, 6C.

"The kid being local and the fact that he went to the trouble to lie about where he was—it puts him up near the top of my list again."

Kate couldn't pull her eyes away from the address. Why would some boy from Manhattan lie about being from Albany? None of the reasons that jumped to mind were good ones.

"Your list?" she asked quietly.

"Of people who are going to stay ruled in, until they can rule themselves out: Dylan, Zadie, the rest of the Magpies, maybe even Woodhouse and the English teacher. They're all still on the list. But a kid who lied about where he was—who he was—and then said he might be on his way to see Amelia right before she died? That's a kid who's definitely got some explaining to do," Lew said. "I just got the address this morning. I should have the details on who lives there soon. That address ring any bells for you?"

"No," Kate said, wishing that it did. "Are we going to go talk to him?"

"Me, *I'm* going," Lew said. "And don't get any ridiculous ideas this time. Going after some kid at Grace Hall is one thing. But we have no idea who this Ben kid is, or what he might be trying to cover up. Being guilty can make anybody dangerous."

When Kate finally arrived home, there was a deliveryman with a large box trudging up her steps. She signed for the box, taking it from him tentatively, as though there might be a bomb nestled inside. She couldn't bear any more documents from Duncan. She'd already had her fill, and she still had stacks of texts and some e-mails left to go through. Once she was inside, Kate peered at a note stuck to the top.

To: Kate Baron
From: Phillip Woodhouse
Personal and Confidential

Kate hauled the heavy box to the kitchen table and stared at it some more. When she finally opened it, there were stacks of photocopied documents inside, some handwritten, others typed. There was also a note, from Woodhouse.

Enclosed are the minutes from school board meetings and rec-ords of Amelia's visit to the Grace Hall guidance counselor. I'm sorry I didn't come forward earlier. I felt like my hands were tied. Now that feels like a stupid excuse. I took this job because Grace Hall was supposed to help me open a charter school in the Bronx. Now I'm realizing that that might have been a lie, too. I'm sorry I couldn't—didn't—do more to help Amelia. The world is a darker place without her in it.

An hour later, Kate knew more than she wanted to about the clubs at Grace Hall and the efforts that had been made—or not made—to stop them. She knew about the Magpies in particular, the members of which were referred to as the Maggies, just as they had been in Amelia's texts and as Kate had expected. Shortly after the Magpies and the other clubs had resurfaced a year and a half earlier, the school board—in consultation with a lawyer hired by Adele Goodwin—had given the administration strict instructions to turn a blind eye to them. According to this conveniently never physically present lawyer—who Kate quickly came to suspect was Adele herself—ignorance would be the school's best defense to future liability. The theory Adele proffered was that because Grace Hall would not be able to successfully stop the clubs' off-campus activities, the only viable alternative was for the school to distance itself as completely from these activities as possible.

From the minutes, some members of the school board—and, most vocally, Woodhouse—had strongly disagreed. Woodhouse went so far as to say he was willing to risk a lawsuit against himself personally if it meant that he could stop the clubs. At one point he called the Maggies "potentially more destructive than any drug, certainly more vicious." He talked about the dangers of hazing and the perils of bullying, all of it cloaked in a veil of secrecy. He even threatened to quit.

But over a series of meetings that had dragged out through the preceding spring, Adele had worn the other board members down. Her most effective approach had been to use Woodhouse's own words against him. If the clubs were so potentially dangerous, Adele reasoned, Grace Hall might be held liable for any wrongs they committed. But the school and its administration could be liable only if they were *aware* of the clubs. Aggressive efforts to remove the clubs from campus—threats of academic suspensions for participating, code of conduct violations for students who wouldn't turn in fellow members, which Woodhouse continued to lobby for—would actually be, Adele cautioned, an implicit admission of the school's responsibility and, hence, liability.

As the school board reluctantly fell into line, Woodhouse had threatened again to resign if he was not permitted to act against the clubs. The only response on record was Adele's. And whoever had been taking the minutes had been sure to take down each and every word:

> Perhaps you should take a look at your contract, Phillip. I think you'll find that you don't need to quit. We can fire you for pursuing any course of action inconsistent with the wishes of this school board. You'd lose your job and your benefits, and you'd have to pay back your moving costs. Not to mention the liquidated damages we're entitled to collect. We set the figure in your contract. You should check, but I think the amount runs well into six figures. A lot of money to prove a point, especially one that—once you're fired—you'll never be able to prove anyway.

There weren't any details in the minutes about the look on Adele's face, of course. But having met her, Kate could imagine it: beautiful but venomous. There wasn't any mention in the notes of Zadie or any other specific student either. But there didn't need to be. It was obvious that Adele hadn't been acting in the best interests of the school. She'd been acting in the best interests of a child she could not control.

The last set of minutes Kate turned to were the ones for the meeting immediately after Amelia died, at which the board had decided to put the security measures into place. "Woodhouse thinks too soon to confirm suicide," read the minutes that followed. After that, Adele asked that the meeting go off the record. When the minutes resumed, the discussion had moved on. According to the minutes, Woodhouse didn't speak again.

Kate was still staring down at them when there was a knock at her door.

Lew was standing there on the stoop.

"Did you talk to Liv?" Kate asked as she swung the door open.

He nodded grimly. "Said that she thought it might get her closer to the kids, that she wasn't trying to hurt anyone."

"That's it? That's the whole explanation?"

"Don't look at me"—Lew shook his head—"it's not my excuse."

"But if she knew all of that, she knew what the Maggies were doing," Kate said. "She could have stopped them. How could she not have? She's responsible."

"You're right," Lew said. "And she knows it. It's not enough, but she'll have to live with that for the rest of her life."

facebook

OCTOBER 23

Amelia Baron

"She felt very young, at the same time unspeakably aged." Virginia Woolf, Mrs. Dalloway

Amelia

"Bye, Mom!" I called as I raced through the kitchen toward the door.

"Whoa!" she said, looking up from the *New York Times*, which was spread in front of her on the kitchen counter. She was dressed in a suit, with her hair pulled back tight. A big meeting, court—those were the only reasons she ever got that dressed up. "What's the big rush?"

"Nothing," I said, breathing hard as I circled back to grab an apple. "Gotta meet Sylvia, that's all."

I wrapped an arm around her shoulder and gave her a quick squeeze.

"Wait, hold on, Amelia." She looked suspicious. "I thought you wanted to talk about the semester in Paris. I set aside time. Let's talk about it, now. While I'm here."

It took me a second to remember what she was even talking about. Then it came to me, Ben's whacky leave-school-and-hide-out-in-Europe plan. I'd almost forgotten about it.

"That's okay," I said, heading for the door. "Never mind."

"Amelia, don't be that way. We really can talk about it." Now she looked worried. "I'm not excited about the idea of you being gone so long, but I am honestly willing to listen with an open mind. I was in a rush yesterday, but I heard how important this is to you. Please don't shut me out."

The look on her face was intense, too, like she'd been up most the night thinking about it. I felt bad for her. My mom was always worried about the wrong things. And it wasn't even her fault. I could have told her everything. I should have, probably, like Dr. Lipton had told me to. But it didn't really matter anymore now. I had a good feeling. The whole thing was going to turn out okay.

"It's not important anymore, Mom. For real," I said, looking her right in the eye. "I'm fine with not going. Better than fine—I want to stay."

"You're sure?"

"Yes, Mom, totally. One hundred percent."

"Okay," she said, hugging me tight. It still didn't look as if she believed me. "As long as you're sure."

I felt good on the walk up to the corner to meet Sylvia. My mom and I were finally back on the straight and narrow, and I'd even put the whole who's-your-daddy thing to bed on my own. After I'd decided I didn't want to read through any more of my mom's journals, I'd decided just not to care who my dad really was. I hadn't known him my whole life. What difference did it make if I knew him now? It helped that the texts about him had stopped coming. I'd even come clean with Sylvia about Dylan and the Magpies, and she'd forgiven me. No more secrets, no more feeling bad. It was all sunny and almost warm, too, like we were on the front edge of spring instead of the backside of fall. All of it felt like a sign. Like maybe everything was going to work out. Like my e-mail to Dylan might even change things back into the awesome way they'd been.

Maybe I could have thought of the answers myself, or whatever, like Dr. Lipton had told me to. But it was way more accurate to go straight to the actual source. It wasn't like I was trying to get Dylan back or anything. I mean, if it happened, that would be fine or great or whatever. But Dylan would have some serious explaining to do first.

I hadn't told Sylvia, or Ben, that part. I'd told them that I wouldn't have gotten back together with Dylan no matter what. Because that was what they had wanted to hear. Sylvia had actually made me promise that wasn't what I was after before she'd even help me write the e-mail. Sylvia said she wasn't going to sit around and let me make an ass out of myself for some girl who definitely didn't deserve me. Sylvia had kept saying that part—about Dylan not being good enough for me—as we worked on the e-mail. She said it a hundred times. Like it was some kind of spell. I knew she was trying to help, but it was kind of annoying. *Really annoying*, actually, especially coming from her. After all, she'd let, like, a million guys treat her like crap over the years.

But it had been worth putting up with Sylvia riding me because the e-mail she wrote to Dylan was awesome. Sylvia really knew how to go right for the gut, without looking totally desperate. It wasn't all nice either. Some of it was even a little harsh, which made me kind of wonder if Sylvia ever would have been that tough on any of the guys in her life. But she convinced me that honey and vinegar was the way to go. If you acted like you weren't going to let anyone disrespect you, they wanted you more. At least that was true with guys, Sylvia said. Maybe it was different with girls, but she didn't think so.

After Sylvia left, I did slip some softer stuff into the e-mail. About how Dylan had been the first person I'd ever been in love with, that she would be that person always. And right before I hit Send, I added a line, right at the bottom: I think I can forget everything bad that happened. All I want is to be together again.

Sylvia wouldn't have liked that part. Ben wouldn't have either. They would have said that it made me look needy and desperate. Maybe I kind of was. Dylan had said before that she thought it was cute. And the truth was, I missed Dylan. And that e-mail was probably my last chance to turn things around. I couldn't risk *not* saying absolutely everything I felt. I crossed my fingers as I hit Send.

"Anything yet?" Sylvia asked when we met up at the corner.

"I don't know," I said. "I mean, not as of when I left."

"Come on, check again," Sylvia said. She sounded almost as wound up as me.

I pulled out my iPhone as we turned up onto Prospect Park West,

shuffling into the crazy-crowded school-traffic flow. I looked around
before I checked my e-mail. I didn't want Dylan to see me obsessing.
Even *I* had more pride than that. But my in-box was empty, except for
a new message from Ben.

"Nothing."

I didn't really think Dylan would write back at that hour, when
everybody was on the way to school. But I wished she had. Sylvia and
I walked on without saying anything else, me staring down at my
phone, her staring down at her pointy ankle boots, until George Mc-
Donnell ran past and smacked Sylvia hard on the ass.

"Asshole!" she screamed after him, but she was smiling a little as she
turned back to me. Things with Ian might not have been completely
over, but she was already lining up new options. "Maybe she didn't get
it yet," Sylvia offered, but it didn't sound like she really believed that.
"And if she doesn't write back, then she's a bitch, which, let's face it,
wouldn't be a total shocker. She *is* best friends with Zadie, you know."

Sylvia's eyebrows were raised hopefully. She was trying to make me
feel better.

"Sure," I said, as we climbed the front steps. Because there didn't
seem to be any point in telling her that it wasn't working. "Totally."

As we moved with the crowd through the front doors of the school,
I noticed Carter and George up ahead looking back at us. Then I saw
some other kids from our class—Kylin, Matt S., Raoul—looking at
us, too. And the more I looked around as we walked on, the more
it seemed like everybody was looking at us. Or me. Really, it seemed
like they were looking at me. They were doing that whisper and nod
thing, too—like the Maggies had done. But the Maggies had done it
so I'd know they were saying something mean about me; these people
seemed like they couldn't help themselves. And the more I looked
around, the more of them there were—staring, whispering.

"Why is everyone looking at me?" I asked Sylvia, backing up
against the rotunda wall, near the creepy photograph of the stripper
lady. It was a bad place to stand.

"What do you mean?" Sylvia asked. I watched her look around. She saw what I did, but tried not to show it. "No one's looking at you."

They totally were, though, and she knew it. I felt my throat tightening as I met eyes with one kid after another—giggling, smirking. Some of them I knew. Some of them I didn't. The ones I knew were sort of trying to hide it, but I could still see the laughter in their eyes.

"Grace girls!" someone in the crowd shouted. "Bringin' out mad love."

A couple of people hooted. Someone shouted, "Yeeah, boyee!"

"Put it up on YouTube, man!"

"Shhh!" Mrs. Pearl hissed, appearing in the rotunda like a ghost. She was holding a long gray finger up in front of her long gray face. "Lower your voices! You are inside, and this is a *school*. Show some respect. And those phones need to be switched off and *stowed*, or they will permanently become my property!"

"Pearly," someone croaked, "stealing the phones."

A tide of shouts and giggles followed.

Sylvia's eyes were all big and round. There was no denying it. She was definitely seeing it, too. And so there we stood, pressed up against the wall as people ignored Mrs. Pearl's squawking about their phones and instead kept on passing them around, dragging their fingers across the screens as they read. Every once in a while, they'd look up. Straight at me.

Suddenly, Sylvia grabbed my arm.

"Come on, let's get out of here," she said as she yanked me through the crowd, shoving at the people in front of us. "Get the fuck out of my way, you stupid shits!"

My feet felt heavy and all huge. I tripped over them as Sylvia dragged me down the hall toward the school's main offices. Halfway there, she turned and banged into the medical clinic. The nurse, Ms. Appleman, startled up from her desk, where she was paging through a Macy's sales flyer. She pressed a hand to her bony collarbone.

"What's the matter?" She looked terrified that she was about to face an actual medical emergency.

"She feels dizzy, and she has her period," Sylvia said. "She needs to sit in here for a few minutes." Then she turned to me. "Stay here. I'll be right back."

As Sylvia disappeared out the door, Nurse Appleman leaned back even more, gripping the edge of her desk like she was afraid I might have Ebola.

"Are you sure it's just your menstruation?" she asked.

The roar of the kids was dying down out in the hall as they made their way to first period. I knew what Sylvia had gone to do, to see for herself what they'd all been looking at on their phones. She'd put together the same thing that I had: a text blast had gone out. Something about me. The Maggies had finally done what they'd been threatening to do all along: send out to everyone a half-naked picture of me. The worst part was that I hadn't even told Sylvia about the pictures; I was too embarrassed. And now, everybody would know.

All of a sudden, I felt sick for real—woozy, hot. My palms were sweaty, and my face was tingly. I dropped myself down hard on the stiff leather sickbed, crinkling its paper covering.

"Are you going to vomit?" Nurse Appleman squeaked. "Please try to make it into the lavatory if you're going to vomit."

I shook my head and stared at the door. Sylvia was taking a really long time out there. Whatever it was must be really bad. So bad she didn't even want to come back in and tell me. I could have looked for myself. My phone was in my bag. Surely I'd gotten the text, too. But I needed Sylvia to give me the edited version. I sat there, staring at the door, waiting.

When the door finally opened, Sylvia shuffled back in slowly. She wouldn't even look at me.

"What does it say?" I asked.

"If you're feeling better," Nurse Appleman said, turning snarky all of a sudden, "you two can have this conversation out in the hallway. This room is reserved for students who are actually ill."

Sylvia and I both ignored her, our eyes locked instead on each other until Sylvia turned and dropped down next to me on the hard bed. She took a deep breath, then rested her forearms against her knees as she stared at the floor.

"Your e-mail to Dylan—somebody sent it around," she said quietly. "The whole thing."

After Nurse Appleman had finally booted us, Sylvia's nervous eyes swiveled the empty hall, assessing the perimeter. "Fuck all of them," she said. "Anyway, you know, everybody will forget about it by the time another *gRaCeFULLY* comes out."

I stared at Sylvia as she kept on looking up and down the hall. She looked more nervous than I'd ever seen her. She knew as well as I did that people wouldn't forget a note like that anytime soon.

It would have been embarrassing if my e-mail had been about a guy, or if everyone had already known I was gay. But to get outed by my own needy e-mail? The kids at Grace Hall would be able to feed off that for years. I wanted to die. I wanted my heart to stop beating. I closed my eyes and willed it to happen.

"I'll be okay," I said to Sylvia after a minute. It was a lie, of course. But I wanted her to go. I needed to be alone. "You should get to class. You'll get suspended if you're late again."

"Hey! What do you think this is, Club Med?" Will yelled down the hall to us. "Get your butts to class or get to Mrs. Pearl's office. Your choice."

The next thing I knew, I was sitting in Liv's class and she was talking about *The Sound and the Fury*. I didn't remember ever leaving the hall. But there I was, and there was Liv, talking about the next book we were going to read. She was saying something about narrative structure. The weird thing was how she was talking about it like it was a thing that actually mattered, instead of its just being another stupid book.

Heather and Bethany were both in Liv's class, too; they sat across the room from me, near the windows. I could feel them staring at me the whole time Liv talked. The whole time I was praying I'd disappear.

I'd written that I loved Dylan. That I wanted her to love me back. She didn't; that was obvious. And now, the whole world knew it.

I needed to get out of Grace Hall. I needed to run away and never come back.

Ben. Maybe he'd help. Do what, I didn't even know. But he was supposed to be coming. He'd promised to try at least. If I could convince him to come now, he'd help me forget about everybody at Grace Hall. Ben had this way of making everything seem not so bad. Sad still—but funny sad, not tragic sad.

I noticed then that people were getting up to leave. Class must have been over. I hadn't even noticed that Liv had stopped talking. I stayed in my seat to write Ben a quick text back, to see if he could come down to Brooklyn soon.

When I looked up, Heather and Bethany were passing by my desk. They strolled by arm in arm, mouthing the word *dyke* at me as they sashayed toward the door. All I could do was sit there and stare.

I felt like I'd slipped out of my body. As though I was standing there next to myself, shaking my head. How had I become this person? This person in the center of some stupid gossip shit storm? Because there'd been this other person, a person who would have never joined a club or chased a girl who didn't want to get caught. Who never would have let herself get made a fool of.

Are you in NYC? I typed to Ben.

I sat there breathless, waiting for him, my exit strategy, to write back. It took forever for him to respond.

BEN

I'm in Times Square!! It's so f-ing rad!! I LVE NYC!!!

AMELIA

When can you get to Bklyn?

BEN

Don't know. Chances are I won't be able to. U know I want to, but . . .

AMELIA

PLEASE. U Have to.

I typed out the address for Grace Hall. I added that I would understand if he couldn't come. As much as I wanted him there, I didn't want him to feel bad for having a good time with his dad. None of this was his fault or his problem. It wasn't Sylvia's either, as much as I'd been hoping she could maybe save me, too.

I was the one who'd been stupid enough to join the Maggies. *I* was the one who'd put all that other stuff into the e-mail, even after Sylvia told me it was a bad, bad idea. Even when, deep down, I'd known she was right. And yet, deep down there in that very same spot, I was still praying there was some kind of magic explanation that made the e-mail getting out not Dylan's fault.

"Amelia?" Liv asked.

I shook my head and looked up. I was so out of it that I was sitting there in the middle of class with my phone totally out in the open. It was one thing for Liv to ignore my sending one quick text, but I should've put my phone away. I didn't want her to think I was taking advantage of her because we were, like, friends or whatever.

"Sorry," I said, shoving my phone back into my bag. "It was just a message from my mom. She asked me to text her right back."

Liv shook her head.

"It's not about your phone." She looked kind of sick as she sat down on the chair in front of me. For a second, I wanted so bad to tell her everything. "I'm afraid it's about your *Lighthouse* paper."

"I know what I wrote about wasn't exactly what we talked about," I said. I felt a little better talking about the paper. It made Dylan, the text—all of it—feel like this weird messed-up dream. "But I thought it would be okay as long as I did it, you know, well."

Liv's forehead wrinkled. "The subject of your paper isn't the problem."

"It wasn't good?" There was no way she could say that.

"It was fine, Amelia. That's not the issue either." She took a deep, shaky breath. "It wasn't *your* paper. That's the problem."

"What are you talking about?"

"I ran your paper through a program designed to catch duplication from published works. All the teachers at Grace Hall do. It's mandatory, starting this year. In any case, your paper was flagged in numerous spots. The paper you handed in, Amelia, was plagiarized."

"No, it wasn't!" My heart was thumping. "I wrote that paper!"

Liv frowned, looked sad. For me.

"This isn't like you, Amelia. I know it's not," she said, looking at me like she was willing me to confess. "If you tell me what happened, I'm sure we can work it out. But you have to start by telling me something."

For a second, I thought maybe I was going crazy. That maybe I had lifted parts of somebody else's paper and just didn't remember doing it. Then it came to me: the Maggies. Of course, it was the Maggies. Bethany was Liv's assistant. She must have switched my paper somehow.

But how could I tell Liv that? They'd—Zadie—had said they'd torture Sylvia, ruin her life if I did. I knew, firsthand, how bad the Maggie torturing could be. Sylvia would never survive it. And after everything she'd done—especially how much she'd been there for me, despite what a shitty friend I'd been—I couldn't throw Sylvia under the bus. I'd just have to take it. Let the world think I was a cheater.

"I want to see it," I said. "The parts where I copied."

"Okay, Amelia," Liv said gently, getting up to retrieve the paper.

She came back with a stapled set of pages. My name was on it, but otherwise, it wasn't my paper. Not even the title. I flipped through the pages, staring down at them. Sections were highlighted, shaded as if by a computer program, their real source typed in the margins.

Texting my private love letters to the whole school hadn't been enough? Zadie had needed to do this, too? It felt like somebody had carved a hole clean through the center of my body. Like there was nothing in the middle of me now but empty space. And yet, somehow, I was still upright.

"Amelia, *please* tell me what's going on," Liv said. "If you can't give me an explanation, I'll have to report this to Mr. Woodhouse, as a violation of the code of conduct. I don't want to do that, believe me. But I'll lose my job if I don't. If you explain, maybe I can find a way out of this, for both of us. This isn't you, Amelia. I know it isn't. Amelia, look at me."

I just shook my head and kept staring down. This was it. The Maggies had finally won. Zadie had wanted to ruin my life, and so she had. Now all that was left was to accept defeat. To lie down on the classroom floor and wait for them to carry my lifeless body away.

Amelia

OCTOBER 24, 12:02 PM

AMELIA

   please tell me you are on ur way

BEN

   not looking good, but still trying.

AMELIA

   please, please, I need you.

BEN

   I'm trying . . .

AMELIA

   that's it? trying? I say I need you here and that's it? WTF? now you're
   lying, too?

BEN

   whoa, lying? I said I would try; that's all I said. I can't tell my dad to fuck
   off

AMELIA

   sorry, u r right; bad shit going down

BEN

   what?

AMELIA

   maggies messed with my English paper; they're saying I cheated

BEN

how did they mess with it?

AMELIA

IDK

BEN

screw those bitches; I wish I could be there to help

AMELIA

I don't want you to get in trouble with ur dad.

BEN

you're more important than my dad getting a little pissed; you're more important than most things

AMELIA

Thanks :). I needed that.

facebook

Amelia Baron

"Alone, condemned, deserted, as those who are about to die are alone, there was a luxury in it, an isolation full of sublimity; a freedom which the attached can never know." Virginia Woolf, Mrs. Dalloway

George McDonnell   can you say, Lexapro?

Kate

OCTOBER 19, 1997, 3:56 AM

To: Kate Baron
From: rowan627@aol.com
Subject: One Last Try . . .

Hi Katie,

Thought I'd throw one last shout out before I head to the hinterlands . . .
Hope you're okay. And don't worry, I'm not going to go all stalkerish and
weird if you don't write back. I get it, totally. Just hang easy and be safe. And
if you ever find yourself over on this side of the world, look me up.

I'll be keeping an eye out, and the light on.

peace,
Rowan

OCTOBER 20, 1997, 9:15 AM

To: rowan627@aol.com
From: Kate Baron
Re: One Last Try . . .

Rowan,

I'm sorry I haven't been in touch. But thank you for writing. I've loved talking
to you and meeting you. But something's happened in my life. Something

unexpected. Anyway, it's changed things for me. I need to take some time out, and just focus on me for a while.

I wish you the best of everything. You're a great spirit. And I feel lucky that I had the chance to know you.

Xo,
Katie

Kate

Kate sat down on a damp park bench across the street from 968 Fifth Avenue. It was dark, past eight p.m. Maybe it wasn't the safest place to sit alone, there along the edge of the park at night, but it was out of sight and had a good view of the building's entrance. Kate still wasn't sure what she planned to do. Though she had known when Lew left with instructions for her to stay home that she would almost certainly be disappointing him again.

A few minutes later, Kate was crossing the street, and a tall, elegant doorman was waving her inside the lobby, making her think for a second that maybe she'd be able to head straight upstairs without having to explain herself to anybody. It was short-lived.

"What apartment?" the doorman asked, effortlessly circling Kate to a stop as he headed toward the phone.

"Oh." Kate felt herself looking guilty. "Six C?"

The doorman squinted at her as he picked up the phone and punched some numbers. "Name?"

"I'm sorry?"

"Your *name*." The doorman drew the word out. He looked as if he were already considering tossing her back out onto the street.

Maybe that would have been for the best. Because what was Kate's plan exactly once she got upstairs? To demand to see this Ben kid?

What would she do when they said there was no Ben who lived there? Not that it mattered. The second the doorman reached whoever lived in 6C and learned that they had no idea who she was, she wasn't going to be going anywhere but home.

"Kate Baron." She smiled hard. "That's my name, Kate Baron."

The doorman didn't seem persuaded by her newfound confidence. His eyes stayed on Kate as he announced her to whoever had picked up on the other end.

"Okay," he said, looking down. "Yes, yes, I understand."

Kate held her breath waiting to endure the humiliation of being turned away. But it would be a relief, too, in a way. Fate intervening to save her from herself. Instead, the doorman pointed toward the back of the lobby.

"Take the last elevator."

Kate's heart was pounding as the gilded elevator doors opened onto a luxurious hallway. When she stepped off, there was a polished sideboard with a huge gold-leaf mirror above it. Kate caught sight of her reflection. Her face was gray and drawn, the color washed out from her hair. How long had she been in such an obvious state of decay? Since Amelia's death? Longer?

Maybe her grief had eaten through her brain, too, because this was wrong—what she was doing—showing up at this Ben's address. She had once been a rational person. Deep down, she still was. She knew that the apartment being exceptionally nice did not preclude the possibility that it housed a psychopath. Kate needed Lew. She had no business there. None. It was disruptive and pointless.

Kate turned around and pressed the Down button. Luckily, the elevator doors sprang right back open. She was about to step on when she heard the apartment door.

"Kate?" a woman's voice called down the hall. "Where are you going?"

When Kate turned, there was Vera standing at the end of the long hall, looking fit and muscular in a tank top and yoga pants, her long black hair pulled back in a low ponytail. She padded in bare feet down the hallway toward Kate. Her strong, beautiful jaw was tilted to the side, her huge brown eyes narrowed in concern.

Vera. Jeremy. Their new apartment. The one that Kate had never been to.

The texts had come from one of Jeremy's sons. Amelia could have easily met one of them somewhere. The world of Manhattan and Brooklyn private schools wasn't that large. They could have even crossed paths at the firm picnic the year before. But why would one of Jeremy's sons have lied about who he was?

"Are you okay, honey?" Vera asked gently. She was right in front of Kate now, her hand on Kate's forearm.

Kate nodded too hard and for too long. Kate couldn't recall Jeremy ever mentioning that any of his sons was gay, but maybe he wouldn't have. Or, like Kate, he didn't know.

"I've got to be honest, you don't look so great," Vera said, ushering Kate toward their apartment. "Come inside and sit down. I'll get you a glass of water."

Vera pushed open the door, and they stepped into the vast living room. A huge wall of windows overlooked the darkness of the park and, in the distance beyond, the lights of the Upper West Side. There was a fireplace to one end separating off a huge dining room and a grand piano at the other. In between, there was enough space to play basketball and about half the amount of furniture to adequately fill it.

"Come, let's sit in the kitchen," Vera said. "It's cozier in there. Out here is still a work in progress."

"I'd forgotten that you'd moved," Kate said, as she sat down on one of the stools alongside the huge granite island in the suburban-size kitchen.

She didn't know if she could do this, talk to Vera. She didn't know whether Vera had read *insidethelaw* or, if she had, whether she'd connected it with Kate.

"You know, sometimes I wish I could forget we moved, too," Vera said. "I don't want to sound ungrateful, but sometimes big is just too

big. Jeremy!" She lifted her chin to yell, then smiled back down at
Kate. "He went to go change. He'll be right back."

"Oh, I'm so sorry to have disturbed you," Kate said. Her voice was
not much louder than a whisper. It was hard to speak with her throat
clenched so tight. "I know it's getting late."

"Please," Vera said, waving a hand. "Considering how late Jeremy
makes all of you work, it's good for him to get disturbed once in a while."

"Thank you for the water," Kate said, hoping to move the conversation away from Jeremy. She wanted to leave the apartment immediately, but she couldn't begin to formulate an excuse for why she was
there, much less for why she suddenly had to leave. "I was feeling a
little light-headed."

"I'm not surprised," Vera said. "When Jeremy told me you were
back at work already—" She made a motion of zipping her lips. "Wait,
sorry, no, I should mind my own business. The boys are always telling
me that I'm the mother hen who pecks people to death. So I'm going to try to keep my mouth shut. Just make sure you don't overdo it.
And that's coming from a woman who ran a half marathon six weeks
postpartum and then argued a motion in the Second Circuit the next
day. Distraction is the best medicine. I get that approach." She paused,
looked sad. "But some things you can't outrun, no matter how fast you
move your legs."

Jeremy appeared in the doorway then. He was pale. *Stop it*, Kate
wanted to shout at him. *You look guilty.*

"I've got a late Bikram class with my name on it," Vera said. "You'll
be okay here, just the two of you?"

Kate tensed for a second, but Jeremy moved quickly to fill the awkward gap.

"Yes, go, go," he said, kissing Vera. "Kate just needs my signature
on something."

Vera seemed to accept this, even though Kate had turned up at
their apartment empty-handed. Vera patted Kate on the hand as she
headed toward the door.

"You take care of yourself," she said. "And try to take your time. Work will always be there."

When Vera was gone, Jeremy headed back out to the living room. He poured himself a short drink at the bar along the wall near the open kitchen. Whiskey or scotch, something amber. He offered a glass to Kate, but she waved it off. He flopped down hard on the couch, resting his head against a hand. He took a few loud breaths.

"She doesn't know yet?" Kate asked.

"I wasn't entirely sure until now." Jeremy shook his head. "She'd been acting a little strange, at least I thought she was. I must have been imagining it. Unless she's planning on coming back with a gun."

Kate stared at him, wide-eyed.

"I'm joking," Jeremy said.

"That's hilarious," Kate said flatly.

He shrugged. "Can you please sit down? You're making me nervous."

Kate set herself down on the edge of a huge round ottoman-cum-coffee-table that she wasn't sure was even for sitting.

"I didn't even know this was your house," she said.

"What do you mean?" Jeremy finished what was left in his glass and set it down on the end table. "You just happened to knock on our apartment door?"

"I came here, to this apartment, on purpose," Kate said. "I just didn't know who lived here."

She was still trying to make sense of it all. If one of Jeremy's sons had been pretending to be Ben, that meant that he also might— at least theoretically—have had something to do with what had happened to Amelia on that roof. How was Kate going to tell Jeremy about one of his sons being Ben without it sounding as if she was accusing his child of hurting, maybe even killing, hers? That wasn't really what she thought anyway. She believed that the Maggies were responsible. Still, as Lew had said, Ben—whoever he really was—had lied. Kate needed to know why.

"I don't understand what you're talking about, Kate," Jeremy said. He sounded and looked exhausted. "Can you just tell me what's going on?"

"There was a boy Amelia was friends with," she began carefully. "Supposedly, another applicant to that Princeton summer program. Their friendship was mostly texts and e-mails, that kind of thing. It seems as if they were close. We've been trying to track him down." She moved quickly to clarify. "Not because he might have done something wrong, but because he might know something. He told Amelia that he lived in Albany and that his name was Ben, but the police traced the text messages." Kate paused, took a breath. "He lives here, Jeremy, in this apartment. One of your sons must have sent the messages to Amelia."

Jeremy closed his eyes and dropped his head again, this time into both hands. He sat there like that for a moment, not moving. Finally, he started shaking his head back and forth. Was he really going to argue? Claim that it couldn't be one of his sons? Maybe he had misunderstood. Kate's disclaimers aside, maybe he thought she was accusing one of his sons of doing something terrible.

"Jeremy, I'm not saying that they did anything wrong. Ben was a good friend to Amelia. A really good—"

"It wasn't one of the boys," Jeremy said quietly. When he looked up from the floor, his eyes were glassy. "It was me."

"What?" Kate snapped, jumping to her feet. "What are you talking about?"

"I wrote to Amelia. *I* was Ben, Kate."

"No." Kate shook her head. This couldn't be happening. Because there were a lot of explanations for a lot of things, but there was only one reason a grown man corresponded with a young girl online, then lied about who he was. "No."

Kate thought then about how she and Amelia had run into Jeremy at the office one Saturday not long ago. How he'd seemed so peculiarly interested in Amelia, staring at her so intently, marveling at how grown up she was. Kate had written it off at the time as Jeremy just trying to seem *interested*, in general. Now the thought made her sick.

"I shouldn't have lied to her." Jeremy went on, more quietly now. He looked down, shaking his head. "That was wrong. But I just— When I was writing that recommendation for Princeton, I spent all this time thinking about Amelia and this amazing person she had become. I wanted the chance to get to know her, at least a little bit, and I thought maybe I could do it without costing anyone anything. I already had her e-mail address from writing the recommendation. All I had to do was set up an e-mail account in a kid's name, get a voice account with an Albany area code, and invent a little backstory, and that was that. Maybe it was selfish, but I couldn't help myself."

"Couldn't help yourself?!" Kate's voice shook. Her face was on fire. She was trying to keep herself from jumping to that most awful, inevitable conclusion. But it was no use. Her mind had already raced there. "She was my *daughter*, Jeremy. She was a *child*."

"Wait a second, Kate." Jeremy was ashen, his eyes panicky. "You don't think that—there's an explana—"

"No. You can't charm your way out of this. I won't let you. Is this how you stay such a good husband these days?" Kate shouted, pointing a finger at Jeremy. "You text teenage girls instead of sleeping with grown women? Or are the texts just the beginning? Were you really planning on meeting Amelia?"

"Kate, come on, that's ridicu—"

"What did you do to her, you bastard?!" Kate screamed, charging at Jeremy.

"*Do to her?* Are you crazy?! I was trying to help her!" Jeremy raised his hands to protect his face. "Anyway, I never even saw her. I mean— I, I thought about seeing her, telling her the truth. But I knew it wasn't my place to make that decision, so I became her friend instead. Why do you think I told her I was *gay*? I wanted to make sure there couldn't be anything weird. Not that it ended up mattering anyway, after Dylan and everything. I was just glad I could be there for her with all that Magpie nonsense going on."

"Oh my God. You *knew*." Kate felt like she was going to be sick. "You fucking— She told you what those girls were doing to her, and you didn't stop it? You could have told *someone*. You could have done *something*."

"You're acting like that would have been so simple. Everything would have come out, Kate. You obviously didn't want that either. You wouldn't have gone to so much trouble to hide the truth." Jeremy seemed angry now, too. *The truth*, it was the second time he'd said that. What it meant, Kate wasn't sure she wanted to know. "Anyway, I did think about telling you when things with those girls started getting out of hand. But before I did, it seemed like Amelia had worked everything out on her own. She told me she was fine. And then, all of a sudden on that last day—" He looked down. "Now, with what happened—Kate, you don't know how much I wish I'd done something."

"Did you go see Amelia that day?" Kate asked, bracing herself. Jeremy had lied about so much. There could be more. There could be something more awful than she could possibly imagine. "You said you were going to in your texts."

"No, Kate, for *the second time*," Jeremy said. There was no anger in his voice anymore, only resignation. He knew exactly what she was accusing him of, and he seemed utterly defeated. "I was with three associates in the office all day. You can check if you want. Anyway, I thought you read her texts. In the end, I said I wasn't coming."

"I haven't gotten through them all yet!" Kate shouted.

"Dad?" came a voice from the doorway then. One of Jeremy's sons was standing there, looking boyish and handsome and scared. "Are you okay?"

Jeremy shot upright and smiled, so quickly and convincingly that it lifted the hairs on Kate's arms.

"Yeah, yeah, Andrew," he said. "I'm fine. Just a problem with a case, nothing to worry about. Go back to your homework. We'll keep it down out here."

"Okay," Andrew said skeptically, letting his eyes drift over to Kate for a second before shuffling for the door. "See you later."

"Yeah, yeah, Drew," Jeremy said. "I'll see you later."

They were both motionless and silent for a long time after Jeremy's son disappeared. Kate hadn't realized Jeremy's children were home. As much as she wanted to scream at him some more, she couldn't do that to his sons. Jeremy's boys already had so much heartbreak headed their way. Once Vera finally did hear about the posts on insidethelaw.com, which she would, sooner or later, there was no way she'd stay with Jeremy. She was not the kind of woman to suffer betrayal lightly. There were other ways to find out if Jeremy was telling the truth anyway. Call those associates, check with his secretary. Better yet, Kate could send Lew. But there was one thing she did need to know.

"Hide the truth about what?" Kate asked. It was still bothering her, what Jeremy had meant.

"What?" he asked, looking battered and confused.

"You said I'd gone to so much trouble to 'hide the truth.' The truth about what?"

"Come on, Kate. I knew," Jeremy said finally. "I've known for years."

"Knew what?" Kate snapped, even though she was trying to keep her temper reined in. "That she was a trusting girl, that she'd—"

"That she was mine," Jeremy said, staring straight at Kate. "I knew that Amelia was my daughter."

"Yours?" Kate choked out. "Amelia was *not* your daughter, Jeremy."

"The timing fits exactly," he said, as if she was just holding out.

How dare he try to claim Amelia, like yet another thing he deserved.

"You are joking, right?" She didn't want to have this conversation with him. She knew what she knew, Jeremy's delusions notwithstanding. "We slept together *once*, Jeremy. One time. And you weren't the only one who was sleeping with more than one person. Trust me, Amelia was not your daughter. I know who her father was, and it wasn't you."

But Jeremy was shaking his head. He didn't look like he was listening to a word Kate was saying. "As soon as I heard you were pregnant, I wondered, obviously," he said. "But after Amelia's eyes changed colors as a baby, then I knew for sure."

"Stop it, Jeremy." Kate's voice was thready and high. She knew what she knew, and so why was she starting to panic? "I mean it."

"Come on, Kate." Jeremy's eyes were clear, guiltless. His voice so utterly calm. He might have been wrong, but he fully believed that Amelia was his daughter. He ran a hand back and forth over his silver hair, tipping his head in Kate's direction like he was making a point. "Look at me. You can't tell me you didn't put two and two together. My hair, her eyes."

His hair? Jeremy had always had gray hair, ever since she'd known him. He'd been almost forty when they'd met, young for a full head of gray hair, but not absurdly so.

"I don't know what you think you know, Jeremy," Kate breathed. She should leave, now, before he said anything more. "But you're wrong."

"I didn't know I had Waardenburg until my hair turned gray freshman year in college. But with Amelia, her eyes, you must have known as soon as they changed."

He was right about that. Amelia had been diagnosed with Waardenburg syndrome when she was ten months old, as soon as her eyes changed from a matching blue-gray to one blue and one hazel. It was a genetic disease and Kate wasn't a carrier. She'd been tested. She'd always assumed that Daniel must have been, and that his disease had just manifested in one of the myriad of less visible ways the syndrome could present itself. It wasn't as though they'd ever spoken about it. That would have required discussing Amelia.

Kate's palms were damp, her hands trembling. But so what if Jeremy had the same disorder? It could be coincidence. It had to be. She'd had sex with Daniel a dozen times, with Jeremy only once.

No. Jeremy couldn't try to rewrite history. It had not been easy, but Kate had made peace with Daniel's being Amelia's father. It was one of the things that defined her life. Amelia had been conceived with a man Kate had never thought much of as a person, and so she'd protected Amelia from knowing him. The sex had been angry and rough, too. It had been the opposite of love that Amelia had been conceived out of. And it had been a noble thing she had done, protecting her daughter from knowing that, from knowing a father who wasn't a fraction of the person she'd grow up to be.

Kate had slept with Daniel in the first place only in a misguided attempt to smother the guilt she'd felt for the one-night stand she'd had with Jeremy, whom she'd slept with . . . why? All these years later, she still didn't even really know. To get over losing Seth? Because she was lonely? Because she'd been swept up by Jeremy's charm? Because he'd made her feel special for a couple of hours? Certainly she hadn't been thinking clearly, as evidenced by the fact that—on top of all her other careless decisions—she'd been less than religious about using her diaphragm during that whole period. She'd taken other precautions, sure, ones any seventh grader half paying attention in health class would have known were far from foolproof.

"I've made a lot of mistakes, Kate," Jeremy said. "But I swear I was trying to help Amelia. You have to believe that. I thought that I could be her friend, even if she couldn't ever know that I was her dad. Now I wish I'd just told her."

"No," Kate said, backing away from Jeremy. She kept backing up until she'd banged against the wall behind her. "Stop it. I won't. You need to—" She shook her head. "I have to go."

Kate looked right, then left. Where had the front door of the apartment gone? It was as if she'd been sunk into some inescapable labyrinth. All these years, Kate had been so sure about who Amelia's father was and why she'd lied about him. She'd been protecting Amelia. But now it felt like the only person her lies had sheltered was Jeremy. And, of course, herself.

"Kate, we have to talk about this."

"No, we don't. We never do," Kate said. "I have to— I can't be here."

"Daniel knows about us, Kate," Jeremy said. "He called earlier from the airport to tell me he was on his way to Scotland and to brag about tipping off *insidethelaw*. He was so drunk that I could barely make out what he was saying, but I did get that someone had sent him an e-mail about us. It was a couple of months ago, I think he said. Your guess is as good as mine who that was. Apparently, my giving you

Associated Mutual Bank—which was already your case, of course—
finally sent Daniel over the edge and made him go public. Personally, I
think the fact that he just accepted a Meyer, Jenkins senior partnership
didn't hurt either." Jeremy shook his head in disgust. "Daniel also told
me about you and him, Kate. I had no idea. And I have to say, I kind
of felt like an ass."

Jeremy actually had the nerve to look wounded.

"I'm glad," Kate said quietly. Then she threw herself forward, praying she was moving in the direction of the front door. "It's about time
you felt like an ass about something."

"Wait, Kate," Jeremy called after her. "We have to figure out what
we're going to do. And there's something else you need to know. It's
about Amelia."

"I don't want to know anything else," Kate said, picking up speed
down the hall, her heart thumping in her chest, tears in her eyes. "Just
leave me alone."

"Kate!" Jeremy called one last time as she dove out the door. "We
still need to talk! There's something else I have to tell you. It's important. It's about another girl at Grace Hall!"

Amelia

AMELIA

where r u? pls. don't tell me u bailed.

BEN

sorry. I suck. but I'm not going to be able to make it.

AMELIA

seriously?

BEN

my dad is all bent out of shape. if I go he'll kill me. but don't hate me, okay. cause I love you.

AMELIA

it's okay. I understand. this isn't your problem. love u too.

BEN

I feel like a douche. promise me you'll be okay.

AMELIA

I promise. I'll be fine

BEN

don't let those crazies beat you down. you're too awesome. besides, you always have me.

AMELIA

xoxo

OCTOBER 24, 1:49 PM

SYLVIA

where are you?

AMELIA

Woodhouse's office

SYLVIA

why?

AMELIA

cheating

SYLVIA

who cheated?

AMELIA

me supposedly

SYLVIA

WTF?! OK I've had enough of this crap. sit tight. I'm coming to get you.

Amelia

I jumped and shoved my phone back into my bag when Woodhouse opened his office door.

"I'm going to pretend I didn't see that," he said as he came around his desk. He was carrying a folder, tapping the edge of it against his open palm like it was a ruler he planned on slapping my knuckles with. Instead, he tossed the folder onto the center of his clean, empty desk. He sat down then and crossed his arms. He looked seriously mad. I'd never seen him like that before. "So, Amelia."

"So," I said back.

"Liv and I both think there must be some logical, perhaps even excusable, explanation for the plagiarism in your paper," he said, using a just-between-us-friends kind of tone that was beyond annoying. Because if we were actually friends, I wouldn't have been down there in the first place. "And I think that explanation has something to do with the Magpies. All I need you to do is tell me the truth, Amelia. Then we can sort this out, together."

"Right," I said. "Sounds totally easy."

Woodhouse made a concerned, kind of disappointed face, bringing an index finger up to his lips and staring at me for a long time.

"Amelia, I'm not saying this is easy. Standing up for yourself never is. But I can see to it that you are protected. You have my word. But it starts with you, Amelia. You need to tell me what happened."

"I didn't cheat on my paper," I said. "That's all I know."

"Your paper was submitted through the e-mail system." Mr. Woodhouse's face got all wrinkly as he rubbed his forehead. "Liv ran that paper through the plagiarism program herself."

Of course, that left out Bethany and the fact that *she* was the one who opened the e-mails first and then did whatever the hell she wanted with them, including switching the papers attached to them. But it wasn't like I could tell Woodhouse that to get the ball rolling. That would definitely count as telling on the Maggies. And Sylvia would pay for it.

I shrugged. "I don't know what to tell you then," I said. I sounded all flip, but I couldn't help it. This was all so unfair and totally ridiculous. "I didn't cheat, and that's not my paper. I don't have anything else to say. So can I go?"

"No, Amelia, you cannot go," Woodhouse said. "This isn't Vaseline on a doorknob. Plagiarism isn't the kind of thing we can just overlook, no matter how great an asset you are to the Grace Hall community. It's a violation of the school's code of conduct, Amelia. We could lose our accreditation if it was made public that we didn't take appropriate action. Not to mention the potential reaction of the other students. There have already been numerous complaints this year about the disciplinary allowances made for academic achievers."

"Academic achievers?" I repeated. "That sounds like a disease."

"This isn't a joke, Amelia!" Woodhouse yelled, scaring the crap out of me. His face was all reddish now, too. I'd never seen him like that. "We might have to expel you if you can't explain what happened. *That* is how serious this is. Come on, let me help you!"

I took a deep breath and closed my eyes. I kept them closed, too, as if the secret to the way out might be written on the insides of my lids.

"I can't."

Woodhouse took a deep, loud breath.

"I can give you a few days to think about it, Amelia. But in the meantime, I have no choice but to suspend you, effective immediately. That's nonnegotiable," Woodhouse said. "Your mother is already on her way to get you."

"Seriously? You called my mom at *work* to come down *here*? *Now*?" All I could think about was that suit she'd been wearing. She'd definitely be missing something important if she had to come to get me. It made me feel bad, and really, really mad. "Can't you just suspend me at the end of the day?"

"No, Amelia, we can't," Woodhouse said. "And you should keep in mind, while you're thinking about what you want to do, that an academic suspension is not the kind of thing Ivy League colleges will overlook. Not even if it was in your sophomore year." Woodhouse seemed even more upset about this than I was. "Your fellowship might even be revoked. I don't know."

"Great," I said, feeling like I was going to cry all of a sudden. First Zadie had taken Dylan; now she was going to take my future, too.

"Amelia, I'm going to give you one last chance. Do you have *anything* you want to say?"

"That's *not my paper!*" I screamed as loud as I could, my stupid voice cracking.

Woodhouse didn't even flinch. Instead, he made a big show of looking down at my name on the front page.

"Your name is on it, Amelia," he said quietly. "Without you telling me something more, that's all I have to go on."

I hated the way he was looking at me, as if I was this huge disappointment. A fraud. A liar. Like there was something *I* should be ashamed of. But I wasn't going to be ashamed. I hadn't done anything wrong, and I wasn't going to feel bad because I didn't want to be the school whistle-blower or whatever. Anyway, the real reason I couldn't do that was Sylvia. Turning in the Maggies would have felt really awesome until they went after her. With Sylvia, they would have so much ammunition to publicly humiliate her with, too. As tough as Sylvia liked to pretend she was, she'd never survive that. After what had happened with her last year, I sometimes worried whether she'd survive, period.

I wouldn't turn the Maggies in and risk their doing that to her. I couldn't. It wasn't my job anyway. If the school wanted to get rid of the Maggies, they could. As far as I could tell, Woodhouse already knew who a lot of them were. What did he need me for? I stared hard at him, willing my eyes to dig into his face, but all they kept doing was sprouting tears.

This bad feeling that had swelled up in my stomach wasn't helping either. Even as I tried to squash it down, there it was, still nibbling at the bottom of my gut. The truth, that's what it was. Because it wasn't just Sylvia who I was protecting. It was Dylan, too. Deep down, maybe I even knew that Woodhouse would make sure that nothing happened to Sylvia if I turned the Maggies in. But I couldn't be so sure what would become of Dylan.

Was I seriously willing to get expelled for her, though? Like Sylvia kept reminding me, Dylan wasn't acting the way someone did when she cared about you. How could I pretend that wasn't true? Because she was a girl? Because I loved her?

Love. Suddenly the word sounded weird. Like I was pronouncing it wrong.

No, I wasn't going to do this. I wasn't going to be *that* pathetic. I was a good student. I'd worked hard my whole life. I wasn't going to give all of that up for the chance to get back together with Dylan.

"I think I know what happened," I said finally, staring down at my hands. My voice was small.

I could do this. I could.

But there was a knock at the door before I could say anything more.

"Come in," Woodhouse called, sounding stressed. He knew I'd been close to coming clean.

Mrs. Pearl popped her head in. "I'm sorry to bother you Mr. Woodhouse," she said, kissing his butt so much it made my mouth hurt. "But there's an issue in the cafeteria that I'm afraid you need to attend to."

"Can't you handle it?" He pointed at me. He was worried that I'd change my mind, and it was a fair thing to worry about. I was on board, but barely. "Can't you see I'm in the middle of a meeting with a student?"

"I wouldn't have interrupted if it wasn't absolutely essential," Mrs. Pearl said testily. "A student saw a rat, a large one. And now it apparently can't be located."

"What do you want me to do? Hunt for it? Delia, this is a really important conversation I'm having." I'd never seen anyone talk to Mrs. Pearl like that. As if she was a pest. It was kind of great. "Why don't you call maintenance?"

"Unfortunately, the student is refusing to move until she speaks with you, personally," Mrs. Pearl said, even saltier. "I assure you, we've tried everything. Honestly, for some reason she's quite hysterical about talking to you, specifically."

Woodhouse closed his eyes.

"Okay," he said finally. "Amelia, I'll be right back. You're doing the right thing. Just sit tight."

As soon as the door closed behind them, my phone alerted with a text. I was hoping it was Ben saying he was going to make it out to Brooklyn after all. I was still fantasizing about ducking out and seeing him. As I pulled out my phone, I looked around for how I'd sneak out. But the text was from Sylvia, not Ben.

Make a run for it. I'll cover you.

Kate

"I'm sorry," Kate said again. She and Lew were standing on Eighth Street, on the meticulous stretch of sidewalk outside the Carmon house. "I just had to go. I know it's not a good excuse, but I had to see who Ben was."

"Hmm," Lew said. He wasn't looking at her. He hadn't since she'd told him about going to Ben's address and discovering Jeremy. "So you've said."

"In the end it was a good thing, right?" Kate tried. But it was hard to focus on her excuses, much less to sound convincing when she still felt so shaken and guilty, for so many different things. "At least now we know that Ben wasn't involved."

"Hmm," Lew said again, looking utterly unmoved. Kate was glad she'd emphasized how upset she'd been to learn that Jeremy was Amelia's father. She suspected that was the only reason Lew wasn't coming down harder on her. "We got the phone company to expedite a response to our subpoena." He checked his small notepad. "The texts to you about Amelia's dad came from a phone registered to Daniel Moore."

"Oh God," Kate said quietly.

If Daniel had been angry enough to tip off *insidethelaw*—an act that could easily be traced back to him—sending some anonymous texts to Kate would have been nothing. Still, thinking of his writing such vicious things was chilling. It was far beyond trying to publicly humiliate Jeremy. It was threatening.

"Why would he write that Amelia didn't jump, though?"

"He didn't. Those first two texts to you about Amelia came from elsewhere. I'm waiting for a call on that. But the texts to Amelia about her dad"—Lew nodded in the direction of the house—"those all came from here."

"Zadie Goodwin sent them?"

"I expect so," he said, looking up at the building. "But all we know for sure is that they were routed through a computer in this house. More than one person lives here." He turned back to Kate, looking directly at her for the first time. "There is something else you should know," Lew said. "The tech guys uncovered some more text messages on Amelia's phone. Deleted ones. They make those little paper notes look like, well, child's play."

"What did they say?" Kate spun around. "I want to see them."

Lew shook his head. "They aren't the kind of thing any parent should ever see."

They rang the bell and waited. Kate squinted up at the converted factory's polished glass and steel facade. The sun was high in the sky now, glinting off the building's huge windows.

"We're sure this is one house?" Lew asked.

"I think so," Kate said, but it was conspicuously large, even compared to Park Slope's largest brownstones. "There's only one bell."

Lew had to ring it three more times before someone cracked the door and pressed her eyeball to it. Through the sliver, Kate spied a small woman with a bent, wary affect.

Lew ducked his head down to make eye contact with her. "We're here to see Zadie Goodwin and her parents."

"One moment. I will check," the woman said in her thick European accent. Her one eye narrowed, then she slammed shut the door.

A beat later, it opened again. Standing there was a towering guy in a flashy gray suit and a pink, French-cuffed shirt. His shiny silver cuff links were shaped like dice, and on his right hand was a ring with a gaudy red jewel in the center. He was handsome, in an overcoiffed, overtanned way that screamed substantial wealth without concomitant sophistication. Even his teeth were too perfect and too white, like someone overcompensating for a history of bad dental hygiene.

"Hi there," he said with a smile that shimmied between friendly and fuck you. "I'm Frank Carmon, and you would be?"

"I'm Lieutenant Thompson, and this is Kate Baron," Lew began. "We'd like to ask your daughter a few questions about Amelia Baron. She died in a fall from the roof of Grace Hall. She was Kate's daughter."

Carmon frowned and shook his head. "That was a goddamn shame. I'm sorry for your loss, ma'am," he said to Kate, then turned back to Lew. "What is it you need to talk to my Zadie about?"

My Zadie. Like she was a toddler or a little porcelain doll. It was disturbing.

"The girls were in some kind of club together," Lew said casually. "We're just trying to gather information about Amelia's state of mind from every possible source."

Carmon stared out over their heads as he ran his tongue over his teeth. Finally, he looked over his shoulder toward the woman who'd answered the door, now looming in the shadows behind him.

"Go get Zadie," he said. "Tell her it's important."

He opened the door then, leading the way into the vast, open living-room-cum-dining-area-cum-kitchen, flushed with sunlight from the floor-to-ceiling windows. Carmon picked up a short glass from the otherwise bare granite countertop.

"Can I get either of you a drink?" he asked.

"No, thank you," Lew said. "You used to be at the Seventy-eighth, right? Here in the neighborhood?"

Carmon laughed, brushing invisible lint from his pants.

"Yeah, for about five minutes a million years ago," he said. "Before I decided that there were easier ways to make a living than getting shot at."

"Looks like you were right." Lew motioned to the house. "Don't know about easier, but it sure looks like it pays better."

"So far, so good." Carmon winked, took a sip.

"You get a lot of your guys from the Seventy-eighth?"

Carmon stared hard at Lew for a minute, then smiled.

"Some."

"Including Detective Molina?"

"Been a long time since I got involved in specific hires," Carmon said smoothly. "I've got people who do that for me these days."

"Molina was the detective assigned to Amelia Baron's case. Looks like he—at a minimum—cut some corners to rule it a suicide. Then a couple of days later, he left to work for you," Lew said, opting for the full-on, direct approach. "Seems like a pretty big coincidence, don't you think? Given that your stepdaughter and Amelia seemed to be butting heads quite a bit in this club of theirs."

Carmon nodded like he was considering this information. "I can't speak to any of that. I don't get involved in the details of my stepdaughter's high-school drama," he said. "But if you want to talk to Molina, Lieutenant, I'm sure I could get him on the phone. Right now, if you want. That is, assuming he does work for me."

Zadie stomped into the living room then, not stopping until she threw herself onto a stool at the kitchen island.

"I was doing my homework, *you know*," she growled. She was wearing a plaid schoolgirl skirt that wasn't much wider than a belt and had a bunch of piercings in her ears and a ring through her nose. It fit nicely with her heavy black eye makeup and short, shaggy black hair, which had a huge chunk of white down one side, like the off-kilter stripe on a skunk. Kate couldn't take her eyes off the stripe. "Just because your friend says they'll probably let me *in*, doesn't mean that Columbia definitely will. I'm not in until I'm actually in."

"Columbia," Lew said. "Impressive. Getting in there sure wouldn't be a thing you'd want to jeopardize."

"Tell me about it." Carmon shook his head in exaggerated disbelief. "Lucky for her, she doesn't have my genes. Come on, my Zadie." He waved her over, then patted the spot on the couch next to him. "These nice folks just need to ask you a couple questions about that girl from your school, the one who died."

Zadie rolled her eyes again, then pounded over and dropped down next to Carmon with a big huff.

"One thing here, before my Zadie answers any of your questions," Carmon said, feigning nonchalance. "She doesn't need a lawyer, does she? This is just informational?"

"She's not under arrest," Lew said, notably skirting the question, "if that's what you're asking."

He wasn't making any promises, and it wasn't lost on Carmon. He stared hard at Lew for a long time.

"She didn't have anything to do with what happened to that girl," Carmon said. "So you can ask whatever you want about that. But we're ending this if we get near anything that could keep her tail out of Columbia. She's worked too hard, and I've spent too much goddamn money—"

The front door opened then. There were voices in the hallway—one sharp and rapid-fire, the other mumbled and apologetic, probably the housekeeper. Then there was the sound of high heels clicking loudly across the concrete floor.

"Oh," Adele said, her pretty face falling as she rounded the corner. She recovered gracefully, though, smiling easily as she headed straight over to Kate, in her fashionable black A-line dress and big hoop earrings, her hair swept up in a soft but flawless chignon. Adele leaned forward, pressing her cheek hard against Kate's as she kissed the empty air next to her ear. "What a nice surprise, Kate. But you didn't have to come all the way over just to talk about PTA matters. I know how busy you are."

"We're not here about that," Kate said, bracing for Lew to make her stop talking. He didn't. "We're here about what happened between Amelia and the Magpies."

"The Magpies?" Adele pursed her red lips and looked over at Carmon, who shrugged and took another sip of his drink. "I'm not sure I—"

"I've read the minutes of the school board meetings," Kate said, hoping things might go better if she kept Adele from embarrassing herself by outright lying to them. "I know that Woodhouse tried to get rid of the clubs and that the school board stopped him."

Adele dropped her purse down hard onto one of the kitchen stools, then turned back slowly. She crossed her arms as she leaned back against the counter.

"Then you also must know that the board was only looking out for the best interests of the school," Adele said calmly.

Kate tried not to get angry, but it wasn't working. "The school had an obligation—"

"The school can't control what students do when they're not on school grounds," Adele said coolly. If she felt defensive, she was hiding it masterfully. "That kind of monitoring is a practical and legal impossibility, particularly in the age of the smartphone. The responsibility for policing off-campus and cyber-behavior must be left to individual families."

The lines were well rehearsed, as though Adele had been waiting for Lew and Kate to come asking. She probably had been, from the very first night she'd shown up at Kate's door. In fact, that could have been the real reason Adele had come by that first night.

Kate turned to Zadie then, hoping she might be less prepared. "Was it because she was gay? Is that why you did it?"

"Zadie, don't answer that," Adele snapped.

"Why? I want to," Zadie bit right back at her, then swiveled her head in Kate's direction. "I wasn't going to let Amelia turn Dylan into some dyke just because that's what *she* wanted." Zadie looked like she was trying to stay tough, but her cheeks were flushed and her voice was getting quaky. "Amelia thought that having sex with Dylan made her more important than me. But sex is easy. With Dylan, it's practically nothing. Trust me, she'll have sex with anyone not at this school. And I know all this because I've been fucking best friends with her for *twelve* years. *That's* something that matters. Not this . . . whatever . . . she had with Amelia for, like, two weeks."

But the look in Zadie's eyes said that it wasn't that simple. She was trying to hide it—working her neck, the tough curl of her lip— but there was something desperate about it, like Dylan was all she'd ever had.

"Zadie, we need to know what happened up on that roof," Lew said calmly. "It's time for the truth, all of it."

"I'm not going to let Zadie get into a discussion that could incriminate her," Adele said, holding up a hand as she stepped between Lew and Zadie. "If you'd like to interview her further, it will be at the police station, with our attorney present. But I assure you, whatever happened on that roof was an accident."

"An accident?" Zadie glared at her mom. "You're acting like I was there. Like *I* did something."

"We know for sure that someone in this house did something to Amelia." Lew pulled from his pocket two printouts and tossed them onto the coffee table. "She got texts harassing her about her relationship with Dylan and about the identity of her father. They came from this house."

Zadie stepped forward and picked the pages up. "What the hell do I care about her dad?"

If she was pretending not to have seen those messages before, she was doing a very good job.

"We were hoping you'd tell us," Lew said. "Because we know for sure that the messages came from here, from this house."

"I didn't— Holy shit, Mom, what is your deal with this girl?" Zadie's eyes were wide as she turned them on Adele. "You told me that you'd had some whole thing with her mom in college, that you wanted to make it up to her." She hooked her thumb toward Kate. "That's why you wanted me to tap Amelia. But you didn't even go to college with her, Mom, did you?"

"Zadie!" Adele snatched the pages out of her daughter's hands. She folded them in half, then visibly tried to regain her composure. It wasn't as successful this time. "Be quiet, honey, please."

Kate watched a tremor of hurt pass over Zadie's face, then rage rise up in her eyes. Why in the world would Adele have asked Zadie to invite Amelia into the Maggies? Kate's eyes moved from Zadie's face to the white stripe in her hair, a stripe that could have been many things, including Waardenburg syndrome.

The most exquisite, unusual eyes, too, Kate now remembered Adele saying when she'd been to the house. *That's a family trait? Two different colors like that?* Why wouldn't Adele have asked about Waardenburg syndrome? Why wouldn't she have mentioned that her daughter had it, too? *I knew people at Slone, Thayer. I still do.* It was too much information for Kate to process all at once.

"So what happened between you and Amelia on the roof was an accident, like your mom said, Zadie?" Lew seemed to be deliberately trying to fan the flames. "The two of you had an argument about Dylan, maybe. It got out of hand?"

"Stop it! Stop talking to her!" Adele screamed at Lew. "I know you don't have an arrest warrant. You would have shown it to us if you did."

"No, ma'am, we don't," Lew said. "We were just trying to get some questions answered. You're within your rights not to cooperate. Of course, innocent people don't usually need to hide behind an attorney."

"Innocent," Adele snorted. "You and I both know that's a relative concept, Lieutenant. I think my daughter would be better served by taking her chances and getting that lawyer."

"Chances?" Zadie snapped. "What the fuck, Mom? Why are you talking about me like I'm a criminal? I didn't do—"

"Zadie," Adele hissed. She looked as if she was coming unglued. A piece of her carefully swept-back hair had fallen loose, and with it the rest of her seemed to be unraveling, too. She waved a finger in her daughter's face. "I mean it. For once in your life, could you not make absolutely everything worse!"

Zadie recoiled, blinking. Her mouth pulled in once, then again, like she was about to cry, but her face quickly set back into stone.

"Come on, Adele, take it easy," Frank Carmon said, finally pushing himself out of his chair and reluctantly into the fray. "There's no need to get crazy."

"Crazy!" Adele screamed, waving her finger in front of Frank now. "It's crazy for a mother to want to protect her child from herself?"

"Right, because you're trying to save me," Zadie laughed, but tears had smeared her black eye makeup. "You don't care about me. All you care about is yourself."

"Zadie, this isn't a game," Adele said, more quietly now. "You say the wrong thing, and you could go to jail for the rest of your life. "

"Um, unless, of course, *I didn't fucking do anything*!" Zadie stared at her mother for a second, then there was a sudden flash of recognition. She laughed in a crazy, manic way. "Oh my God, Mom. You *actually* think I pushed her?"

"No," Adele said, though it was clear she did. "That's not what I—"

"Holy shit, you do. You seriously think I killed Amelia. That I *murdered* somebody." Zadie turned to Kate. "She's the one who wouldn't shut up about her. She was obsessed. 'She's the daughter of my long-lost friend, blah, blah, fucking, blah.' She even made me find out where you worked so she could get back in touch with you. All of that was bullshit, obviously. She doesn't even know you. You are such a fucking liar, Mom. Who knows, maybe *you* pushed Amelia."

"Okay," Frank said again as he walked over and rested his glass on the counter. "I think all the ladies here need to take a deep breath."

"I wouldn't take her side if I were you, Frank," Zadie said. "You know the only person she has ever really cared about is him." She pointed toward the framed photographs on the bookshelf. "When she gets into her third glass of Merlot and you're not here, she says she doesn't belong stuck with some wannabe mafioso from Bay Ridge. She loves your money. But you, Frank? I'm not so sure. Isn't that right, Mommy?"

Kate stared at the framed pictures on the bookcase where Zadie had pointed, slowly moving across the room toward them.

Adele had turned to Frank, who was taking another long swallow of his drink. "Frank," she pleaded, "you know that's not true."

Frank's mouth pulled in as he nodded. "Sure thing, Adele." He reached for the bottle of whiskey and refilled his glass. "Whatever you say."

As Kate drifted closer to the photographs, she saw a familiar banner at the back of one, and she recognized the school photo arrangement of the two dozen adults pictured, too. Even from a distance, she knew she'd seen the photograph somewhere before.

"Frank, I'm serious." Adele sounded frantic. "You can't listen to Zadie. She lies all the time. You *know* that."

Kate was at the bookshelf now, bracing for someone to stop her before she laid hands on the photo. No one did. They were all too focused on one another.

"I don't know what happened to Amelia on that roof," Zadie said to Lew. Her voice was low and quiet now, almost unrecognizable. "But I can prove I wasn't up there."

Kate lifted the photograph from the shelf, running her hand across the glass, then tracing her finger down the sides of the heavy silver frame. It was a photo from a Bar Association Public Service Award ceremony from seventeen years earlier. And there was Jeremy in the center of the photo, shaking Adele's hand as he accepted a plaque.

Kate had seen the photo so many times before, sitting on a shelf behind Jeremy's head whenever they were meeting in his office. She'd never even noticed the woman handing him the award, until now.

"I was here when Amelia died," Zadie said finally.

"In the middle of a school day?" Lew asked.

Kate turned around, the photo still in her hands. She looked at Adele, who was still staring at Zadie. Adele had one hand over her mouth, for the first time looking upset instead of enraged.

"And I wasn't alone." Zadie shrugged. "You can ask him, if you want. I guess he might lie. He's kind of a prick that way."

"What's his name?" Lew asked.

"Ian Greene," Zadie said.

"You can check the house security tapes for confirmation. They're all dated and time-stamped," Carmon said to Lew. But Zadie was telling the truth. Kate already felt sure of it. "As for Molina, you should ask her about him." He nodded his head in the direction of Adele.

"Last time I checked our phone records, she was still finding a reason to talk to him every day."

"Her hair," Kate finally managed to say. She pointed to Zadie's streak. "It's Waardenburg syndrome, isn't it?"

Adele turned around slowly. She looked first at the picture in Kate's hands, then up at Kate. When she did, there were tears in Adele's eyes.

"I have to give you credit, you're a good liar," Adele said, her voice wavering. "I went to your house because Molina told me about the text you'd gotten about Amelia. I wanted to see for myself what you planned to do about it. I almost believed you when you said there was no family history of Waardenburg even though you and I both know that's impossible. Jeremy must love the way you protect him. It's very convincing."

"I said that because it was the truth," Kate said. "*I'm* Amelia's family and I don't have Waardenburg."

Adele shook her head like she was sure Kate was still covering for Jeremy.

"I guess that's why he's kept you around all these years. Me, he wanted nothing to do with. He was worried I was going to make him accountable. The funny part is that I would have kept his secret, too, if he'd done something to keep his *other* illegitimate child away from *my* daughter." Adele shook her head, then wiped at her eyes. "He was talking about leaving Vera for me, you know. He would have, too, if you hadn't come along. I realize that now. At the time, he told me he'd decided he had to stop cheating on Vera. But it was actually about you. I had no idea there was another *child* until I saw Amelia at Grace Hall this fall, when she volunteered for the Harvest Festival. I noticed her eyes, but I never would have made the connection to Jeremy if Julia Golde hadn't mentioned how it was so amazing that Amelia was so great, given that she was being raised by a single mother—a lawyer— with a crazy schedule." Adele was staring at her clenched hands now, looking closer to the edge of tears. "It took only one call to find out about you and Jeremy. It's not the best-kept secret. I wasn't just going to let Jeremy get away with lying to me for all these years. He made me think *I* was the only one. That what we'd had actually meant something. He should have at least had the decency to keep Amelia out of Grace Hall, and away from me."

Kate tried to breathe, but she felt like someone was sitting on her chest. She'd been even more responsible for everything that had happened to Amelia than she ever could have imagined.

"It was you who e-mailed Daniel Moore?"

"We're on the Bar Ethics Committee together. Daniel has been complaining about Jeremy to me for years," she said. "He was looking for a way to get back at him. Of course, he waited months before finally doing something about it. I didn't think he was ever going to."

"So you dragged Amelia into it?"

"It was time that someone held Jeremy accountable," Adele said. "And Jeremy made clear a long time ago that he'd make me pay if I ever opened my mouth. He plays golf with my general counsel. He could have destroyed my career before the first tee." She shrugged. "He'd never have done anything to Amelia. I obviously had no way of knowing"—she motioned toward Zadie, who glared again at her mother—"that things with Amelia and the club, with Dylan, would get so out of hand. How could I possibly have predicted any of that?"

They sat in Lew's car in silence. Kate had walked out of the Carmon house still holding the photograph. She sat in the passenger seat, staring down at it.

"Are you going to be okay?" Lew asked, after they'd sat there like that for at least five minutes.

"I keep thinking things can't get worse, but then they do." Kate shook her head. "If I'd been honest with Amelia about who her father was, or at least who I thought he was, maybe none of this would have happened. She might still be alive."

Lew shook his head. "Wouldn't have made a difference."

"You don't know that."

"Maybe not," he said quietly, then looked Kate hard in the eye. "But you need to."

Lew's phone rang then. He answered it and, after a few curt yeses, hung up. He stared at the steering wheel for a minute, his finger tracing the outside of the circle.

"Who was that?" Kate asked.

"We got an address on those first texts sent to you about Amelia," he said as he started the car.

Julia did not look happy to see them. She opened the door and forced something that didn't even approximate a smile.

"Sylvia isn't feeling well," she said. "I'm not sure she'll be up for visitors."

"I'm afraid, ma'am, this isn't an optional discussion," Lew said. "I wish that it were."

Julia stared hard at Lew, then, for even longer, at Kate.

"In that case, come in, I guess." Julia looked away from Kate and moved begrudgingly to the side. "I'll need to make sure that she's awake."

But as soon as they stepped inside, there was Sylvia, standing like a gray specter in the doorway to the kitchen.

"Oh, there you are," Julia said nervously. She went over and wrapped an arm around Sylvia's shoulders, then closed her eyes as she kissed the top of Sylvia's head. "Kate and the detective have a few more questions they want to ask you. If you're not up to it, honey, that's okay." Then she turned to Lew, apparently suddenly realizing something. "Speaking of which, what exactly did you mean when you said this wasn't an optional discussion?"

"Your daughter left out some facts surrounding Amelia's death," Lew said matter-of-factly. "We need for her to supply them now. Kate's waited a long time to know what happened to her daughter. It's time now, Sylvia, that she knows."

Julia looked from Lew to Kate, then down to Sylvia, considering. Finally, she nodded.

"Sylvia doesn't have anything to hide. We loved Amelia like she was family. We want to know what happened to her, too."

"You knew Amelia was a Magpie, isn't that right, Sylvia?" Lew asked. His tone wasn't exactly aggressive, but it was as forceful as Kate had seen him be.

Sylvia stared down at her hands for a minute. When she looked up, there were tears in her eyes.

"Do you know the stuff they did to her?" her voice squeaked out. "I was afraid— I thought they would do the same thing to me if I told you about them. That stuff . . . it doesn't even matter if it's true, people don't forget."

"Do you think it was one of the Magpies who pushed her off the roof?" Kate asked.

Her heart was pounding. *Yes, say yes. Say you saw it happen.*

Sylvia shook her head. "Like I told you before, I think that Ben kid did it. Have you even found him? He was supposed to be visiting Amelia *that day.*"

"We found Ben," Lew said quietly. "It wasn't him."

"Oh." Sylvia wrapped her thin arms around herself. "Never mind then."

"These clubs," Julia said, crossing her arms and shaking her head, "I'm getting on the phone today about this. We pay tens of thousands of dollars to send our children to Grace Hall, and this is what we get: *Lord of the Flies?*"

"I agree, ma'am, you should contact the school. All the parents should." Lew took a deep breath, as if he were relieved the hard part was over. Kate wondered if it was genuine, or if he was just trying to get Sylvia to relax. "Now what about Dylan? Is there a reason you didn't mention her to us before?"

Kate stared at Sylvia, waiting for her to look confused, worried, something. But she just looked worn-out.

"She didn't even tell me about Dylan until after it was over," Sylvia said finally. "I told her that girl wasn't worth it. But Amelia was crazy upset about it and totally obsessed with getting Dylan back. She wouldn't listen to me."

"She was 'crazy upset'?" Kate asked.

"Like nutso." Sylvia shook her head

"And you didn't think maybe you should tell somebody? Like an adult?" Kate snapped. It sounded like an accusation. She couldn't help it. What if Amelia really had killed herself? Because for the first time, it suddenly seemed possible. "Maybe she needed help."

"Kate, that is *not* fair," Julia shot back. "I'm not going to let you blame *my* child for *your* oversights. It wasn't her job to be Amelia's mother. It was yours."

Kate closed her eyes and tried not to cry. Because Julia was right, of course. Kate was the one who'd really failed Amelia.

"I think Amelia was in that club because she was lonely." Sylvia's voice cracked, and there were tears in her eyes. Julia put her hands on Sylvia's shoulders, trying to calm her down, but she shrugged her mother off. "She needed a family. Maybe if you'd been around more, instead of spending all your time at your stupid job, she'd still be alive."

"Okay, okay." Lew stepped forward. "Let's take a step back here. We're just trying to fill in some blanks. I think you know more than you're telling about what happened to Amelia. I think you were there."

"What?" Julia's eyes were wide. "Sylvia, what are they talking about?"

"No." Sylvia shook her head. "I helped her get out of Woodhouse's office, but then when I came out of the bathroom afterward, she was gone. I don't know where she went."

Lew nodded, looking down at his notepad without writing until the weight of his silence grew unbearable.

"I don't know anything else, really," Sylvia added, caving to the pressure. Her eyes had welled up, and her voice was scratchy. "I swear."

"Except that I think you do." Lew pulled a page out from his back pocket and held it out to Julia. "I think you know a lot more than you're telling us."

Julia looked down at it, confused. "I don't understand. What is this?"

"It's a report tracing some anonymous texts that Sylvia sent to Kate," Lew said. "The texts said that Amelia didn't jump. Isn't that right, Sylvia?"

There were tears streaming down Sylvia's face now. She tried to speak but only sucked in air. Then she dropped herself down onto a kitchen chair and put her head in her hands as she sobbed. Julia went over and knelt beside her daughter.

"Whatever it is, we'll figure it out," Julia said, rubbing Sylvia's arms. "But you have to tell them, honey. You have to tell them why you wrote that."

Finally, Sylvia sniffled hard and looked up. Her brown eyes were wet and red-rimmed, her cheeks still slick.

"After Amelia died, I started walking by your house sometimes after school. I stayed on the other side of the street so you wouldn't see me," Sylvia said to Kate. She was hugging herself now. "One time, it was, like, late afternoon, and you were standing there in your doorway in a robe. Just standing there, staring. At nothing. Maybe you went out to get the paper or something, but then it was like you'd forgot what you were doing. You were frozen. And it was totally"—Sylvia was staring at a blank space on the floor, as if she were seeing it play out there again—"awful. Like, so much worse than you crying at the funeral, and that was really bad." Sylvia shook her head and pulled in a quaky breath. "I thought maybe if you didn't think she'd jumped . . . if you didn't think it was your fault . . . maybe that would make it better for you."

"So you pretended you knew," Julia said, sounding relieved. "To make Kate feel better."

"No," Sylvia said, her wet eyes were still locked on Kate's. "Amelia didn't jump. I know that she didn't."

facebook

Amelia Baron

"A ghostly roll of drums, remorselessly beat the measure of life . . . and warned her whose day had slipped past in one quick doing after another that it was all ephemeral as a rainbow." Virginia Woolf, To the Lighthouse

Carter Rose	Dude, TMI
Sylvia Golde	Shut up, Carter, you moron

Amelia

When I poked my head out of Woodhouse's office, I could see Sylvia there, in front of Mrs. Pearl's office next door, blocking her view of the hallway and of me as I made my escape.

"What I'm *saying* is that it makes me kind of uncomfortable that Grace Hall doesn't offer alternatives to evolution." Sylvia was talking loudly, and in this really superior voice. She was waving an index finger through the air. "Where's the intellectual *dialogue* if you only present one point of view?"

"*This* is why you had to be excused from biology to come down here immediately?" Mrs. Pearl asked.

"I happen to take my religious beliefs *very* seriously," Sylvia said, sounding appalled.

I noticed Sylvia's other hand down behind her back. Her fingers were waving me out of the office. I ducked down and made my way toward the door.

"I'm sorry, Ms. Golde, I must have missed the memo about you being born again," Mrs. Pearl said sarcastically. "And here I'd been thinking this whole time that you were Jewish."

"I am Jewish, and I am *also* born again," Sylvia said as I stepped out into the hall and tiptoed past Mrs. Pearl's door. "You have something against interfaith marriage, too?"

I pressed myself against the wall, praying that Sylvia would hurry up before someone noticed me hanging out there in the hall in the middle of third period.

"Okay, that's officially enough, Ms. Golde," Mrs. Pearl began. "You need to return to class and—"

"Fine, I was about to leave anyway." Sylvia said. "But this isn't over. I won't be marginalized for my beliefs."

When Sylvia finally dove down the hall toward me, she had a huge grin on her face. It made me smile. And I would have sworn at that moment that I would never smile again.

"Come on," Sylvia said, grabbing my hand and yanking me down the hall.

"I can't *leave*," I whispered. "Woodhouse is going to come back. If I'm not there, he is going to be really pissed off."

Sylvia stared at me then. "So what?" she said. "Let him be. You didn't do anything wrong."

"They can kick me out of school."

"Hello? You are the victim here. Woodhouse will back off the second you tell him that Zadie and her friends were harassing you for being gay. It is the truth, after all."

She did have a point, except that was leaving out the part about the Maggies going after her.

"Come on," Sylvia said, tugging my arm again. "We both need some cheering up, and I have a plan."

The first stop was the Grace Hall auditorium, which was so fancy and huge, it was shared by both the Upper School and the Lower School next door. With its cushy, newly upholstered seats and polished mahogany stage, it was nicer than a lot of Broadway theaters.

"If I'd known this place just sat here, open all the time," Sylvia said, her left hand smacking down the back of the seats as she made her way down the center aisle, "I would have totally had sex up on the stage."

"Ugh, Sylvia, gross."

"Oh please," she said as she neared the stage, "don't even try to play that prude crap with me anymore. You and I both know it's bullshit."

I followed her, but more slowly. The good girl in me still didn't like being somewhere I wasn't supposed to be. And we definitely weren't allowed to be in the auditorium unattended. There was a reason the place stayed so nice. Sylvia ran up and onto the dark stage and stood in the shadows at the center. The glow from the few lights made her look spooky, but in a pretty way.

"What are we doing here, Sylvia?" I called from the first row of seats.

I'd tried not to sound nervous—Sylvia would just make me stay there longer—but I kind of did anyway.

"We're going on a tour of some of our finest moments, my dear maiden," she said from center stage with a bad English accent and a dramatic flourish of her hands. "I'd say we both need a reminder of how utterly fabulous we are. *This*, my fair lady, is your first stop."

I was smiling and shaking my head. Sylvia was nuts, but sometimes in the best possible way. She was also a great friend. Despite everything I'd done, all the lies I had told, there she was. At the exact moment I needed her most.

"How is this one of my stops?" I asked. "What does the auditorium have to do with me?"

"Come up here to center stage, madam," she said, calling to me like a circus announcer. "And I will show you."

I climbed the steps onto the stage, feeling self-conscious even though there wasn't a soul in the audience.

"Okay," I said, once I was standing next to her under the ghostly lights. I stared out over all those empty seats. "I think maybe you have me confused with someone else because this seriously isn't ringing any bells."

"Just wait," she said, putting her hands on my upper arms and staring out past my shoulder at an imaginary crowd. "It was here that I decided you had to stay my best friend forever. Second grade, Ms. Ritter's class, Presidents' Day presentation. You were scared shitless to go out onstage, even though it was going to be with everyone else and all you had to do was hold up your sign that had the letter *G* on it. But that's neither here nor there. The point is, you actually had to go throw up beforehand. You *must* remember that."

"Oh yeah," I said, feeling kind of sick just thinking about it. I'd blocked it out, mostly. But I did have this vivid image of Ms. Ritter handing me tissues and asking me if I always threw up when I was nervous. "Now I remember. Thanks, yeah, that was awesome times."

"It was seriously like a marquee moment for me."

"Me throwing up is your big defining moment? That's so pathetic." Looking out over all those empty seats, I was starting to feel hollow. The high that had come from jetting out of Woodhouse's office was fading. Whenever this little field trip of Sylvia's ended, all of it—the plagiarism, the Maggies, Dylan, my embarrassing e-mail—would still be there waiting for me. "By the way, I'm still totally terrified to be onstage. It's making me nervous right now, and there's not even anyone in the audience."

"It wasn't the throwing up, stupid," Sylvia said. She crossed her arms and rolled her eyes. "It was what you did afterward."

"And what was that?"

"You came back from the bathroom with this, like, wad of tissues and this, like, *True Grit* look on your face, you went right out onstage with the rest of us. Not a whimper, not a shake, nothing," Sylvia said. "You were totally my hero."

"Thanks, Sylvia," I said. "I still think it makes me kind of lame, but thanks."

And then I remembered something else about that day. Once I'd gotten out onto the stage, I had actually kind of started to waver again. I'd looked back at Ms. Ritter, and when she'd ignored me, I'd looked for a way out on the other side of the stage. But then I saw my mom, rushing in the side doors, fifteen minutes late as usual, looking all panicked and frazzled and lost. But she was there, and when she finally spotted me—back row, left side, big *G* pressed against my chest—she had this look on her face. Like I was the most amazing thing she'd ever seen. It was her looking at me like that that had really kept me standing out there.

I was still lost in the memory when there was a sound at the back of the auditorium: the doors opening.

"Shit, come on," Sylvia said, grabbing my hand and tugging me off the stage. "We're headed to the cafeteria."

The cafeteria was empty, except for two janitors mopping the floor.

"You can't be in here," one of them barked, without looking up.

"We're doing research for a book report," Sylvia said, waving him off. "This is where you told Whitman Price to fuck off. You do re-member *that*, right?"

It took a second for that to come back to me, too, but it did. Back in the sixth grade, Whitman had been, like, the ringleader of a pack of boys who had picked on all the girls. He'd pointed out one girl's too-big ankles and the ugly mole on someone else's neck. He'd called us too fat or too skinny or misshapen. Of course, Whitman was kind of fat himself, with an acne-dotted face, but everybody was too scared of him to point that out. Luckily, he'd moved away back in eighth grade when his parents got divorced. I hadn't thought about him in years.

But now that I had, I did remember the day he came over to the table where I'd been sitting with Sylvia and a few of the other less popular girls. Whitman had stood at one end of the table and started giving each of us a score on how cute or not cute we were. Most of us weren't cute, according to Whitman. Then he let us know what it was exactly about the way we looked that had kept our score down. He was trying to help us out, he said. By the time he got around the table to me, a couple of the other girls were crying and a half dozen other boys had come around to watch.

"And you," he'd said, pointing at me, "you've got a horse face. It's, like, all long and flat and like three times normal size."

I'd never been the type to stand up to people. But on that day, with Whitman picking us off like we were fish in a barrel, something in me had snapped.

"And you're really fat, Whitman," I'd said. "So fuck you."

I'd never said a swear word out loud before. Much less *that* swear word. It felt like my mouth was going to burst into flames.

"Oooh, snap!" one of the other boys had hooted.

"Damn, Whitman, she called you *out*," somebody else had said.

And Whitman had looked so mad, I'd thought for a second he might punch me. But then he'd just turned around and disappeared into the crowd. He was back at it a few days later. Not the next day, though. That next day he'd stayed by himself, far on the other side of the cafeteria.

"Come on," Sylvia said, stepping toward the door. "We've got to get out of here. I think one of the janitors just went to call somebody."

We went on like that through the school, dodging and weaving and ducking our way past teachers and staff and administration. Sylvia took me to where I'd once won the science fair with my project on magnetism and plants, and the place where, in eighth grade, Chris Mellon had told me he liked me. We stopped at the place on the second floor where I'd told Sylvia—in the seventh grade—that I was going to be a writer someday, no matter how hard it was.

None of the stops on Sylvia's tour could change anything. They didn't make Dylan love me, or swap my excellent *Lighthouse* paper for that copied one. None of the memories took back all the awful things Zadie had done or erased the embarrassment of everyone's seeing my e-mail.

But the tour did remind me that my life had been bigger than just that one moment. One girl. One set of words on paper. That I had gone through other things before—good and terrible, funny and awful—and I had survived.

We were back in the hallway when the bell rang. We dove into a janitor's closet to hide while classes changed, pressing ourselves against the wall next to the mop and bucket. We held our breath for as long as we could so we didn't choke on the bleach smell.

"Thank you," I said to Sylvia, when the hallway was quiet again and we were about to head back out, "I needed this."

"We're not done yet," Sylvia said. "It's my turn now."

Crap. I should have been thinking of where to go on Sylvia's tour. Because totally nothing was jumping to mind. What had been her marquee moments?

"Don't worry," Sylvia said, reading my mind. "You're off the hook. I've already got where we're going all worked out."

From the closet, we hit an empty classroom in the north wing, then the library and the courtyard, visiting Sylvia's most important places— which mostly (no, all) had to do with boys—giggling as we dodged teachers and staff. It felt as if we were little again, wrapped tight in our own pretend world.

But by the fourth of Sylvia's stops, things had started to take a turn for the worse. Every place we were stopping wasn't just about a guy. It was where a guy had *broken up* with Sylvia. At first she didn't seem upset, but then all of a sudden it was like she'd hit some kind of tipping point and she looked all shaky and sad.

"None of them deserved you," I said as we headed toward the fire door. "You're better off without them."

"I know," she said. "That's why I'm reminding myself."

But I didn't believe her. It was like the awesome light inside her had been snuffed out.

"Where are we going now?" I asked as we headed up the stairs, hoping we were going to end her little merryless march of men soon.

"To the roof," she said with a sad smile, trudging onward. "And cheer up. It'll be the last stop on Sylvia Golde's trail of tears."

I stopped. That was exactly what I'd been afraid of. She was really upset, even if she'd been trying to act like the whole thing was about how *not* upset she was.

"Sylvia, come on," I said. "What do those stupid boys know about anything anyway?" My mind was racing, trying to think of anyplace maybe I could take her. Someplace she had done something remarkable. But I was coming up totally blank, even though there had to be cool things Sylvia had done. Big, like, impressive moments she'd had. Except I seriously couldn't think of any. "You are mad creative and

supertalented. You are a crazy style icon. You're going to be an amazing fashion designer someday, I just know it. It'll be like you and Steve
McQueen at fashion week together."

"It's Alexander McQueen." Sylvia rolled her eyes. "And he's dead.
So is Steve McQueen."

"Fine, then Donna Karan."

"Donna Karan? Seriously? She might as well be dead."

"Come on, Sylvia."

"I know, I know, you're trying to make me feel better. But you
know, you actually sound kind of desperate," Sylvia said, trudging on
up the steps without looking back at me. She shrugged. "And it's okay.
I know who I am. I accept it. You don't have to try to cover for me.
Now come on."

When we were finally at the top, Sylvia pushed open the door to the
roof and we stepped out onto the south side of the building.

"Didn't they catch a bunch of kids smoking up here once?" I looked
around at the tops of the trees. Above, the sky was a crisp, cloudless
blue, and it was a little cold, but still nice in the glow of the afternoon
sun. In the distance to the north, you could just see the Empire State
Building peeking between the buildings. "I thought they locked it up
here after that."

"They did, but the construction guys working on the music an-
nex unlocked it so they could eat lunch up here." She looked around,
then smiled, kind of bittersweetly. "You know, Ian and I had sex up
here once."

"Seriously?" The crazy things Sylvia did never stopped amazing me.

She nodded, then looked down and bit on her lower lip like she was
trying not to cry. Something had happened. Something bad.

"Sylvia, what's—"

We heard someone on the stairs then, the sound of keys jingling,
echoing in the stairwell.

"Shit," Sylvia whispered, waving for me to follow her. "Come on."

We crept around and ducked into a cramped little alcove on the far side of the roof and squatted down. A minute later, Liv came around the corner. Sylvia and I looked at each other, mouthing "OMG" in unison as she pulled out her phone to call somebody.

"Hi, yes, this is Liv Britton," she said. "Oh, thank you. I'm so glad. That's a huge compliment coming from you. But I think I'm going to have to retract the manuscript. Things have gotten complicated at my school, and—"

She was quiet for a minute, probably as the other person talked. She was chewing on one of her fingernails.

"Yes, I was definitely assuming I'd change all the names. But even so, I think—" She nodded through another pause. "Yes, I am aware of that. Okay, yes, I'll think about it. Thank you for your time. I'll be in touch."

Liv hung up and stared down at her phone for a minute. She took a deep breath and blew it out loudly before heading back toward the steps. We stayed down until we heard the door close behind her. Luckily, she was long gone when my phone signaled with a text.

BEN

Not mad are u? I know I suck . . .

AMELIA

It's ok, really

BEN

R u sure?

AMELIA

Totally.

BEN

U'll b okay?

AMELIA

Yes. Def. Have fun. Xoxox; we'll still meet soon! I'll make sure of it ;)

"Who was that?" Sylvia asked.

"Ben, he's in town," I said, already knowing what her reaction would be.

"You're not actually planning on seeing him, are you?" she asked. "Because over my dead, lifeless body are you meeting up with that psycho."

Sylvia walked over to the edge of the roof then, which had a weirdly low wall around the top. Just seeing her that close to the creepy edge gave me vertigo. She was standing with her back to me.

"Can you step back?" I asked. "You're freaking me out. What if you trip?"

Sylvia took one tiny half step back, which didn't make me feel any better.

"Ian broke up with me," she said. "He brought me up here an hour ago to do it. Maybe he thought the view would soften the blow."

Crap. It was bound to happen sooner or later, but that didn't actually make it any better.

"Are you okay? I mean, I'm sure that sucked. He's such a douche."

Sylvia tilted her face a little then, so that it faced the sun. In the glow, she looked even more sad. Poor Sylvia. If I'd totally seen it coming, she must have, too. But I still felt awful for her. And I wanted so much to have something more to say, something really great, the kind of thing Sylvia had said to me about Dylan. But everything jumping to mind sounded hollow and stale, even just in my head.

"You want to know what he said to me?"

"What does it even matter what that dickhead thinks?" I asked.

But it mattered to Sylvia. She needed for me to know.

"He said he wasn't *sexually* attracted to me. And when I was, like, 'What are you talking about? We have sex all the time.' He was, like, 'Yeah, we do, but basically I've only been doing that because I felt bad for you.'"

When she turned toward me, she was full-on bawling. I went over and wrapped my arms around her shoulders.

"He's just saying that," I said, burying my face in her neck. "You know that, right? You're beautiful."

She shook her head and sniffled. "I'm not as pretty as I used to be. I know that."

"That's nuts, Sylvia. What are you talking about?"

The worst part was that she was kind of right. Sylvia had been a crazy-looking little kid, like off-the-charts cute. The kind of kid people stopped on the street and gawked at in restaurants. It wasn't that she was ugly now or anything. But she was a lot more average.

"I'm not like you," she whispered as I squeezed her even tighter. "Pretty is all I have."

I pulled back to look her in the eye.

"Sylvia, that is not true," I said, and suddenly everything that was so amazing about her rushed at me. "You are funny and loyal and supportive and honest, and I wish I had a quarter of the passion that you have. You're my best friend, Sylvia, and I don't know what I'd do—"

Her phone alerted with a text. I prayed it wouldn't be from Ian. As bad as this was, it would be worse for him to get back together with her only to break up with her again later, which he definitely would, eventually. And from the way Sylvia was frantically digging for her phone, I could tell that a text from Ian was exactly what she was hoping for.

"Who's this?" Sylvia asked, looking down at the screen when she'd finally found it. "Blocked number . . ." Her voice drifted as she tapped open a message.

"What is it?" I asked.

"I don't know . . . some picture. The note says, 'Look in mirror.'" She tapped the screen again. Made a confused face at me. "It's you. Why are you in your underwear? Was this some kinky thing you did with Dylan?" She sounded totally entertained. "I'm kind of impressed, Baron. It's ballsier than I would have given you credit for."

She turned her phone toward me. Sure enough, there I was making my sexy face. It was the furthest I'd gone in any of the shots, my legs open, leaning over toward the camera. I hated seeing the picture again. It was so humiliating. I handed the phone back to Sylvia.

"Ugh, gross," I said. "It's a long story. But trust me, there was nothing sexy about it."

"Look in mirror," Sylvia muttered as she turned back down to her phone. "It's, like, a clue." She used her fingers then to enlarge the picture. "Holy shit," she whispered as I watched the color drain from her face. When she looked up at me, her eyes were wild, crazy. "Holy fucking shit!"

"What?" I asked, leaning forward to see what she'd seen. But she was swinging her phone in the air like a lunatic. "Sylvia, calm down! What is it?"

"You fucking bitch!" she shouted, suddenly charging at me with those crazy eyes.

"Who's a bitch? What are you talking about, Sylvia?!"

"You!" She screamed like some kind of animal. I'd never heard a person make that kind of noise. "*You're* a fucking bitch!"

Finally, she shoved her phone in my face. There in the photograph, in the blown-up reflection of the mirror, was Ian Greene.

"Sylvia, no," I said, my heart pounding. I took a step backward, as if that could somehow move time back to a place where she'd never seen the picture. "It's not what it looks like."

"Oh no?!" she screamed again. Her face was all red and veiny, and she was holding her phone back like she was going to whack me across the face with it. "Because what it looks like is that *you* were the Magpie that was fucking around with *my* boyfriend!"

"Zadie set the whole thing up. Come on, think about it, Sylvia."

"You fucked him because the *Maggies* told you to!"

"No, Sylvia, no," I panted. I'd backed up so much that my legs were jammed against the little wall. "I didn't have sex with Ian. *Nothing* happened between us."

"Except fucking this!" She jammed the phone at me harder this time and I bent back, trying to stay clear. "Naked fucking pictures! Do you even like girls? Or is that just a thing you made up so you could try to steal my boyfriend!"

She swung her arm back then and slammed the phone down hard against my collarbone. I winced and leaned back, my chest throbbing from where she'd hit me. It was too much. All too much. They were never going to stop. They were never going to leave me alone. I tried to move, to get farther away from Sylvia before she tried to hit me again.

Then, all of a sudden, it was like something behind me gave way. I put my hands out to catch the wall, braced myself for pain when my back scraped against it. But there was nothing there, no pain. Just gravity. And I kept going, and going.

And then I saw this look on Sylvia's face. I saw in her eyes the awful thing that had already happened. That we were powerless to stop

"No!" she screamed, trying to grab me. "Oh my God, Amelia!"

And I tried. I tried to grab her back. I tried so hard to hold on.

facebook

Amelia Baron
"I am rooted, but I flow." Virginia Woolf, The Waves

Epilogue

"It's getting warmer," Kate said as she lowered herself onto a patch of cold, manicured grass. It was unseasonably mild for early March but still coat weather. The words were barely out of Kate's mouth, though, when the wind picked up, cutting into her. "Okay, maybe only a tiny bit warmer, but if you were here, you'd probably think it was time for summer. That was always you, asking to wear short sleeves as soon as the snow melted. 'I won't be cold, Momma.'" Kate smiled, thinking of Amelia's round little face, making all those little-girl promises. So fervent and sure. "The funniest part was how I'd always bring along your coat, counting on you to change your mind when you felt the cold. But you never did. Not once. So perfectly stubborn. So perfectly perfect."

Kate teared up as her voice drifted. Sometimes she made herself promise that she wouldn't cry when she went to visit Amelia at the cemetery. Sometimes she just accepted that she would. Either way, she cried every time.

Still, inch by slow inch, the darkest of her grief had begun to lift or perhaps shift, leaving behind only her longing for Amelia. Kate was even coming to accept that no matter how tight she tried to hold on to each and every detail about her daughter, she could not prevent their gradual fade. She could only mourn their loss.

In the few months since Amelia had died, there were things Kate had already forgotten. She could no longer remember what Amelia had smelled like, even though she hadn't given up searching for some hint of it still buried in her pillows. Kate couldn't remember either that thing Amelia would do when she was eager to end a conversation: had it been two snaps of her fingers and then a thumbs-down, or three snaps and then a finger point? Lost, too, were the ages Amelia had been when she'd finally learned to ride a bike, which tooth she'd lost first, and how much money Kate had left under her pillow.

But what Kate did recall was frozen to crystalized perfection. She could still feel the weight of Amelia's newborn head resting in the crook of her neck as they slept upright in the rocking chair. She remembered how she'd shouted in delight when Amelia had said her first word—*dog*—but so loudly that Amelia had burst right into tears. Kate remembered the time she sent Amelia to nursery school without a diaper on. And the horrified look on Amelia's face when she was eight and Kate had tried to explain sex one morning on their way to school. Kate remembered the sweet, infrequent bliss of Amelia hugging her as a teenager. And what it had felt like to see her cry hard at that same age, nearly grown-up tears.

In the end, Kate recalled all that she needed to. Everything that had ever really mattered. Especially, how very much she had loved her daughter. And how very hard she had tried. The rest—the shortcomings, the mistakes, the things Kate would have done differently—she was working to forget. Because Seth was right. So much of how it turned out now seemed like luck, good and bad.

"I saw Julia today," Kate said. "Sylvia wants to come to see you here, to tell you how sorry she is. I said that I thought that would be fine. I hope I'm right to believe what Sylvia says happened on the roof. That it was an accident. I think I am. But I'm still not sure what the police are going to do. Even if she's telling the truth now, she lied about so much and for such a long time." Kate took a breath, running her hand over the well-tended grass. "Zadie is gone finally, some boarding school in upstate Connecticut for troubled girls. Her mom is off the school board and the clubs are shut down for good, too, at least as far as everyone knows. It's not enough; nothing will ever be enough. But it's a start, I guess."

Kate wanted to be able to tell Amelia that Dylan had written, saying that she really had loved Amelia after all. But she hadn't heard from Dylan, not a single word. Kate pulled her coat tighter around herself and looked out from the top of the hill where Amelia was buried over the rolling hills of Green-Wood Cemetery, past an ugly strip of worn-out bodegas and the huge Home Depot, to the horizon of New York Bay.

"I feel like I owe you an apology, that I've owed you one for a long time. I should have told you everything about your dad from the start," Kate said. She had been planning this speech for a while, but it was still hard to get the words out. "You had a right to know what I knew, even if I was wrong about what the truth was. It turns out that your father is Jeremy Firth. Yes, *that* Jeremy. We only had sex once and he was married and it was wrong. I was confused and lonely, and it was just something that happened. But it led to something great: you."

Kate shook her head and twisted some strands of grass through her fingers. She thought then about Phillip. So far it had been only one cup of coffee and a couple of e-mails. With his short salt-and-pepper hair, the soft lines around his eyes, and his clean-shaven face, he looked nothing like Rowan had. But Phillip reminded her so much of that passionate boy she'd known so very briefly, so many years ago. She wondered whether or not Amelia would approve, but she had to believe that she would. Gretchen had been right about that much: Amelia would want Kate to be happy.

"There was a boy in the bar . . . I didn't lie about that," Kate said. "Maybe you already know that. Maybe you read all those old journals of mine, I'll never know for sure. I think all along I just wished he'd been your father. Not even him, really—I mean, I barely knew him—but the idea of him. And over the years, that idea of him became all the greatest parts of you. I believe Phillip when he says he knows that you were one of a kind. He saw in you what I always saw, and I need that right now. To be with people who know that the world is a darker place without you in it."

Kate took a deep, shaky breath, and tried not to cry.

"I want you to know, too, that even though Jeremy was a mistake for me," Kate went on, her voice breaking up, dissolving in the wind. "*you* were never a mistake, Amelia. You were the best thing that ever happened to me. You always will be."

It was too late to change anything. Too late to make different choices. To be a better mother than she had been. Kate could only be the mother that she was, Amelia's mother—the curator of her memory, the keeper of her secrets, the cherisher of her heart. That, she would always be.

Acknowledgments

My deepest gratitude to my agent and personal superhero, Marly Rusoff, the most compassionate and dedicated advocate an author could hope for. I can't thank you enough for standing by me through this book's many iterations, and those of the manuscripts that came before it. To Michael Radulescu, for all your help and your much-appreciated levity; and Julie Mosow, a keen editor, a great creative partner, and a wonderful friend.

To my amazing editor, Claire Wachtel, your incomparable insights have improved not only this book but also me as a writer. Working with you has been an honor. Thank you to Jonathan Burnham for giving me this incredible opportunity. Thanks also to Elizabeth Perrella and everyone in HarperCollins's marketing and sales departments for your enthusiasm and all of your hard work on my behalf.

To Megan Crane, thank you for leading by example, for always being willing to read yet another draft, for telling me the truth when it mattered, and for lying to me when I needed you to. Most important, thank you for your remarkable friendship. Without you to talk about writing and life with over the years, this sometimes harrowing journey would have ended a long time ago.

Thank you to Victoria Cook, for her excellent cheerleading and for swooping in to save the day so many times. To Elena Evangelo, for her warmth and boundless optimism; and to Cara Cragan for her faith.

Thank you to my dedicated readers and precious friends whose feedback and encouragement have been invaluable: Cindy Buzzeo, Heather Frattone, Nicole Kear, and Tara Pometti.

To the very many of you out there who offered such generous words of encouragement over the past decade—Catherine and David Bohigian, the Cragan family, the Crane family, Jeremy Creelan, Joe and Naomi Daniels, Larry and Suzy Daniels, Charmaine De Grate, Dave and Joannie Fischer, David Kear, Merrie Koehlert, Hallie Levin, Brian and Laura Mayer, Diane Mehta, Brian McCreight, the Metzger Family, Jason Miller, Sarah Moore, Frank Pometti, Jon Reinish, the Thomatos Family, the members of my very talented Park Slope writer's group, and everyone else I've forgotten—thank you for believing in me, especially at those moments when I no longer believed in myself.

Thank you also to my parents, stepparents, and family, as well as the Prentices—Martin, Clare, Becky, Mike, and Steve—whom I feel so very lucky to call my family now, too.

To my husband, Tony, this book is truly yours as much as it is mine. Without you, I never would have had the courage to write a single word, much less the hope to see it through. Thank you for your generosity and your honesty, your patience and your belief. Thank you for making me laugh, for challenging me to think, and for making me feel understood. I could not ask for a more incredible husband and best friend.

And to my own perfectly perfect girls. Thank you, Harper, for your amazing empathy, outstanding hugs, and for telling me that you were proud of me on days when it felt like no one was. Thank you, Emerson, for standing printer-side, counting pages, for telling me that you want to be an artist someday, and for your incredible smile, which could lighten even the darkest day. Know that no matter how big you girls get, no matter where you go, or who you grow into, I will always love the whole of each of you, without reservation. And your secrets, whatever they end up being, will forever be safe with me.

Reconstructing Amelia
Discussion Group Guide

1. What is Amelia's relationship with her mother like? Why doesn't she share more with Kate? Why are adolescents often so reluctant to talk to their parents about the events in their lives—especially problems they are having with friends?

2. Describe Amelia. Is she a typical teenager? Talk about her friendship with Sylvia. What drew the girls together? What about her relationships with Zadie and Dylan? What made her feel so close to her Internet friend, Ben?

3. Might Amelia's situation have been different if she'd had a larger family around her? What if that family had been larger, but more filled with conflict?

4. Is Kate a good mother? She believes she knows her daughter well, but does she? What does she discover about Amelia that surprises her? What does she discover that confirms her deepest beliefs about Amelia and their relationship?

5. What kind of support network does Kate have to rely on? Does she bear any blame for the events that occur? Is there any way she could have prevented the tragedy? What about Grace Hall—how much, if any, responsibility does the school bear for Amelia's death?

Who can you turn to for help in handling a problem involving your child?

6. Why is being popular so important in adolescence? Has the Internet and social networking added to the pressures teenagers must cope with?

7. What impact does class play in the story? What about sexuality—Amelia's recognition of her own desires? What about Amelia's need to be perfect—her drive to be a good student?

8. Why does such a smart girl like Amelia fall into the trap of the secret clubs? Why isn't she more suspicious of the Magpies and the boys around them? How did her keeping the secret about the Maggies impact her relationship with Sylvia? Why are some children cruel to others? Did your school have a hierarchy or clubs like the Magpies? Where did you fit in?

9. If you have a child, how much do you know about his or her life? How far should parents go to monitor their child's life? Do children have a right to privacy the way adults do? What might someone learn if they tried to "reconstruct" you from your e-mails, correspondence, texts, tweets, messages, blog posts, and Facebook updates? Does social media make us too connected? What is your opinion of social media—do you think it's a positive development or an erosion of who we are and how we interact?

10. How does the author ratchet up the suspense in the story? What clues does she provide to point you toward the truth—or away from it?

11. Bullying is a major topic across the media and throughout society. Do you believe it is a serious issue, or do you think it's a phase that all children go through? How has the rise of the Internet contributed to the severity of bullying and to our awareness of it? Can we decrease the incidents of bullying? How do we learn to stand up to mean people?

12. Does Kate get closure when she discovers the truth? Where do you think she will go from here?

13. What inspired you or your group to choose *Reconstructing Amelia*? Did it meet your expectations? Is it an accurate representation of modern parenting and growing up in twenty-first-century America? What did you take away from reading the book?